ROLLING *the* BONES

ROLLING *the* BONES

a novel by

Kyle Jarrard

STEERFORTH PRESS
SOUTH ROYALTON, VERMONT

For information about permission to reproduce
selections from this book, write to:
Steerforth Press L.C., P.O. Box 70,
South Royalton, Vermont 05068

Library of Congress Cataloging-in-Publication Data

Jarrard, Kyle, 1955-
Rolling the bones : a novel / Kyle Jarrard.
p. cm.
ISBN 1-58642-026-7 (alk. paper)
1. Swindlers and swindling—Fiction. 2. Americans—Mexico—Fiction.
3. Drowning victims—Fiction. 4. Married people—Fiction. 5.
Gamblers—Fiction. 6. Thieves—Fiction. 7. Mexico—Fiction. 8.
Texas—Fiction. I. Title.
PS3560.A546 R65 2001
813'.54—dc21
2001002705

FIRST EDITION

For John L. Phillips

I learned not to fear infinity,
The far field, the windy cliffs of forever,
The dying of time in the white light of tomorrow,
The wheel turning away from itself,
The sprawl of the wave,
The on-coming water.

— from "The Far Field" by Theodore Roethke

Carl Blalock

The guy pulled up to my hardware and lumber store just after I opened up the Saturday before Thanksgiving. He had an old white Falcon, and it'd been awhile since I'd seen one of those. Wisconsin plates. He made the woman stay in the car. Then he came in through the door with his hands in his jacket like he might've had a gun on him.

I was at the cash register and kind of jumped back. Damn giant, at least six-six. Wearing red high-top tennis shoes, green trousers a size too big, and a blue denim shirt. But the hands came out and he wasn't armed.

"'Morning," I said, all five-five of me. "What can I do you for?"

He didn't stop until he got to the bathroom door. Then he turned and asked, "Use your facilities? Nothing else open yet."

"Have at it," I called.

But as he wheeled around to go in, his knee knocked a bottle of Spot-Off from a shelf. I can still see that sucker tipping through the air.

"Damn it to hell," he let out. "I can't believe I did that."

Well, you did, you son of a bitch, I wanted to shout.

But it didn't really matter. Because I could see right away that there was something else going on here. Not just a pit stop. Not even a bona fide robbery. Something else.

"Don't worry about it," I assured him. "Happens all the time."

And it did. Permanent stink in there, like in a hospital or rest home.

"I'm real sorry. Really."

He was thirty-something. Headed to Houston to get an oil rig job? That paid big, and he looked strong enough for anything. He squatted and started carefully picking up the bits of glass with his bare hands.

"Leave it," I said. "I'll get it."

He straightened up. "What is it, anyway?"

"Trichloroethylene and a few other things."

He shot me a look like I had to be nuts sitting in there with those bottles getting poisoned. Then he bent into the bathroom. The light shone under the door. I could hear him shuffling the *Democrat*.

The woman in the car was maybe twenty-five, and a looker. With mounds of curly blond hair that caught the morning sun and seemed all lit up, and a happy round face with green eyes peering steadily out at the world like it was the most interesting place imaginable. It wasn't often, or hardly ever, that this would happen, but this woman, on the big scale of women, was right up there with my Venus, who, of course, is the most beautiful black-haired, black-eyed creature ever to walk Texas.

Anyway, I ignored the mess on the floor, went outside, and made like I was counting up the cement stepping-stones. I'm not nosy, but I was bored stiff. There were the ads to do, but here I had a little story going.

The morning was warming up. She saw me watching her, rolled down the window, and hung her sunburned arm out. It was skinny, like a little girl's, and bobbed up and down like it weighed almost nothing.

"Howdy," I said.

She nodded, smiled lightly, waved the arm and hand.

Her man was coming out. "You sure you don't want me to mop up that mess? I can't leave you with that."

"Nah," I said.

"Mop what?" she asked.

"Knocked over a bottle of solvent. Fingers are burning."

"Where're y'all headed?" I asked.

"He says we're getting there," she said.

I didn't press it. "Well, that's good."

"What's good?" he said, looking at me, then at her.

She said, "I think he was being polite. Hoping we're coming to the place we want to be. Just like you said we were. But when was that? Five hundred miles ago? A thousand? I just want to get out of the car. Permanently."

I made like I couldn't care less what that was about and went on counting stones — twenty-three, twenty-four, twenty-five — and marking on my clipboard.

He kept examining his fingertips.

Then it occurred to me that he was going to get sick or something on account of touching that Spot-Off. "You take care now."

"What's that?" he asked.

That funny mustard-yellow hair of his, Scandinavian or something, puffed up in the breeze. His white face shone like a full moon.

"I said y'all take care."

"We're from Wisconsin," he said, "and —"

"Saw your plates," I said. "Long ways."

She said, "Nine thousand four hundred and twelve miles."

He jabbed his head her way to say butt out and she rolled her eyes in response and didn't care if I saw it.

"Mister, I need a job." He held his chin high, as if he were talking to someone much taller than himself, which almost made me look to see if there wasn't something above me he was addressing.

"Looks like you took the long road to get here," I said.

"That's counting all the side roads to all the little towns," she said. "If only we could get out of the car for more than a month at a time . . ."

"I've helped at a store like this before," he went on. "I'm a builder, too."

"They got stores good as this one in Wisconsin?"

"Yes sir. Worked at three of them. I mean one after the other. I didn't get fired or anything. We moved around."

"You can say that again," she said.

I let him off the hook. "Name's Carl," I said.

He lowered his face toward me and his smile opened up on a huge set of teeth, some as big as a thumbnail. "That's my name, too." The voice had kicked up higher, lost its dangerous edge.

"Well, now," I said. "Your name Blalock, too?"

"No, it's Stein," he said. "This is my wife, May."

"Mrs. Stein," I said.

"May will do," she said.

Could he spray flock on a Douglas fir? That was my moneymaking sideline and we were fixing to fire up the blowers. It'd be nonstop until Christmas, and if the past was any guide we'd rake in the dough.

Then he said, "Heard you could use some help out on the D & D deal."

That was a big plant that was going to be making men's socks, of all things, outside Red Rock and for now my number one building contract. You never saw so much glass. I don't know how much we sold them. Or how many board feet of pine or barrels of nails.

True, I'd fired my foreman, but this guy somehow didn't seem experienced enough to handle a team of twenty men. I did need somebody to flock Christmas trees, though.

"You ran into Tommy Atherton, then," I said. "He was drinking out there on the job. I couldn't have that, you know."

"Don't know any Tommy Atherton."

"Then how'd you find out about my foreman?"

"Only heard there was an opening out here."

"Who you been talking to?"

"Guy at Kendal. Said you were the one who had the big D & D deal and might be wanting help."

That was Kendal & Co., the Dallas outfit that'd been trying to buy out us little guys. I was ready to bet a thousand bucks they'd recruited this fellow as a spy. "Kendal, huh," I said. "Look, I've got everybody I need right now. But thanks all the same for dropping by."

I started back counting. Heck with the flocking job, too. I'd get some high school kid and do like before.

He didn't move. "I need a job, Mr. Blalock."

"Can't help you, Mr. Stein. But I do wish you luck."

He stood there like he hadn't understood plain English.

So I shouted, "Boy, you can tell those Kendals I said go straight to hell. You got that? I ain't going to sell to him."

"Do what?" he shrieked.

"You want work? They'll give you work. Now get out of here."

"They didn't have a job."

"Whatever."

"But one of the workers came up to me on the parking lot and said you might be hiring up here. Guy said he'd worked for you before. McKnight?"

"Danny McKnight. Bailed his ass out a hundred times. Well . . ."

"So we came straight here, Mr. Blalock. That's it."

I counted some more stones, took my time. Either they were poor people in real need or damn good actors. I couldn't decide.

Then my mouth opened before I'd finished thinking. "Can you flock?"

"Flock? Mister, I'm the world's number one flocker. Right, May?"

"How long a job is that? Just for the holidays?"

I could see dark exasperation in her face and felt bad for her. "We can see about that when the time comes. You never know . . ."

"That right?" said Carl.

"Sure," I said.

If this was all a trick and the Kendals were up to something, well then everything would come to a head, wouldn't it? That might be for the best.

We had Carl and May over to our house south of town for turkey supper, and Venus liked them right off. There was a lot of quick talking and laughter, which felt good because our table can be a quiet place through the year, and the rich food was piled up so high it seemed like all you had to do was lean forward and eat to your heart's content. That's the way I like Thanksgiving, the night of succulent meat and delicious gravies. Venus had lit a couple of dozen long yellow candles and turned off the lights so that each of our faces was cast in a warm glow that spoke of contentment and well-being. I said grace, which definitely is rare for me, but Venus nodded at me grinning to say it was all right to be praying that night because there was a joy at work there.

Carl said, "We haven't had a meal like this since . . . I don't know!"

Venus was wearing a red dress I'd bought her in Dallas, a simple straight thing that was too tight now. She wouldn't wear it in public, saying it was way too vulgar, so once in a while I tried to get her to wear it when we were having dinner together at home alone on one of our birthdays or something. But she wouldn't ever do it, left it in the closet and told me to think about a cold shower. That night, though, there it was in plain view, and I had the hardest time keeping my eyes off her bosom filling that deep V-cut. I guess it was the other pretty woman being in our company that'd helped her get up the nerve to put it on again.

"Well, we haven't had company for Thanksgiving in a long time," said Venus. "So everyone's getting something special tonight."

"Where are you staying?" I asked Carl.

"At the Roadway up north. I'll find us a house next week."

"I'll find it," May insisted. "You're going to be working."

"Maybe I could help you," Venus said to her. "Go through the ads and whatnot. I may know a house or two for rent."

"That would be very nice." She poked her hand into all those curls and then pulled it out again, and I watched to see if she hadn't found something in there that she was going to show us. "I just can't believe it all," she said. "It's been not just months but years. Years."

"What?" I asked.

"A bona fide sit-down dinner with fine people welcoming us into their home, the portion of the earth that is beneath my derriere not moving at seventy miles an hour, the things to the right and left of me not moving backward and out of my vision, the look of these candles, the smell of this food and of the women's perfume and the men's cologne, and the color of all your eyes like colors I'm seeing for the first time."

"Too much wine," said Carl, poking his food with his fork.

May hiked her pretty white shoulders in the blue summer dress she wore as if to say, Wine or no wine, it was a rare evening full of things and people to be grateful for if one would take the time to see.

Venus leaned to give her a hug and pull the strap back up her shoulder, as if that could somehow make up for the fact that the girl needed a real dress to wear in November.

"I kind of agree with all that," she said. "As for the wine . . . drink all you want because you can spend the night if you want to."

"Can't be out driving around drunk anyway," I said. "We have cops here who'll throw you in jail on New Year's Eve, for Christ's sake. Guys who'll sit behind a billboard waiting on you for hours and straight-out salivate giving you a ticket. They end up in the front row at church Sunday playing deacon or what have you, but they aren't the least bit sorry for all the misery they deal out during the week."

"We don't go to church anymore, though," said Venus.

"Church?" said May. "The last thing I remember was Bible school. And the fat man who kept touching the girls in places he shouldn't have been whenever he leaned over us at the table to point out some passage or other. I told Mama that was the end of religion for me. She didn't argue with me. Unbelievable."

Venus clapped her hands, and I couldn't remember the last time I saw my wife clap her hands. They were big hands with long fingers, and the sound was loud, silly somehow for someone forty-four years old like me, and I laughed.

Carl said, "I don't think we can spend the night."

"Come on, Carl," I said. "Loosen up here. Don't have to work tomorrow."

He nodded and examined his food like he was considering the veracity of that. Then he gave May a look that meant, Calm down, we're in these people's home, don't get out of control. That's what I saw in his eyes, anyway. For her part, she answered him by picking up her wineglass and throwing back the rest of the ruby contents.

"Tell me some of the places you've been," I said to Carl.

"Everywhere. Wherever the money is."

"Why is it always about money?" May asked.

"Got to eat, honey."

"We've never starved."

"Jobs play out. You move on."

"Seems like we run."

Venus repeated my question. "So where have you lived, then?"

May answered. "I think the sweetest place was Tahlequah, Oklahoma, and that's where we just came from. We had a little white house. Stayed the whole summer."

"I wouldn't have wanted to heat that place in winter," said Carl.

"That bad?" I asked.

"Oh, boy."

"I liked Mrs. Johnson a lot," said May.

"Who was she?" Venus asked.

"Widow who lived next door. She had a peach orchard and I helped her put up preserves. Dozens of jars. Best stuff on earth. She had this huge white kitchen with blue curtains and on account of her age she had trouble getting into the root cellar, which was down some stairs under the kitchen, and so I'd take all the jars we'd done down there and set them on the shelves and smell the sweet earth. Carl cut trees in the Ozarks and came in very late because they worked him to death and I'd sit out back under the peach trees with Elaine Johnson and watch the stars come out over Oklahoma and maybe there wouldn't be a sound on the earth save the crickets in the tall grass out where her lot ended and the countryside began. I'd sit there thinking there was no reason to move my body an inch because everything was perfect."

"There was something spooky about cutting down trees in the Ozarks," said Carl. "Like I was doing something wrong."

"You were earning your living," his wife said.

"We were cutting the oldest trees up there."

I said, "The Ozarks are the oldest mountains in North America."

"What's that, Carl?" Venus asked.

"I read that, anyway. That they were once like the Rockies. They've eroded down. Might even be true."

May and Carl studied me with surprise and then waited gently for me to make my point, though there really wasn't one.

"I guess that was the wine talking," I said.

"I think so," Venus agreed.

"Why not," said May. "Once like the Rockies! I can believe that. That's how old things are. But how many people ever think about how old things are? People don't even know much about their country's own history, much less how old its rocks are. I think you have to care about the rocks, and the people who live by the rocks, and the trees that grow between the rocks, and the people who tend to those trees, and what kind of fruit they give, and what makes it taste like it does. There was a cinnamon flavor to those peaches. I'm not kidding."

Venus gazed at May and shook her head slowly side to side like she was hearing unheard-of things, which she was. And I thought, Here is one of the brightest people ever to enter this house, and she's just a woman who happened to show up with her lanky husband after wandering all over the heartland. What were the chances of this happening, this particular pair waltzing into our lives? Why did it feel like we were being given a gift by some unseen benefactor?

They had a light to their faces and it came from the youth of their hearts. A hardworking boy and maybe his dream girl, out making their way through the rough-and-tumble of the world, trying not to let the sheer fatigue of it all rend them apart. I wondered if they would make love when we put them in the guest room in the back of the house, and I kind of hoped they would because me and Venus would surely hear it and it would not be lurid or shameful but very nice.

I pondered Venus, and I swear she could see my thoughts. Then she popped up to get the dessert and May went running after her.

They stayed in the kitchen a long time, and so I poured more wine for me and Carl and he thanked me and kept his hands on either side of his glass, as if it needed steadying or as if he were sheltering his thoughts.

"It's been a good Thanksgiving," he said.

"I'm only glad you stopped at my store to use the can."

He laughed. "Well. We'll see."

"You're doing fine on the job. I'm not worried."

"Thanks for the vote. I won't let you down."

"Why would you do that?" I asked.

Then it was all the pecan pie and vanilla ice cream you could eat, and the talk slowed and the windows turned deep blue as the last of the light went its way and May announced that, Yes, they could spend the night. I saw Venus's eyes light up and I was sure she was going to start clapping again, but then she didn't, and we all carried dishes to the kitchen where Venus declared that we would in fact abandon the mess. After which she and May brought all the candles from the dining table into the living room and set them around and then got on the couch and started talking. As if someone had opened a giant old box and let out all the years of desire for talking, for saying everything that could possibly be said whenever a breath was not being taken.

Carl and I let them be. Went out on the porch to see the land stretching out broad and overlit by uncountable stars in the vault.

"I think they'll be friends," he said.

"That's true."

We sat on the steps and witnessed the night like grown men.

"I guess I've kept her moving too much."

"You do what you have to."

"Yeah, but I can't put down roots."

"There'll come a time."

"I don't know."

"She'll take you there."

"Where?"

"It's like that orchard, Carl. She's not just talking about the peaches."

"I know."

"Venus taught me that."

"What?"

"Listening to the words behind the words. You'll hear them."

"You think so?"

We watched the glow of the town shining up over the chalk hill that stood between here and there.

"I think so, Carl. Question of time. Question of need."

"May is frightening sometimes."

I wanted to laugh, but held it. "How so?"

"Just being that beautiful. Like if I lost her I'd just . . . what? Stumble and fall. Everything I do is for her. Every stroke of work. Every minute of my day. It's like I'm only here because of her."

"That's not so bad, friend."

"I don't know . . ."

"And I bet she'd say she's only here because of you. Works both ways."

"I hope it does."

"You can't see that?"

"Do you?"

"Plain as day."

Once in a while a pair of headlights came toward us and then the car or truck zoomed on past. White dust floated off the road through the mulberry trees and dogs barked far off.

"Damn dust," I said. "I swear my head is full of it."

"Your head?"

"I swear . . ."

"You know, I think May might be one of those people you call gifted."

"I'd have to agree."

"Not for all the things she can do, though. Not for all the things she can say, either, because she can really say a lot of things when she gets going."

"Can she now?"

"It's those times that pop up out of the blue when she'll notice something you'd never imagined, though maybe it was right there all along, and then get you to see it, too. I remember once when we were in the desert out West and she got this notion that we had to climb up on top of this big pile of orange rocks that we were driving past and damn it if I didn't give in and march right out there. Middle of the blazing afternoon. We got up there and she squinted at the desert and I said, 'What?' And she said, 'Hush up and listen to this.' I shut up and there was nothing. Just the wind. I said, 'What?' She said, 'The wind. Listen.' It was hot as an oven and I was sure rattlesnakes were gathering around that hill to cut us off —"

"But they weren't."

May stood right behind us, and Venus behind her. They sat down on the step above us and May passed a wine bottle forward to Carl. He peered at it and I smiled and said, "Hurry up." He had a big swallow and then I did and then I set the bottle on the step.

It was like there was nobody but us four in the world, though I don't exactly know where that notion came from. Maybe because we had created such a sanctuary for ourselves that night, or maybe because we knew inside that maybe there weren't going to be half a dozen such evenings in a lifetime. Where quiet harmony and trust were the gold.

"No, the snakes weren't circling, Carl, but they might've been watching, for we were a sight to see perched on those rocks miles from the car without a water jug. The desert is a weird place. It's like it's all one big thing, dry, empty, monotonous. Until you start listening to it."

"We listened a very long time."

"Standing out there in the sun?" I asked.

"We were sitting down," May said. "Feet over the edge of a big drop-off. The rock was blazing hot, but we didn't feel it after a while.

That's right. We forgot about the heat and stared out into this desolate void before us. I remember moving my head lightly this way and then that way to make the breeze that was moving around us make a different sound on a different part of my ears. I couldn't think of anything but how little movement it took to make the sound change utterly. I wanted to tell Carl to try it but when I looked at him I could see him smiling because he'd already been doing the same thing. Catching the strange power of the wind in his ears."

"What was wonderful," Carl said, "was that after we left there —"

"We stayed there all the rest of the afternoon," she said.

"— and went on down the road into the night toward Bakersfield, I could still hear the wind when it had barely been blowing at all."

"It was the permanent wind," said May. "The one that's always there. Has blown for all time. Has never ceased."

"All that from sitting on a rock," he said.

"Why not," said Venus, and it wasn't a question.

May said, "Whenever I think things are out of kilter, I think about those orange rocks and the wind that was speaking to us."

I thought how the evening had a familiar feel to it, as if Venus and I maybe had had this kind of communion some time back, but if we did, habit and familiarity had erased a lot of that ancient feeling, leaving us to awe at the glow being cast across our world now as if some new star were rising to startle us and make us think again about wind.

I had another hit of wine, finishing it, and then saw them all looking at me. "What?"

"Nothing," said Carl.

"It's been a good supper," said Venus.

I saw that May had borrowed one of Venus's sweaters. Just the same, she was leaning hard against her, trying to get warm.

Not only did Carl Stein know how to flock a Christmas tree, he flocked like I'd never seen anybody flock. All we'd ever had was some idiot who could hold the sprayer and be willing to choke on that crap. Carl had style, was good with the colors, even got funny with black ones. When the holiday had come and gone, we'd sold three trailer loads of trees and I kept him on full time at the store.

Carl Stein, from Fergus Falls, Wisconsin, from the other side of the moon. But the way we got along we could've grown up together and been friends for life.

First and foremost, he was as nuts as me about bowling Monday afternoons when the store was closed. May and Venus often went, too, but bowled only a game or two before going to the snack bar. We drank beer and watched our scores slide. But we couldn't have cared less.

This was January, which meant a lot of downtime, and I was fixing to take Venus to Mexico for a week. To Puerto Azul, a vacation spot on the Pacific about as close as you can get to paradise.

"I'm telling you, it's not a problem," he said.

"You only have to keep the D&D boys supplied and then take care of the customers like always. It won't be busy."

"No problem."

I picked up my spare in the tenth, rolled my extra one for an eight, which made a hundred and thirty-two. I've been stuck in the hundred thirties since nineteen sixty-eight and the summer I bowled maybe a thousand games drinking and whooping it up after I got out of going to 'Nam on account of my nine-toe birth defect.

He hit a strike, then got another. Then he guttered.

"I can trust you," I said.

"Take your wife to Mexico and have a good time."

I had to reach up to put my hand on his shoulder.

The girls stopped talking when we walked up.

"Venus?" I said.

"What, honey?"

"Carl's going to run the store while we're in Mexico."

It caught May by surprise and she looked up at Carl, who was smiling. It was as if I'd announced an engagement. The wives got up and hugged, and then me and Carl hugged, and then we all hugged.

We celebrated over a catfish dinner on Red Rock Lake. There was a dock out in back of the restaurant. From there, you could look out over the water and see lights along the Oklahoma shore.

"Daddy had a boat," I said, "and he'd park it up next to the dam and catch the biggest old things. Long as your leg, some. Fish, Carl?"

"Not too much."

"We got catfish in this lake big as a man."

"They say there were giant fish like that in Dead Lake."

"Dead Lake?"

"Dead Lake. Near Fergus Falls."

"Weird name."

"So is Wisconsin."

"Never been anywhere near that far north."

"It just happened to be the place I went first when I left home. Don't ask me why. I was just going. From there, you keep picking and choosing. May thinks any direction toward the south is probably right. Long as it's toward sun and heat."

"That's why I like Mexico."

"Never been there," he said, with no hint of jealousy.

"Where is it you want to be, do you think?"

"I've often thought Alaska might be good. They say the glaciers break off into the ocean. Ice is sky blue. I'd like to see that. Catch the North Pole wind up there. Then again, California wouldn't be bad."

"Nutty place, I hear."

"Unless you've got money. Then it can be pretty good, I think."

A fish rose from the deep and flopped out there in the dark and we watched for its circle on the surface but it never came.

"That was a big one," I said.

As usual, Mexico was fantastic. We rented an apartment on a mountain overlooking the bay, the bluest on earth. That was a thing I liked to do. Take a lady by the hand and show her paradise. No skimping. Set her up in high style and make sure everything was just so, then kick back and watch her melt right into it like she'd been doing it all her life. Watch her smile as she stared off the balcony at all that tropical beauty as if she'd never really been that happy before. It made me feel taller than I'll ever be and of a piece with men who could provide.

We slept late every morning, hit Playa Linda at noon, had cocorums and barbecued shrimp under a thatch umbrella, swam some, went on back to the apartment about four, showered, then napped or didn't nap.

Most of the time we didn't feel like going out for dinner, made salad and sat watching ships pull in and out all lit up.

"I'll call Carl and see how things are going," I said one night.

Venus went on in to bed.

It was after midnight but I knew he'd be up watching TV or something. I let it ring a good ten times. Then someone picked it up.

"Carl?"

Either they hung up or it got cut off. I tried it again. It rang and rang, but nobody answered. Third time it was busy. I gave up and started for the kitchen. Phone rang, and I jumped. It was Carl.

"Been trying to get you," he said. "Everything's fine, though."

"I was just trying to call you," I said.

"I'm at the store. Lumber truck got here at midnight."

"Jesus."

"Anyway, they say it won't wait, so I'm unloading."

"Call some of the boys in."

"I can get it. No big deal. Be done by breakfast."

Things seemed under control. "I'll be in Sunday."

"Take your time. Having fun?"

"Sure are. We've been — "

The connection went dead.

Venus was leaning on the doorjamb, not a stitch on. "Come to bed."

I obeyed.

She had me lie still next to her while the moonlight worked its way across the tile floor. It barely seemed to move and then it would move quickly, as if suddenly borne along by an unseen power, and yet we didn't start one toward the other or make any sound or speak. The heat rose out of our bodies and hovered blue in the air as we lay on our sides, my back to her belly, and let the Mexican night carry us where it would.

The moon had rushed out of sight when she said, "I think it was like this when May and Carl sat on the orange rocks in the desert."

I reached around and put my hand on the high curve of her hip, but that was all, and then we slept.

I dream of May holding hands with Venus in an orchard that somehow stands full and green out in the middle of a desert. Carl and I are watching them from the front seat of a brand-new Falcon. For some reason we have all the windows rolled up and as soon as I notice this I see that there are no window handles or door handles and that we are locked in. I am about to ask him what's going on when he reaches for the key and fires her up and hits the gas and starts steering for the orchard. And it isn't like he's going to stop when we get there, either. Venus and May see us coming and run to get out of the way. I start yelling at Carl and grabbing the wheel but we are almost there already and the women cannot run fast enough in their dresses.

It wasn't dawn yet when I awoke and went out on the balcony. The air was still, cool, and a light was emerging from it, scattered here already from below the horizon where the sun was struggling to rise. He did seem to have something in him that would do such a thing, though I couldn't say for sure what made me think that. An undefined mystery.

And yet Carl had taken care of everything like he was supposed to. Business had been slow, as expected. But all was in order.

Venus and I had rested, and there seemed to be a new sense of curiosity between us, as if it were possible that we could discover something more about each other after all the years. I found myself coming home earlier, leaving Carl to close up the store, and cornering Venus in whatever room she was in, nudging her up against a wall or a door. She would laugh genuinely at my antics and then drop all indifference and resistance and make a universe of wonder with me. Sometimes we'd just stay in bed those evenings.

Unless May came around, and then Venus would pop up and rush to the door and begin carrying on as if they hadn't seen each other in countless days when maybe it'd been only twelve hours. I didn't mind all this, though. May was bringing something alive into our drab home, and if I had to venture a guess as to the funny feeling that seemed to be hanging in the air around there, I'd say it was something that May was spreading like the bounty that only some people can dispense.

They would sit and talk and giggle while I wandered around the place enjoying the sound of them. Somehow it was kind of like they were both mine, though I would never have said that.

May told Venus much about her past, and it was like flipping through postcards. As if there were no places she and Carl had stayed for more than a few weeks, which made it seem like they'd been on the road forever. Places like Storm Lake, Iowa, and Elizabethton, Tennessee, and Frankfort, Kentucky, and Alamosa, Colorado. Exotic, hardly, but strange, yes. Places nobody went to, but maybe only came from, or escaped from.

"Carl would get this look in his eye and I knew what it meant. That we were leaving within twenty-four hours, no questions asked."

"What's that mean?" Venus said.

"It meant, Don't ask because you're not going to get much of anything back. A shrug. Some vague words. So I gave up asking."

"I guess some men are turned that way," I said, butting in at the door to the spare bedroom where they were sitting cross-legged on the bed facing each other like girls playing a game. "Needing to move."

"That must be right, Carl," she said. "He showed up in my town out of the blue from New Mexico. Kind of strange to go from New

Mexico to Wisconsin. What for? He'd have to be a pure wanderer."

"Must be hard to keep up with him," Venus said.

"Not after a while. I've adapted because I love him. No matter where we are I try to make it like it's the final place, the place we've always dreamed of being. I fix everything up just so and hope that it will be so powerfully . . . what is the word? Radiant? Yes . . . so radiant with living that he won't want to go out on the road and drive in insane directions smoking cigarettes and hardly talking to me while I spin the radio dial and feel like a doll he trundles along because he doesn't know what else to do. Whoa. I'm bitching now, aren't I?"

"Amen," said Venus. "Go ahead."

"You know, I liked the life I had in Fergus Falls. I liked my parents, good people, both of them. I liked being with them, talking with them, sleeping in their house, eating food with them, everything. Which isn't normal."

"Why not?" asked Venus.

"Everybody else I knew hated life in Fergus Falls, hated their parents, thought they were bad people, did not like being with them, and so forth. So I felt like something was wrong with me not to be like everybody. And here came Carl tugging on me. Saying, Go! So I went. Left my pediatrician father and my volunteering mother behind."

"Don't you talk with them?"

"No. I don't write, either. It hurts too much. I'm their only child. I went away without a word. They don't know whether I'm dead, alive, in heaven, or in hell. Nothing. Carl says that's just as well, too. I'm not so sure anymore, though. More and more I'm thinking I need to get in touch with them. They'll listen. They'll understand."

"They love you, no matter what."

"I think you're right. But it's very hard to begin again. I guess that's because being out on the road most of the time is like being on another planet . . . Anyway, enough moaning. Who'd want to hear all this?"

"We would," I said.

"That's right," said Venus. "We're people like anybody."

"Like anybody? No, you're more than that. I can see this for sure. You're two people with all this settled peacefulness that comes from years of trying. Not like me and Carl. We're still kids. We don't have a stick of furniture. We rent the stuff, then turn it in on moving day."

"Maybe right here is where you're going to buy furniture," I said.

"But what're we going to do with it when it's time to go?"

"Maybe he won't go this time."

"You don't know Carl Stein."

"I've got work for him for as far as I can see down the calendar. Give it a chance."

"I am, Carl," she said. "I am. But I don't know about my Carl. He's not one for holding out all that long. Some bell'll go off . . ."

"Let's stick a sock in that bell," said Venus. "And keep you here."

May blinked and smiled. "Now there's an idea."

Spring was our busy time. I hired on more boys to help out on D&D and let Carl ride herd on them. He did such a good job that I quit going out there to the site five times a day to check up on everything. I only drove by in the evening on my way home. They'd all be climbing like ants on the buildings. I could see Carl's huge straw hat.

Sometimes I'd sit there in my Suburban thinking how the world in which I lived was a painting, of strong, living colors, full of strong, living people doing things like putting up buildings in a powerful golden light that would shine like the pictures in my boyhood Bible. It was silly, maybe, but everything seemed clear to me those days, as if something had been removed from my eyes. Spring will do that to me. Set the planet to hovering like it had only just been made, like we had only just ventured out of the forests of yore to bust up prairie sod and erect our feeble boxes upon the land, to claim it, to make it ours.

One time I stayed out there watching them work until sundown, and Carl came by in his Falcon and saw me and stopped.

"Spying on me?"

"You know it," I said.

He could tell I hadn't had anything better to do. "She's coming along. I figure we'll be there by mid-July. If it doesn't rain."

That was a month ahead of schedule, and I looked at the building, back at him, then back at the building. "Maybe."

"Maybe nothing. Going to happen. See you, boss."

And off he went, fishtailing his car on the road in his haste to get back to the house. To May, waiting for him in a yellow-lit room with all those curls of hers softly glowing. It made me want Venus again. I was always wanting Venus those days.

Along about the first of May, I brought Carl back into the store Saturday mornings. That way I could sleep in sometimes, or take my time, while he opened up. I figured I'd earned the right to drag ass some. And Carl needed the break from all that outdoor backbreaking, especially now that they were so far ahead of schedule, a miracle I never was quite able to figure out. I gave him a raise, too.

Like before, we went out bowling, messing around, something somewhere every few nights without fail. Then we got really restless and went kicker dancing all the way down in Fort Worth one Saturday. And got so drunk we had to check in to a motel. There was only one room left when we pulled in carrying on like idiots at dawn. And only one bed.

"I'm not sleeping with you idiots," Carl boomed, dropping onto the lounge chair by the window and tipping straight back onto the floor with his blue cowboy boots pointing straight up. "Holy Christ!"

May rushed to help him and had him up and resettled in a flash. Like maybe she'd had to do that before. But the cloud that blew across her face lasted only a few seconds, and then she was May again, center of the fun, the fire around which we'd danced like the possessed all evening, the heat of all that exuberance reaching out and into our bodies.

I was pretty far gone and feeling generous. "I don't see why we couldn't take you two to Mexico with us next time."

"Sure we can," said Venus. "It'd be the greatest thing. Being there with you two. You've never seen anything like it."

"That's right," I said. "There is nothing in this world like it."

"I've got this feeling," May said, growing quiet, "that going down into Mexico will be like going down into some dream place that changes you in ways you never imagined possible."

Carl said, "That's a little extravagant."

"Is it? I don't know. Have you ever been to Mexico?"

Carl shrugged. "Girls at the border's about it."

"That's disgusting," said May, but she wasn't angry. "That wasn't Mexico, anyway. Right, Venus?"

"We go way down into the southern part. Down on the Pacific. Takes days to get there but when you come up over that last ridge and the blue of the ocean hits your eyes, you fall back on the car seat stunned. There's nothing like it. And maybe not like it in the next world, either."

"My," said May. "I can't not see this."

"You'll see it," said Venus.

"Can you imagine?"

"It's realer than real, honey. An indigo ocean. Not like the damn Gulf of Mexico. This is alive. Whitecaps racing along like thousands of boats all going the same way in a big hurry. We always come down out of the mountains way faster than we ought to. Carl will barely touch the brake. Our ears pop. And then we're there in Puerto Azul. Parking and running down to the beach and sticking our feet in the sea and smelling the fish and feeling the salt air on our faces like we've never felt it before."

"Count me in," said Carl, giving a wave from the chair and shutting his eyes. "Night-night."

The rest of us slept it off lined up like sardines on the bed. Well, not right away. Somebody said something, I don't remember what, and then we couldn't quit laughing. It went on and on and then the girls started bopping me with their fists as if I'd started it. When I hadn't. But I had no desire to resist. What for? I let them pound me like a drum.

It turned summer, and then late summer.

One day Venus said, Why don't we all go on the Oklahoma side of the lake, up by Arrowhead Point, and so off we went the next Monday in my Suburban with enough barbecue fixings and beer and wine for an army.

It was a red dirt beach below a bluff lined with oaks, nobody around. Must've been ninety-five when we got there. The girls went on in swimming while me and Carl got the briquettes going in the pit.

Carl said, "I've got something to say about Covington."

I didn't want to hear it. "No shop talk today."

"What if I told you —"

"Don't tell me anything."

I'd been up since seven running around getting everything Venus wanted for the picnic. All I wanted was my rear on a lawn chair.

Carl said, "I got you the Covington factory extension. New wing on the north side. That's a lot of square feet, Blalock."

Covington made cowboy boots and the old man had been talking about a new wing for ten years. So I didn't believe it for a minute.

"Did you hear what I said?"

"You got me a contract with Covington. Now it's Monday and . . ."

He threw up his hands. "Whatever you say."

"Tell me tomorrow."

He waited, gave the charcoal a squirt of lighter fluid. Flames shot up and fried gunk off the grill. Then he said, "What's wrong?"

I'd gotten my chair set like I wanted under a tree. I was watching the girls swimming and a speedboat buzzing back and forth. "Not a thing."

"Right," he said.

I watched him fooling with the hot dogs, putting out the plates and cups and stuff, doing the women's work. "Let them do that."

"I don't mind."

"Grab a chair and sit down."

He chucked down a handful of plastic silverware, brought over a chair, and popped it open.

I stared out at the brown water. "Covington," I said.

"Covington," he said back.

"You got me Covington."

"That's right."

"You're not kidding."

"Nope." Then he jumped up, grinning. "Can you believe it!"

Venus and May waved from their air mattresses. They'd drifted off some, though. You had old river currents moving under that lake.

"We got Covington!" Carl shouted at them.

I said, "Tell them to come back in some."

"You what?" Venus called.

"Covington! We got the Covington contract!"

They couldn't hear us.

"Come on," I said. "Let's take a dip before we do the dogs."

I had my suit on already and waited around eating some potato chips while Carl changed over by the Suburban.

"We're going to make a fortune," he said.

"I can't believe you did that."

"Why not?"

"All these years. How'd —"

"That's secret."

I turned around just as he was pulling the trunks on. Then I looked away.

"We're not going to have secrets, Carl. What'd you do?"

He came up behind me. "Relax. All I did was go over there and ask. I said we'd appreciate their business if they did build the new wing and they said they'd think about it. Next thing I knew this Covington car pulled into the D & D site when we were finishing up and a guy put his head out the window with a smile and said he wanted to talk."

We started down to the water.

"Which one?"

"Dick something."

"Dick Aldrich. Manager over there."

"That's it. Right away he said Covington would like to offer us the contract. I said I'd tell you. And he said fine, and that was that. Simple."

"Why didn't you call me?"

"I was saving it for today."

Something felt funny, out of place.

"When do we sign?"

"Tuesday."

"Tomorrow."

"Tomorrow. They're coming by. That all right?"

I wanted it to be true. Still, I couldn't concentrate.

"Let's get wet," I said.

We went on down to the water. It felt like a hot bath at first. We waded out on the muddy bottom to where the girls were. There, I could feel a cold current going around my ankles. The top of the water was as still as a table.

"Can be peaceful out here," I said.

Everyone shook their heads yes.

Then Carl filled them in on the good news. Venus questioned me with her eyes, and I winked to say, Yes, it did seem true. We were going to make a bundle, get our own house in Puerto Azul in no time.

Then no one knew what to say. As if too many good things had been suddenly lined up for us to contemplate them all at once.

Maybe five minutes passed with the world turning its slow way and the four of us riding along upon it in contentment.

Then Carl said to May, "You're getting out too far," and tugged on her mattress.

"It's not deep here," I said to him. "Pretty much flat."

"I don't swim," he said.

"All right," I said, "we'll stay in close. Let's back on up here."

I pulled on Venus's mattress, too, and we moved closer to shore.

Smoke was coming up lighter off the grill. Coals were ready.

"Better get wet, girls," I said, "then we'll eat. Come on, Carl, let's throw on the dogs."

We waded away as the girls rolled off their floats. I squatted down to cool off a last time before getting out.

"Get wet, Carl. Hot as hell out here."

He looked nervous. Only the bottom half of his suit was wet.

"How come you never learned how to swim?"

He squatted. "Cold." He was feeling the mud with his hands. "There's a spring down here. Coming right out."

I cut the water, got him right in the eyes. "Covington. Son of a bitch."

He splashed me. "You owe me one."

"Sure do." I let out my Mexican cry. I can do it right, too.

Then he said, "Look where they are now."

The girls were out farther again, wading along.

"Old river runs by out there somewhere," I said. "Good buddy of mine who was a fighter pilot said it's a sight to behold when you fly over. You can see the channel. There's towns down there that got abandoned when they filled the lake. You can see the old streets. "

"I'd love to learn to fly," he said. "Bet I never will, though."

There was a yell and then May dropped out of sight.

"Hey," said Carl. "Hey."

Venus was looking around at the water, at us, then at the water. Neither of us moved. Then Venus's scream hit our ears.

"Go get help!" I yelled at him. "There's a phone in the Suburban. Go!"

But he wouldn't move.

"Goddamn it, Carl, run and call!"

I started swimming out as fast as I could. But every muscle in my body seemed to have turned into rock and the water felt thick as sand. What do I do, what do I do, I kept saying. Damn current get her? Drag her off? No head had popped back up, nothing. It was like ink was bleeding in from the edges of everything, leaving only the center and my wife standing there screaming and waving her arms.

Then I saw Carl following me. Wading with all his strength, slipping on the bottom. I hollered at him to go back. But he was losing it.

Venus was bellowing and pointing at a dark place in the water, probably an old cistern, lunging toward it. I pulled her back and she started hitting me and I had to not think and slap her once hard on the cheek. The screams stopped.

I put her on an air mattress, pushed her toward Carl. "Take her back."

He caught hold of her mattress but stayed there.

"Take her back," I told him. "And phone for help!"

"Find May!"

"Take her back. Take Venus back, Carl."

"Find my May!"

It was too late. I didn't want to say it but it was. That cold current was grabbing my legs. I got down and put my head under the water. You couldn't see much. A black hole going down. The water pulling that way. There was a brick edge to it but no cover or anything. I couldn't feel her, either, no matter how far I stretched out my hands. She was too far down.

I backed away some.

"What're you doing?" Carl demanded. "Keep looking, keep looking!"

"It's a hole, Carl. I go in there, I'll drown."

I had to say this again and again.

And then he let go of my wife on the mattress and charged over and pushed me back toward the cistern. I was slipping, losing my footing.

"Keep looking! You've got to keep looking!"

I got my balance and shoved him back. May was drowned. Nobody could stay down that long. She was drowned.

"Carl, come on! Got to use the phone. Got to get help."

He cursed me, said he was going to kill me.

I kept my head and got Venus back to shore, carried her to the

Suburban, sat her on the front seat. She was shaking and the towel kept falling off. I made the emergency call. Carl stood out there yelling, at me, at God, at Venus, everything. His spit flew and he yanked on his hair.

I don't know how long it was but after a while he stumbled away from the cistern and sat down on the bottom with only his head showing. Like some creature that'd come up from the depths and turned to stone.

I don't know how long it was before the rescue folks made him come to shore and sit in the Suburban with us. A long time, a century, more . . .

Then a boy in a wet suit went down in there. It took him a long while to get her up. They had to cut her out from a mess of barbed wire and trotlines. The boy said the cistern was full of junk, that if she'd been much farther down he would've had to leave her.

They put the body into the ambulance after we'd stood staring down at her on the stretcher in the shadows of the oaks long enough that there was no more sense to it. I'd never seen a body so white, like every last bit of life had been withdrawn from it with a vengeance, which is what had happened, and the three of us were full of anger and black desperation and raging blood because the earth would not stop its tilting as if it wanted to shake us off for remaining alive.

We had this house by the Brazos River down near Glen Rose when I was growing up, and I can tell you for sure that my mama and daddy never once gave a thought to anything but fishing Sunday mornings down in the grass by the mud bank where the current cut through hard and deep. They'd fish with flour-dough bait for carp, useless carp, catch the biggest ones you'd ever seen. They'd start — I mean, we'd start — before dawn and we wouldn't stop until eleven, when Mama'd say, "Time to fry the chicken."

Mama never wore anything on her feet but flip-flops. I'd watch her go off through the grass, those pink rubber flaps flopping and her fishing poles twitching this way and that like insect antennae, and then Daddy and me would sit there awhile longer.

Daddy didn't concentrate much on his fishing, I don't think. Instead he was always watching that brown river pulling right to left. I used to think it was like melted chocolate. I don't know what he thought it looked like, I never asked, but it didn't matter because I could tell by his eyes that he was in love with that river more than you could be in love with any person or any thing on this planet. It was a she, no doubt about it, and she was a luscious one, running sweet to the sea, cardboard brown by day, dirty milk in the moonlight.

Once in a while my line would tug hard and I'd pull out a carp.

"Why can't we keep one?"

"A million fish bones. Put it back."

I'd give the fish a nudge with my foot and it'd slip into the chocolate drink and be gone. It made me mad to have to do that, and I'd pout.

Then Daddy'd say, "Let me tell you something about life. It's kind of like that five-pound carp you let go. I know that was hard to do. After all, you caught the thing, right? It was yours, you caught it, right?"

I felt guilty and didn't answer.

"But you did it. Did the right thing. Even when you didn't want to, you did. I had to coax you some, but you did it yourself. All by yourself. Someday I'm not going to be here and you'll be a big guy and you'll have to decide for yourself whether the fish needs to go back or not. And you'll decide, and you'll do the right thing. I think that's God."

"God?"

"God is the other side of everybody. The smart side. The side that says, Be careful now, do the right thing. That side. That voice. That's God to me. And that's God to your mama."

Then the bell'd ring up in the yard and we'd reel in and take the bait off our hooks and chuck it into the river and go up to lunch on that shiny white table on the back porch. Where there wasn't a breath of wind but it was somehow cool. Where the only sound was our forks against the big colored plates piled with the most delicious food ever cooked.

I gave Carl a month off after his wife's funeral, but he came back after a few days saying that if he stayed around the house he'd kill himself. I didn't argue, and he went about his work like always.

We got the Covington deal, and I gave Carl a thousand dollars cash.

He came and ate supper with us sometimes, but it wasn't like before. There were tremendous silences. I took him bowling a couple of times, too, but he played poorly, lost his temper in public.

One night that fall I told Venus we ought to take him to Puerto Azul for a while. I wanted to go see our new place down there, show it off to him. After all, he'd had a lot to do with it, having finished D&D so early and having bagged the Covington deal, which would see us through for another year or more easy. If anybody should get to enjoy it with us, Carl should. She had no trouble agreeing that we owed him a good turn.

He opened up the store the Saturday before the three of us were going to go on the trip, and I didn't get there until about eleven. I was going to get the last deposit ready, decide about the newspaper ads.

It irritated me to see there wasn't one car on the lot. Usually I won't do it, because the customers come first, but I parked up by the door. CLOSED, the sign said. He hadn't turned it around. I got out, started over. Hadn't turned on the lights, either. All the doors were open, though.

"Carl?"

No answer.

"Carl, you here? Yo!"

Then it was my turn to bump into the shelf and knock over a bottle of ammonia. The crap went everywhere.

"Carl!"

The light was shining in my office. I peered in there. Nobody. I went around the desk. The floor safe was open. All gone. Five or six grand, maybe more. It hadn't been forced. The knob was turned to the final number in the sequence, three.

"Son of a bitch."

Maybe I'm stupid or something. But I looked for a note. Maybe he'd explained. You didn't do that to people. Or did you?

There was no note.

I drove over to his house. Of course, everything was gone as if he'd cleared out weeks before. A neighbor woman came up to me in the yard to see if I needed any help. But I didn't answer.

Barber Brown

I said to Shirley, "That woman who drowned today didn't have to drown," and she said, "How's that, Barber?" And I said, "I think the idiots with her didn't do a thing when she fell in there," and she said, "What do you mean?" And I said, "Well, it looks like she fell in there and they didn't save her real fast like they could have." Shirley stared at me like a wife will sometimes. So I dropped it, went out in the backyard, sat on a lawn chair, and scratched my nuts. I don't like our yard much, but it's ours. Can't get any grass to grow back there on account of the sewage leaching out of the hill from the church. You'd think living next to a church with bad pipes wouldn't really be a problem, except maybe Sundays. But let me straighten you out on that. You've never seen people going to church as much as these people. Hell, I think a lot of them live there. The lights are always shining, and you can hear them carrying on at the oddest times. Maybe it's a cult. Maybe it's a sex cult. I wouldn't say that out loud, though. Not in Fill-in-the-Blank, Oklahoma, I wouldn't. If only because about everybody belongs to that damn church now. Weirdos. I don't need to go to no church to know right from wrong. I've known the difference since I was this high and I'll tell you this: Those people out there at the lake didn't lift a finger to help that woman who drowned. Now why is that? They weren't drunk, I would've seen that right off. They were stupid, I figure. Stupid cowards. Two grown men and a grown woman and they didn't do anything. All they had to do was to reach down in that hole real quick when she first went down in it and they would've caught her right up. But they stood there and didn't do anything and the woman sank down and down and then got stuck. Few seconds later she was all the way down in there and then it was too late. This shit happens all the time. People dying of stupid shit they don't have to die of. Dying for no reason, really, other than people not doing the right thing at the right time. It's like they'd had to think about it or something. Why think? What was there to think? And there came the phone call from the department. "Barber? Barber, come on out to Arrowhead Point. We got you a cistern drowning. Bring all your gear." I load up my scuba stuff, kiss the wife, peel out with my flashers going. People get out of the way and then I'm getting suited up and there are those three people carrying on and the police are asking them questions and nothing's getting anywhere. I go out there and down into that hole. There she is. Like meat on a hook. Jesus I hate this work. I hate holes in the lake. I hate dead people. I hate sewage and Christians and stupid people. I pull her up and out and the cowards are flipping out with grief. Flip out, you idiots. It's your own fault. Here's your body. My job is done here. Shirley says, "You think about it too much." I say, "What's too much, Shirley?" She says, "Too much is too much." Whatever that means. I don't know. I sat there pondering the church and the gunk oozing into my yard until night came and then went on into the house. It was hot as a parking lot in there. Shirley looked dead on the couch. I stared at her a long time, and then my mind was as empty as that dead woman's eyes under the water looking at me while I got her out.

Venus Blalock

Venus knew she was the kind of person who could walk out to the edge of light and say boo to the dark no matter how pitch black it was. And maybe she hadn't been truly frightened a day in her life.

So she had no problem when she decided that, well, yes, it would be all right to run around on her husband, an idea that had positively never occurred to her before. It was May who got her going. Telling her it was a natural thing, a part of a woman's life that she need not broadcast but that she definitely had no interest depriving herself of. For if all women halted themselves, said this couldn't or shouldn't be done, feared pleasure for the sake of pleasure after a certain age, then where would women be if not mired in unspoken misery as they'd been down through the ages?

At first, though, Venus had flinched. No other woman had ever spoken to her about sex, not straight out, not without walls and codes.

"You did it with other men before your husband, no?" May asked.

"No."

"Oh, my."

"That's not wrong. That's the way I was raised."

"Me, too, honey. But . . . no one?"

"No."

"It's not wrong to do this."

"Probably not, but Carl and I have a good thing. In fact, it's gotten better lately. And I mean in bed, too."

"Aren't you curious?"

"At times."

"I am all the time. But that doesn't make it vulgar or whorish. I love the power of the mystery, and of the body, and you know what? I like it when they don't talk, don't say a word. That's very sexy."

"I guess so."

"Damn right it is so. Unbelievable."

They were sitting in Venus's old red Impala parked in the shadow of the grocery store with the windows up and the air-conditioning going full blast and all the shopping left to do. They smoked cigarettes and if they'd had a fifth of something strong they'd have cracked it and chugged it right there. Because the world at large did not matter so much when they were together, except to the degree that May would suggest what might best be taken from it and enjoyed while their breasts were round and high and their asses hadn't sunk to faraway places and fun in bed with a stranger was a scrumptious delicacy to be consumed without guilt.

"We love our Carls. This has nothing to do with that."

"And yet it does."

"Well, then, some. But only as much as you allow. So don't allow."

"Easy to say."

"A stranger whose name you don't ever ask taking your clothes off slowly without speaking in a blue room. Putting his hand behind your neck and then the other hand behind your back and leaning you onto the bed. Oh, my."

Venus studied the cases of soft drinks sitting in the sunshine. Wouldn't they blow up one day? Go off like bombs? The car throbbed as it idled and the air conditioner sputtered.

"You simply give more and more life to your body," said May, "and then your body will give more and more life back to your soul, and you'll know that doing this for Venus can only be a good thing. You know, there have been times when I see Carl gazing down into my eyes as he makes love to me as if to say, Now where is all that coming from? And I shut my eyes to say, Don't ask me questions, just take the woman I'm giving you now, and then I move my body against his in a way maybe he's never known before and he's positively out of his mind with joy because there is no space between him and me and I make him believe that life can be anything we want it to be if only we don't shut doors or quit trying or doze our way through the show. A pageant. A glorious pageant."

No one had ever spoken of these things with Venus, and she sat staring at May leaning against the other door smoking. Venus imagined May's body moving against a man's, and then without a pause she imagined it moving against her own, and then the two of them moving together, in silence, in sunlight, on a broad white bed. She saw their hands buried in each other's hair. She saw their eyes locked straight on. But she did not say this to May, though the thought moved inside her as if it would never cease again, so that when they went into the store together buying groceries seemed like the most banal thing on earth.

"But who would I sleep with?" she asked near the chips section.

"Start with someone very tall."

They laughed, and kept laughing, and then people were sniffing at them like they truly might have been drinking. Which, of course, made them laugh all the more as they threw their purchases into their shiny carts and then rolled them along very slowly over the cool floor as if they relished some grand privilege others could only long for.

So Venus went and slept with Bob Hightower.

It was in a motel in Tishomingo, over in Oklahoma, where you went to do the things you didn't want anyone to know. A perfect place to break the vow she'd made to the man she married as a teenager. In a place full of down-and-out Indians and whites, all drunk. Hearing all their carrying-on in the other rooms. Hightower, a part-time cop she'd see at the highway coffee shop now and again, raising up and saying not to worry, if anybody tried anything he'd finish it, and giving a nod to his pistol on the nightstand. Staring up past him at the velvet Mexican nude on the wall and turning to an icicle when the woman in the next room started her rhythmic scream. Pushing Hightower off the second he finished his business and feeling like she'd throw up if she moved.

Then his silly words. "Are you okay?"

"No, I'm not okay."

"Is it this place?"

"I can't do this."

"But you did."

"I don't like you talking to me like that."

"Why not, Venus? You liked it, didn't you?"

Venus didn't answer him and lay flat and still on the rumpled sheets while he showered and sang cowboy songs off key.

On the way back to Red Rock he pulled the silent treatment on her as he whisked across the low bridges over the lake in the orange dusk. He wasn't going to lift a finger to save her from her questions.

So she took away his name and told herself that he was no one. Vowed that from then on, with the next man, she wouldn't know who he was, his name or anything. Like May had told her. So that it wouldn't just be this one ugly time, which she decided she wouldn't tell her about in a million years. So that nothing would get in the way of the pageant.

Once Venus had decided to take a particular road, she went down it with unstoppable determination. And so it was that she quickly worked through the question of how to sleep around some more by thinking of May's body doing things that Venus then wished to do with her own. Building a wave of desire that carried her without fear the next time into a motel room in Wichita Falls with a man she'd met in a bar at lunch.

"Don't tell me your name."

"All right. Another drink?"

"Vodka-tonic."

The clinking of the bottles in the minibar made her feel sick again, for a moment, but then they drank and the alcohol helped.

Not much else was very memorable in these encounters, except how hungry the men were. Kind of like puppies waiting to be fed? She liked that. She liked puppies. Come here, you, she'd say when the moment came. Come on up in here and get yourself some loving, puppy.

"What'd you call me?"

One time she got slapped for that. But it was still good puppy loving. She only had to put on some extra makeup to hide it.

She never worried when she was with Blalock, never feared he might find out because the question would never arise in his contented mind. And they made love unboundedly and he stayed happy as a puppy, too. It made her want to go on, be every woman to every man.

"A goddess who extinguishes all pain with a single touch of her soft, pink-painted nails." So said May in Venus's kitchen after dinner one night. Which got them to laughing hard.

The Carls were on the front porch. "What's so funny?" one of them called.

"The whole damn world," May replied.

"Oh," one of them said.

Then May said, "I went shopping Thursday."

"You did? How was it?"

"Thursday afternoon. I like the afternoon, you know."

"I went yesterday. In the morning."

"Morning is nice, too."

"Yes."

They almost started laughing again, but then they didn't and watched each other quietly. It was okay. They had some natural red color to their cheeks those days. Everything seemed alive and good.

"Kiss me good night, Venus. We have to go home."

Venus leaned forward to peck her on the cheek, but May moved her mouth right in the way, and then they were kissing. It was over in a few seconds, and they pondered each other. But they didn't say anything, and then May and her Carl went home.

May. Teacher of Temptations. First and Last Best Friend.

They'd buried her in late summer. May's Carl had stood there with them listening to the Methodist preacher say the departing words, and then they had run to the limos when the thunderhead broke and it started hailing and the driver tore out of there to get the car under something. In the rush it turned out that Blalock had ended up in another limo, leaving Venus alone with Stein while they waited out the storm in a carport next to the White Cloud Laundry. It was coming down big as pecans and they couldn't see half a block.

"You better have insurance today," said the driver, a Mexican kid.

Venus tried some Spanish, to say hello, how are you.

"Lady, I don't have to talk to you," the kid answered.

"Problem, son?" Stein asked him.

"I'm no son of yours, mister."

Venus smiled at Stein to let him know what he'd done was okay. It also meant to take it easy.

Then the boy said, "Leak," got out and walked off.

The hail had almost stopped.

Stein put his hand on Venus's lap.

She looked down at it and recalled being a girl in the backseat of a car helping a boy come in his jeans because they couldn't do it for real. Watching him grunt and carry on, but raking her fingers through his hair and saying she loved him so he would hurry up and finish.

Stein did nothing with his hand. Left it there.

Then Venus lifted it away.

Nothing was said.

His eyes dropped. Hers shifted away.

Where was that Mexican boy? Only now, she thought, were the grave diggers filling the hole back up with all that gray clay and slapping the huge mound of it with their shovels. Only now was the casket being sealed into the silence of the earth. Maybe half an hour passed, maybe a lifetime, then the kid showed up and drove them to the funeral home.

Blalock was standing under the green awning.

"I won't tell him," Venus said to Stein.

Stein stared at a spot near Venus's feet. Then he climbed out, glanced at Blalock, walked off.

"What the hell," said Blalock.

"Let him be," said Venus. "That was his wife we buried."

There was hail slush all over the ground. Stein walked on it like it wasn't there, bent, older, his breath making clouds.

To Venus, May was the exotic bird that will sometimes land outside your window in winter. You marvel at it because it shouldn't be there at all. Then in a moment it is gone. Never to come back.

Blalock found Stein a couple of nights later in a bar and told him to take the month off. Stein'd sat there like a mental patient. So when Blalock said he'd showed up at the store three days later neatly dressed and freshly shaved, Venus was certain something strange was going on.

"Could you do that? Come right back to work like it'd been nothing?"

"I don't know, Venus."

"Don't you think it's odd?"

"I think he knows what he's doing."

"What's that?"

Blalock slammed shut a ledger on the kitchen table. "Go ask him!"

But she never did, and then it got odder when he took to smiling at her when she hung around the store, like he was coming on to her for real. It went on a long time one afternoon. There hadn't been a customer for hours and Blalock had gone to Dallas to see about a paneling shipment. So Venus leaned on the counter and watched Stein doing inventory.

"Why do you keep smiling at me?"

"Smiling at you?" A bottle of something slipped and broke. "Shit," he said. "Why would I smile at you?"

And then he was out the door, gone.

Venus went and stared at the black, oily mess. It was fizzing, eating the linoleum. Somebody was going to have to do something.

Venus missed May and took long walks and then when she had taken enough walks she stayed in bed and let the world do without her.

One time someone rang the doorbell in the middle of the afternoon. She didn't get up. The bell rang and rang, and she lay there thinking it was Stein come to solace himself with her. Blalock was at work.

She wasn't about to answer it. Because she would only have seen May's eyes gazing out of his eyes and she would have become angry.

Then the ringing stopped.

She rested on the pillows and told herself that the only goodness left on this earth was the goodness you had within you like a secret fire. That you could do any number of things on earth, go anywhere almost, do anything almost, so long as you didn't let it drown the fire. The flame that May had possessed and given. The flame that Venus knew she had inside her, too, and that she must keep safe from forces that would put it out.

The knock on the window would've scared anybody. A man banging with a hammer on the screen frame, calling, "May? You in there, May?"

Venus got down low in the bed. He was cupping his eyes and peering. She knew he could see her.

"Go away!"

He banged and banged.

"Venus! Venus!"

Or was it Blalock, lost his keys, locked out? She sat up. "Carl?"

"Open this window, honey!"

She went over, pushed the thin curtains out of the way.

But there was no one there.

Only the motionless mulberry tree. She got hold of the window and pulled it up. Stood looking out through at the hot afternoon air and waiting for her heart to slow. There was no sound at all.

Then a burst of wind came and the limbs of the tree flew against the house, almost into her face. She jumped back.

"Damn you! Damn you!"

The limbs whacked the house again and again.

Then halted. As if the air had never moved.

"Damn," she said again.

Then she shut the window and the dusty curtains and sat on the edge of the bed without moving until evening, when the room turned deep red.

Sometimes in the night Venus would think how a light will come along in this life if you're lucky, and how if you're very lucky it will shine upon you. The light's name will be May Stein. And she will penetrate every corner of your life, turn everything inside out, expose your soul to the air, shine into it and through it and cast out its shadows. She will urge celebration, demand recklessness, stir up storms of desire and questions never asked or long ago disallowed. She will discard fear, impermanence, all that is not joy. Turn life into something astonishing where before there had only been a man with a very hairy back who ran a hardware-lumber store and the neat grid of curbed streets and the slow car ride down Pecan to the grocery or down Lamar to the library, then the slow car ride back home to evenings that went on and on. She will pour new colors into the world and set all things to shimmering, vibrating in the air, and make you see marvels everywhere.

May Stein had remade all things in this way until the chance hand of destruction swiped the table clean like a drunk man angry or jealous at the new turn of the game, at his opponent's vain conviction that she could win, crush him with her will to live ecstatically and without fear. And then the light called May was flung away, and in the ferocious power of the movement all people and things close to her were drawn in that direction, too, the way trees will tilt after a big wind, toward that lightless place, a pit that Venus imagined rising all around her.

Other days Venus went out and it did not matter so much where she went but that she went anywhere. A bar in a motel, most often. A place with thick mildew-stinking curtains and an older woman for a bartender. Maybe they'd talk, maybe even about May.

"This great light that just appeared," Venus always said.

"It sure sounds like it."

"There is not a doubt in my mind but that she came into my life and gave it everything I didn't know was missing."

"You're very lucky, sister."

"Is it luck? Or are these things supposed to be?"

"I don't know. Isn't it enough that it happens?"

"But it doesn't. Hardly ever. This is like . . . I don't know."

"Touch of God? If you're religious. Refill?"

Venus drank her vodka-tonic and then a stranger came in and he was all over her and they drifted out to the lobby and he got a room and May was alive and smiling within Venus as she let the man remove her clothes in front of the air conditioner. It was a very quiet motel, nobody there, not even when evening came and the weary should've been pulling in off the road with their children.

It was Blalock who suggested they all three go out to the rock Red Rock was named for. This was only a couple of days before the rip-off. All they'd do was eat pimento cheese sandwiches and watch idiots climbing that rock. A big brown thing not at all red.

Blalock got drunk the fastest. It didn't take Stein long to catch up, and then they were high school kids again on a fall afternoon. "Check out that one, Stein. Whew, how'd you like that next to you?"

"Not in my worst nightmare."

"Bet she was pretty back when. Real pretty, even. But then they'll blow up on you like that. Boom!"

"Whoop, yer fat!" Stein said, like he was umpiring a ball game.

Maybe the woman heard them, maybe not. Her husband had, though, and started toward them, then saw how big one of them was, dropped it. Blalock and Stein had another laugh.

Venus was thinking about May and about how neither Carl was giving the dead person a thought.

"Anybody want to climb?" she asked.

"Out of your mind?" Stein said.

Blalock threw in with him. "No way."

Venus went ahead anyway. How long had it been since she'd gone up on Red Rock? Ages. The steps cut into it were rounded off.

When she arrived at the summit, nearly out of breath, she squatted and scanned the earth. The lake looked like oil spilled onto the colored quilt of the land. Would she ever let herself get into it again? she wondered. What was the point of climbing up there anyway? Just to see again where all the spinning mess began?

"Bet you can see ten miles," said Stein, also breathless from climbing.

"If you wanted to," Venus said.

"I want to. I always want to see as far as I can. I like being high up."

Venus wasn't going to turn and look at him.

"It's like when you have the open road in front of you, too," he said. "You're not tied to anything. You're free to go forward or backward or sideways. And there's this feeling of not knowing what's over the next rise, who'll be there, what people you'll meet, what they'll say, what you'll do. I guess what I'm saying is I can't do without that for long."

Venus didn't answer. A mother and child came by. The woman had on a green dress and a yellow hat. The boy was dressed in green shorts, a white T-shirt, and a red cap. It seemed like they hadn't seen each other in a long while because they kept stopping and hugging, then pointing all around and talking, then clutching each other again. A man who had to be the boy's father arrived, meantime. But he kept apart, smoking, gazing around. Though he seemed like he wanted to join them.

"You don't talk much to me," Stein said.

He found a stone and chucked it off the rock. It sailed and sailed and landed way out there without a sound. The other man who was waiting for the mother and the boy stared hard at Stein and then he threw a stone, too. It flew as far. Then the two men eyed each other.

"Don't you want to go somewhere, Venus?" Stein asked.

"Go where?" It was Blalock, gasping.

"To get another beer," said Stein, not missing a beat. "Bring some?"

"What, am I the waiter? So how about this view, huh?"

"Nice," said Stein.

"Yeah," said Venus. "Paradise."

"Hey, you can see all the way over there where we were with May," Blalock announced, pointing.

"Is there something wrong with you?" Venus demanded.

"I'm sorry . . . I —"

"Why would we want to look at that place? Why?" she asked.

Blalock put his hand on Stein's shoulder. "I'm sorry. I didn't mean —"

"Forget it," Stein said.

"I'm going back down," said Venus.

"We just got up here," said Blalock.

"Let her go, Blalock," Stein said.

It sounded like an order.

Venus started down off the rock.

"Women," Blalock said, loud enough that she heard.

"Shut up," said Stein.

"Ho! Who're you telling to shut up?"

Venus didn't look back. Maybe they'd end up punching each other out, maybe they'd push each other off the rock. Did it matter?

When she got to the ground again, she waited in the car and watched for the troubled couple and their kid. Enjoyed feeling the sunlight on her arm in the window. Glanced up at the broad sapphire sky.

Of course their boy had to be named something innocent, like Jimmy, the first boy to ever pull on her hand and take her behind a pear tree for a mouth kiss in the middle of the wasp-swarming summer, and Venus didn't have to keep her eyes open any longer to see him coming down from up there ahead of his parents, leaping along on those steps. One miss and he'd tumble to his death, the furthest thing from anybody's mind.

Like Jimmy the farm boy who hadn't come back to school that fall long ago, who'd been caught under his horse one summer day when it stumbled drinking in the cow tank and drowned. Like May. When no one could have conceived such a thing ever happening.

No, she didn't look at him doing that scary stuff, or see his mom and dad still way above, now holding hands, helping each other, then stopping to hug long and hard like everything was all right again. No, she wouldn't see him fall off that rock onto the sandy earth and lie there on his back dead as his newly reunited parents froze in horror.

But Venus would hear him when he busted out laughing like it was the funniest thing that had ever happened, him falling all that way and not the least thing broke or scratched, look!

She would not look, though. How could she?

Not even when the adults' voices got loud and almost washed away the laughter, and not even when the three of them, talking and moving along in light-filled harmony, went right past the Suburban where she was sitting in the sun with her eyes shut firmly.

She wouldn't look because this couldn't be. Things couldn't get that close to death and then suddenly be right again in a flash. That just couldn't be. Or didn't everyone else know?

It was a fiercely windy day. Blalock had left before lunch and didn't show up again until the middle of the afternoon. He was dazed, like he'd been knocked with a board. The wind had parted his hair on the wrong side and his face was red-brown, as if he'd been out in the wind for hours. Venus listened to the story about the empty safe and the empty Stein house and the possible reasons for it all for hours, deep into the evening, into the night. On and on, Blalock talked, trying to find the why. But it was like trying to stop the wind. It would stop only when it was ready, and it blew as if it would strip the earth bare to its stone base. Venus didn't say much back, waited until he lowered his head and didn't say the next thing. Then she got him to bed and went and sat in the kitchen and drank coffee and listened to the grit hitting the window screens. People did these things to each other, but she couldn't understand how. Or, yes, she could understand how, but only if people were no longer people. And if that was it, if that was what had happened, then what was Carl Stein? She could feel his hand on her lap again. Like wet clay. And the hand going for it, going for the money in the floor safe.

Telling her that to go and live their lives as they had been intending to was the best medicine of all, Carl shut his store and took her on down through Mexico to the Pacific Ocean like they'd planned.

For the first time, though, Venus thought that the road was far too long, that every mile seemed like the one before, leaving her with no choice but to sleep in long stretches while he drove, there being nothing to see, nothing at all in the unbroken sprawl of brown rock.

She awoke from her first long slumber, all the way from Monterrey, at a Pemex station outside Querétaro, in the highlands. Carl was watching the boy pump gas into the Suburban, and she had walked across the huge parking area past dozens of stinking trucks and gawking drivers until she came to the edge of a wasteland of sand and trash and scrub where she could see a long ways. The heated wind off the desert dried her mouth and made her squint. And she thought how this squinting made it feel like she was looking hard for something out there. It was midday and men catcalled from their oil-spattered rigs.

"What are you doing?"

Carl. Nervous and worried.

"Looking at this view."

He waited a moment. Then touched her elbow and said, "Let's get out of here. Don't you want to see the ocean?"

"I'm coming."

"Come on."

"I'm coming, Carl."

The truckers yapped and Carl went back to the Suburban.

Venus stayed there awhile more, thinking, Here I am wondering whether I do or do not love Carl Blalock now that May Stein has died. It was a strange question, as odd as the waste into which she stared for an answer. Which came, as on one of those whirlwinds that will spin into the road out of nowhere. Dust skipped up out of the desert and flew at Venus and forced her to turn away. As if the earth itself had tired of her. Wanted her to get out of there and stop asking questions. She did love Carl. She would always love May. Where was the problem? The wind blew and pushed her back to Carl.

"All done?" he asked quietly.

"Done."

"Let's get to the ocean. It can only be good for us both."

She believed that he had somehow understood what she'd been looking for out there and sat closer to him as they plunged southward.

They'd been in Puerto Azul maybe a month, she couldn't remember, when one night, from the deck of their new house, she looked down into the jungle below and saw a cemetery. Maybe fifty yards down among the trees and boulders, a pale orange light hanging over it, the glow of hundreds of candles. Between the black and green trunks and branches, people dressed in white moving in slow motion.

"Do you see them?"

"Hell, yes, I see them," Carl said.

"What are they doing?"

"Day of the Dead. It's like a picnic or something. Right here."

He took a long drink, then planted his glass on the table, offended.

The air smelled of wood smoke and meat. Venus pictured herself among the women laying out the food for the dead, and then waiting and looking at the food and at each other, maybe nibbling something, and the candles spitting and the wax running down the headstones. Imagined the cemetery back home where mounds of grave dirt had melted down and the grass had grown back as if there'd never been a vulgar cut in the dirt, as if there'd never been a casket going down in there with May in it.

"Are you angry, Carl?"

"I was thinking no one would dare drink a cup of water out there in the cemetery where Mama's buried. But this is all right."

"Like a supper."

"Long as they don't make noise."

Venus frowned at him. "You're kidding, right?"

"Certainly am not."

But then he lifted his glass and rattled the ice cubes hard, to make sound, and smiled, and after this they could hear voices rising from the graveyard as though headed toward some higher place, whispered prayers. It lasted deep into the night.

Another night, Carl said, "Did you know it's almost time, honey?"

"For?"

"For Mr. Pullman to put on 'Strangers in the Night.'"

Venus looked up with Carl at the white stone mansion on the top of the mountain above. "No lights. Not home."

"No, no, I just saw him. He even waved. I think."

"That's progress."

"He'll put that record on any minute. I'm telling you, he's a close friend of Frank Sinatra's. The real estate man told me this."

"You're like a child about it," Venus said.

Carl glanced at her drink, as if to gauge how much she'd had. "I wouldn't mind meeting Frank Sinatra, Venus."

"Whatever for?"

"Because we can now."

"Excuse me?"

"I mean, look where we're living now, Venus. It's our place, our stone walls, our pool, our furniture, our everything. We can meet Frank Sinatra, our neighbor."

"He's not our neighbor, Carl."

"You know what I'm saying, Venus. It's what I busted my bottom selling truckloads of two-bys and plate glass and mirrors and toilets and nails and bolts and industrial solvents for. To have this place and say it's mine and sit out here like I like and hope that whoever that guy is up there he really knows Frank Sinatra. We're not low folks anymore. Don't you kind of like the idea of telling your friends how you met Sinatra and invited him over and sat around with him and talked about the things he's done? Can you imagine that? I don't know, it's like we're not what we were anymore. I'd like to never have to go back. We have money and —"

"Money? Carl took our money."

"That was only petty cash, for Christ's sake. We have money. Plenty enough. We have seven contracts going last I counted."

"There's more to life than Frank Sinatra."

"What's that mean?"

Venus watched the cemetery. "Do you think about May?"

"No. I think about Frank."

Was he trying to be funny? Or sick funny?

"I keep thinking of her," she said. "More and more."

"I don't know what good it does. Best to let go. It's time now."

Something went crashing through the jungle, likely an iguana. The insects' song stopped. A bell clanged on an ocean liner below.

"I think about May, and also about you and me," she said.

Blalock waited a long time.

Then he said, "It's like she and Carl made everything fuller than it'd ever been. Especially her, the way she filled a room with something. And he was my friend. I told him everything. I laid out all the crap of my life right there in front of him. And then he went and did that. You ever wonder if she knew all along what he did for a living, ripping people off?"

"I'm certain she didn't know."

"I don't know. This may have been a long-term act or —"

"She was good, I believe that. And the bad lives on. Gets away with it. Do you think he'll spend his whole life that way?"

"He's cut that way."

"He mourned over May, didn't he? Really mourned?"

"He better have."

"Maybe he didn't."

"I think he did, Venus."

She frowned. "You and me, then."

Again, he waited, looking out at the jungle. "What about us?"

"Were we looking for something to happen to us?"

"I don't follow you."

"Did we get our wish?"

"What wish?"

"A very bad wish, maybe. Like we'd hoped something dramatic would happen, to shake us up. Only it just happened to involve the death of this young woman?"

"You don't mean that, do you?"

"It feels that way."

"That's crazy."

"There were so many things about them we didn't understand."

"Yes."

"Why is it like she had to die so we could sit here and talk about it?"

"You lose me, Venus."

"It seems wrong that we can be alive and everything about her still inside us and yet she isn't allowed to live."

"It was an accident."

"All the worse."

Carl went and stuck a hand in the pool. "Want to swim naked?"

His voice had that anxious edge to it, and she knew what he wanted. She said no. He lifted his nightcap to toast her, then went on in to bed.

Venus went and draped a hand in the warm pool and knew he'd

been right about it being good for swimming naked. She might have gone to wake him and bring him out, to make it good between them for a while, but already she found herself dropping her clothes and stepping in and going down the steps. There was no moon and she swam in a circle without a sound. Hearing again the voices rising from the jungle below.

Later on, seeing a man dressed in white waiting on the veranda of the mansion high above. Later still, hearing the Sinatra record come on and whine oddly as if the air in which the music moved were warped.

It would play that way until dawn.

William Pullman

The ocean moves inside me and I move inside the ocean and it could be no other way for us since my Gloria crossed the borderland where air meets water and went into the ancient depths. *El mar,* the place where all roads end if you take them, if you go to the far edges of the rocks. From this high place I can see the sea curving away like a slender shoulder, and I can see Gloria's eyes in the waves when they glitter far out there.

I only got as far as the Arrowhead Point Motel, there on the bluff near the place where May died. The log cabins had red curtains, which felt strange because we'd had red curtains in our home, and late that first night I went outside as if to pay my dead wife a visit. It had turned cold and the north wind made the oaks creak as I sat at the edge of the drop-off and stared at the wraparound dark until daylight returned and the lake began to glow gray as if it were covered with ice.

At sunup the few people who'd stopped there for the night came out into the chilly pink air and stretched their limbs and talked loudly, then climbed into their cars, struggled to get them going, and drove away slowly. By eight o'clock the place was empty.

The road out of there lay only a few feet away. But I couldn't manage to get into my Falcon and go. The ridge felt safe, the bow of a sturdy ship cutting out into that lake. I could see back across the water to Texas, the rolling countryside, and recalled many a good drunk night with Blalock roaring down the back roads with a bottle of bourbon propped between us on the seat and deer cutting through the headlights. I had stolen his money and I would miss him, and his pretty Venus, but I had no real regrets at this point. The other side of me, the part that takes and does not return, was used to this. I'd done it to countless people, in countless towns, and I'd do the same thing to many more folks.

A week passed, then two, and the cold snap settled in like it was going to stay for the winter. To keep from going goofy while I made up my mind just when to get out of there, I begged the manager, Virgil McKown, for odd jobs. I fixed windows, doors, beds, raked leaves, emptied trash, scrubbed toilets. I worked for chicken feed and he skipped the questions because, being a Vietnam War invalid, he was glad to have me do anything for him that required much physical effort.

Cynthia, the Cherokee cleaning girl, once came and sat on the bluff and watched the lake with me after I was done tinkering for the day.

"Is there something wrong with you?" she asked.

I didn't answer, which was an answer anyway.

A guy was coming by in a boat. I don't know what he thought he was going to catch in that biting wind. He stopped over a dark spot down in the water. Which, the longer I looked at it, I realized was the very cistern that May had drowned in. He cast his line like he was just anywhere.

"If you told me, then we'd be able to talk," she said.

I didn't like the guy fishing there like that at all.

"Nothing," I said.

She stared at me a long time, then watched what I was watching. Which was the guy fishing right over the cistern. He'd known where it was. You'd think they'd have covered the damn thing after the death.

"You lost something here," she said. "Now you're finding it again."

It was real cold, but I could tell that guy was going to sit there in that boat over that hole and leave his line down in there for as long as it took.

Maybe a whole frigid hour went by. Then Cynthia sighed, got up, and left. I watched the guy fishing until dusk. Then he reeled in, buzzed away. Somehow the scene left me kind of sick to my stomach. Like the boat on which I was riding had entered rough waters I hadn't expected.

I worked days fixing up the motel, and then at night I drank a lot and did things with Cynthia in bed. She put candles all over the room, and then we lay speculating about each other, and I felt the strength in her limbs and would put May's face where hers was, May's blond hair where her black strands lay. The fire in the fireplace burned hot and I could sit naked in its glow and lose my dark thoughts among the flames while that woman rubbed my back in a way that made me forget pain.

Then Virgil put up Christmas lights around the office door, got an aluminum tree out of a box, and stuck it on the counter.

"Not the spirit of the season," he said, "but I've run out of work."

The place sparkled, nothing banged, every light burned, not one shower dripped. But it was blowing snow and there were no customers.

"You've been good to me, Virgil."

"You could sure say that again."

"I'm getting that old road chill anyway."

"What's that you say?"

"Ever been out in the middle of nowhere, Virgil? Like when you were hunting or walking back in the woods? So far out there you have this flash that goes through you saying maybe I'll never make it back from out here, maybe I'm so far out here I'm lost and no one will ever find me and I'll never have the strength to get back through all that empty space. Ever feel that?"

"Damn right I have. In 'Nam. More than once, too."

"I didn't mean anything. Sorry."

"Don't worry about it. 'Nam sucked. I'm just trying to keep my head on my shoulders here. You do the same, friend. Only way to go."

I tore a string of popcorn off the tree and looped it around my coat collar and thought about my older brother coming home in a bag from over there. "Only way to go is right."

"Leave my tree alone!"

"I'm out of here, Virgil. Keep Cynthia warm for me."

"You know it."

I went to the bluff for a last look. At the water freezing along the shore. At the cistern waiting for its next victim. I pondered the open road. To anywhere I wanted to go. Hundreds of miles of wind and asphalt and peanut butter crackers and soft drinks, radio playing full blast, nobody to tell me no. Going town to town like I did with May.

Hooking into lives, making strangers into best friends. But I didn't get so close to these people that they made me forget my game. I kept some unspoken space there, enough so I could go without any trouble or regret when the time came. And I had this way of knowing when it was time. I'd get up from whatever I was doing that day, grab some cash, steal a checkbook, lift credit cards, anything I could take, no matter who they were. It worked because I always managed to have their total confidence. And so it was easy. And even fun, too, especially when I was with May, who was always ready to go — well, most of the time anyway — and who sat on the car seat bent forward toward the world as if it were there for her to be discovered. I liked taking her down the road through it.

But I never told her where the wads of money suddenly came from. I wouldn't have wanted to spoil the look on her face. I wouldn't have wanted her to turn away from me saying that it was wrong. When it wasn't wrong at all. When it was simply a matter of survival, Stein style.

"Some people will work their lives away in lightbulb factories," I said to myself. "Or down at the dog food plant."

I knew what I meant. And I knew what the wind did to me in my gut whenever I was standing in the open night a hundred miles from the nearest town, out under the unending stars with May next to me breathing slowly and holding on to me. My baby. Gone. I stood close to the edge of the bluff and looked at that spot in the water as the snow thickened and wind picked up. Then a hand fastened on my shoulder. Cynthia.

"Going to leave without saying?"

I looked at her long brown face.

What was there to say? Of course I was. And she knew it.

She walked off and I watched her until I couldn't see anything but swirling white stuff.

When I checked the lake again, the dark spot in the water was gone. Snow skittered over the thin ice. I was a deer. I could run a thousand miles. I looked around. Then started away. Quickly.

I recalled being in the desert the night my ma ran away from Pa. I was maybe six. There was so much stuff in the car I couldn't move. My brother, who was starting to have a mustache, was stuffed in there, too, asleep and snoring. Ma was holding the steering wheel with both fists. No cars, no trucks, nothing but the silvery-shiny road and the yellow stripes flying under the hood as she ran them down. Every so often long-armed cacti jumped up out of the darkness to try to get us. But Ma saved us every time. Sang church songs real loud. And the cacti fell back.

You picked a dot on the map. Then went there. Of course, this time, it did have to be a ways down the road. But that was no problem. My Falcon could've gotten me to Africa. Like last time, I went about it in very much less than a straight line, drove long distances and often very slowly for days, days that then clumped together into a number of weeks, then looked out over the hood and realized I'd gotten to the dot, the small town, which was any town. A place where a stranger was an oddity but where my talents worked best.

I bought a fifth of bourbon and pulled into a public park and drank it kicking on a swing. There was no hurry. All that had come before and all the unknown that lay ahead didn't matter a hoot. The booze went down fast. Then I started thinking how pretty a town I'd found. I could see the whole thing laid out like in a magazine — winding river, main street, neat wooden and brick houses, white steeple every few blocks. Everything anybody would want in a town. A place like eternity. A place to turn honest and settle down? That was stupid, because I knew myself. And who can change who he is? I capped the bottle. Enough of that.

I had come uncountable miles and I was beat. But it hadn't been a crazy run, like it used to be with May, flying along and carrying on, turning any way we wanted, hurtling through the countryside. This time it'd been stone quiet, as if I were crossing abandoned land. I'd rolled. Filled her up and kept going. Again and again. I didn't recall state lines, only the changes, hills here, flats there, pines here, oaks there. Dust. Freezing wind. Headlights. A bar for a beer. A motel for a rest. Again and again.

It was late and cold, and here came a police car, shining a light on me, and then an officer ordered me to stand up. But I couldn't. My road legs had given out. So he took me in. Just as well. It turned out lucky, too. For the first time in as long as I could remember, I slept like a child.

The Falcon was full of our stuff and the police got all over me the next morning about that. Asked lots of questions. I kept it friendly, told them what they needed to know, even showed my billfold pictures. "And this is my deceased wife, May. Drowning accident."

The thirty-something guy who was playing detective probably hadn't been laid in years. Wide-eyed, testy. "Where was that?"

I was drinking their good coffee.

"Beaver Lake," I lied. "Up in the Ozarks."

"Beaver Lake, huh. Green, didn't you used to go fishing up in the Ozarks?"

Green was maybe seventy. They had him propped at a small desk by the water bottle. "What's that?" he shouted.

"Forget it! Well, Mr. Stein, I'm very sorry about your loss. Nevertheless, we're going to have to fine you for public drunkenness and disorderly."

"Disorderly?"

"Three hundred."

"Bucks?"

"We don't take pesos . . ."

The old guy somehow heard that one and laughed and chucked a clump of papers from one side of his desk to the other.

"I was only drunk, sir," I said. "Bothering nobody."

"Sir? I like that. I like that a lot. Will you say it again?"

He patted his pot like he was proud of it.

I said, "No sir."

"There you go! I like this guy. That's pretty funny."

They laughed. It was like that stupid movie where the cops are aliens from some planet. Nobody ever came out of those aliens' jail and at long last the town figured it out and attacked. But then the mother spaceship got involved and started zapping the town with its blue laser.

Then he said, "You're going to have to pay the three hundred, though. It's that or twenty-one days."

I paid with twenties and he counted it up.

He sat back, relaxed. "Welcome to Iona, Louisiana. Looks like you've been on the road awhile, buddy. Nicky Blair."

It was a different man speaking to me then.

Then Green came over. "Yep, a real traveler."

I didn't say anything.

Green said, "Real sorry about your wife. I lost mine twenty-seven years ago this winter. Don't know why, but I'm still here."

"Green's been with us forty-two years," said Blair.

"Took this job before you were even born, kiddo. I shot Dick Owen."

I looked at them. And they looked at me like I was supposed to know who Dick Owen was. So I said, kind of loud, "You're kidding!"

"Nope," said Blair. "This here is the man."

"Can I shake your hand?" I asked him.

He grinned, poked his hand out. "Put her there."

We shook and then I said, "Dick Owen. Goddamn!"

"Yep," he said. "Right in the yahoos."

He pointed at his crotch. I laughed and Blair laughed and the old boy bent over playing the wounded Dick Owen. God, who was Dick Owen?

"Sure hope you'll tell me all about it sometime," I said.

"We could do that," Green said. "Coffee shop on Cypress. Sunup."

"Maybe sometime," I said. You didn't commit. But you stayed polite. Then I said to Blair, "Bet you've heard it."

"Oh, Lord," he said. "'And he came into the room and there we were face-to-face and I drew my pistol and squatted down and fired and . . .'"

"Ho there, that's my story!"

"The Ballad of Dick Owen?" I asked.

"Takes all day and all night, that ballad," said Blair.

I said thanks a lot again for taking my three hundred dollars, and they said think nothing of it, and then I walked out. I wanted to find a doughnut place. I like doughnuts more than some men like life. As I was driving off I imagined those boys sitting there in silence for a while. Then Green saying, "Better watch that one." And Blair nodding and going to the percolator for more coffee.

I found a doughnut joint, bought half a dozen plain ones, ate them all, and despite that peaceful rest I'd gotten in the Iona jail fell asleep in my Falcon in the parking lot to thoughts of sweet sugar glaze and the lips of the cute girl who'd sold me the doughnuts.

John Wayne plays Dick Owen standing at the bar next to me. It's in a ghost town in Nevada and there's nothing to drink, no bartender, only me and Owen leaning on the counter and studying each other in the mirror. The shine on the mirror is mostly eaten away and our faces appear to be gouged. We've been there a long time, waiting on Green. I say, "You got a gun, Owen?" He doesn't answer, and so I reach over and pat him down. No gun. Then I have my hand in his back pocket where he keeps his billfold. Only I can't pull it out. It's thick and I know damn well there's a lot of money in it, but the thing won't come free. He's watching me in the mirror while I do this, expressionless, as if dead. "What'd you do, glue the damn thing in your pants, Owen?" I say to him. "That what you do to keep boys from stealing your goodies, Owen? That what your ma taught you, Owen?" He seems to be sobbing in fear but I can't see tears. Then Green is there, snub-nosed pistol drawn and pointed at us. I forget about the billfold and step back. "All yours, Green." Owen turns, facing Green, and says, "Why, hi there, Green! I've been waiting on you, good buddy." Owen reaches for something in his pocket to give to Green, but Green lets him have it right in the crotch. Owen falls and the fat billfold pops free. I grab it and scurry away and then Green is shooting at me and the bullets are buzzing like bees in slow motion around my head. It's for sure I'm going to get stung bad by these babies, so I run and run, but it's no use because the ground is being pulled out from under me like a cloth off a table.

You found an apartment to live in the same way you found a town. Stuck your finger on an ad, went there, and moved in. Not very difficult.

I stayed quiet for weeks watching TV and then the spring rain came down. The paper said holes were opening in the streets. Every retaining wall in creation flopped over and contractors' phones rang off the hook. There were prayer meetings to stop the rain. It kept pouring.

I laid very low wishing May were alive. Drank coffee and observed the rain and worried about whether there would ever be another decent lady in my life. Because it has got to be a rare thing to have what I had with May. There was the heat and fire of it, yeah, and that was fast and great, but there was also the cold and ice of it, and that was slow and easy, like things up in the mountains where nothing disturbs the natural order unless there's a violent storm. I met her in a downpour, in fact. Trying to get into the same phone booth late one April morning in Fergus Falls, Wisconsin, the place I'd picked out by stabbing the map when I up and left Ma and my bad job out in Albuquerque. I'd pulled up in my Falcon and gotten out just as the girl came rushing along in a short dress with all that hair curling this way and that, and then we collided at the flap doors like kids.

"Somebody about to die?" she demanded.

I stopped, backed off. "No."

"Good, because my best friend is in the hospital in Minneapolis and is waiting for this call."

And with that, she slipped into the booth and proceeded to have what I am certain was the longest conversation ever held on this earth. She had a big cloth bag of coins, which she kept feeding into the phone like there would never be an end to coins.

I stood there and stood there and then it was afternoon and the girl began to notice that I was still there and to watch me, but in that distant way people do when they are chatting their heads off with someone. I thought, Now here is a fine and shapely specimen of womanhood in a powder-blue dress who is perhaps in need of company and surely in need of someone to speak with directly.

She gabbed and gabbed and stared at me more and more, up and down, down and up, side to side, and I leaned against the glass door and did the same without flinching, and the rain still came down.

Finally she hung up and pulled the door open. I stepped in. It was a deeply warm place. From which I will never emerge again except perhaps when my time is up for good.

Then the sun came out over Iona and fried up creation again. People were thrilled. Shouting, Hello, how're you doing, and how about that rain. I nodded and continued on wherever I was headed, never far, maybe to the corner for smokes or beer or to peek at the girlie magazines.

"My God, look at those hooters!"

It was the cop who'd taken all those twenties of mine. I stayed calm, acted like running into him was no sweat. "Yeah, she's got it."

"I'd say she's got it all. Mamasita!"

"Going to arrest me again?"

"No. Where you been?"

"Home watching the rain."

"All this time? Wasn't that something? We haven't had that much rain since nineteen fifteen."

"Kept you busy?"

"You bet. Had about three hours of sleep a night the last two weeks, which is only somewhat better than the two hours of sleep a night I got the two weeks prior. You been getting along all right?"

I shut the magazine. "Fair enough."

"Live around here?"

"Down the street."

"This street?"

I pointed. "Right there."

"Those red brick ones?"

"You got it."

"See that gray brick house there under the mimosa trees? That's my place. Funny, I haven't seen you around."

"I don't get out much."

"That's all right. Hey, can I tell you something personal?"

"What's that?"

"I am in deep need of a fishing partner. How about it? Seeing that we're neighbors and all."

"I don't fish much."

"It's not a contest or anything. Somebody to fish with. Crappie."

"Crappie?"

"Yeah. You've been crappie fishing, ain't you?"

"Been awhile."

"Well, want to?"

"I guess."

I'd never had a cop friend.

"All right, then," he said. "You got a job yet?"

"Not yet."

"Guess we could go anytime, then. How's Tuesday sound?"

"All right."

I opened the magazine again, right on the same girl.

"She's smoking!" he said.

It was my cigarette burning.

He laughed, went his way. I bought the magazine.

Maybe a week went by before me and Blair, I mean Nicky, were driving out to a place called Moon Lake one morning in his souped-up Mustang pulling a bass boat. He pointed off at the tall wire fencing that we'd been following for a while and said, "One of the biggest penitentiaries in the country back there. The stink makes men vomit."

I gazed across the fields. There was nothing out there. "How far?"

"Three, four miles. Only one road in. And fence after fence. Hundred jillion volts a whack. It's gotten to where they don't necessarily need guards. They put up the volts and stand back."

"You've been out there, I guess. For your job."

"Bunch of times. Smell hits way before you get there. Hell on earth."

I kept looking. Hoped to see something. Some orange-suited prisoners tramping around.

"Lots of people in there?" I said.

"More than you'd want to know. Lots of them are piddly players, though. We're filling up the prisons with people who haven't really done anything. But then, that will keep your crime stats down. And if your crime stats are down, then you can get elected to office, ain't that right? I'm no freaking liberal, but we can't lock up the whole goddamn nation."

I thought, Why couldn't we, and watched the scenery. Screw his politics or whatever that was. I didn't care. It was just good to be out and about and doing something. Going fishing even, of all things.

The drive took another thirty minutes or so, during which we rode along not talking much. It was still very early.

I got to thinking about May again. Are there other men who've loved a woman so hard that they thought they'd go soft in the head?

It'd been so good that when it all turned bad without warning it hurt like it wasn't ever going to stop, which in my book is more than enough reason to put your head in a gas oven. Or go shoot a bunch of people and end up in that prison out there. I mean, I could easily perceive why a man would do that, lash out in a rage against the indifferent power of blind fate.

When we could see the lake through the trees, my thoughts halted, froze, sank into the depths again. Going down through there to the edge of the water and parking, you wouldn't have known a thing was wrong with me, though. We put the tackle in the boat, got her in the water, put on life jackets, and headed out. Two guys going to fish.

We'd hadn't had our lines in ten minutes when Nicky said, sort of like he'd been holding it back, "You know, we can talk about anything."

"Sure."

"Anything. That's the kind of guy I am."

I didn't want to talk about May, if that's what he meant. I wanted to fish. Listen to hollow sounds out there, the clicking of our reels, the cries of crows back in the trees, and all that slow dripping as if we were in a glass dome. Those were the things that would help me anyway. Not talking. Not going through the tangles and knots as if you could make everything straight again. That was not the way the world worked.

"I'm not much of a talker in that regard," I said.

"That's all right."

No bite, but I started bringing in my line.

"You keep pulling it up, they won't bite for anybody," he said.

"Checking my bait."

Which I did. It was still there. I cast again.

"Be still awhile now," he said.

And so I was.

Neither of us got very many bites, which Nicky said was strange.

"Conditions are perfect," he whispered. "I don't get it."

"That's fishing for you."

"Something's wrong."

We were quiet again a long time, and then Nicky caught one. Nothing to write home about, but a keeper. And it wasn't five minutes later he had another, and then another. Bang, bang. My line didn't even wiggle.

He messed with his fish and I thought, Look how proud he is of himself. "I don't get it, either," I finally said.

"My good luck?"

"Where's mine?"

"That's always the question, isn't it."

"Huh?"

"Where your luck is. Got to keep it close."

"I guess."

"No guess to it. Keep it close so you can grab it when you need it."

Whatever, I thought. He seemed kind of strange and that worried me some, because it was the ones who said or did things you couldn't predict who would sometimes get a glimpse of your hand, catch on to your game. If they were smart that way, then you had to watch them like a hawk.

"You a lucky man, Nicky?"

"Sometimes. And sometimes very."

"How so?"

"At the tables. You know."

"Gambling. That's not easy."

"It is if you keep your luck close, and listen."

"Listen?"

"To your instincts."

There was a tug on my line and I yanked back hard on my rod, but it was gone. I slumped and started to reel in. "If only I could get me one."

"You must be thinking about something awful."

"Huh?"

"And it's chasing your luck off."

"Get out of here."

Then out of the blue he poked my chest. "Get out of here?"

It got my blood up. "What the hell? Back off."

He was calm as a cucumber, and smiling. "Back off?"

"Yeah, back the fuck off," I said.

"When you're screwing up our luck out here?"

"What?"

"Stop thinking about your beloved. She's gone."

Yeah, I had me a nut. "Back off, Nicky. Back all the way off."

"People don't grieve for the dead," he insisted. "They only feel sorry for themselves. Is that what you're doing, friend?"

"It ain't your business."

He poked me again. "Yeah? Why not?"

"Hey! You cruising for a fight?"

He laughed, slapped his khaki pants at the knee. "Jesus, man. A fight? Get real, will you?"

I looked away. What next?

"I'm trying to help you is all, Carl."

"You ain't helping anything."

"I think shaking people up is the only way of helping them."

"Bet that goes over well with people."

"You have to pick your audience, Carl."

"Let's just fish."

"Yeah, let's take the easy way out. Not say what's true."

He cast again. It went far, landed right where he'd aimed.

"All right, what is it you want?" I asked.

"I don't want anything."

I cast, missed the spot I'd wanted, cast again, missed another time. I swung my hook and bait close. All still there. I cast. Got my spot.

Maybe fifteen minutes passed.

Then Nicky leaped up and the boat tilted sharply

"Look over there!" he shouted. "Look!"

Everything spilled out of the tackle box into the bottom of the boat and I spun on my chair, sure we were going to fall in. "Jesus fucking Christ! I don't know how to swim, you asshole!"

"Look over there, Carl! Quick! Look!"

The boat rocked some more, then settled back flat and I looked where he was pointing toward the east. The sun hung back in there like a car light in fog. But that was all.

I turned back around. "What?"

He was picking up tackle.

"What the hell?" I said.

"We needed a perspective change."

"A fucking what change?"

"I was ganging up on you."

"What?"

"I get overexuberant sometimes. But we can be friends. I know that now. You're just a good old boy who's had some trouble. And, hey, I'm just a good old boy, too. But I won't bullshit you. You'll get only truth out of me. What did the freaking hippies say, Tell it like it is? Yeah."

"I don't swim, goddamn it."

"You've got a life jacket. What's the problem?"

My line tugged.

"You got one," he said.

I brought that sucker in. It gave no fight, as if it wasn't there. A little thing not worth a shit. I jerked the hook out, tossed it back.

"You're scaring them off, damn it!"

"Fuck this," I said. "The fish are all long gone."

"Quiet down!"

"You're the one causing all the commotion!"

"Lord God above . . ."

"So now you're going to save me?"

"Be quiet."

"Going to save me even if I don't want you to?"

"Get a preacher if you need that kind of help, Carl."

"Then what do you want?"

"Nothing. To fish. Relax. You may end up liking this life."

I fixed up my line once more and got it back in the water.

He said, "I don't get the feeling you're going to stay in Iona forever. Am I right?"

"Can't really say . . ."

"I'm pretty sure you've never stayed put much anywhere. Not that that's not all right or anything. Some people are that way. I used to be. Then I came here. It's the place that does it to you, finally. Quiets down that part of you that's like a cat, always needing to move, to hunt."

I watched my line sagging, thinking, Maybe this guy really is just trying to be friendly, to do what he thinks is the right thing.

"Now I have my own mimosa trees," he said. "Mimosas I planted in my yard myself. And they're big now and they hang over the roof. And you know what else? I even put a white china cat up there in one of them. Like my granddad did in the old oak out in back of his place. I liked that."

I tightened my line again. Kept quiet.

"I don't think people change much from generation to generation," he went on. "We all kind of like the same things when it comes down to it."

But putting down roots was not me. Do that and you ended up like him, which was no more than those who came before him. Do that and your thirsty being dug down into the dirt and anchored you. Do that and day after day you grew taller and stronger. Sure that you'd begun to understand the grand scheme of things.

Maybe half an hour went by with us fiddling with our poles.

He said, "Well, they don't like us today. Let's get out of here."

He'd gotten three keepers, I had zero. I heard them flipping in the cooler all the way back to town. Despite the bullshit Nicky'd laid on me, I thanked him for dragging me out there. He seemed pleased with that and nodded. Like he'd won his point, whatever it had been.

I knew I had to try to resist some if I wasn't going to have the apartment walls collapse in on me, and so late one afternoon maybe a week after the fishing trip I went and knocked on my neighbor's door. College girl. Not a looker, kind of roly-poly, but if you didn't try to make something happen, nothing was going to occur and there'd you be.

"Carl Stein," I said. "New around here. Thought I'd introduce myself."

"New? You've been here forever already! I'm Lisa Joyner."

She had just washed her red hair and looked better, maybe even a tad thinner, than I'd remembered.

"Come in. Have a seat. Beer? Wine? I've got chardonnay."

"Beer."

It was some foreign brand, but cold. We sat far apart on some towering floor pillows. The TV showed educational stuff.

She smiled and lifted her glass. "Toast?"

"All right. To what?"

"What about the sunset?"

The day's last rays streaked in golden and bounced off the walls in odd directions on account of the dozens of small mirrors she'd hung up.

"To the sunset," I said.

The potpourri stink in there was something else again. I began scratching.

"You allergic to lavender?" she asked.

"I don't know."

"Well, I hope not, because I do have a lot of lavender."

The beer tasted like cherry soda.

I said, "Lisa, I don't mean to be rude, but this beer is about the worst beer I've ever tasted."

"Really? Emile bought it. Emile, my boyfriend from France."

"Emile?"

"Ex-boyfriend."

"So, Lisa, when did Emile buy this beer?"

"Long time ago. Emile's been gone since . . . awhile."

"And it's been in the fridge all this time?"

"Did it mess it up to leave it in the fridge?"

"Nah. But after a while, though, any beer will —"

"Flip out from old age?"

I smiled and then we started watching rhinos on the TV. They were trying to get it on and it was taking a long time. Lisa laughed and I watched her laughing in those red and orange blades of mirror-thrown light. I drained the beer and, in spite of its foul flavor, called for another.

"You sure?" she asked.

"Why not. It's growing on me."

The rhinos humped while she was gone. A lot of dust got kicked up.

"You missed it," I said when she came back.

She hissed. "Seen it."

"Pretty dusty."

"Hmm. So, you don't work, do you?"

"Not yet."

"What kind of work would you do?"

"Everything."

"You're not an older student? I mean, you're not here to study?"

"Study? Is there a college here in Iona?"

"Junior college. I'm studying French. And mirror making."

"These your mirrors, then? They're really good."

"Thank you."

I stood up and let the sunset-light knives pierce me. Each one had a little heat to it. A need to laugh came over me, and then I was turning in circles in those light blades.

"Mirror making!" she called, giggling now, too.

But I could see she was nervous, so I stopped turning.

"Yeah, nice mirrors, Lisa."

"Thank you."

"You sell them, don't you?"

"Sell mirrors? I hadn't thought of that."

"You could make a fortune off what you've got in this room."

"I don't know . . ."

"Sure you could. Flea markets, art shows."

"Sell my mirrors?"

"It's not like you can't."

Shut up, I told myself. She doesn't want to sell the mirrors.

"I'll give you one if you want."

"Nah, they're your mirrors, Lisa."

"I'd like to give you one."

"What would I do with it?" I asked, without thinking.

"Hang it up. Look into it. The usual things one does with mirrors."

"Sure," I said quickly.

She gave me one the size of a cigarette pack. I could see myself being copied way down into it, how I don't know. Very weird. I tried to kiss her as I left, but she hissed again, and then I went back to my apartment and shut the flimsy door and fiddled around looking into that mirror.

Nicky Blair

Carl Stein's wife drowned in a lake one day. I don't think he's come up from that. But he seems like the kind of man who will. Like a fish that has to come up sometime for air. And then I'll see him for what he is. Right now, though, he's dragging bottom. I would, too, I guess. He seems so tired. Like he's been all over the earth and can't clear his mind of all those places. I catch him staring into the water when we're fishing and it's like he's seeing straight into his past. I want to know that past. And I want him to know that I want to know that past and not be chickenshit about it. There's not a lot of things I can't stand, but if there's one, it's people who won't go the mile. You go the mile, you've got my vote. You make the effort, I'll be there. Who knows, I might be able to do him good. And when I do good, if only a little, then I feel good, too. That's the way I am, that's the way my daddy was, and his daddy, all the way back. Good people, one and all, even if I do say so myself.

Carl Blalock

When a guy comes in on you like that out of nowhere, makes himself your closest friend, and then turns out to be a damn thief, you start asking hard questions. Why didn't I see it happening? What else was I not seeing while this happened? Who could be trusted? It made me look hard at everything.

And what I saw early that fall after May left us was Venus's Impala parked out in front of motel rooms in nearby towns I happened to be going through. Her red bomb and maybe only one other car, right next to it, both as obvious as the sun and making the loudest statement imaginable.

The first time, I stopped across the road and sat there gazing out my rolled-down window while all the energy of my body fogged away like dry ice. I didn't even consider that the sky-blue motel door might pop open and out she'd come with whoever it was. That she would see me sitting there with all the color gone from my face and my eyes fallen away to the place eyes recede when they can't suffer this reality. And I was there a long time, too, long enough for the sunlight to swing down low and fill the scene with sickening despair. Then I drove away and drank a lot in a bar in another town and said nothing to anyone — and vowed to especially never say a word of it to her.

What was there to say? What was there to say that would not bring what we had left crashing down? I knew better than that. I knew better than to throw everything away when it was only broken and in need of repair. Because what could these men be that I was not? She was still the woman who moved beneath me in the way a woman will when it's for you and not just for now but through all days and nights no matter what. I believed that. I didn't believe the Impala parked at a motel meant anything beyond a moment out of time, a single page in a very big book. Something she took in quickly before moving on.

The second and third times it was some other motel, and I thought, Why are you parking your Impala out in the open like this, Venus, as if you wanted me to see it? But she had only been in a thoughtless hurry. Driven to distraction by the idea of distraction, I finally learned.

Once in a while a man would come in my store and glance at me a funny way, and I knew without question that he'd been with Venus. But I said nothing. I didn't look at them twice, either. Whatever would that have changed?

Meantime May Stein sank down in her grave, and Carl Stein hauled ass to the other end of the nation with the goods of mine he'd had his eyes on. Left his dead wife's bones there in the ground and disappeared.

Then I knew Venus and I had to get out of there, that we could wait no longer. Get back to the only place that could mean anything to us anymore. Wild, sweet Mexico. Where we could take our sins — her rambunctious infidelity, my trusting foolishness — and try to live with them in another light, in the yellow-green glow that radiates from dense, wet depths. Where perhaps we could forgive each other these things. She said, Of course we should go. She had only been waiting on me to give the word. Which kind of stopped me. But I didn't say it.

Every summer for years Venus and I would drive up into the Panhandle to visit Mama. She'd moved out there, back to the place she'd come from, after Daddy died of a stroke working too hard at the lumber and hardware store. I never knew just why she wanted to be so far out there away from us, but I wasn't one to argue with

Mama about anything. And so we forced ourselves to make the long drive and when we arrived all worn out we'd go into the hot little house she'd bought in Amarillo, the town she'd been born in, and talk to her, but she was getting old and tired and wouldn't know who we were. Maybe just two soft lights. When Venus and I were done talking she'd reach out with her spotted hands and we'd go toward her. It was always too much to bear and Venus would slip back and I'd stay close and hold Mama. Carefully, like a cicada shell. She'd say, I don't know who you are, and I'd say, It's all right, Mama.

I finally buried her weightless body in hard earth north of town, next to her parents like she'd once asked me, out there where the only thing to hear was a truck whining down the highway or the wind carrying the moan of the plain. I thought of cycles and knew that this was the last one, because of something rare and unfair that had been dealt me so that I wouldn't be able to be a father or make Venus a mother to a child. That my child would never be, never live and come to stand at that spot someday and see the dirt and hear the wind after planting me with the others. Out among the tilted tombstones and wrought-iron fences. Not a tree in all creation. Where no one ever goes unless they have something to dispose of for always. I picked up a handful of grave dirt, crushed it with considerable effort, and let it glide between my fingers. Then turned away.

Mexico. I even bought a new navy blue Suburban for the trip, though the old navy blue one was still kind of new. Nothing was going to get in our way. And if you had to spend money, lots of money, to help set life right again, then you did. You wrote off losses and took your lady by the hand and went. To Mexico. Where things could be in limbo while we sorted out our lives away from the motel men who would have her for their own and all the con men who would have everything that was mine. I honestly believed we both had hopes along these lines.

But then the electric windows on the Suburban flew down and refused to come back up in the middle of a traffic jam in Mexico City.

We'd bought every vase, pot, mirror, lamp, and chair we'd seen from the border on down, which with all our supplies for the new Puerto Azul house filled the car. I remember the locals all staring at us and Venus saying, "I'm going to kill Larry." That was Sutherland, our car dealer. "I'm going to kill him," she said. "Then I'm going to kill you."

"Wait, I didn't break the windows," I said.

"Like hell," Venus said.

Then she got out, slammed her door with both hands so hard I thought it would fall off, and started away. We were miles from the hotel.

Quickly she was almost out of sight between the cars, and yet I didn't do anything. People were laughing and pointing and the light was changing and everybody was inching forward and honking. Then I couldn't see her anymore. I got over to the side and drove slowly.

A crowd formed around the Suburban and I didn't like their eyes. Children's hands reached in and poked packs of cigarettes and chewing gum into my face. I said, No no no, and yet more hands flew in, touching me, the wheel, knobs on the dash. I said, No thank you, no *gracias*, get away now, and when some of the others started reaching in through the windows, I jammed the accelerator and screeched out of there.

It took me three hours to find a dealership and be told, Sorry, but there's nothing we can do about the windows, and then get to the hotel, where I hired a boy to stay with the Suburban. Venus hadn't come in. Somehow I wasn't afraid for her, though. She'd show up.

I had a bourbon-Coke in the hotel bar. The bartender was no talker, so I just enjoyed my booze and tried to get the bad day out of my head.

After a while an American hollered at me, "How about those Dolphins?"

I couldn't have cared less about the Dolphins. But I said, "Yeah, how about them."

"All the way to the Super Bowl. All the way!"

He parked himself on the next stool, ordered a rum, and flashed his teeth. I thought of Stein's big teeth, but these were fence posts.

"Arnold Seidensticker. Miami. U.S.A."

I introduced myself, let a respectable silence play itself out during which we both sipped our drinks. Then I said, "Mexico City." As if naming a smell that'd just wafted by.

"Pure hellhole!" he boomed.

I wanted to hold my ears. But nobody else seemed to notice. And the place was full of customers lingering in the purple-shadowed corners, murmuring, gazing into each other's eyes.

"Business or pleasure?" I asked.

"Pleasure," he said quietly. "Always."

"We're going to Puerto Azul."

"As am I, friend. Something to drink to."

We sipped our drinks.

"So what do you do, Mr. Seidensticker?"

"Legal work."

"Lawyer?"

"Sometimes. And you, sir?"

"Lumber, mostly."

"Ah, trees. You must love it down here. Thousands of square kilometers of exotic trees!"

"Lots of trees all right."

"So did you ever want to sculpt it?"

"Sculpt what?"

"Why, tropical wood, of course."

"No, no. No artist in me. I do flock Christmas trees, though."

"Flock. Flock! Sounds like wooden shoes on a wooden floor. Ah, the Netherlands!"

"Pays the bills."

"Yes . . . one must pay the bills."

I like a little story, so I ordered us another round.

"Obsessions," he said. "We must have them, you know. Married?"

"Yes. That's an obsession, all right. From day one."

"Where is she?"

"Out messing around." I waved at a window and the darkening street.

"Shopping, no doubt."

"Or lost."

"Lost? Seidensticker at your service."

"I'm only kidding. She's shopping."

"If you say so."

Then he leaned near, whispered. It was like a mouse's squeak.

"What?" I asked.

He leaned near again. I still didn't hear.

"What're you saying?"

He produced a neat blue handkerchief and blew his nose with a duck honk. But he didn't answer me, and then he stared into his drink.

"I really didn't hear what you said," I said.

"Discretion is the key."

"What're you talking about?"

"The lady."

"What?"

"I lost mine the same way. In Beijing. Been there?"

"No."

"Typical thing. A spat. Words flew. She departed in the midst of a tie-up. Never saw her again."

My head spun. Had I said we'd had a fight in traffic?

"A sad world, isn't it?" he said. "So easy for things to turn ugly."

"Look, how did —"

Then he started singing something from an opera in a booming bass voice. And I thought, Oh, boy, I've got me crazy one for sure.

"Stop that," I said. "Something wrong with you?"

He halted, but not like on my order. More like he'd heard something from afar and wanted to confirm it, whatever it was.

"Twenty-five years from now Mexico City will be full of lost wives, tens of thousands of them, and then the city will become the birthplace of a plague that will eat the earth alive in a matter of weeks."

"Look —"

"We're talking fifty million people living in the bowl here then. We're talking Armageddon, Carl Blalock, and the boiling madness of flesh. Cross borders, it will, and eat cities in the north, it will, suck us dry, it will. So . . . how about those Dolphins?"

Dolphins? I couldn't speak.

He grabbed my shirt like he didn't intend to let go.

"I asked you a question, son."

"Get off me."

He let go, smirking, then looked at his fingertips.

"Now I'm going to confess something to you. You look like a nice guy. I'd wager you're always polite and a gentleman and all. In fact, I know you are. And I respect that. But I'm going confess, Carl."

"Whatever."

"I hate women."

"I bet you do."

"Carl, I also have another confession. I hate men, too."

I didn't know what to say.

"Carl, can I confess something else?"

"No, Arnold."

"I hate the Dolphins as well. And I hate you. Very much."

With that he stalked out of the bar with his drink, stepping high like a stork, and straight through the lobby to the front door of the hotel. Where he paused, looked back majestically, raised his glass in a grandiose toast to some mysterious thing, then wheeled around and vaporized.

I jiggled my drink, got the ice to swirling. Thinking, Goddamn do I ever hate traveling Americans, because they can never hold their liquor. Every single one of them gets stupid-high and insists on thinking he or she is the center of the universe and that each and every single thing they say is fundamentally right, important, and significant. Jesus.

Skipping supper, I went up to the room, got my clothes off, made another bourbon-Coke, and sat on the balcony watching the blinking neon lights. Later on a tan lump of moon struggled up out of the soup.

I was stretched out on the bed when Venus showed up after midnight. It was too late for a fight, so I let her be. Watched her undress like I wasn't even there, get her nightie on, then go check the view.

After a while she said, quietly, "I think the building's on fire."

I went out. "Yeah?"

"Up there. No?"

Orange and red sparks were raining down from the top floor.

"We're out of here," I said.

"Let me dress first."

"No." Loudly, firmly. Like that day at the lake when I yelled at Stein to go phone for help. I seized her hand and pulled her toward the door.

"Aren't we supposed to crawl?" she asked.

"The smoke's on the top floor, Venus. Damn."

She put a hand on the door. "You're supposed to feel the door. Warm to you?"

I touched it. Cold. "It's okay."

The hall was empty. Not thinking, we got in the elevator. Me in my boxer shorts, Venus in that blue nightie. Going down, I kissed her in there. We had twenty-eight floors. She didn't resist at first, then she did, and pulled away angry like I'd had too much booze.

It was the fancy Mexico City jet-set hour in the plush lobby.

Venus called out, "There's a fire upstairs!"

The people milling around in their swank evening attire stopped and gawked with mock concern. A man in a white suit stepped forward and offered Venus his jacket, much to his wife's displeasure.

I went to the desk. "There's a fire."

"Sir?"

"There's a fire. Up on the top floor."

"Let me see, sir."

Calm. No problem. A call was made.

"No, sir. No fire."

"I'm telling you —"

"We saw it!" Venus exclaimed. "Sparks, smoke. Even flames!"

More people were slowing to watch. Most were laughing.

"There is no fire, madam. I assure you."

"Look," I said. "We saw the fire. Have someone check."

"Sir?"

"Have someone go look!"

"Sir?"

"What!"

"It's a fireworks show, sir."

The fancy crowd burst into vigorous applause.

"For Christ's sake," said Venus.

She beat me to the elevator. There are times when you have the fight of fights and that night had to be one of the worst in our career of fights. It went on and on. We drank and argued and slept far apart.

A few things were missing from the overnight shift in the street, but by some miracle the rest was right where I'd left it. So I paid the boy a few bucks like I'd promised and we zoomed out of there for the coast.

Coming down off the heights of Cuernavaca we hit a pothole and the windows buzzed up. After that we never opened them again.

Again and again in my dreams May plunges out of sight and Venus's cry tears the air. Most times I charge out there — only to stop short again, stand knee-deep in the lake while May drowns below the unmoving surface. Other times Carl and I are sitting on our lawn chairs when the scream goes up. "What a racket," I say. "Just girls," he says. "May hasn't come up in a while." "Nope. Not in a long while." "She'll come up." "Yeah." Then we get more beers out of the cooler.

Our new place was way out by the mouth of the bay and faced back north so that we saw the entire port with one sweep of the eyes.

Perched a couple of hundred yards from the water, a third of the way up the jungle-covered mountain. Other houses were going up around there, but ours was the first one finished. So that we had no neighbors yet except for William Pullman in the white mansion on the crest above. An American-turned-Mexican who had been around there since the beginning of everything. A very highly regarded gentleman who also knew Frank Sinatra, who sometimes came there for visits and stayed awhile. Meaning that even if it was only a sixth of an acre and a stone house with one bedroom, a galley kitchen, a small deck, and a tiny pool, all on a ninety-nine year lease, we were in the most exclusive spot on the whole bay. And we had good fun fixing the place up, nailing and painting and cleaning, being together. In a week it felt like home. Our new home.

We had come in early from the beach. I made drinks, and then we went out on the deck as the sun passed behind the mountain. The bay was dark blue, as if it were filling up from below with the night. We finished our first round without talking. Then I made another.

Iguanas crawled up on boulders at the edge of the jungle. Venus trained the binoculars on them. "There's Henry," she said.

He was the fattest and longest one of the bunch. Venus had given him the name, but I had no idea why she had or where she'd gotten it.

"I think you love Henry," I said.

"King of the iguanas. My prehistoric pal."

Venus had eyebrows with wisps that stuck up straight and sharp, and I got to looking at them like I'd never seen them.

She handed me the binoculars. "Your turn, honey."

I looked. "Hey, Henry."

"He's been around here for ages," she said. "Be here when we're gone. Somebody said they can live two hundred years."

"That all?" I swung the binoculars around and looked across the bay to the north. "There's that tree again."

"Let me see."

I handed them over.

"There it is!" Venus said.

We'd spotted it our first evening there. A single tree atop the mountain opposite, up there on a bare ridge where no one climbed. Red again with the fire of the sunset. A big old tree, all alone.

"We ought to go see it up close someday," she said.

"Not like climbing the rock in Red Rock. This'd be work."

"I could do it."

"Well, then we could. That'd make it worthwhile."

"That's sweet, Carl."

The booze felt good and our glasses were empty again, so I made a third round and hoped that things might keep going long enough for us to drop all the unsaid crap and stumble into each other's embrace.

"There comes the moon, Venus."

"I prefer our tree. Let's name it."

"Are we going to name everything?"

I hadn't meant to sound negative.

"Something wrong with naming a tree?"

"Not a thing."

She leaned on the railing. "Henry, tell him it's all right to name the tree."

A couple of the iguanas crawled away, but not Henry.

"Henry?" she called. "Are you spontaneous?"

"Maybe not all that spontaneous when I should be," I answered for him.

"No matter. I'm now going to name the tree. Tree, you're Ellen."

I laughed. "A tree named Ellen."

"Yes . . . Ellen."

She turned and glared at me, then whipped back around and raked her hair back hard. Huffed.

I beheld her bare back and the thin black straps of the bathing suit top crossing her shoulders. I followed the slender length of her spine down, and then looked up and saw that the sunset fire had gone out of the tree called Ellen and that the night coming up through the bay would soon fill the air until it, too, was deep blue.

Venus watched her tree, trying like a big girl to let go of whatever it was that'd gotten hold of her so suddenly.

I wanted to stay in that place unmoving. Low down in my chair with a drink in my hand. Venus's backside there for my eyes to wander over. Twinkling boat lights thrown like gems onto the bay below. High-rise hotels across the way poking up like ivory dominoes.

But then she groaned and flung her drink, glass and all, off the deck, spooking Henry and just about everything else out there.

"Two drinks and I'm thinking about May Ellen Stein. Don't give me three drinks again. Don't make me drink."

"I wasn't."

"You did."

"I'm sorry."

"Don't say that."

"Easy, easy . . ."

The last time we'd made love was early one morning back in Texas when she turned over to me after I'd sat up on my side of the bed and put her hand on my back. Touched me that way that meant, Don't get up, come here and get into my arms. I thought of her Impala sitting in the sun on a parking lot. I thought of her taking off her white panties and dropping them on the blue shag carpet of a room. Of being the man who might come up from behind and ease her forward onto the bed, onto its edge, and take her that way. Venus's hand moved up and down my back and I saw how erect I was and felt anger with myself for wanting her but turned to her just the same. She turned, too, back the other way, and I lay alongside her and pressed my hand against her spine and then took hold of her shoulder and eased her over toward me. It was maybe five in the morning out there in that house not far from town and our bed clanged like a struggling washing machine, which made me want to laugh. But I didn't, because it was far too perfect, too right.

We were at Playa Linda, brooding as the sun went down.

"The water here sometimes looks like the lake that day," she said.

"Not at all. This is the Pacific Ocean, Venus."

"Exactly like at the lake."

"As you wish."

"What does that mean?"

"Nothing."

"I'm not arguing with you, Carl. I know what I remember."

"All right."

"Can't you let me remember it the way I want to?"

We watched the sun depart, the water redden. Then a cool wind blew.

"Carl Blalock?"

A towering man in starched white swimming trunks. There were two young boys with him, Mexicans, smiling down at us. Then I recalled.

"Seidensticker."

"Indeed! So is this the guilty lady?"

"Pardon me?"

"You wanderlust wife?"

"Carl, who is this?"

"Venus, Arnold Seidensticker. Met him at the hotel in Mexico City."

"Nice to meet you."

"And you, madam. I've heard a lot about you."

"Have you?"

"Not true," I said. "So, Arnold, how're you getting along?"

"Fine." He patted the boys on their heads and they smiled up at him. "Miguel and Enrique are keeping me company."

"They're your boys?" Venus asked.

I didn't think anybody could be that stupid.

"So, Venus, how was it being lost in the big city?" he asked.

"Pardon me?"

"Lost in Mexico City. Must've been terribly frightening."

"Lost? When?"

"Why, during your last visit to Mexico City, dear."

"I don't understand."

"Skip it, Seidensticker," I said.

"Did he tell you, Venus, that I lost my wife in Beijing?"

"Pardon me?"

"They found you, or you found your way. But they never found her. She simply disappeared. Twenty-two years ago now."

I didn't like the way he kept smiling as he spoke.

"That's terrible," Venus said. "I'm very sorry."

"Not nearly as terrible as you might think, though."

"Oh?"

"You find new passions. Mexico is all about passions, isn't it? A little money, and you can have nearly any part of it you want. So no, I don't think about Maggie anymore. I've gotten past it. And on with my life."

He rubbed the boys' heads and they smiled up at him.

"How old are your boys?" Venus asked.

"How old?"

"Look, Seidensticker," I said, fed up, "we're sitting here watching the evening and, well —"

"Yes, Carl?"

"It was good seeing you."

"All right, I'll leave you two with your sadness. Enrique, Miguel, come along. We'll let these people be alone. Bye-bye now."

Off they went, the boys' arms around his thick waist, walking slowly across the sand and then toward the street.

My mouth had gone dry.

"What does he know about our 'sadness'?" Venus asked.

"I don't know."

"I don't like that."

"Venus, those weren't his boys, you know."

"I know. Sick jerk."

I looked toward the street again. They were gone.

We stayed there alone on the beach much longer than we ever had, into the night. Until it was black out on the ocean.

I said, "Now it looks like that day at the lake."

She turned her head and stared at me.

"But that's only to say that if we sat here long enough, Venus, the pink and orange would come up over our shoulders and light up everything again. Because the world is going to keep going."

"No, Carl. The world has stopped and we are on the night side looking out into nothingness."

"Would May agree with you?"

"Stop."

"Of course she wouldn't. Not in a million years."

"That's enough, Carl Blalock."

"Is it?"

"Stop."

One night out on the deck she grabbed the binoculars off the table between us, pointed them at me. I laughed, thinking she was playing.

"Feeling better, Mrs. Blalock?"

"I can see you up close, Carl."

"And I can see you up close, Venus."

"Can you? What do you see?"

"A woman with binoculars spying on her husband."

"Something to hide?"

"Not a thing. And you?"

She set down the binoculars, pursed her lips. "Game over."

I wished I hadn't opened my mouth.

A liner's horn boomed below and she went to the railing to watch the boat head out of the bay.

"I was in love with May," she said. "Did you know that?"

I said nothing.

She firmed her grip on the railing, leaned against it, then over it, but not dangerously, balancing herself, rocking slowly forward and back. Like a girl considering a decision.

"I'm not trying to hurt you," she said.

"I know. You're trying to explain."

"No, I'm not."

"All right . . ."

"The words are just coming out."

"That's fine."

"Not really. We say things and then we forget. It's easy."

"Better to let it go, though."

"Even about the other men?"

"Let that go, too."

"I wasn't in love with any of them."

"Better not have been."

"Please."

"What?"

"You're making it too easy for me. You've already forgiven me."

"Is that wrong?"

She turned to face me. Moonlight made green shadows around her eyes. "That makes you either very good or someone who's letting me walk on him."

"Or someone who's slept beside you twenty-six years."

"You're a good man, Carl. But the truth is I can't stay here in Puerto Azul with you. I thought I could, but I can't."

I went to the railing next to her. Not touching her. Listening. My eyes poring over paradise, watching boat lights shimmer.

"I came to get away from her death," she said, "from the place her body lies down in the ground. Only to find this place makes me think of death and her even more. What does this to me, Carl? The stillness? All this deep water staring back at me? Do you know?"

"Where do you want to go?"

"Everywhere May went. Which is everywhere. Without stopping."

"But you need to let —"

"No, it's May who needs to let me go. But she won't."

She held herself tightly in her own arms.

"Don't you see?" she asked.

I frowned at the inevitable. "How long?"

Her body became rigid. "I don't know."

"When?"

"I don't know. But it has to be this way."

I said nothing. And went in to bed. Lay curled up with my knees to my chest. Slept quickly and dreamed of an earthquake, which woke me up only to find her sitting on the bed crying like I'd never heard her cry.

I touched her shoulder. But she didn't turn to me, and then I lay watching her look out the door at the bay lights. Nothing moved anywhere, maybe not even the earth, like she'd said, and there was no other sound but the jungle speaking in many voices at once.

And yet she made no move to go away. Though the conversation lingered heavy as the air before a storm. She stayed right beside me as we went through the motions of living the life of leisure, rising late and eating in our café behind Playa Linda and sunbathing and swimming until the twilight before going back up the mountain. To shower and comb our hair and put on clean clothes and eat something from the bowl of fruit and then open the bar and unscrew caps and crack ice out of trays and mix and pour. I would sit at the rim of the deck and smell sweetness rising out of the jungle and listen to Sinatra sing, the voice drifting away or surging near depending on the breeze. She would sit by the pool whose lights shone pale blue upon her face and I could not stop thinking how she was already as far away as the moon, or the back of an iguana's ancient eyes.

What was she doing? Trying to prepare me for the time when she would be gone, staying longer to somehow make the end less painful when it came? I didn't ask. Because it would be like asking her if she did truly pity me. Which is something no one should ever ask anyone.

It went on long enough this way that I became restless, stayed with her at the house for the length of a drink each evening but then went out, took walks up the mountain. I'd climb stone steps though the jungle to an abandoned hotel that had a gigantic deck where I could look out at the Pacific and see the lights of freighters. At first the place spooked me, what with rattan chairs rotting in the swimming pool water and the moonlight hitting it all just so. But then the desolation beckoned me to stay, and so I'd sit on a beat-up chair and nurse a glass of bourbon half the night. Thinking through our story, watching for a solution.

The facts were simple. I ran my dead daddy's lumber and hardware store in the town my parents had moved to because by some great miracle they'd saved up enough money selling fishing bait in Glen Rose to start their lives over anew. I sold plywood and tar paper and stepping-stones and Christmas trees and made some money and then hightailed it to Mexico the first chance I got. I had a wife who'd decided she needed something more than all that. An orphan girl who'd grown up in the town and married me when we were eighteen. Who'd decided after twenty-six years to go to bed with other men. The creature I adored and sometimes hated. A girl who had loved another girl in ways I might never begin to fathom and who had named a tree in Puerto Azul after this other girl and thought the paradise I handed her was deeply oppressive, where she could not linger and go with the flow, a place she absolutely had to flee.

But it was not a simple story. And I knew that any answer would come from some great distance, and maybe only at a whisper. So that I had to be quiet and listen carefully and wait for as long as it took.

Somehow, every night, the contents of the pool made a full revolution, the same broken chair with its three legs poking out in different directions returning to rest at my feet. Then it was time to go. To get in the bed with her but not touch her. To dream of never leaving Mexico, of remaining there in the ocean air until I was very old. Only to wake full of the sadness of seeing her lying there looking at me.

Christmas came and we hung gray moss on a knee-high spruce, drank some champagne I'd scrounged up, stood looking out at the bay.

"I get twenty-four," she said.

"I see twenty-three."

It was a game we played, seeing how many fishing boat lanterns there were on the bay each night. Almost every time we got two different numbers, but it didn't matter.

"Merry Christmas, Carl," she said.

I kissed her mouth but she did not kiss me back, and then we studied the tree. It was like a funeral, and we both knew it.

One night there was a man parked on my chair by the hotel pool when I got up there. An old guy, maybe eighty, sitting ramrod straight.

"Hello there," I said.

He didn't answer.

I went closer. "Hello?"

His bald head sat low in the collar of his white shirt.

"Never," he said, turning to me, "ever get into a hotel deal. Period."

"What happened?"

"Some of Frank's pals. Put the money in. Took the money out. No warning. No reason. Nothing."

He went back to studying the debris in the pool. Then he seemed to awaken. "But excuse me. William Pullman. You're Carl Blalock."

A thin white hand came toward me like a fin. I reached out and grabbed it. Hard, damp.

"The hotel went under three years ago now. I still haven't made up my mind what to do with her. Another hotel, a disco, a restaurant? Don't you hate deciding all the time?"

"It can do you in."

"To say the least. But I've forgiven Frank. It wasn't his fault. It was his pals. Creeps, one and all."

"How did you know my name?"

"That's my property you're leasing down there."

"You own this whole mountain, then?"

"Something like that. But I want company again now. It's a long way out here, you know. Nobody comes out this far, there being nothing here anymore to come to. Agent told me the first lot went to a couple from Texas. That's you two, then."

"That's right."

"Well, welcome to the club." He slid his head back, smiled at the stars. "Sirius. The Dog Star. Nine light-years. That's close, actually."

I looked up at the star. "You're an astronomer?"

"I wished to be. But no. Are there things you regret like that? Things you wish very much you'd done? These tell a lot about a man."

"Maybe that I didn't study petroleum engineering."

"The oil business. Risky, but highly profitable."

"And you?"

"I wish I'd studied astronomy, yes."

"No, I meant what do you do?"

"Nothing! I'm an old man."

"I see . . ."

"But to answer your question, real estate."

"Ah."

Then he said, "Listen, Carl. I'm concerned about you and your wife. You two seem quite sad about something."

"Pardon?"

"From my veranda I can hear things very clearly, all the way down to the water. I don't know how it works, but your voices drift straight up to me and it's like I'm there with you. With you and Venus."

I gazed at him, annoyed at the intrusion. "I sometimes can see you watching us from up there."

"Don't be upset now," he said. "I feel like I already know you, and so I hope you will bear with me."

"You move fast, Mr. Pullman."

"I'm a busybody old man. I don't mean to offend, though. Forget I said anything."

"It's all right," I said.

"I may simply be bored. That, in addition to the weight of all the years and the things I've seen and lived and suffered, well, it might add up to a penchant for voyeurism. Do you follow me?"

"Of course," I said.

I liked him, in spite of, or because of, the strangeness.

He said nothing more and I walked slowly around the trash-filled pool. For the first time. Seeing it from the other end, the other side. The darkly shining surface seemed like a dangerous mirror, the kind that sooner or later would tempt you, make you fall, then take you down.

"Isn't there another chair around here somewhere for you? I'm afraid I've taken yours. Would you like it back?"

I looked. There was no other chair.

Then he was ogling again at the sky as if seeing a friend for the first time in ages. "Betelgeuse, on the other hand, is much much farther. More than three hundred light-years. And yet its light —"

"Why do you play that Sinatra record every night?"

He didn't answer, continued to peer aloft.

"Will you be here tomorrow?" I asked.

"Perhaps I will."

"What do you like to drink?"

"Vodka on ice. Sliver of lime."

"Sure," I said.

I turned to go.

"Don't worry about the things I said to you," he called. "They don't mean anything. And if my record playing offends —"

I felt I'd been rude. "Don't worry about it, Mr. Pullman."

"William."

"William. Good night."

"Yes," he said. "It is a good night."

He hadn't lowered his eyes from the stars.

Going back home, I felt sure there hadn't been a night that he had not taken my place on that chair and stayed until dawn. While one of his maids played the record over in his house. While I sat on my deck below. While he hummed and listened, all the way from up there, to me thinking.

Any number of weeks went by, the barely felt winter passing through the air like some creature that only brushed this reality, and then Venus gathered up a suitcase of things and went back north. There were no angry words, no scenes of hatred, no tears or final embraces. She'd simply found the moment to go, to escape our lifeless waiting and drinking. I wished she would snap awake from the bad dream afflicting her, but there was nothing I could do. Except let her go. As one lets go of something in the vain hope that it will return because you have not kept it prisoner.

Miguel

It is the hour you know someone will come. My dirty enemies. Mateo, Blas, Andrés, they are the worst. I try not to be frightened, keep my hands high on the gringo's wheel, which is smooth as glass and makes you want to drive away. The gringo is going to pay me ten American dollars. My mother will want it. My father will want it. But I want it, too. To buy gas and drive this car called Suburban to the end of the earth. To be sitting in an American vehicle is to be in a spaceship ready to take off for places where the air does not make you want to throw up every morning. If I only had the keys. I do not know how to steal a car. If only I had somehow gotten him to leave me the keys. Americans are stupid, everyone knows this except them. But maybe this one isn't. Short, black haired, friendly. The doorman turned his American into Spanish. I was told to sit in the car until morning and not let anything be stolen. All the windows are down and the car is full of things. And don't fall asleep, they told me, or someone will come and take things and you won't get a dime for your work! Why did he leave the windows down? For a while I worry that I will fall asleep like they said. But it is very scary to be sitting there with the windows down. I have to sit on the front seat turned like this to be able to keep an eye on every opening. Mateo will come, though. He'll bring the others and they will circle like dogs. They will. Everything will be stolen, sold and resold through the neighborhood. By dawn the Suburban will be gone. I look at the hotel. Full of rich people. Lights everywhere. The man whose car this is is in there somewhere and he is not thinking of it nor of all the things about to be taken from it. He is not thinking of me nor how scared I am and how much I wish to go take a whiz. Mateo and the rest of them know this and they are watching with yellow eyes. Over there. See them? There.

Because May would have said, Of course that's what you should do, Venus had pushed herself and her body back out in her Impala not too long after the funeral and parked on the broad motel parking lots and gone into the lukewarm rooms. May lived again within her as she stood with her back to the door after hooking the chain and watched the man undress and heard him start to call her from the sunken bed and then to ask, in a way that meant there better not be, Is something wrong? Yes, my best friend is lying in her grave. But she said nothing, not even when she'd had too much to drink and felt deeply angry that goodness had been snatched away as soon as she'd found it. No, she only smiled at the stranger and let herself also be May taking off her clothes and walking toward him with the boldness of a goddess. His hands reached out for her, and she went quickly into them and the man groaned with pleasure. How could he not, with the power of two women upon him at the same time? And time came to a halt, or very nearly so, everything falling into the most unimaginable slow motion, every detail becoming the intricate essential of some greater whole as if the order of things were made plain, every breath a lifetime of breaths, and the ugliness and pain that stalked the world were nowhere to be seen, were cast out, banished, if only for the length of an hour or so in a cheap room with stained carpeting and a dripping shower and a running toilet. She insisted that there be no talking in there, not before, not after, and the strangers liked that, made their bodies be all the sexier, like May had said they would. And when they had rested and when time had taken up its old pace again and the burning light of evening came to frame the heavy curtains, she dressed and threw off the door chain and went out. Drove fast in any direction, so long as it meant hurtling the red bomb through the ends of the day with nothing to bind her, no one to say it wasn't all right to imagine May with her there every mile of the way. As if she and May had never been apart. As if May had intended all along for Venus to take over her life if ever it were to halt or be halted and live out of the rest of it.

Venus went back to Texas in style on three airplanes, one from Puerto Azul to Mexico City, another from there to Dallas, and a last one from there up to Red Rock, all in a few hours. Everything in the yard was in the throes of spring, as if God could have cared less that no one lived there any longer. Drawn by the wild glory of it all, Venus surprised herself and stayed there nearly a month, sleeping in the old bed for countless hours, then waking and pondering her next move, watching nature rise up all around as if to engulf her. Gradually she began to pace through the house, day and night, as through the run-down compartments of her mind, stopping only to peer through the scarred windowpanes at the entwining greenery, ever more sure that choices can only be born of motion, and not the other way around, that she must now live the opposite of Carl, immobile down there on his mountain. Then one morning there were no more questions. It was time to go, as May would want her to, and explore and open her life to all the possibilities that she'd spent so many years putting off. So she packed for a lady's first solo road trip.

She had her Impala, credit cards, and the road was there, and all she had to do was go down it. The light over the land seemed pale and innocent, so she decided to make her voyage the same, a fearless run where whatever happened happened, no second thoughts.

"Hit that radio, honey," she said in some man's voice. "All right, sweetheart," she had herself say. It was a hog report. But then came Bob Wills and she sang along.

Sometimes people in a passing car would see her lips moving and stare. That's right, she'd call out, I'm a crazy! Crazy Venus, taking to the road trying to outpace the power of death. If she could, she'd be better off than most. She'd be free awhile.

The hum of the road sounded like that weird signal from the spaceship in that movie, very high, wavering, *ooo-eee, ooo-eee.* It made her laugh and look out at the wide open sky.

Carl had gotten weird at the end. On account of the he-knows-Sinatra guy up the mountain and that record's mystery voice drawing him in. He'd go up the mountain with two drinks, one for each of them, and come down hours later. There'd be a flashing in his black eyes. He wouldn't be smiling, but he would be at ease. And he'd sit out at the edge of the deck and prop his feet on the railing and study the bay until dawn. Assuming she was asleep in the bedroom when most nights she was parked back in the shadows on the sofa, watching like an iguana. While the record up there played and played. While everyone was a stranger in the night and the night was full of growing vines and sprawling leaves and sweet opened fruit lit by the moon, always silvered and close. Night after strange night, the record needle sometimes sticking — and then someone unsticking it after the longest time.

The gas station boy at a bend in the road in Louisiana was the first to ask her where she was headed. The sun had long gone down on another of the many strung-out days of driving from here to there with no direction in mind. "Who wants to know?"

"Just asking, lady. That'll be nine dollars and thirty-five cents."

She handed him a card.

"That's not our card, ma'am."

Venus handed him another one.

"Missed again. It's the green one, ma'am."

Venus slipped a nail down the row. "Which one?"

"That green one. There."

Venus got it and the boy huffed.

"You in a hurry?" she asked.

"No ma'am."

"Then why'd I make you mad?"

"You going to tell my boss, lady? I didn't mean anything."

Venus examined the young man. Born in this place, raised in this place, slaving in this place, sure to get married in this place, raise a family in this place, abuse his wife in this place, hate his kids and his in-laws and himself in this place, watch everybody die in this place, and then wait until it was time to die himself right here. That's what she saw.

"What're you looking at me like that for?" he asked.

"Nothing. I won't tell your boss."

"You promise?"

"And if I don't promise?"

He stood there. "Lady?"

"What?"

"You're not funny."

The boss came out, a kid maybe two or three years older than the other one but who swaggered like he'd been through war.

"Problem here, Neal?"

"No problem, sir. Going to ring up this charge. Lady's from out of state."

"That so? How're you today, ma'am?"

Venus nodded, hoped he wouldn't try to talk.

"Clean your screen?"

"Pardon?"

"Your windshield. I see Neal forgot. Neal!"

"It's all right, really. Going to get dirty again anyway."

"We do have bugs down here. Where you headed?"

"How long does it take to ring up a charge?"

"Neal! Boy is real slow. Having lots of trouble with him. Neal!"

"He's only nervous. Give him a break and he'll do fine. You give people a break and they'll give you one back, you know."

"Break, hell. That's all he does. 'I'm taking a break, boss. Okay?' 'Neal, that's your tenth break today.' 'It's not either, boss. I've only had five.' Only five. More like a dozen. Lazy. I don't know . . ."

"What don't you know?" said Neal, coming back.

"How much of a raise to give you," Venus said. "Whether a dollar more an hour is enough."

"I did not!" the boss protested. "I did not say that!"

"A dollar! Lady, did you hear that? A dollar."

"Yeah, that's what he told me. A dollar more an hour."

The boss wadded and chucked down the paper towel he was going to use on the windshield and stomped off. "No way . . . no way . . ."

"Thanks anyway, lady," Neal said. He tried to reach in and shake her hand, then stopped himself. "Really."

"He'll come around," Venus said. "Give him time. And you know what might be even better?"

"What's that?"

"Show him ways he can make more money. Easy stuff. Like cleaning up the place. For starters. More people'll stop."

"Hadn't thought of that."

"Do it and see what he says. Bet you he comes around."

"Are you an angel?"

Venus laughed and started the car. "Yes, I am."

"I thought so."

"Is there a motel around here?"

"Excuse me?"

"You know, a place to sleep."

"Blue Oaks isn't bad, they say. On the casino highway."

"Casino highway?"

"Yeah, highway thirty-seven. Runs to where they've got a casino now. You seen it?"

"A casino? Out here?"

"Yeah, gigantic thing, brand new! Hottest thing going. Boss's been there. Says it's crazier than all get-out. People in there from all over the country. I thought sure that was where you were headed."

"Thought they only had casinos in Vegas."

"Hey, I don't know, lady. All I know is we've got one down here now. And you have a good time now, all right?"

He stepped back and waved. As if her Impala were a steamship pulling out for a round-the-world cruise.

Venus grinned back. "Casino, huh."

"Bigger than all get-out," the boy said. He pointed at the road. "Thirty-seven south is right at the next light. Take you half an hour before you start hitting the motels in Iona. That's the town. Watch for the cops."

"Thank you."

"Lady?"

"Yeah?"

"Don't take all your money out there to the casino, though, okay? You don't know how many people I get coming back through here with about half their shirt on." Then he saw Venus's blouse that she'd left a little unbuttoned. "I mean, with about half their stuff. I mean, broke."

"I understand."

"Yeah. You got it."

Venus had tried to follow Carl up the mountain one night but found herself on a new road that wound on around the mountain, neither rising nor falling, only curving through the jungle. There were no houses yet out this way, only the nameless street leading on and her hard sandals slapping against it. Only heaped-up walls of jungle and all its urgent sounds. She could go on down the street or go back, it didn't matter. And so she walked some more and then even farther until it came to an end at a barricade of oil drums. Beyond, more jungle. The unknown. The raw stuff of the world where mere people didn't go. She peered into the green tangles and saw the lights of flowers that bloom only at night. No animals roared at her, nothing slithered up her leg, nothing alit on her back. There was simply the velvet calm. Which she seized and held inside herself, looking left and right as if to be sure no one were watching, as if the ladies of the cemetery might emerge at any second and ask her what business she could possibly have there. At the frontier of the known and the unknown, sweat on her palms and on her neck, her scalp tingling in the night heat. And then she took the next step past the barricade and bent into the green and let the wet weight of the jungle seal her in, as if to be reabsorbed and then remade. Into a flower that opened only at night. Into May, who came to her through the jungle to take her hands in hers and tell her that this was no place for a living woman, no place for a woman with all the rest of her life to live with passion — as if it were to be the single exception to the ugliness of the universe. Who then abruptly let go of Venus's hands and admonished her, told her to go forth, leave that wet and shadowed place and refind the light in broad unbounded places where the soul could breathe in sunlight. Who pushed her back out onto the road over which an eye of lead-colored moon waited.

The Blue Oaks was actually the Green Oaks, but anybody could get a name wrong and the sign was cobalt. It had a nineteen-sixties funk about it, but it seemed safe and the rooms were clean. She took a downstairs unit with a kitchenette, put the air-conditioning on max, opened a beer, and stretched out on the queen bed. Like the Queen of Sheba, she declared to herself. Lording it over the men there, in charge. Her beauty a sword. Cutting them to ribbons with a bat of her eyelashes. Or Queen of Venus. Better. Queen of a whole planet. Why not.

She decided to stay for a while, maybe go to the casino. Then she'd wander down the road, or not, or whatever. There was no reason to make big decisions, which felt only fair and right.

She lay there enjoying the cool air pouring over her legs, wondering if she didn't need to be a better person now that the deck had been cleared. The thought had come out of nowhere like a fly. She observed it, tried to make up her mind whether to smash it or let it be. Then she decided it could live, be a thought to think about some. Not a lot, though, because maybe it didn't mean anything. Be better? Did that mean being nice to people? When had she not been nice to somebody on purpose? Never. And you couldn't count leaving Blalock as not being nice, either. That was different. That was getting off a sinking ship. Being with other men, then? Well, that wasn't exactly angel-like behavior, but then it was time for the world to grow up and live with these things. It wasn't the Dark Ages anymore, hell. A light had come into the world named May and taught through its shining. And Venus had learned. And so, no, she'd always been good down inside.

So she went ahead and swatted the thought. Guilt wouldn't be allowed to tag along on this trip. She'd make sure of that. Keep her head screwed on straight about who she was. Someone with a few problems. But someone nice. No one could take that away.

She got another beer from the fridge and cracked it, surprised how fast she'd knocked off the first one. The second one was colder, better. She scrounged up some saltines she'd dropped into her purse back somewhere, looked out the window. A guy in his street clothes was lurking by the pool. Some hick looking at the lights in the water. Then he turned around like he'd been waiting all along for her to show her face. Venus pulled back but was sure he could still see her. Then she went over by the door, turned off the overhead. Peeked out. He was gone.

The rap on the door sent her stumbling back.

"What do you want!"

"Hello?" The voice was high pitched, far off. "Hello?"

"Who is it?"

"Night service, ma'am. It's eight o'clock."

"Night service?"

"Do you not wish night service?"

"No thank you."

"Thank you. Good night, ma'am."

"Good night."

What bullshit. This was no fancy motel. That'd been some asshole trying to come in on her. She rechecked the lock and chain. Had another beer and thought again about what being good meant, how it was something you never let go of, no more than you let go of your life. Being good was painting Easter eggs in Bible school. Being good was thinking God would step in when the time came and lift you up on his hand and take you aloft into the eternal blue. Being good was letting your soul fly out of you and into the body of the women preparing food for the dead in a Mexican cemetery. Being good was exchanging places with an orphan being sold at the side of the road in the Sierra Madre. Being good was thinking of May and remembering her.

Venus slept in the big bed. Dreamed that she kept her eyes half open. That she saw her tall Indian man again. With his black eyes and thick pigtails to his waist. Walking in through the door as through air and standing before her without speaking. Like he'd always done ever since she was a child hearing her grandfather's tales of living out on the West Texas plains with his grandfather, who had related many a time in a shaking voice how Indians came at night and surrounded the homestead and made owl sounds. They'd never attacked, though, not like they had the other farms, and no one had ever understood why, though Venus thought she knew, all these generations later, seeing the Indian man standing over her as though simply curious but also to guard her, to keep his strong back turned against the night and all that might leap for her. A guardian, a man the way men were before they became white men venturing loudly and righteously across the land by day but cowering in their cabins by night. He stands over her and once again she tries to ask him how tall he is but she cannot speak, only smile.

Someone always flushes a toilet at four in the morning, and it woke her. The air conditioner was off for some reason and she was sweating.

"I'm sorry," a man said.

Venus sat up. Somebody outside the window.

A woman answered, "Shh. It's okay."

"No, I really am sorry. I shouldn't have done that."

"Well, you did, and now it's done. You've hurt me bad."

"I know."

"I know you know. And you know what else I know?"

"No."

"That you're going to know what you know right now for the rest of your life. It'll be like a knife in your head."

"Fuck you."

"Yeah, fuck you, too."

A door slammed. Footsteps trailed off.

Venus turned on the lamp. No Indian. No May. Nothing but a moth batting around. She picked up the phone and called Mexico for the first time since she'd left. Someone answered, but said nothing. "Carl? That you, Carl?" Whoever it was hung up. She did not call back, the words she'd intended to say having already escaped her.

There was no staying away too long from the Iona Belle. Everybody was there. All sizes, shapes, colors, one of everything from every corner of everywhere, and all of them working hard to throw away as much money as possible in the insane hope of making it all back and plenty more on top of that though the odds were billions to one.

Venus went to a keno parlor upstairs and marked up a seven-spot, paid one dollar, sat down on one of the chairs.

A waitress waddled over. "Drink?"

Venus saw a vulture.

"Vodka-tonic. Stoli."

"We only have domestic vodka, ma'am. No imports."

"Whatever. Make it a double."

"Now calling game number eight eight six," the announcer said. "And wish me luck here."

Indifferent, the waitress tapped a red fingernail on Venus's sheet.

The chairs were lined up as if in a classroom. Venus straightened up, like a good student.

A fat guy slowly read numbers into a microphone. "Number nineteen, number thirty, number three, number five, number . . ."

When it was over Venus had an eighty-dollar ticket. Beaming, she hurried to cash it in.

"How about that?" the cashier girl said, shrugging. "A winner."

"Nobody wins at keno," said an old guy behind Venus.

Venus nodded happily, took her twenties, and returned to her chair.

The guy came and sat next to her. "That's real good luck."

He was past seventy and studying her money like a starving man.

"Take twenty," Venus said, handing him one.

"Now, I couldn't do that."

She could tell he was a guy who'd kind of lost his way or been forgotten. Tears welled in his red eyes and he thanked her again and again until Venus told him to stop.

"We can't have that, can we? This is just about sharing the wealth. So, what's your name?"

"Mort Cageot."

"Mort, I'm Venus. We're adults here, right?"

"Yes ma'am, we are."

"Playing a little keno, right?"

"Yes ma'am, we are."

"Nothing to get upset about, right?"

"No ma'am, there ain't."

"All right, then."

They marked up new seven-spots together and then the vulture swooped in with Venus's drink.

"Get one for Mort, too," she said.

"Sorry, ma'am, can't do that."

"Why not?"

"He's been cut off."

"That true?" Venus asked him.

"You want your twenty back?"

"I do not. Why'd they cut you off? What'd he do, anyway?"

The waitress set Venus's drink in a hole on the armrest.

Venus tipped her five. "Well?"

"Well what?" the girl said.

"What did he do?"

"We've cut him off."

Venus forgot to be good and lashed out. "Are you ignoring my question on purpose, or what?"

"Lord above, look down," said Mort.

"Back off, lady," said the waitress.

"What did you say?"

"I said, 'Back . . . off.' Are you deaf?"

Venus handed her drink to Mort. "There you go, buddy. Drink up."

Mort began gulping.

"I can throw you people out of here," the waitress said.

Venus jammed two twenties into her tip cup. "Not if you want to make a nickel or two. So keep them coming, hear?"

The vulture gawked at the money. Then looked around to see if somebody, like her boss, had witnessed the altercation.

"All right," she said hurriedly, "but I do have the power to throw you both out. If either of you gets out of line. All I have to do is snap my fingers and you're out of here."

"I think we can handle that," Venus said. "Right, Mort?"

"You bet we can, honey."

The vulture flew away.

"Have to tip them right these days," Venus said. "Otherwise they go ballistic."

"You got that right," he said. "I didn't do nothing. They got nervous when I started winning. Said I was drunk out of my mind. Then I started losing and they said I was being too loud and —"

"You don't have to tell me," said Venus. "Let's get this game in."

They went up front, paid, came back.

"Nice way to spend an evening," he said. "And cheap."

"I believe in tipping, though, Mort."

"I can see that."

"Game number eight eight seven is now closed," the announcer said.

Of course neither one of them won a thing on game eight eight seven, or eight eight eight, or eight eight nine, or any other game all the way up to nine-o'-something when Mort fell asleep facedown on his chair's writing tablet and Venus gave him a pat and got up to wander.

She stopped at a bathroom, splashed water on her face, and vowed to leave before too much longer. She only had to get a cab and go. There'd be other nights, so no sense overdoing it at the outset, she decided.

"Honey, do I look like total shit?" asked a young brunette washing her hands and sneering at her messed-up makeup in the mirror.

"You sure do," Venus said.

"That's what I thought. Thank you."

The girl teetered out clutching a big pink purse. Venus followed her a ways through the crowd, as if to assure herself that the creature made it back to her table or whatever, but then lost her in the swirl of people and stepped up to a bar for another vodka-tonic.

It went down agreeably and she felt a pleasant sense of detachment from everything and began to think again how May had changed her into someone much more than a woman going through life in a little Texas town without even the notion that there could be promise again, desire and anticipation. She thought of the many men without names who had traversed her existence because of May, their rapid and vigorous passage warming the depths of her to a degree she'd never known. She thought about the joy and excitement in May's voice whenever she'd spoken of life's possibilities, its unbounded grandeur. She thought about holding May again and squeezing her hard and being squeezed back hard until they'd hurt each other again and laughing and gasping and then marveling at all the goodness when they were together.

"Big crowd, huh," the bartender said. Chubby kid, twenty-five.

"Where do they all come from?" she asked.

"Soon as this casino opened up down here every critter in creation came out of hiding. Like they'd spent all their lives before this casino got here dreaming of it. But this crowd's nothing."

"How so?"

"This is only Monday."

She had a second drink, then tipped him ten and said she'd see him again, and he said that would be good and dropped her gratuity into a jar.

Then she went back up and woke up Mort. Got them going again, got the miracle machine revved back up, got the many intricate parts of chance and fate to do their thing like they were supposed to. Venus, giver of order, of combustion, of life and winnings and smiles.

By dawn she'd won two hundred forty-seven dollars at keno and he was singing songs of joy to her and touching her again and again on the arm like she was saintly, had performed a miracle — which she had.

Then she gave him all the money.

"You can't do this."

"It's done, Mort."

"No, I can't take your money, Venus."

"Would you argue with me, Mort? Really?"

"No ma'am. Not if it did not please you."

"All right, then."

She hugged him and he hugged her back, putting every last ounce of his energy into it, which wasn't much, as light as a tired child's. Then she kissed him on the cheek. A blue-haired couple gawked and shook their heads.

Venus walked out of the Iona Belle into the light of the new day feeling slightly off the ground, as if May were right at her side helping her float along, which she was, once again.

The barkeep was right. Tuesday's crowd was thicker, Wednesday's even more so, and Thursday's a flood of bodies. She came and went without watching the time, poured down vodka-tonics and watched for Mort, as if he needed someone watching for him. But he never showed up and so she played keno alone. No one hit on her, which was a nice break, and she watched people come and go, take seats in the parlor for a while, laugh and carry on, or perch there very serious, maybe even desperate, then wash away as a game ended. The number callers would change every so often, but it was always the same bored voice. Announcements about misparked cars drifted down from speakers above. Toilets flushed beyond the wall behind her head. The cocktail girls all looked the same, dumpy and sassy, and though she tipped them well they got into a game of ignoring her. Which turned out all right, in the end, because otherwise she might well have ended up sprawled on the blue carpet.

It was like being at the back of a cruise ship rolling side to side as it plowed the seas of money and chance, never coming to shore, never arriving. She thought of all the ocean liners that would creep into the bay at Puerto Azul just before dawn while she slept and that would be sitting there in all their impossible hugeness when she arose and went out into the day, the tiny launches already buzzing back and forth. And of all the sunburned tourists from Australia or England or Germany whom they'd run in to shopping at the market, loudmouthed rubberneckers buying up trinkets and waddling this way and that in their plaid shorts and sandals and white socks. All having the time of their lives, like the people there in the casino, unleashed, set free in the parlor of their dreams to do as they wished, their only worry their little wads of money and how long this would last as they struggled up and down the decks while the great ocean pounded them from all directions just like they'd hoped.

She played it easy, the better to stay on the big boat another night and another. For there was nothing calling her yet to go elsewhere.

Once you find an all right bar in a casino, you go to that same bar over and over again because that way you feel like you know someone, like you have a kind of home that's yours.

The bartender kid said, "You've survived."

"Have I?"

"How're you making out?"

"I don't know if I'm bold enough."

"Better not to be."

"I'm a keno queen, though."

"Nothing wrong with that. Keno ain't easy."

She liked his quiet certainty, and stayed with him there for several drinks minding her own business and playing video blackjack.

He didn't talk much and she liked that and tried not to look up from her monitor to watch him moving back and forth serving people with all the solid assurance of someone who knows exactly the score.

Then he went off shift, with a nod to her on the way past.

She lost a couple of dozen more hands of blackjack, then conducted a long, narrowed-eyed survey of the electric heart of the casino and concluded that it might be all right to think about getting out of there.

"'Morning, my angel."

It was Mort, down and out.

"Where have you been?"

"I was here."

"Not with me, you weren't."

"I was downstairs. In that parlor."

He pointed.

"Didn't know there was one down there."

"Looks right out over the river. But I lost all you gave me that time, angel."

"It's okay."

"Silly Mort."

"That's ridiculous. It's only keno."

"All two hundred and nearly fifty."

She opened her purse and handed him a twenty. "Here."

He backed off. "No, no. Going home. My daughter's going to pick me up any minute. Soon as she gets off from the hospital."

"Take it. Come on."

"No, no, Charlene's coming. Mort's going home."

Venus poked the bill into his shirt pocket. "Go make some more with that until she gets here. You've got time."

"I do?"

"Sure you do."

"Well, it is only five. She's not off until seven."

"There you go."

"Join me?"

Venus thought no, but then said, Why not. He was right. It was only five o'clock. And she didn't have a damn thing to do but sleep and why sleep when a sweetheart like Mort needed your company?

"I'm with you."

Mort grinned and poked out his elbow, and she hooked on.

Mort Cageot

That girl? I tell you she is an angel from on high. She hit every number in the book. One right after the other like it was raining luck. Never seen anything like it. On fire! I sat there and baked in the heat. Put my hands out into it. Felt it. Whew, I am telling you, I wanted to kiss her. I wanted to be twenty-five and dancing with her in the woods back where you used to take a gal. An angel. A white angel for this old black bastard. They say there's one for everybody. One angel for every man, woman, and child in America, if only you will live right. Live by the truth. Then the angel will come to you. And take her keno card and fill it out like it is nothing and hit every number in creation. Pardon my tongue, but this bitch knows the bad from the good. Casts the devil out and makes those numbers fly up on the winning board and flash red. Yes, two hundred and forty-seven dollars' worth of angel love is mine. And I'm going to sit here and play it out, one dollar after one dollar after one dollar until there isn't a dollar left and they come throw me out again. I love her. I do. Crank me up that old Hammond organ, honey, and let the silken choir sing out! Hallelujah, Lord! Thy will be done! Praise you, Lord!

Nicky came over one night when I'd almost quit thinking about him and his preachy ways and the goofy fishing trip and said, "Let's go down to the Iona Belle. And we won't talk about crappie fishing or mourning your life away or anything like that. Promise."

"Deal."

"But we will talk about gambling. This might be paradise."

It was Friday night in America, everybody was going somewhere, and it felt great to be getting out. I definitely had had enough of four walls like a cell and of creeping once in a while over to Lisa's and back but no farther. Here, then, was the living world again showing me the green light to go about my business freely, the Blalock heist now an old story that no one could possibly know of. What better place to start than in a casino?

Nicky hauled ass down the highway like he owned it, and people got out of the way of his Mustang, which made him snicker like a teenager and shoot me that look that said, Any doubt who's in charge here, buddy?

The Iona Belle was maybe ten miles back in the boondocks where the cotton runs out and the swamp takes over. The building was made like a steamboat, thousands of lights streaming this way and that all over it.

The lots were full and there must've been a hundred cars circling. Nicky found some kid he knew and slipped him some money, and then we had a place to park up by the door.

Let me say it now, Nicky knows gambling. I got a thorough

overview on the way in, though he never asked me if I'd ever gambled. First off, he said, you skipped the slots. Guaranteed loser there. Next, you blew off blackjack, because you had to be a genius to win and there wasn't one person in ten million that smart. And you didn't play baccarat, either, same reasons. After that, there was roulette, where you had the zero and the double-zero against you, but which was as safe a place as any to have some fun.

"Let's put in twenty bucks each and you stand right behind me," Nicky said. "We hit, we stay. We miss, we're gone from the table. Okay?"

I handed him my money. He dropped the bills onto the green felt.

The Asian gal said, "Forty coming in."

Nicky sat at the end where the high numbers were, and she pushed the chips out to him. Bets were five-dollar minimum.

"Here goes," said Nicky.

He put one chip on thirty-six and four on the thirty-five/thirty-six split.

The Asian got the wheel going and dropped the marble. "No more bets," she said, slowly passing her hand over the table.

Number thirty-five came up. Like that.

I didn't shout out, though I wanted to. Neither did Nicky. The four chips on the split paid seventeen-to-one each.

"Have a color preference, sir?" the Asian asked.

"Purple."

The Asian pushed over our winnings in bright purple chips.

Down at the other end of the table was a poor boy who'd maybe been playing since lunch. He was up some, but not much. Passing time.

"Dead tables are good," Nicky said. "Get us a drink."

All I had to do was turn and there was a gal. "Help you?" she said.

"Two Scotch and waters."

Nicky handed me some dollar chips he'd had squirreled away. "Drinks are free, but tip. One drink, one chip."

On he played. Hitting splits and corners, once in a while right on a number for thirty-five-to-one. Then he'd lose on one or two spins, and I'd give him a new number and we'd win one or two back. Pretty soon we had several good-sized stacks of chips.

"This ain't going to last," Nicky kept saying.

But then it did. I had a couple of drinks, watched the people slowing to watch, then got to thinking I needed to move around, stretch my legs.

"I'll be back."

"Don't leave me hanging here long, bud."

A casino is a spooky circus. Everyone jostling, flinging themselves at each other, shoving, leaping, groaning, dancing in circles, holding their heads, crying their eyes out, pleading, begging, hanging on each other. I saw dozens of people who'd definitely been at those slots ever since the day the things had been turned on, never missing a minute, their fingers dark gray with coin dust, insane grins on their faces. Card tables, craps tables, roulette tables, and giant spinning money wheels stretched as far as I could see, on and on, all the way back in there where maybe the universe itself began. Colored lights flashed in every direction, grabbed on to my eyes and spun me around and around until, no choice left, I let go and joined the fantastic rhythm. Started smiling at it all, greeting people, wishing them luck, going with the flow. Wherever it took me. Let myself be led through the Big Throwaway. Like the boys behind the mirrors and in the camera booths way upstairs somewhere wanted me to do. Let that wild-ass gambling fever take me over.

"Get out of my way," he said.

A boy, maybe fifteen, maybe not even, had stopped in front of me.

"You talking to me, son?"

"You don't have a son. You don't have anything."

"Who do you think you're talking to?"

"Who says you even have a name?"

Was this one of those gang kids from out West? Did he maybe have a large gun stuck in his baggy clothes? How'd he gotten in there?

I went around him.

"Hey, where you going?"

"To piss."

I wished I'd had the guts to deck him, but your life didn't mean anything to a kid like that. You got out of his possible line of fire. I headed upstairs to the john.

Then the kid was pissing right next to me. "Trying to get away?"

"What do you want?"

"Gamble."

"You're in a casino, bud."

"Never been in one."

He shook his thing a lot like nobody'd ever told him not to overdo it.

"My first time, too," I said.

He smiled, if that's what you call it.

"How'd you get in here?"

"Just here."

"What's that mean?"

"I's here, okay? You got money."

"How old are you?"

"Twenty dollars."

"You want twenty dollars?"

"Twenty."

"You want me to just give you twenty dollars?"

Then there was something cold on my neck and a voice to that side may have said, Give it to him. I looked but there was no one there.

"You got friends in here?"

"I want to gamble."

"Your friends are gambling?"

"Twenty dollars."

"Are you on drugs or something?"

"Lay off, man! You got a twenty, give it!"

He held out his hand. It shook.

I peeled him off twenty. He didn't say anything, just crammed it into a pocket of his pants and shuffled out.

I laughed at myself for being such an idiot, and then someone else came in to take a leak and saw me laughing and so I finished washing my hands in silence. When I came out I had the thirst of a man who's worked all day clearing brush under the summer sun, and found a water fountain. There is always somebody ahead of you when you're thirsty like that.

"Hope it was good," I said when she finished.

Then she looked at me. Venus Blalock.

"Carl Stein?"

I started away like I hadn't seen her. If her old man was around, something bad was going to happen. I told my feet to keep moving.

"Where are you going? Carl?"

Then I stopped. Don't know why. But I did. And turned around.

She was wearing clothes for a gal half her age: red high heels, short red leather skirt, kind of a see-through red blouse.

"What?"

"What?" she squealed.

"Yeah, what?"

"You took our money," she said. "Goddamn seven grand, Carl said! And you just look at me and say, 'What?'"

I laughed at her. "Yeah, and?"

"Hey, give her her money back, man!" a guy said.

"Let her gamble with it!" a woman called.

People clapped and the woman, a plump retiree in a Hawaiian shirt, stepped forward, took a bow, and ashed her cigarette.

I looked around for Blalock. Would he leap out with a gun and bring this to an ugly head? Was it all going to climax right here, real fast?

A security guy came along.

"Sir, this man has stolen money from me," Venus said.

"Yeah, arrest the bastard!" a man said.

"Stole her purse!" a woman yelled. "I saw it!"

The cop reached around like he was going to take something off his belt, his service pistol maybe, and I took off down the stairs. Hit the main floor, cut through the crowd, shot out the front door and into a cab.

"Iona!" I told the guy. "Move it."

"Uh-huh. You got twenty?"

I wagged the cash. "Go, go."

"Uh-huh," he said, adjusting his cap. "Here we go."

A few minutes later we were out of the swamp and back in the cotton.

"You believe in ghosts?" I asked the guy.

"Don't you?"

I hung my head out, saw the stars in the steamy night. "Maybe."

"You better. They're all over the place now."

I wondered what I'd tell Nicky. I needed to think, come up with something good.

"That's right. Many ghosts. All sizes."

"Yeah?"

"Most of the time they're like real people. Bet you didn't know that."

"No."

"Yes sir, like you and me. Real. But they're ghosts, all right. Real live ghosts. Tricky bastards."

"Would you know it if you yourself were a ghost?"

He watched me in the mirror. "You're not a ghost, pal."

"How do you know?"

"I can tell."

That night I got out Lisa's mirror and tried to see myself in it again. Talk about ghosts. There was a crowd of them in the back of that mirror. A bunch of guys, all me. There I was pumping gas by the interstate in Albuquerque. Having a fistfight with Sandy Shoemaker in a Flagstaff motel. Shooting buckshot at the moon out in the middle of nowhere in Montana. Frying chicken legs in a fast-food joint in Boulder. Making love with May in the Mojave out on a pile of orange rocks under the sun. I don't know how Lisa did it, but her mirror was without a doubt haunted. I wasn't even drunk. I almost went over there to ask her about it. But then you don't do crap like that unless you want to blow your setup.

Venus kept popping up in the other mirror in my mind. Blalock, too. The two of them staring me down. Would they somehow find me here? It took me half the night to get to sleep. Every time I shut my eyes, they came open like someone'd just busted in through the door.

I sat in my apartment a few days, watched TV, but every few minutes I'd look toward the door again, thinking I heard something. Then I thought it out carefully and decided that it was a freak thing for Venus to have been there in that casino. A total accident. Nothing at all to fear.

Deep-sixing my paranoia, I finally did the necessary and opened the morning paper and spotted a job that suited me. It was to ride up with a pilot in a two-seater and be the one to chuck out bales of leaflets, ads for stuff. What better place for me to be than way up there over everything, free as a bird? Turned out I was the first to call, and so first to get a tryout.

I called Nicky to tell him about it and, not missing a beat, he insisted on driving me out to the Iona airfield for the test.

"We did damn well on the roulette, you know," he told me.

"How's that?"

"Thirty-six kept hitting, that's how. Two times in a row, then it went over to thirty-five, and then right back it came. I was piling it in. Thirty-five-to-one. You know those guys who were standing back in the pit watching? Well, after all that one of them came over to the girl at the wheel and said something. After that, downhill. But I pulled up fast."

"How much?"

"Four hundred bucks for our forty-dollar investment. Not bad."

He pulled a couple of hundreds and a couple of twenties out of his shirt pocket. "There you go, dude." It was more than half, and he saw I was confused. "That's called tipping," he said. "For good luck. Like when I hit a big one, make a thousand dollars? I'll toss you a hundred."

I gave a twenty back. "Tip back, too?"

"You got it," he said. "Now we'll both have good luck next time we go out there. So, want to tell me what happened to you?"

"Got sick. Puked."

He winced and laughed. I said nothing, then thought better. "Yeah, overdid it. Those free drinks. Cabbed it home."

"You missed me on the dice."

"Do good?"

"No. So, Carl, I want to talk you out of this flying job. I can help you get a regular job. This is goofy. You know that, don't you?"

"I've always wanted to fly."

"This isn't flying, Carl. They dive-bomb. Talk about throwing up!"

"Nah."

"I bet I could get you on the police force. How about it?"

"No thanks."

I watched the cotton fields. One step too far and Nicky could find out much more than I'd want him to know. I imagined men squatting and staring at dripping walls in that smelly penitentiary way back in there.

"I take it back," he said. "You haven't got enough guts for the force."

"That's right. Not enough guts."

"Of course, you can be trained."

"Terrible trainee. Army hated me."

"Figures."

The airfield was coming up.

"We can't have you doing this, though. This is stupid."

"It's money."

"Let's go have a beer and read the other want ads."

"Forget it," I said.

We went in through the gate. A yellow plane was sitting outside its shed, and guys were standing around visibly pissed from waiting.

"An old girlfriend," I said.

"What?"

"I wasn't sick. It was an old girlfriend from New Mexico I saw in there."

"All the way from New Mexico? Jesus. And?"

"She was drunk. Real drunk. Anyway, I said hello and that was about it. But I couldn't stay in there anymore. Had to get out."

"Hell, you only had to say so. Women. I ain't been laid since —"

"Thanks for the ride."

"Sure you want to do this?"

"Hey!" one of the guys called. "You here for this job or not?"

"Got to go, Nicky."

"Don't fall out."

For a second I thought about how good a liar I am, then I went over and shook hands with the men. Bunch of wise guys who thought I wouldn't last fifteen minutes. The boss, a coot named Curtis Blankenship, started in about how some air force pilot had strangled on his vomit and then ejected. The jet had gone *boom* and the guy had been booted down to something so low he was begging for a discharge. But they didn't give it to him. They made him stay, suffer, mop up shit. He had an entire eighteen-million-dollar plane to work off. And let that be a lesson to you. It meant, Don't puke in my plane. "Now load up them bundles."

Chucking ads over the town was not my idea of doing the right thing. But in some silly way it was pretty with those things drifting down like confetti. We rose and dove and dropped, rose and dove and dropped ten big loads. I wasn't sick at all. I landed the job as chief thrower-outer.

A few days later Nicky came over and hung out awhile.

"You going to see that old girlfriend again?" he asked. "Maybe you might get laid. I mean, if you've already done a woman, sometimes she'll do you again, even if she's tied up with somebody else. For old time's sake. You might want to work that angle."

I'd had some beers. Said nothing, looked at the horse race they were fixing to run on the TV.

"Well?" he asked.

"Well, what?"

"Why aren't you answering me?"

"I answered."

"You did not."

"You just didn't hear it."

He paused, then said, "Hear what?"

"My answer, goddamn it."

"What's wrong with you?"

"Nothing's wrong with me," I shot back. "Who do you like in this race?"

"Hellfire," he said, getting up. "You don't know squat about horse racing."

I stood up, too. "You're right. But what else is on? Nothing. Everything's dead."

"I'm out of here. By the way, you spent your two hundred yet?"

"What do you think?"

"Nah. You've got it squirreled away. That's you."

"What?"

"That's you. Cheap ass. Where you got it?"

"Get out of here, Nicky."

"What day is it?"

"Shit if I know. Thursday. Wednesday. No, Thursday. Go home."

They were getting the horses into the starting gates — or trying to. Three or four of them were kicking and making trouble.

"It's been eight years," Nicky said.

"What?" I said.

"Eight years, no pussy."

I shoved him toward the door. "I've got a headache. Get out of here."

"Yeah, me too."

Then he was gone.

I turned the race off and stood there scratching my gut. Things would come to me about what next if I just let them, but I decided I was too tired and too drunk for anything to come to me. I knew where I was headed and that was on down a road wherever it went. Who needed to think, meantime? Wasn't all my thinking already done for me anyway?

I turned the race back on. Sure enough, all those expensive horses were hurtling down the track at full speed, and the crowd was going wild.

But then it happened. There was May staring at me from the TV. Her black-and-white face, no smile, nothing, staring. I knew the look. Not the love look, but the other one, the sex look, the look she had when that was what she wanted and nothing else, the look that said, Don't kiss me, don't hug me, just satisfy me. It was the face of the last time, five or six days before she drowned. When we made love on the floor in the front room of our house in Red Rock, in a warm pool of afternoon sunshine.

Sometimes I'd get out my two hundreds and feel how crisp they were, then put them back in the envelope under the vanilla ice cream. Sometimes doing that would make me think about sticking my hands down in Blalock's floor safe and taking all those twenties, seven bunches of them in all, and jamming them into that rubber bank bag. It'd been cold enough that morning to get me shaking while I was kneeling there stealing and thinking, Where did he get all these goddamn twenties? Now there was the bag, minus only what I'd absolutely had to take out, stuffed into a big box emptied of its frozen black-eyed peas. You'd think I'd've put the two hundreds in with all those pretty twenties, but I never did. I kept them on the side.

"Mexican food do you all right?" Nicky asked as we got in his Mustang.

"Sure."

"Hey, listen to this rev! Got me a brand-new motor, friend."

He revved her up to about three billion RPMs there on my parking lot. Sounded like a jet fighter, but he wouldn't let up. I didn't think, just reached over and turned her off. There was a big jolt, like we'd landed.

The cop face appeared. He turned her back on. "Don't do that again."

So I did. *Bang*, she was dead again.

"What the hell's wrong with you, Carl?"

"You're making too much racket. I live here. I have neighbors."

He looked like he wanted to slug me one. But he only turned her back on, guided her into the street, and headed downtown. Cars went around us, people honked, but he never took her over fifteen.

"Who're you to say anything about how much racket I make?"

"Who're you to make so much racket?"

Then we didn't say anything for several blocks.

"I was only kidding around," I finally said, lying.

"I don't like people messing with my car."

"A fucking joke, Nicky."

"Yeah? All right, ha-ha."

"Jesus."

"So what're we doing? Oh, yeah. Mexican food. Here we come. Hey, you ever been to Mexico?"

"Nah. Blalock invited me once, but —"

"Who?"

"A buddy."

"So you have had friends. Which life was this in?"

"What?"

"When'd you have a friend named Blalock?"

"Back in the army."

"Y'all were going to Mexico in the army?"

"No, that was after. Later on, when we ran into each other again."

"Where was that?"

I said anything. "Del Rio, Texas."

"Del Rio?"

"Yeah."

"What year?"

We were going past a graveyard on one side and the river on the other. Up ahead was the Mexican part of town, the tall yellow sign flashing over Garza's restaurant.

"Five, six years ago."

"You were living in Del Rio?"

"Visiting."

"All the way from Wisconsin?"

"Yeah. Have family there. On my ma's side. Conables. Mitzi Conable, my aunt. Hadn't seen her since I was eight. But she's still living out there. Pa had always said Del Rio was like death. He'd finally gotten Ma out of there, moved her up north to Wisconsin. But Mitzi had stayed put on account of her husband being in the Border Patrol and all."

"Good for them," Nicky said. "Hey, Garza's is packed."

"Neither one of them, you know, would ever eat Mexican food again after living in Del Rio."

"I wouldn't go to Del Rio if you paid me."

Nicky pulled into the parking lot, found a place in the back, cut the motor, and stared at me like he had something to say.

"Let's eat," I said, and got out.

We'd gotten a beer and ordered our number two combination plates when he said, "Why am I thinking you've never been to Del Rio?"

"I don't know, Nicky. Why are you thinking that?"

"Don't know. But I am."

I shook my head like he was being silly and shrugged, and then we scarfed down all the chips and sauce. It was a full house and so noisy you could barely hear yourself think.

I was riding the sky over Iona with Curtis those mornings chucking out ads for a special night coming up at the casino where they had guaranteed somebody would walk out a millionaire.

Nicky asked, "What would you do with a million?"

"Probably lose it in ten minutes."

"Don't say that. You'll jinx it. Shit!"

"Didn't you tell me nobody ever really wins in a casino?"

"That's all negative. You're jinxing it, Carl."

"Jinx, my ass."

"Don't say that!"

In fact, everything I said before the big night made Nicky suspicious. And so it got old real fast, and then I wasn't sure I would even go.

Still, flying over town, Curtis shooting us up and down like on a roller coaster for no reason other than to try to make me lose my cookies, the idea of a cool one million dollars looked pretty good. Just the ticket.

Lisa came over for a drink late one afternoon, and I poured her one of my domestic beers and pulled the blinds high so the sunset would hit that mirror she gave me. I knew she appreciated that. There wasn't a lot to talk about and I sure wasn't going to say anything about the things I had seen in that mirror or ask if she was a witch. So we stayed quiet. Lisa sat with her legs folded underneath herself like she was going to meditate.

Then she pulled out a joint and fired it up. We smoked it and the silences filled with soft bells and the red light streamed in through my windows like a floating river. A million and one things came to mind with the force of a hurricane. Lisa was certainly more practiced with weed, so she didn't say much. But me, once my mouth opened, it wouldn't shut until she was laughing so hard I cut the party short.

What I'd been saying was that Ma once decided I needed some education about people and set it up so that I'd go over to this young lady's house Thursdays to sit and talk with her for an hour. This lady was a cripple, a polio victim, laid up in a pink bed like a doll. With a big girl's head and a baby body and skin like white soap with liver spots on it. She was the sweetest girl on earth and collected postage stamps in big green books, and when she had too many postage stamps she'd put a bunch of them in a shoe box and give them to me for my own collection. I couldn't remember what all we talked about, but it wasn't the words that counted those afternoons. It was the being together, quiet, looking at stamps, knowing that life sometimes didn't treat you right, that sometimes you came out a cripple in a pink bed. This went on for about six months and then one Thursday Ma picked me up at school all red-eyed and quivering and said the girl had died. I think maybe I'd been in love with that girl. And so I cried for days inside. Not on the outside, I was too big for that, but for days deep down within where you really cry when you cry. Then Ma said she had another project for me and started leaving me at this rest home in a desolate part of Albuquerque where it was all ancient Indians and I played a few hymns on the piano. I sometimes sang while I played, and the old Indians gathered around like rabbits from the forest.

"You're making that up!"

"How could I make that up?"

Then she started laughing. I don't know why, guess it was the dope after all, but she went off the deep end. Maybe I should learn to have pity again, but I won't have somebody laughing at me. I ordered Lisa out and she obeyed and then laughed her head off over in her apartment.

I showered a long time to get that weed out of me. While I was in there, I actually remembered that crippled girl's name. Venus. Like the other one. That sent shivers through me and I kept saying to myself, "Think about something else. Anything else." Which meant I couldn't. Which meant the girl with the soap skin and the liver spots was on my bed when I came out. Lying there, ruined legs spread. Saying, "Hello there, Carl."

The day before the big casino night Curtis said, "Going to have to lay you off, son." He'd never called me son. "Haven't got a thing lined up. Sorry."

He had my little check ready.

Leaving, I got stupid and kicked the door of my Falcon. But once I was rolling, heading back to town, I felt better, kind of liberated. I even went to a motel bar out there someplace and drank myself goofy with the afternoon crowd.

A few hours into this, and after a long, ignorant discussion with a husband-and-wife drunk team about nothing I can remember, the waitress got skinnier and prettier. So I asked her home with me. She said yes so fast I dropped forty dollars on the table for the tab and ran out. Last thing I saw was her head poking between the window drapes to watch me go.

I drove to that park I'd gone to my first night in Iona. There was a wind like ocean waves. I wanted to ride them, go where they were going, and began to push myself on a swing again like a child. Slowly and then faster, and up pretty high, up far enough until I was able to fling myself out into the sea, which lifted me up and carried me away, light as paper.

Lisa Joyner

Mirror, mirror on the wall, who's the whitest of them all? Carl Stein. He's like an ocean of milk on a bright day. But I don't want to be insulting or rude. There's much more to a man than that, and I'm glad to have such an interesting neighbor. Mirror, mirror on the wall . . . and I think he likes me. Is that possible? He does like my mirrors. And I'm more than happy to share them with him. I mean, what good is there in going to mirror classes if you don't share your mirrors? Did you know part of you becomes part of a mirror when you look into one? It's a fact. And I also know that this part of you that stays in the mirror can't get back out. Does this part of you know it's stuck in a mirror, though? I think the part of you that's stuck in there doesn't really know where it's stuck once it's stuck. Then other times I think this part of you, once stuck like that, starts thinking backward. I mean it realizes it can't go forward from where it is, so it goes back. Into the past. All you have to do is watch the movie. I've seen this. I've seen Carl in my mirrors doing this. Carl comes from trouble, lots of it. It shines off that pure white skin of his, bounces off those huge teeth right out of my mirrors, gleams in that goofy smile. I know he wants me, too. I may not be smart but I'm not ugly. I may not know everything, either. Like, where exactly is France? I mean, I know it's over there somewhere near England because Emile said it was. Does it matter just where, though? I mean, what are we talking about here? Why would you have to know that? When I've got my life right here. This life during which I eat trash food at night, during which I iron bad if I ever even bother, during which I don't like to take walks, and during which mirror class is all there is besides volts. That's right, and who would've guessed, huh? Lisa Joyner wires houses. Top to bottom. Want to talk amperes, volts, fuses, plugs, or grounds? We can. I never have with Carl. Maybe he'd think I was lesbian. People think that kind of crap and he might think so. Until he touches me, that is. Then he'll know . . . I wonder if he thinks of me in my mirrors when he looks down in them. I wonder if he touches himself in my mirrors, too. Why do I feel like a slut? Give a man a mirror or two and he'll take your body away, too. Only maybe not in the good sense, not in the loving way. Maybe he'll take your body and hurt it and then discard it in a lonely place where officers will tread many months later and find just pieces of you, dried out, bits of clothing, hair . . . Make me sick, will you . . . Mirror, mirror, on the wall, what do I need, do I need a dog? I've always wanted one. I'll name it Rabbit and it'll be a she and we'll play. Maybe I'll teach her to jump into the mirrors with me. Late at night. When everyone is sleeping on earth. When the streetlight hits my mirrors real pretty and if I put my ear to the wall, I can hear him in there sleeping. Carl. Me, Carl, and Rabbit. Flowing on enough natural juice that we could light up the Iona casino if we thought about it. Into the mirror, I go laughing and smiling. Into the silver lake I dive. Down and down. Through the heavy liquid of the past. What do I see? I see Carl down in there floating along. I see another woman. I see roads and truck lights and filthy rest-stop bathrooms and oily gravel. It is a love story without words, without direction. It will turn out bad, you can be sure, and she will not be a part of what comes after. And him? He'll end up in a tiny apartment somewhere all alone again. Until then, though, he's still here and he's mine. Mine every night he sits over there trying to figure out how I make my mirrors so you can see yourself down in there again and again, twelve whole times, one inside the other. Trying to figure out old Lisa's tricks. And I've got a whole bag of them, baby. Waiting to travel. Waiting to kick out of the past and into the future like a bolt of juice down that copper cable at the root of your mind.

Carl Blalock

I went back to Texas that spring for one last shot, something having bubbled up after a few weeks without her down in Mexico, something angry born out of drinking that said, Enough is enough, she's got no cause to be tramping away, spitting on the past, casting what we had into the trash, acting like none of it ever happened, giving up, quitting. I went back all puffed up and agitated like a father going to fetch a child who's misbehaved, my temper carrying me along, that and my bitterness and my good bourbon. Only to find Venus wasn't there. Had taken some of her things and gone. No notes, no message. Which made sense. She didn't want me to find her. I waited a few days, slugging bourbon on the porch and remembering long talks with Stein but none of the words. Recalled watching his wife glide about the green yard in a white dress in the evening and my wife floating alongside her in a blue dress and the glow of the two of them amazing me and Carl in a way that got us to smiling at each other as if maybe we'd had something to do with the happiness those two had found. I missed him in spite of his nasty turn, and I missed May's strong alto voice telling us to be awake to all possibilities, and I missed Venus's big feet and the horn-rims she wore when she read and the curve of her back in the evening light. I drank as much bourbon as I could and then deep in the bottom of one starry night after I'd been stumbling around on the overgrown lawn trying to find constellations I'd learned as a child, I fell flat on my back and in the ferocious gravity pulling me down I realized how senseless it was to wait any longer for Venus to come down out of the heavens to me again. And so I got up off that yard and picked the stickers off my pants and shirt and out of my hair and went inside to sleep on my side of our bed and did not dream of her being there or of anything else. The next morning I set a plan in motion. Put the business and house up for sale, moved everything into storage or dumped it with the charity people, arranged for all loose ends to be tied up. Shut down our existence there. Erased our marks upon the earth. She had gone away. But I knew where she was. Out there. Getting whatever it was she wanted, so long as it didn't involve me. I went back to Mexico. Wondering why I'd ever left.

She'd always had every boy in Red Rock running after her, and I still don't know how I won that contest, especially when I hadn't even entered it. I wasn't any good at sports and all that flashy stuff, so that definitely wasn't it. In fact I was nearly invisible from the day Daddy moved us there and opened that store. A no-count kid from another town like this one. Minding my own business and going fishing out on Red Rock Lake in Daddy's boat every chance I got. I'd putter back up in the farthest reaches and cast and make notes on a map and pretty soon I could tell you about good spots a lot of guys didn't know were there. It was like I was a scientist explaining the world under the surface of that lake. It being Daddy's boat and all, he'd sometimes go out there with me — that is, when he could leave the store — but he wouldn't want to do any of that exploring around and insist that we stay by the dam. Deep was good in his book. The deeper, the bigger the fish. It didn't always work that way, but sometimes he'd pull in something so big we'd get in the newspaper. His fish. Never one of mine. And that was why Venus Miller, the orphan girl with enough sex appeal to light up a stadium, came up to me at school one day and said, "I saw your daddy's picture in the *Democrat* with that gigantic fish. That was really something." I looked at her standing there in the hall by the lockers and tried to imagine why on earth she'd give a hoot about a big fish, and I waited there looking for the answer to this question so long that she said, "Did you hear me, Carl?"

"I sure did. It was a big fish."

"Like something prehistoric!" she shouted. Then she clapped her hand over her mouth. "Oops."

"Oops?"

Then she whispered. "How long do you figure that fish had been down there?"

"Don't know."

"Guess."

"Fifty years, I don't know."

"Jesus."

Then we stood there and the kids went around us, some of them looking at us wide-eyed, some giggling. I started feeling a cold burning in my stomach and wanted nothing more than to run out of there and keep running until my legs collapsed under me way out somewhere.

"You all right?" she asked.

"Why not?"

"You look funny."

"Nah, I'm okay. Anyway, I'll tell Daddy you liked the picture."

"Did you keep the fish?"

"Huh?"

"Going to have it mounted?"

She had to be pulling my leg. "I don't know. Guess."

"You guess?"

"How come you care about this fish so much?"

"I don't know. But I'd been watching you."

"Watching me?"

"Yeah. And then your daddy went and did this thing. Kind of neat."

"Neat?"

"Give me a chance, Carl."

I looked around. She just had to be talking to someone else.

"Chance?"

Then she took her black penny loafer and kicked me in the shin. Like might happen in elementary school, only we were juniors in high school.

I looked down at my leg. "What was that for?"

"Not being nice to an orphan girl."

"Sorry."

"All right, then. So, are we understanding each other?"

"I guess."

"What?"

"Yeah, sure. Sure we are."

"Good."

Sure enough, Daddy did have that catfish mounted, though someone later actually stole it out of the living room of our house, and sure enough, the next time I crossed paths at school with Venus Miller she announced that I would be taking her out, unless, of course, I wanted to feel pain in my shin again. It was the most insane start of a romance that I've ever heard of. Two years later, we were married, my mama and my daddy and Miss Brown, Venus's good-looking spinster aunt, who sure did smile a lot at Daddy, who smiled back a lot, looking on with joy because this was one gorgeous couple with every hope. And we were.

I felt neither pained nor well when I got back to Puerto Azul. More like I didn't exist any longer, like I was neither here nor there.

I made it a point not to look at the Ellen tree on the mountain across the way. Because the stupid things couples did together were ridiculous when the couple was over. I also did not count fishing boat lights.

Pullman showed up at the abandoned hotel pool and sat and drank with me. He let me talk, I think because he knew I needed to push the past out if I was ever going to let the present refill me.

I told him about that final day in Texas when the neighbor widow came into my yard while I was emptying the house and asked, "Is there is anything I can do, Mr. Blalock? I'm so very sorry it turned out this way. You were such a beautiful couple for so long."

How I said, "I've always wanted to ravage you, Marge Pickens. Bend you over the couch and ride you home."

How she collapsed and how I stood in the sun looking at her very well-shaped ass until the real estate agent came waving papers.

"Going to sell this one in nothing flat, Mr. Blalock. You're going to have to come down a touch, though. My, my, though, don't you ever take care of your yard or anything around here?"

"How much is a touch?"

But it would sell, and he and I both stepped over Marge like she wasn't there for all to see and went out into the deep grass and searched for a spot to stick the sign into the earth.

"Here's a spot!" he cried. "Ram it in here. Wait, you got a hose? We could soften up the dirt some first. It'd go in deeper that way. You know what my youngest boy says, don't you?"

I wanted to grab the front of his seersucker suit and shake him, rattle all the goddamn stupidity out of him.

"My boy he says, 'Daddy, can we run the garden hose into that hole out by the dead hackberry? Can we, Daddy, please?' And I say, 'What the heck for, Randy?' And he says, 'To send some water to those poor people in China, Daddy.' 'China?' 'They ain't got water in China, I heard.' 'You did? Well, why wouldn't they have water in China?' 'There're so many of them there they ran clean out, I heard.' Can you imagine him asking —"

"Excuse me," I said.

I went back for the hose and stood over Marge Pickens lying there passed out and squirted her up and down until I could see her blue panties. Then I sprayed water through the front door onto the elm floor.

"What're you doing, Mr. Blalock?" the agent screeched.

Then I squirted the agent's suit and backed away laughing. Dropped the hose and ran out of the yard and down the chalk road and then out into a pasture and then into another pasture. Black clouds boiled above and spits of hail flew down and I barreled ahead through the gray-green light with nothing to stop me, my head full of visions of cities cut in half by howling funnels and of bodies thrown high into the sky and landing in other counties along with a million and one pictures, everybody's family snapshots, piss-poor photographs of everybody doing little forever poses, fake smiles telling all, everything sucked aloft and spewed all over creation. Everybody and their porker kids and all their hopes. I ran through rain that flew whipping like wire and didn't stop until I got to Mexico. The rest of the world ceasing to be, all illusions discarded.

Pullman only said, "We've both got bad storms in our heads."

Stein and I are going through the desert, and we come to a mountain of pale blue rock that you can see into like ice. There are fish suspended in it. Shad, cat, bass, bonito, all big ones.

"I'd pay anything to fish some of those," he says.

"Me, too. Makes me think about Daddy talking about fishing off the Baja. That all you had to do was think and fish jumped into the boat."

"How nice."

He's carrying my bank bag like a purse, and it has a new chain strap that goes over his shoulder and lies heavy against his pink shirt.

"Ready to let me show you a good time?" he asks.

"Why?"

"Least I can do. You're not still pouting about the money, are you?"

"I don't want to do this. I want to wake up."

"What, am I making you uncomfortable?"

"Some."

"Well, get used to it. I'm not the same man anymore. I may not even be a man at all." He pokes the bag toward me and draws back the zipper. There are dozens of mirrors in it, every one of them shining like a weak flashlight. "Is this a man's stuff?"

"I thought you had my money."

"You thought, you thought . . ." He zips shut the bag, hikes it back on his shoulder. "Shall we proceed, sir?"

Ahead is the entrance to a mine shaft into the mountain. We go inside and down steps that make me think of the grand staircase on the *Titanic*, pictures of which I'd stared at for hours as a child out in the middle of Texas, the last place on earth you'd think anyone would think of the ocean or doomed liners or the deep black sea at night and the lights going out one by one as the ship stood upright and dropped into the abyss. The steps go down steeply, turn at right angles, descend farther, and then we are in a Far West saloon where it's raining hard and the patrons are yelling to be heard above the roar of the downpour and crazily amplified tinkling of the player piano.

"Drink?" Stein asks. "Or are you on the wagon?"

"You're wasting my time, Stein."

"Relax. Just showing you a good time. Least I can do, yes."

"It's raining, Stein."

"Oh?"

The beer is a mug of cloudy rainwater. Stein guzzles his. I give up after a mouthful. Pretty women yell things at me I can't understand and examine me. Their nipples poke out like lemons in their T-shirts.

"Time to skedaddle," Stein commands.

I obey. We go out a back door and down more stairs. Into another bar, a big-city-style place, where it's raining again. I wait while he drinks another beer. Then he points to another back door, and we go through it and down more stairs into another bar, in some tropical setting, and so on. Every so often Stein whirls around, seizes my shoulders, squeezes them in an overfamiliar way, and shouts, "We're almost there!"

Finally we find ourselves high and dry on stools in a place that looks just like that hotel bar in Mexico City where I'd met Seidensticker.

I'm fed up and say, "Why don't you just apologize for what you did? Even if you don't have the money. I could still use the apology."

"Say I'm sorry?"

"That's right. Say you're sorry."

"But I'm not, Carl."

"Not at all?"

"You were a sucker. A big bumbling sucker. Swallowed the whole thing. From the day I stopped at your store to take a leak."

"But what about your wife?"

"What about her?"

"You conned her, too?"

"Don't be a bitch, Blalock."

He lifts that purse full of mirrors and swings it at my face. It misses but comes open and out fly the lighted mirrors all over the bar and onto the floor. None of them breaks, though. Even stranger, all of them land mirror-side up, and then there are these thin sticks of lights shining out of them and twitching this way and that like we're in a hopping disco.

"Help me pick them up!" Stein shouts, leaping around. "Before somebody tries to steal them! Help me, Blalock!"

I sit there thinking, Why should I lift a finger?

To my surprise Pullman came down to my place one afternoon to pay his first visit since we'd met. "Good view," he said. "Look at them go." Sailboats of all colors sliced back and forth across the bay.

I had never seen him in the daytime. He was even older than I'd thought, and very pale, but there was a liveliness in his movements, a springing energy, like he might be strong as a bull.

"Do you sail?" I asked.

"Gloria and I sailed to Panama once. Gloria was my wife. It was in the middle of the war and we'd bought a yacht and named it the *Tres Estrellas*. Three Stars. Because we weren't three yet. We were only two. But we hoped to be three. It was kind of a pleasant joke that way. Every day was as nice as today as we followed the coast. I was thirty-two and Gloria was twenty-six and of a beauty that would choke you. Did you ever fall in love like that, Carl?"

"Sure I have," I said. "But we didn't have a yacht to ride around on."

"It was the one moment when all the pieces fit," he said. "I had left my destitute family and crossed the border. There was land for sale down here, so I came to see. It was going for pennies an acre."

"Pennies?"

"That's right. I became a Mexican national and bought everything I could. All the way around this bay. Which was nothing but a small port. Within a few short years I had the beginnings of a considerable fortune."

I whistled at his good luck. "What a way to go."

"Which meant that I could do anything I pleased."

"Like sailing to Panama?"

"Why didn't we go to California?"

"Pardon me?"

"She'd wanted to go up to California. But I'd said Panama."

I wanted to ask, but didn't. Waited for him to say it.

"We navigated always a few miles off the coast, where you could still see land but didn't feel like you were next to it. Out where the water was blue enough for her. She had to have that deep blue, purest blue there is. We went very slowly, hardly parting the water, and there was no sound out there except the feeble wind and the low groan of the motor. You woke, you slept, you stopped counting time, you stopped thinking.

"Gloria sometimes cooked a fish in the galley and brought it out and we'd lie on our sides on the deck and nibble it and watch each other. You know, I don't think there's a man who has spent as much time staring at his wife as I have. I could do it for days. Until my eyes hurt. And even when I shut my eyes she would still be there, blinding me in my sleep, as if I were looking at the sun. A lot of the time she would stare back just as intensely, but then after a while she would stop and look around at the ocean. While I kept staring. And I imagined that my staring could soak into her and make me part of her. And then she would lie all the way back and look at the sky and I would do the same. Our heads touching. Carl, have you ever awakened under the stars? It's as if you're being watched by a million eyes. The colors set your heart racing. Blue, orange, red. People are wrong to think stars are white. It's not true!"

His fist rose up and came down hard on the chair arm.

"Have you ever made love under stars on a yacht on the ocean? I'm not saying, Carl, look at us, look at me. I'm saying, Look at the moment. Does everyone have at least one like that in life? Isn't it the ones who never have that kind of moment who suffer? Or is it the ones who do?"

I wasn't sure what to say. Everything that came to my mind seemed worthless. Because I knew Gloria would die on that trip.

After a while the wind carried all the boats out of the bay.

Did I tell you that in Mexico I wouldn't be caught not wearing a sharp white wedding shirt? Because you are made very tall by those shirts. Elegant, too. Even after Venus went her way, I never quit wearing those shirts. I liked them so much I bought one every time I went into *el centro*. There was nothing I enjoyed more on those outings than going into those high-ceilinged department stores and walking up and down the aisles of those shirts. Each wrapped in a plastic bag, lying in wait for men to pass by in that violet glow cast down from the fluorescent lights. Each a four-pocketed possibility, each another chance for you to hold your head higher in the street or on the beach or on your deck. *Mucho más grande. Y muy hermoso.* You became the little bit of Mexican you could become. Took another step away from all that you had been.

Then it started raining every day. I'd sit on my chair just back off the deck under the stone arches that formed the front of the house and stare at the emerald wall of rain that cut off everything — bay, hotels, jungle, swimming pool, potted palms, all.

Hours would go by, and then days and nights, and just when I had ceased to think the world existed at all, I heard, "Blalock? What're you doing?" And Pullman stepped out of the rain in his white raincoat.

"Hello, William."

"It's going to do this for a while. We have to go."

"Go?"

"Isn't there someplace you've always wanted to go, Carl?"

The rain had deadened my nerves. "I'm there now."

"I was thinking China. Gloria and I were going to go. What say?"

"What do you mean?"

"Will you go with me?"

"To China?"

"Yes."

"Just like that."

"And why not?"

I said no. Because there would've been everything to overcome. I would've had to stand and walk out through the green wall of rain and leave my corner of paradise. I no more wanted to do that than to go to the empty moon. Pullman said nothing. But you could hear him thinking of China as the rain fell and the light faded until we were staring into the black roar of it and lost again in the hours of waiting.

My thoughts wandered to a village in the Sierra Madre where Venus and I visited the tomb of some royal somebodies from way back when. They had a sheet of glass over the tomb in the ground so you could look down in the hole and see the two skeletons. Husband and wife. Some pottery. Some colorless shreds of clothing. The boy guide told us the story of their lives, and we gave him a hundred pesos and got out of there. I remember Venus said, "He made that up. That was somebody's grandparents' bones he was showing." I said that that could well be and she scooted over closer to me as we wound our way back down to the sizzling plain. I'd never seen a skeleton in the ground like that. There'd been beads of humidity on the inside of the glass cover from the heat.

Far back in the night there was a sound like a door being slammed, and then the wall of rain pulled away and everything lay open, the pool, railing, lights along the bay.

Pullman said, "Ah, a pause," and then rose to go.

"It's a long way to China," I said.

"Not that far. 'Night."

"Good night."

I listened to his sandals clacking on the steps back up the mountain until I could hear them no more. He could go to China. But not me. I was where I wanted to be, as on a comfortable balcony with the show just starting, I was sure. A liner had come in. The air was cool. I told myself to thank him again anyway for the offer. For perhaps I had been rude.

"Did I tell you that I never once learned her real name?" Pullman asked.

We were up at the hotel pool again one night.

"It wasn't Gloria. She took that name when she came to Mexico with her father. To start anew. He was German and a champion rowing coach and a fantastic pianist, a student of a student of Liszt, or some such. I never knew him, but Gloria said having him for a father was like heaven.

"From the earliest times she could remember he took her out rowing on all the rivers and lakes of Europe. Her mother had died of tuberculosis not long after she was born, leaving the father to raise the child alone. But they were wealthy and it was a time to travel.

"They went from city to city, never staying anywhere more than six months or a year, living in the nicest districts with the finest schools, visiting every monument of European civilization they could find, but quickly, as if fulfilling an age-old duty, and with lots of laughter — and then heading directly for the nearest body of water to go rowing.

"It was the laughter that she spoke of most. How it rang hard across the water, as if someone were banging hammers on tin. When they'd fly under the bridges, the old man and the young girl with the blond hair, people in their huge winter coats would point down and stare. And then one day her father pointed back at some people and shouted out, 'Look at the people, dear! Why aren't they rowing?' Someone tossed down a paper sack and it smashed straight into his chest and exploded. Flour. Full of bleached flour. There was a roar of cheering above, and when they came out on the other side of the bridge a crowd began tossing all manner of things, papers, books, umbrellas, anything. Her father looked up at the rain of things and laughed at them and pointed. 'Look at the people, dear!' Gloria worked the oars to bring them downstream and out of the way. 'Stinking Parisians,' she told him. But as he wiped off his face, he was smiling. 'Dear, they are only people. We, however, are rowers.'

"She said he would have gone rowing even at night. If not for the piano, if not for Liszt. Nights were for playing and playing. Perhaps while he dreamed, she said, of finding the right country with high lakes, where the people were scarce and it was always warm, where the piano would not bother, could ring out at any hour into the clean air, where they would have great racing teams for his daughter. Because there was no question but that he intended to see to it that she became an Olympic champion.

"To have such a father is beyond the craziest dreams of any of us. My own father was a steelworker in Pennsylvania and my mother was his wife. And all I have to say about them is that the day I was old enough to walk away from them for good, they didn't look up. I don't think they could have looked up. Their faces had been locked staring down. For me, coming here to Mexico was to climb over a wall to freedom, and now I can scarcely imagine having lived anywhere else.

"You know the oddest thing? When Gloria's father fainted the day they landed here, I was the one he fell on. I didn't know it yet, but he had died right there at my feet, as if he had simply collapsed after completing the long task of bringing her to that time and place where I was standing, ready to take over. A crowd gathered and everyone was swept into the fury these things provoke. I lost sight of her in the confusion and it was months before I saw her again.

"How can I say how beautiful she was, Carl? It begins with an ache throughout your body and never abates. Now, all these years later, the same pain fills me when I imagine her. When I see her walking again in front of me on soft sand. When I follow her over the rough rocks to wherever it is she wants to go that day under the sun. It doesn't matter where, because I'm like the one who sees not the real light of the world but another, the light of her, and just to be with her is enough to fulfill me completely. How beautiful was she? I have been thinking about it for untold years but any words I used would be less than she.

"The woman who said her name was Gloria. From Bocheim, Germany. Championship rower. Member of the recent Olympic team. Onetime voyager on the Seven Seas with her father, now deceased. Having tea in the afternoon at a restaurant behind the beach. And didn't she remember me from somewhere? Hadn't I been there on the landing that awful morning? My body began to sail, like a dry leaf, dropping, rising, falling again, and then we were sitting face-to-face and the talk flowed like water. As if it had always been that way.

"Seconds later we are man and wife, and in a few seconds more we are entertaining everyone in our mansion. I especially remember the Chinese ambassador, a midget of a man in red silk pants who kept wanting to kiss her hand. I hired men with dynamite to blast open a cove in the rocks down where this mountain plunges into the open ocean and make a deep swimming pool for her. Businessmen, dignitaries, movie stars, politicians, they all came and stayed awhile and swam in the ocean pool and drank and feasted and gazed at our pretty maids and swore allegiance and friendship. We had everything we needed and the breezes made the long pink curtains in our blue bedroom fly in and out day after day. Sometimes we did nothing, sent everyone home and remained quiet. And these times I sat watching her go back and forth, her wet brown feet leaving black prints on the clay tiles. While the sea swelled into the pool, sometimes bringing in schools of colored fish that stayed there turning and glittering for just as long as we stared down at them. We went days without talking, all the while listening, but many words passed between us. The words that cannot be said.

"We knew nothing of time and there was everything still to do.

"You know, I still don't know why I wanted to take the yacht to Panama. She'd wanted to see the coast of California, but I didn't listen. I don't know why I didn't want to hear her. There was nothing to see in Panama except the canal, but I wanted my way, even if it was for nothing. Had we poisoned each other being too close? Had it begun to rot? We did not know it, but it had happened, we had made the false move, the mistake, the error that, like a drop falling on still water, fans out perfectly until it has reached all edges. It could not be undone, no more than a storm can be made to blow back where it came from, no more than the swell that heaved the boat and threw her into the sea in the night can put her back on the deck, no more than everything in me that flew into the water to find her can climb back out and live again, no more than the deep can give back the light it takes away.

"At dawn, long strands of weeds rode the fast and milky current and I let the yacht drift. While I watched for something to rise, while I held to the edge wanting to slip into the water and swim down and die with her. But nothing happened, nothing appeared."

Then he announced that he was leaving for China. Would I mind staying in his house while he was gone? Would I do him that favor?

"But you have plenty of people to look after it," I said.

"I'm giving them a long-overdue vacation. I will leave my cook Elena, though, to look after you."

I could not refuse.

"I'm going to go deep into the western parts. I want to see the Taklimakan Desert." There was a red haze in his eyes. "It might be as far away from the ocean as you can get. And think of the stars I'll see!"

I didn't ask questions. I only marveled at his energy.

"You're not obliged to stay there, though," he said. "If you feel like leaving, do it. Elena will watch things. I'd feel better, though, knowing she's not alone. And that the house is being watched by the two of you."

I said I would stay there as long as he needed me to.

"You understand, though, that after the desert, a man might wish to go elsewhere. Turn south into Tibet? I can't be sure what I'll do."

I said, All right.

He gave me a strong hug.

Maybe it was the long rain that night, but still I somehow committed the crime, went ahead without thinking and told him the story I hadn't had the courage to tell, of May and the drowning. I seldom talked during his stories, and he stayed quiet as I rambled. It was the first pink light when I finished. He stared at me, exhausted. I had only worn him out, punished him. Made him feel Gloria's drowning again, the depths of all he'd suffered. Once more, I wished I hadn't said a word.

Then he said, "Let's go up to the house now."

I followed him, tired and small, listening to birds waking in the jungle, watching the damp steps carefully. Slip and I could tumble all the way down into the bay.

Gustavo Cabeza de Vaca

There is not one visitor I wouldn't like to throw into the tomb with these Amado bastards. Damn the Amado family. Damn the tourists. Damn their fancy cars and children. Fuck all the gringa virgins until their tripes pour out. Then throw them away like sacks. The people of the village scorn me but I make my living on the bones of Don and Doña Amado. The people say I should stop living in the past. Damn them all. These are my bones to do with as I please. This is my land now. My family's land. All the Amados are dead and we killed them with the delicious pleasure one gets from the slow draining away of life as you watch and grin. A hundred years of servitude rose like a spring from the rocks and poured out onto their land and soaked it in blood. Nothing would grow and everything died and the Amados wandered around in their fine clothes while we hounded them, became snakes to bite them, scorpions to sting them, the sun to beat them down and draw every last drop of water from them. The Amados are dead and I collected the bones of the don and the doña and dug a hole in this hill and bought a sheet of glass and tell everyone this is ancient history, skeletons from the deep Mexican past, very authentic, look down into the ground and see the bones of the conquistador and his royal wife from long ago . . . This name I have that is not mine by birth? A master's joke, and yes I will keep it. Keep it like a snake in a bag. Reach inside, and it will strike . . . Tourists come, one or two a day. I explain everything to them and they hardly understand a word. Then they go their way again and I sit on my rock and wait in the sun next to the bones and imagine the blood and tripes of gringas running into the earth. When night comes I go up the mountain to the old Amado hacienda and watch the village lights below. They have electricity now and sixteen streetlights shine all night in the valley. What do I care? I have the hacienda where the don and doña whipped my father late at night for some trifle, some uncompleted thing, before retiring to their huge bedroom with its orange walls and red floor and high black bed to make love while my mother fanned them until it was her turn to be called to come and lie on the white sheets. No, I have riches. I have their souls.

Carl Stein shot out of that casino like a bat and there she stood with strangers gathered around asking her questions and swearing up and down about the man being a scoundrel to have ripped off a woman such as herself. Instant friends kept patting her, asking if there was anything they could get her, and then the cop came back out of breath to say he'd lost him. The crowd burst out shouting and the cop didn't like that and backed away as if maybe they intended to jump him. Venus called to him, said she wanted to give him the particulars of the tale. But he kept backing up and shaking his head like there was no way that he was going to get involved in this story, he was just an underpaid security guard after all, and then he rushed away. There were more howls of protest and Venus broke away from the group because it had changed from regular people trying to help her to nutty people getting out of control. She looked for the guard, but she could no more find an individual in that place than locate a fish in the ocean. Bells rang, lights flashed, screams rose and fell, fortunes came and went, and the air-conditioning blew down from the ceiling in icy gales. Carl Stein had brushed that close to her again, the tall white man straight out of the blackly spinning past.

She felt sick, all the sleepless carousing catching up with her all at once and shoving her body meanly forward. Another push and she stumbled in front of everyone. But an older man helped her up right away, as if he'd always stood at that spot right next to the baccarat table waiting to lend a hand. She thanked him, apologized, thanked him again.

"Think nothing of it, little lady."

"I'm no lady," she said.

He waved away the remark and looked around for the next person who might fall. She headed back to her bar, but the young man she liked wasn't there. She had another drink anyway. And it was one too many.

There was someone on the steps outside her motel room who spoke like he knew her. He had a liquor bottle propped between his legs. She halted at the ice machine and tried to pick a path. But one side of the world rose up and she waved for a railing that wasn't there.

He had a nasty laugh. "Having trouble?"

Venus got her balance. No, it wasn't Stein. "Who're you?"

"Don't remember me, angel? It's your buddy Neal."

"Who?"

"At the gas station, remember? Hey, but how could I forget the smile you gave me? You're the first person in my life to tell me she was an angel and I kept thinking about it, you know?"

"I don't remember you."

"Sure you do, angel."

"Let me by. I need to sleep."

"You just need to get angeled up again. Here, have a hit."

"It's late."

"Five o'clock in the morning. And here I am at the Blue Oaks with the angel lady. Don't you want a hit?"

"Green Oaks," said Venus. "Green."

"Whatever you want, honey."

Venus gasped and then finished her voyage at the bottom step, sat and poked her hand back up over her shoulder to take the bottle.

"There she is," he said.

One gulp of the stuff and she was sure the ice machine needed a good swift kick. She passed the bottle back. "Damn that ice machine."

"That's right!" he shouted. "Damn that thing."

"What does it do all day but sit there and spit out about half the ice it's supposed to. Am I right?"

"Yes, you are. That ice machine does not deserve to keep living."

Maybe it was better not to go over and kick it, though, Venus concluded. "Hell, if I were an ice machine I'd . . . whatever . . ."

"That's right," he said.

"What is?"

"What you said."

"What'd I say?"

"Look, tell me something. What's your whole name, anyway? Only said V. Blalock on your credit card. I can't be talking here to an initial."

"Venus."

"Venus, really?"

"Why wouldn't it be?"

"I know girls who sometimes change their names. There was this Tracy I knew, but when she got on at the Kitty-Kat Club she was Darby and whenever I'd say, 'Hey there, Tracy,' she'd say, 'I'm sorry, you must be mistaken. The name's Darby.' 'Come on, Tracy, I know it's you. Why don't you just say hello?' I'd say that and she'd look through me like I was the biggest asshole on earth. Darby. Her name was Tracy Higgins. We were in the same second-grade class together, for Christ's sake."

Venus had another hit. "Mine's just Venus. Now it's late and —"

"I know how angels are."

"Are?"

"May sound strange, but they don't talk."

"You're the one who's talking."

"No, no. I mean, they're quiet, saying nothing. Thinking lots of nice things, but not saying them. Keeping all that inside until they become superangels." His hands touched her shoulders. "Superangels can love with their wings. They move them and that's all it takes to get it started." He pressed her shoulders back, eased them forward. "Like this."

He was right, Venus decided. She was a superangel. Now being handled like a rare bird by a backwoods boy. His rough fingers were soft. Or maybe it was the hour when all edges are smoothed. The superangel hour. When Venus felt she could be sweeter than the warmth of summer light as she slowly turned and gathered him up.

They didn't come out for anything and no one knocked on the door and it seemed like time could have gone on indefinitely with Venus lying there watching this twenty-year-old read his cowboy-story paperback when they rested. No, there was no hurry at all to return to the places beyond the pink curtains. As he read he stroked her leg lightly, as if dragging his hand over the side of a boat. While Venus slowly counted the smooth river rocks that his muscles made, touching them stone by stone. Until they added something bolder, and something more, and then lunged toward each other yet again like hunters.

It was that time of year long ago when Venus's dad would drive her and her mama from Red Rock all the way up into the Ozarks to see the dogwood. It took hours to get there and the transmission leaked a stripe down the road and then it took hours to get home. Oh, but the blossoms! White lights in the wet forest! Mama hung out the window and cried. As if winter had been some fierce ocean they'd crossed.

Venus thought maybe she understood but knew Dad couldn't see what the fuss was. All was well, wasn't it? Annie Louise, how can you cry when you have an angel riding here in this car with us? But he wouldn't say things like that out loud. No, he'd let her sniffle, and smile at the carpet of dogwood flowers lying across the mountainsides like they were on tour of the best acres of heaven, try to get her to smile, too.

Mama said Jesus' Cross was made of dogwood. But then Venus questioned that because Jesus surely hadn't ever lived in Arkansas. She never contradicted Mama, though. Do that and those pretty tears of hers would dry up in nothing flat and you'd get a slap across your twelve-year-old face. Mama wasn't mean, though. She just wasn't good all the time.

Dad took it all in stride, stayed quiet, drove through the hills all afternoon. Changing gears, smoking cigarettes, keeping them safe from everything. There were hillbillies living back in those woods, half people ready to jump out and shoot you with antique guns. So they never stopped anywhere for very long. And when they did Dad was calm about it, easygoing, and Venus liked to think she was like him. The kind of person who'd go dogwood looking all day if that's what it took to please. A dad who gazed at you the longest time in the rearview and smiled the way that said he loved you. She knew Mama had loved her, too, but she was more rules and authority, never a friend. Which left a lot of things unsaid and Venus in the dark. Until she became a woman and found out things for herself. Simple things, but that could maybe save you. Like giving and expecting nothing in return. Clinging to nothing, not even the precious things you hold inside your soul, the dogwood blooms, the rain in those trees in the mountains, your dad's smooth brown face and your mama's silver tears. And you looked neither too far ahead nor too far back and tried to be satisfied with the way things were. That was another thing she'd found out. This was harder, though, now that her life had veered so far, taken a dive into the trees like that time the car left the road in the mountains and flipped once. So fast it seemed it hadn't happened. Except there were dogwood branches poking in through the windows and into her dead parents' faces. While she, Venus Marie Miller, sat there in the back without a scratch, the motor still murmuring. She remembered waiting in that car a long time thinking that she was no longer a little girl if she could look at those flowers and see a face of death in each. For girls did not think such awful things. Girls knew only life and fruit trees, sunlight and warm wind. Not death. Nor the sudden desire for death.

Venus did not speak to the boy in her motel bed and he did not ask if anything was wrong. He only whispered that she was a superangel. Superangel with dogwood blooms to be plucked from between her legs, she thought, now there's an interesting image of me. One that, of course, Jesus would never have approved of, but May would have adored. Then early one afternoon he dressed and departed.

He'd been gone maybe two hours when Venus finally opened the door. There was no one around. For that matter, it didn't look like anyone would ever stop at that motel for the rest of time. She went out there in her robe, removed it, stepped naked down the pool steps, and walked along the scratchy blue bottom until the water reached her chin. Then she let herself go, sinking. Hung like a jellyfish for a while, then started to choke and cough and quickly got to the edge and gripped the cement overhang. The light hit her eyes hard, as if someone had flipped on projectors. She thought that she was going to faint and that maybe it would be good, because then she'd slide under and not choke and have to come back up. But then the sun slid behind a roof and a chill rose through her and the water began to smell like sewage and she felt revulsion and pulled herself out. Got out and pushed back, put her arms around her knees, and shook. Why hadn't she saved May herself? Why had she just stood there screaming? Why hadn't she put her head under the water and looked down where May was dying? She rocked herself hard forward and back. These questions had come to her before but never this loudly. She didn't know why it was happening again now, and it was like a crowd had formed around her once more, only this one was against her.

The casino drew her in day after day, and then there was no use in counting how long she'd been there because she cared only for wandering through random flames. More men came back with her to the motel and some were gentlemen and some weren't, and others thought it required to leave dollar bills on the nightstand. No laughter ever rang out in the room, even when she and the man were drunk and stripped naked and bounding this way and that over the bed, and no talking troubled the stale air. Nor radio music, nor questioning stares, nor pauses, nor honest embraces. All movement was rushed, an eager search, his body flooding with blood until he glowed over her like a dark sun, her body taking flight through unfettered light over a patchwork of green fields and blue lakes and orange rocks where people made love out in the open thinking no one was watching when Venus was, jealously, transfixed, dazed by the strength of the woman's legs and the man's back, wanting to be her, to be May pushing her body up into his and taking his into hers out there where the wind spoke along the edges of ears so that lovers both heard it at the same time and flowed with it one into the other.

The green motel room door opening or shutting at odd hours, she came and went, sought strength in instant encounters, found little if anything remaining to lean upon for long once the lust had spent itself, hoped for answers watching the ways of people as they tempted insanity in the name of money but only found herself asking more questions.

At times she pondered Blalock, but did not call. For fear that he might speak this time, ask her how much longer he must wait, how long she'd be throwing herself against the mayhem, want to know what she didn't yet know herself and wasn't sure she wanted to know. What she wanted, what she was seeking, the mysteries obsessing her whenever it poured rain and she sat in the motel room watching it come down onto the lifeless swimming pool and turn it the frightening color of slate.

Vodka lifted her up, slammed her down, spun her this way and that. But she didn't resist. Went with the flow of the abuse, let the fire move freely through. So that everything slowly began to hurt less and less, as if there were something beyond the flames, beyond the bottom of the pit into which May had plunged. As if she would, having endured, someday believe in her life again.

The electronic cash tellers kept giving her enough money to keep going, and she knew she had Blalock to thank for keeping the credit cards alive. If thanks were in order for letting her do what she was doing.

Then one hot night she declared to the four walls that now was the end to wasting away in that place, paid her bill, got into her dirty Impala, and went swerving back up the road she had taken there.

All the way back to their house outside Red Rock, the car radio booming out cowboy music nonstop, arriving sleepless and ruined by bad coffee in the midday brightness that removed all colors. Driving the Impala not down the driveway but straight onto the lawn and stopping with a sharp jab on the brake that caused the motor to stall.

Which left her sitting in the silent car studying the FOR SALE sign and the curtainless windows and the air of abandonment all around. Unbelievably, he had come home, if only for long enough to empty the place out and put it on the market. It seemed so avoidable, though, an utter trashing of effort, all of it, from the ground up, every nail, every swipe of paint, every pause in a sunny corner to embrace and then wait there taking the heat into the body as though breathing it in. Now all sat discarded in the wind and the unfeeling light. If only they had kept control of their lives, she thought, not let them be invaded by Carl Stein of Wisconsin, by the bad one come stalking from afar. If only she hadn't let herself be possessed by May, by the good one come running like a child into her heart to shake all its old trees back to life.

She gazed through the bug-spattered windshield at the house that was no one's home anymore and recalled a dream from one black-drunk night in Louisiana. Of showing up like this and finding Blalock sitting on the porch waiting for her. Of getting out of the car and walking toward him in a clean summer dress and moving into his arms and staying with him contemplating the yard filled with summer wildflowers. Saying nothing because all was forgiven, put aside, buried like the dead should be. Marveling with him at the beams of sunlight coming down between billowing blue-white clouds. Because that was the image of heaven they taught in Bible school, because that was the place one goes when the living here below is done, because that was the light that comes down from the eyes of God as he watches over the earth and over people like them, like Venus and Carl Blalock, if only they would try to live their lives and not succumb to bitterness, not be blinded, not grant themselves the liberty of guilt and self-loathing. Because they had not killed May Stein; she had fallen into a hole, stepped directly into it, and it was no one's fault, it had happened for no reason, in that country that knows nothing of why, a blank land with no signs into which people stare but never understand.

Carl had come back from Mexico and quickly drawn his conclusions. That this need not be preserved. Not the warped boards of the porch, not the unmoving weather vane, or the towering mulberries. That this could be given up without regret. That he had the house in Puerto Azul to which he would return. For where else would he go? Surely not out into the unknown like her. She knew better than that.

But it didn't hurt to know this, and a part of her allowed that he was waiting down there unmoving on the Mexican coast so that she would come to him there if ever it were time again for her to seek a home and to rest. She could see all this in the washed-out light in which everything trembled as a storm of loneliness began to break inside her.

She recalled the neighbors they'd had back when they lived in town packing up everything and leaving one stifling morning, and their child, the girl, coming home from school for lunch and climbing the steps to the porch and opening the door. As onto a furnace of emptiness, the floors stretching back, all lines coming together at a patch of blue light at the back door. And the girl stepping slowly inside, seeing the dust clinging to the air as if unable to fall, walking through the middle of the house, finding nothing, not the least scrap of anything of their lives, as if she had never lived there, had never had her parents' love or homemade ice cream or hot chicken soup in winter or her father's beard to put her hands into, touching the bare walls on either side of the hall, pushing off one and then the other, then speeding up, moving quickly toward the blue light, then bursting out into it and down the steps. Running as hard as she could. Her small white shoes splitting open on hard ground.

Venus drove without direction again on one of the windiest days she could recall. She took back road after back road, always turning at right angles, at corners of endless tracts of farmland, first one way, then the other. Out there where the dirt sailed up in clouds and bucked the Impala. The mighty wind that bore down on the earth and on the ragged people who managed to cling to it, stone-faced folks out there watching her go by. Rust-brown people who neither smiled nor frowned, who sat atop their hunks of machinery and observed her, a woman alone. Lead-eyed people who'd lost a limb, or a child, to an accident, or a wife to disease, people leaning like the telephone poles but held together by all that old wire, all the years of being out in the middle of nowhere.

And when she had driven long enough to begin to believe that she could well be lost in place and in time, she came over a rise in the tableland and saw a large pasture of blue-green grass grown up as high as her head all around an abandoned farmhouse with its windows shot out and its roof sagging like an old hat.

No, there'd never been a day this windy in Venus's recollection. Wind that shoved her as she left the car on the dirt road, walked through the grass toward the island that was the house, and came into the yard like a child, slowly. Fruit trees in the side yard quarreled, poked each other, and fruit sailed to the ground. Over there was the frame of a swing set with a length of rope on it popping in the air. A vine with orange trumpet flowers trailed out of a bathtub by the front porch, onto which she went to look out at the surrounding grass. It was a warm wind that swept through it like a hand through a woman's hair, now pressing it this way and that in soft circles, then pulling it hard back and forth as if in passion.

She wanted one of those pears from the orchard but there was the house to see first. It didn't feel like the floor was going to bust through, so she didn't worry. No, this house had been lived in a minute ago. It was the wind that'd aged it in no time, made it seem a lifetime had passed since kids ran through here, or a mother called or scolded, or a father demanded help with chores. Since a girl cried over something she'd lost out in the waving grass, or a boy pouted in the sun, blue shadow of his straw hat hiding his face from the others. Dry-skinned, freckled, often hoarse creatures with nothing better to do than sit up in the pear trees eating until they couldn't eat any more and watching for Mama's ship to come over the horizon. For Mama's ship was going to show up any day now and they'd all get in it and sail out of there. They watched the horizon for the big white hull of it, listened for the boom of the horn. Mama, when will it get here, your ship? Any day now, any time now, hush. And they'd all lie in bed awake watching the light die at the windows and the rainwater stains on the ceiling turning to monsters or maps of old countries or new countries, dragons, great-great-grandfathers, the Devil himself or sweet Jesus the Lord, until the light flared a last time and plunged away, leaving the children alone with the sound of the grass sweeping this way and that like an ocean. Will we ever get to go and see the sea, Mama? Go swim in it? We'll see . . . now everybody quiet down and get to sleep! And the wind would blow all night. Maybe so hard something out there would break and everybody would wake up and ask, What was that? A tree limb, now go back to sleep. Are you sure? Sure I'm sure, and in the morning they'd find it hadn't been a limb but a whole tree that'd keeled over. All the leaves still green and the fruit right there for the taking and wasps swarming. A ball of black roots sticking up in the air, vulgar and ugly. The men standing around awhile until one of them started chopping with an ax and white chunks of tree flesh flew and the firewood pile rose by the house, tree after tree, windswept year after windswept year, leaving only the ten or so gnarled survivors carrying on just off the end of the porch as if annoyed to have never been invited in.

She stood at the front door and stared all the way through out the back door and saw with a leap of her heart how this was so much like the place in the memory of the abandoned child. She squatted and put her hand on the floor. It felt as soft as an old quilt. She held her hand there for a long time, taking in the lingering warmth, then looked up to find a girl in a pink sundress standing in the tilted frame of the back door, bonnet in hand. "What are you doing, ma'am?"

"Looking at this house. And you?"

"I play here."

"Where is your house?"

"Over there."

She pointed beyond the grass.

"Is it okay for you to play here alone?"

"Sure it is. Do you want a pear?"

"Sure I do."

"I'll get you one!"

She flew down the back steps.

Venus advanced through the house, passing through a main room, then into the hall, which gave onto other empty rooms, and to the back. Everything was clean, and she suspected the girl kept it that way. Wind moaned along the walls. When she went out the child was at the bottom of the steps holding up a pear the size of a softball. Venus took it. "My."

"Ever seen one that big before?"

"Can't say I have. You want some of it?"

"Oh, no. That's your pear. I've had plenty. They grow here all year. Isn't that something?"

"It sure is," said Venus.

She tasted it and then asked the girl her name.

Sharla. Sharla Fail, will be nine Thanksgiving, makes straight As but hates Ricky Beaman, who thinks he knows everything and will not leave her alone. Used to live in this very house, but now lives over there.

"Where?"

"You can't see it. Maybe on the roof you could."

"Break your neck."

"Yeah."

Venus sat on the steps and took the longest time she'd ever taken to eat a pear. The child watched her like she was water in the desert, or a snake, or a very interesting flower. "You didn't tell me your name."

"Venus."

"I heard about a Venus once. She was gorgeous and all the old-time men liked her."

"That so?"

"Yes, and they courted her something fierce. That was back before there were tractors and windmills. There weren't towns like our towns, either. People wore white clothes and talked to each other a lot and Venus was this goddess who looked down from heaven. The other heaven, not the one where Jesus is. The first heaven. You know? Venus was watching everybody and she was so beautiful sitting up there that the men on earth went crazy looking at her. Well, she figured she had to do something to keep them from suffering like that, so you know what she did?"

"What?"

"Well, that Venus of the olden days, she up and decided one day to wave good-bye to all those men pining away like that and she ran away."

"To where?"

"Where no one could find her. Not even the old-time gods."

"That is sad."

"Wait, that's not all. After that she became ugly. Very ugly. Like a witch. Then she became a planet that's covered with poison gas and so hot it'd melt your bicycle to stand there. Know what I mean?"

"I think so. Very sad."

"Yeah. Funny name, Venus. Do you like it?"

"Why, yes."

"You're very beautiful."

"As are you, Sharla."

"Don't say that. That might ruin things."

"I doubt that. You'll always be a beauty."

"Mama said that."

"She's right."

"She doesn't come over here with me. It makes her sad, she says, on account of all the things it makes her remember. But she says I can play here all I want. Long as I don't try to get on the roof or anything silly like that. I take home as much fruit as I can carry each time. Are you going to buy this place and live here or something?"

"No, I only stopped to rest. Saw this beautiful tall grass . . ."

"Where are you going then?"

"I don't know."

Sharla began walking toward the swirling grass. Venus followed her.

"Old-time Venus didn't know either. She went out into space. Became a planet."

"Hmm."

"Do you think they could do something to fix Venus?"

"Fix her?"

"Make her like the earth? Couldn't they fly some things up there and make the place new again? Make her beautiful?"

"I don't know, Sharla."

"Probably not, huh. Too messed up."

"It would take a lot of work. But maybe someday . . ."

"Maybe." The girl smiled at the prospect, and then they came to the edge of the grass. "Want to walk out into it with me?"

"Sure I do."

She held out her small hand for the taking and led the way. And they walked deep into the wavering grass until there was nothing but the cool ocean of it all around and the bleached sky far above.

"Are you going to go away real soon?"

"I have to."

"Like Venus. Do you love God?"

"I think so. Do you?"

"I don't know yet. Maybe I will, maybe I won't. But let's have another pear. Then you go."

"Sure."

They passed the second pear back and forth and smiled at each other and then shut their eyes and lay down and watched the wind bend the grass and the sky, far away, come and go. There was no other sound but the dry waves of the grass and their low heartbeats in their ears as they breathed in and out and tasted the sugar on their lips.

"I had a friend named May who died."

"A long time ago?"

"Not so long ago."

"Did you ever eat pears with her?"

"I don't think I did."

"I'm sorry about your friend."

"Don't worry, Sharla."

"But now you're eating miracle pears with me here in this field."

"I think my friend would smile and eat miracle pears with us."

"Sure she would. These are the best pears around."

"Are you okay, dear?" the manager gal asked. "We have good doctors in Iona, you know. Would you like me to call one for you?"

"No, I wouldn't. Just a room."

Same motel, another downstairs unit.

"Will you be staying with us a long time again?"

Venus didn't know, said nothing. Her ears were ringing after driving around again for days.

"Well, if you don't know yet, you can tell me tomorrow. Why don't we work it that way? That all right?"

Anything you want, Venus wanted to say.

"You think about the doctor, too, huh?"

"I'm not going to die on you if that's what you're worried about."

"Well, I hope not, honey."

Venus shut the door and sat in there as in a tomb. The room was all brown, like it had burned halfway. Upstairs there was a loud man who'd gotten himself a screamer, a young girl learning the ways. It went on and on and then there was some stomping and the toilet went *ka-shung.*

The girl called, "That was awful, Don. I didn't come. Again!"

"Yeah?" Don called back. "Is that my job?"

Venus got into the bed and lay on her side with her knees to chest and tried to make herself sleep staring at the vents of the air conditioner as it spewed humid air into the room and something in its guts clanged like a big old bell being rung at a great distance beyond the earth.

"Why don't you go back to the casino?" the manager gal said. They had crossed paths on the sidewalk as Venus was coming back to her room with a bucket of half-moon ice cubes. "You look like you got some money left, anyway. Not like most people around here. Why not?"

"It's not the wisest place," Venus said. "Get in trouble."

"Me, I've never been. You have to have enough money, for one thing. But, hey, you look like you could go. Why don't you?"

"Is there some reason you're trying to get me to go?"

"Is there some reason you're cranky? People can actually be nice to each other, you know. It isn't against the law."

The poor thing stalked off wagging her head. Venus almost went after her to tell her thanks for trying, for giving a damn. But she didn't. Instead she went and sat by the pool.

Not two minutes passed before someone said, "Somebody's going to come out of that casino a millionaire tonight. They've guaranteed it."

Who was it now? A bent old guy in a rumpled light blue suit and his wispy wife in a daisy-print dress.

"One million dollars is a lot of money," he said.

"That's the truth," the woman said.

Venus peered at them.

"We're Grover and Emma Hudspeth," the old man said. "We drove all the way over here from Gunnison again. You ever been to Gunnison?"

"Not far from Tackney," Emma said.

"Can't say I have," said Venus.

"Well," they both said together.

The air smelled of cologne and chlorine.

"Hon, I was born in o'-nine and never had a dime," said Grover. "Tonight might be it. Who's to predict, eh?"

"That's right," Emma said.

"So. You going, hon?"

Venus didn't know. "Maybe."

"Are you here alone?" Emma asked.

It was like having grandparents show up out of nowhere.

"Quite alone."

"That's no good," said Grover.

"It's all right," said Emma. "If that's what she wants . . ."

"Hmm . . . don't know about that."

Then they scooted some chairs close to hers and took turns telling her all about their last trip to Vegas and how they'd sat out on their balcony and watched the fire in the other hotel and the firemen getting the hundreds of people to safety. It went on and on, through other trips all up and down the country, until one thing rolled into another as if there could be no stopping it and the two old folks were waiting in Venus's door for her to finish fixing herself up and come along with them. It was the night of the millionaire. They didn't care if they won or not. All they wanted to do was to be standing there when the lucky son of a gun won. See the eyes of whoever it was whose life had changed in a single instant pop straight out. Venus wasn't sure she understood all what she was doing, but she kept going, put on a short blue skirt, white blouse, and white pumps. While the old folks gabbed. Granma and Granpa. Heading out in their pink Imperial into the Saturday night of a lifetime for somebody.

Neal Wiley

I'm telling you that woman was one messed-up lady. I called her superangel on account of I'm a nice guy that way but, hey, she was weird. Good lay, though. But I don't know, there was something wrong with her. Like she couldn't shake a bad dream or something. Hey, what do I give a shit, though. I got cancer of the brain maybe. Talk about a problem. You ever think about that? Or what it'd be like to get born without any luck, like me? Yeah, sure, I get pussy and stuff. Lots of it, but you know maybe I've got cancer of the nuts even. I mean I could be dying right now, so could any of us. There ain't no salvation, and who can afford a doctor? I don't know, I feel like a stone in a field of stones on a hill that's just steep enough that all the stones are quietly rolling down, clicking slowly one over the other, on and on, but there isn't one of the rocks that knows it's a rock and there's not one rock that can see what's going on, how they're all headed for the edge of the cliff and that this is one of the slowest landslides in history. You see? Rocks are people. Who among us can see an inch past his nose? Not me, not any of the rocks, not that superangel, either. Poor thing. Probably the first time she'd been laid right in her life. Was she fifty? Did I do a fifty-year-old woman? Hey, if so, so what. We both got what we wanted and time is rolling on. I'm going to pump gas until I throw up from pumping gas, this I know. And that Venus? Let's hope she's going to figure it all out. Whatever it is. While she's out there running around. For it to work, though, I kind of think you have to be running away from something. Something ugly and mean. Only way you're going to get anywhere is if there's a fire underneath you, you know? I'll never have that kind of fire under me, I figure. Except maybe cancer. Yeah, it'll come. But then it'll be too late to run. It was too late to run the day I was born. You know? Yeah, I see things all black. Because it is completely jet black, Jack, out there in the wide world. Blacker than even empty space. Blacker than a gunslinger's black hat, too. God, I wish I'd been a cowboy out in the open away from this stinking swamp. I wish I'd been born on a horse with nothing to do all day but watch them little dogies move this way and that in grass reaching all the way from here to there and then some. Out there in the open where you can see. Where if you're going to run into a superangel, she'll come walking through that grass in a white dress and be about nineteen and as sweet as a fruit off a tree. You and her and the wind and all that open land. And the cows moving around and nobody watching you take her into your arms out there and lay her down. Man, oh, man. That'd be a superangel, all right. Down from heaven. For me. Cowboy Neal.

It took Nicky a good hour to park, not being able to find the kid he'd paid off the last time, and then on top of it we had to stand in line.

"Getting impossible to go anywhere," I said to him.

Nicky brushed some invisible dirt off his white jacket. He had that business gaze going. You knew he'd brought his last dime with him.

But I asked anyway. "How much money did you bring?"

"Who goes in saying shit like that?"

"I brought eighty-one bucks," a punk just behind us said. "I'd give eighty of it to get in the door. Y'all see all that snatch? Ow!"

Nicky glared at the boy. "Get away."

"Lighten up," I said to Nicky.

"Don't ever ask how much money I brought."

I said to the kid, "I bet you get laid, son."

"Why, thanks, mister. You, too."

None of us said anything more and the line was slow. Maybe fifteen minutes went by. I got the feeling we were desperadoes waiting to ambush somebody. Then, at last, we were getting close to the door, and at some unseen signal everybody started talking like they all knew each other.

Nicky whispered, "Curtis said you were in the petty cash."

I ignored him, pulled out my two hundreds, all I'd brought, and waved them in his face. "Here. Let's do like last time. Roulette."

"Quit showing it," he said, snatching the bills away and jamming them into his pants pocket. "So what about it?"

"About what?"

"What's your real name?"

I thought, No time to think, just to act. And keep acting. "You keep bullshitting like that and you'll jinx the whole night, Nicky."

"Arthur Lansing? Daniel Horst?"

"Jinxing it, jinxing the whole night," I said, hard and forceful, like I might be able to carry out my own prophecy.

"Cut that out!" somebody far behind us said.

"I dusted that cash box, Carl," he hissed into my ear. "Six aliases popped up on my computer off your prints. You've been all over and they're looking for you all over. So it's you who can cut the bullshit."

The doormen handed us hats and tooters, and then in we went, chucking them into the first trash can we found. I'm no church boy but I thought about Jonah being swallowed by the whale. There was no telling if I'd ever get out of there in one piece.

Sure, I'd seen that box on Curtis's desk, but it'd been too soon since the deal with Blalock for me to think about taking a dip. I remembered how it felt like Curtis had put the thing out as if he were trying to get me to do it. Maybe I'd touched it once or twice. But I hadn't stolen.

"Box was always out," I said. "Doesn't mean a thing."

"Your prints do, though. Now don't they?"

I thought, I'm going to have to say something because if I don't say anything then it'll mean yes. But nothing came into my mind and he saw this and it was like he had flown really close to my face where he could see way back in my eyes only to sweep away again just as fast.

"Know how much money this place is going to make tonight, Carl?" he hollered, as if trying to outroar the roar. "That million dollars they're going to give away? Drop in the bucket. Huge syndicates own these things, and they're raking it in by the van loads. People will give their lives to own even a sliver of one of these babies. Give away a million? They don't feel it. Pocket change." Then he shifted down low again, said into my ear, "Like the hundred forty-seven dollars you lifted from Curtis. Hundred forty-seven fucking dollars. Goddamn."

I don't like a man preaching at me. "Arrest me then."

"For a hundred forty-seven dollars? I could, buster. Nail your ass."

"You can't prove I took it out of the box. Because I didn't."

We advanced slowly into the maw of the beast, and for me, anyway, it was like time stood still. Rock-solid still. Like for Jonah.

"What I want to know is who you are," he said.

"Carl Taylor Stein."

"What was it now, Frederick Johnston Knapp? That's a whopper."

"That's not my name."

"It used to be. A name you told yourself to never think about again. One of many. And now it's back. Catching up with you."

"My name's Carl Taylor Stein and you know it."

"The hell I do."

"Suit yourself."

"What?"

"Whatever, Nicky."

He shook his head side to side and had this poor-dog look in his eyes. It was incredible, but the guy really didn't look angry. More like I'd hurt his feelings, something simple. I thought, Yeah, sure. Then I wanted to laugh. I also wanted to turn around and walk straight out of there. This was getting way too close to something going bad wrong for me.

He stopped in front of a spinning three-foot money wheel where a lot of people were having the time of their lives.

"Look, Carl," he said.

But he was looking more at the carpet.

"What?"

"Carl, I want to help you out."

"Yeah? Why?"

"Friendship?" he asked, looking up again. "Maybe. But then I don't know who you are. Because I think you're a good man who's been through a lot of bad shit? Yeah. Because of what would prison do to you? Finish you off is all. I'm not going to be the one to send you in."

"Are you even a cop?"

"Look, Carl, if we're going to make loads of money tonight I'm not going to be able to do it alone. Going to need your help. Like last time when you were so hot on the numbers. Remember?"

There was a begging sound to his words.

"I remember," I said.

"Do it again, help me, and then I'll help you on this other thing."

"Help me?"

"Stay out of prison. Because it's not the hundred forty-seven dollars. It's the whole mountain that's fixing to come tumbling down on you."

"What mountain?"

"Con schemes you rigged up in half a dozen states."

I watched someone make a bunch of money on the wheel, and all the other people around the man were clutching him and whopping his back.

"What do you say?" Nicky asked.

"I guess."

"This is not a guessing question."

"All right. I'm with you."

"Yeah?"

"Yeah."

"All right, then. Let's do it." He charged ahead like a general into battle. "Roulette first. Like last time. We're going to nail them again."

I had to run to keep up.

"Look! There's the Chinese gal we had, too. Let's do it."

Then we were at our table, right back where we'd started.

"When we come out ahead tonight," he said, "I want you to take yours and go. I'll say you slipped through the net. It happens."

"You don't sound like any cop I've ever known."

"Nicky Blair," he said, poking his hand out. "Pleased to meet you."

Was this real? I guessed so. Shook the hand. "Carl Taylor Stein."

"Ready to gamble, friend?"

"Ready."

A stool got freed up. Nicky climbed on.

"Shooting for the big one!" He put down my two bills, then two of his own. "Five-dollar chips, if you please."

"Four hundred, coming in," the dealer lady said.

A pit guy glanced at the four notes, nodded.

"Color?" the lady asked.

"Yellow," said Nicky. "How you been, dear?"

She didn't acknowledge him.

"Stand right behind me," he said. "And think of a number."

I got into position. Like that last time. There were chips all over that table. I don't know how, but I relaxed. Everything was clear.

"Nine," I said.

"Okay," he said. "Let's do it."

He put a chip on nine.

Fifteen seconds later we were up a hundred and seventy-five dollars.

Nicky's eyes filled with a happy light, a believing light, that red feverish light, and the grinning big-boob drink gals closed in around us.

"Damn if you're not hot again!" he let out. "He's the man!"

I thought about being ten in Albuquerque. That was right along in there when Ma told us kids we didn't have to go to church no more if we didn't want. We were heading home from Sunday service in the rain and she was mad and crying at the same time and there we were, us snot-noseds, staring at her from the backseat. Ma said, real slow, that she'd up and decided to resign from the church after the elders declared that the extra cash they'd come up with that year was not going to be spent on a carton of brand-new Bibles for Indian children out at the reservation. That's what Ma'd asked them to do. They said no way. So we didn't have to go to church anymore. Did that explain how I turned out bad? For sure, some people'd say. I kind of doubted it, though. In any case, I answered only to myself anymore. Not God, not Ma. Poor thing. Spun her Skylark off the road and into a ditch in a storm. Bibles for Indian kids! Look what all that goodness did for her! We'd left Pa out in California a very long time ago already. I heard that he ended up putting a gun to his head after losing everything at a poker table in Pomona. And there I was calling out numbers to another gambling nut. When the jig was up there in Iona and I should've been long gone. When I knew better than to keep standing there and yet I kept standing there. Like I had no choice. When I still did. He wasn't going to shoot me in the back. He wasn't going to put the cuffs on me and take me away. All had I to do was walk off. But I didn't.

Soon we were up enough to be putting lots of money out there. Their money, Nicky liked to say. Never gamble big with yours, always bet big with theirs. Meaning that it wasn't long before a pit boss came up and said, "Y'all brought Lady Luck in with you. You know that's illegal."

Nicky paid him no mind, said to me, "What's the number?"

"Two."

He steered ten chips toward the Asian. "Cover the two, darling."

She placed the stack, passed her hand over the table. "No more bets."

The white ball clicked and popped and dropped. Two it was.

"Yes, yes, yes!" Nicky cried.

I gave him a bear hug from behind and shouted with joy.

He elbowed me away. "Don't be getting on me!"

"Whoa, man," I said, backing off.

The Asian got the winnings together. "One thousand seven hundred fifty going out."

The pit boss eyed the payout before she let go of it, counting it, nodded and withdrew. We were marked, sure as shit.

Nicky's hands were steady as he straightened the stacks of chips.

Then she came and took the empty stool. A pretty young redhead with great jelly-roll hooters you wanted to bury your face in.

"Well, hello," I said. "Is that you, Lady Luck?"

She counted Nicky's chips in a glance. Nicky sniffed the air, then gave her a look like, See, I'm the hotshot. Watch me, honey.

She came in for a thousand. Took it in fives like us, got red chips.

"One thousand coming in."

The boss nodded from way off.

Every stool was taken.

"Let's have another number," Nicky said.

"Eighteen," I said.

He put fifty on eighteen, and the redhead piggybacked with the same.

It came up seventeen.

"Shit," she said quietly, shooting me a go-die look.

"It's all right," said Nicky. "You won't do that again, will you?"

He was talking to the Asian. She eyed us like we were the enemy, which of course we were, and I fell to wondering if some Vietnamese relative of hers had been the one who killed my brother, Paul, over there.

"Nineteen," I said. And I wanted to add seventy, the year he died, but that number isn't on any roulette table. "Nineteen it is."

"You sure?" asked Red. "You miss this one and I'm out of here."

"Nineteen."

"It hits nineteen and I'll make you smile."

I considered the prospect and swallowed dramatically for her, as if everything in my life depended on the next spin.

"Concentrate," Nicky hissed. "Don't you know they send these girls in here to get us to lose our concentration? You hear me?"

I'd never seen him that wound up.

The girl said, "I'm a spy, huh? Well, if we hit nineteen, I'll make you smile, too, honey. You hear? I'll make everybody smile!"

I liked the idea of her making me smile and moved closer to her. Lo and behold, she slipped her hand in there on my thigh.

"Nineteen all the way," I said.

Everybody piled on. Nicky went with a hundred-dollar bet, the inside maximum on that table that night. Lady Luck was in for the same. It took a long time to get all the bets placed before the Asian snapped the marble around that wheel and sneered at us all like we were total scum.

I felt fire moving through my legs.

A black man leaned in and threw in a twenty. "Place nineteen!"

The Asian waved her hand over the table again. "No more bets."

A pocket of silence formed and everyone leaned forward, as over the proverbial cliff, the one out there at the edge of the ocean where it just drops off into oblivion. The redhead moved her hand directly onto my goods and began rubbing me up like a friendly kitty.

"Yes!" someone cried out down by the wheel.

"Nineteen it is," the Asian said.

"Right on! You did it! Way to go! All right!" everyone shouted.

Thirty-five hundred more American dollars.

Half a dozen bosses rushed over. And I think about half the casino. Or maybe half the planet, but I lost track somewhere in there, because that redhead got off her stool, turned it around to face me, sat down again, and, with everybody pushing and cramming all around, grabbed my fly.

"Go for it!" somebody said. "Do it, do it!"

"Pull up," said Nicky. "We're out of here. You hear me, Carl?"

"I hear you, I hear you."

"We're out of here," Nicky said to the Asian. Then he gave Red a shove. "Leave him alone."

She tried to slap him but he caught her arm.

I zipped up.

"Sixty-two hundred, going out," the Asian announced. The pit bosses leaned near to check the amount. Then she shoved the chips to us.

A cry went up like a touchdown at the Super Bowl. Pit bosses scribbled on their clipboards. Hidden cameras filmed us up close.

Red's payout was four thousand four hundred fifty.

The Asian had turned white. A couple of the bosses were saying things to her and she moved her thin gray lips but it wasn't like she was talking or anything, more like she was unable to keep them still.

Then there was this black guy in my face. "Thank you, thank you, thank you." He was cradling the seven hundred-dollar chips he'd won.

I patted his shoulder. "Damn luck is all."

"You got the spell."

"That's right!" somebody cried out. "You did it, buddy!"

"All right!" I said, and waved to the crowd. People waved back and then the whirlwind shifted and blew me and Nicky down to the bank, Red trailing and saying, "Am I ever going to make you smile! God!"

Nicky got in her face. "Cut it out with that shit."

"Was I talking to you?"

"Could we hold it down, please?" the teller asked.

"Give me my damn money," Nicky told him.

The teller got up and left. We'd gone too far. They weren't going to cash out our chips.

"Now you've done it," I said.

"They're stalling," Nicky said. "Bet they're reviewing film of us on that table. Making sure we weren't cheating. Cheating!"

The other deadhead tellers looked at us.

Red said to Nicky, "You're weird." Then poked his cheek like it was a loaf of bread to be tested. "Scared of women or something?"

"Don't touch me," he said.

She backed off. "Fuck you both. Find somebody else to make you smile. Boys! That's what y'all want, ain't it? Boys!"

"Ship out, bitch," Nicky said.

"Queers," she whined.

Then she slunk away to go play elsewhere.

Another teller, some higher-up in a double-breasted black suit, showed up and counted out the correct amount.

Nicky divided it in half. "Number nineteen, huh. Good work."

"Can't believe it," I said.

"Here. Thirty-one hundred dollars."

I pondered that money. Leave now? Play more?

Nicky said, "I'm going to the craps table now."

No telling how many eyes were watching us. I could feel them all.

My mind went blank and I handed him a thousand. "Catch up with you in a while. Got to wander some."

"A demonstration of the very spirit of winning," he said, tucking away the ten hundred-dollar bills. "Don't be long. I may need help."

"But we've got the spell," I said, believing it. "Nothing can get you."

"That's absolutely correct," he replied, as if there were no doubt in the world. "So correct it couldn't be correcter. The spell will triumph."

"Go for it!" somebody hollered. "Clean this place out!"

Even if a lot of life's decided in advance, you have to hope deep down that, with luck, you'll eventually come out where you want to be. I think it will be like going through a time tunnel. Remember that wild-ass spinning one they had on that TV show? I like to think I'll come out wealthy and retired in . . . Carmel, California. Where all I have to do is strut out my front door, take a big deep breath of the ocean air, then step into my golf cart and buzz out onto the course with my rich buddies and every day is sunny and full of pussy. Only thing is, I have to find the time tunnel. Where is it? I like to think that someday, somewhere, I'll go through some door and then there'll be a man in a red suit up waving me along with a white-gloved hand and calling me sir. Right this way, sir. Straight ahead to the time tunnel. The tube to paradise, sir. Cute girls in skimpy outfits will come up and take off my clothes and spray me all over with a musky oil and giggle. Going to get you through that tunnel real fast, our handsome friend! And off I'll run into the tunnel, slipping and sliding, and I'll hear music and it'll be the Godfather of Soul himself screaming out, Ow, I feel good!

A couple of drinks later and it was like I was flying over the crowd with my new money laughing my head off. I tipped strangers, ten bucks here, five there. To keep the spell alive. I even stepped into a roulette crowd while everybody was betting and cried, "Sixteen to win!" Then left. Seconds later there was a roar behind me. A good roar.

Yet another drink and I began hearing classical music in my head, and then there was the smell of roses. I hate classical music, but it kept getting louder, and the roses were about to gag me.

"Found you." Red with headphones. "Dump your boyfriend?"

"You were nasty back there."

"Hey, don't I get a tip, too?"

"Sure." I dug in the stash, got a twenty.

Then someone tugged on my sleeve. "Mister, mister." It was the kid I'd told would get laid. "Give me one of your magic numbers, mister."

"You want help?"

"I sure do." He wagged a ten in my face. "This is all I got left and it's Saturday night. Do me one? Roll your eyes back and let it fly."

I said, "How about a woman?"

"What?"

"Only number I've got left. Here she is."

I pushed Lady Luck toward him.

He went, "My God."

"No way," she said.

The kid started backing off.

I pulled her aside. "You'd do him for a hundred, wouldn't you?"

"Sure thing," she said, snatching the bill away and going for her prey.

She said something to him and they headed off through the crowd. Last thing I saw she was fixing her headphones back on. She was going to finish that symphony doing him in one of the restrooms. I hoped he liked the stink of roses.

Time to find Nicky again. I steered toward the biggest thicket of people I could see. You knew it was a craps table, a hot one. Of course he had the dice. And he'd had them a long time. In his other hand was a drink. It was like wading into a mass of guys fighting over a lifeboat. Loud, rough, dead serious. Playing for keeps, big time.

"Roll them, Daddy! Make those babies sing! Come on, come on!"

He rolled a six. Joyous shouts went up and the stickman did his work moving the dice back to him for the next throw.

Then Nicky saw me. "You stayed gone too long."

"Roll on, Daddy!"

"Chase out that devil, chase him out!"

"Get it on this," Nicky barked. "I'm on a roll."

There were black hundred-dollar chips in his tray and a lot more of them on the table. But you could tell it was one of those deals where he'd forgotten his own rules about pulling up.

"Fixing to lose it all?"

"Don't say that shit!"

A guy as tall as me said, "That's right, get out of here with that talk."

"Yeah, buster, you go play with the snake-eye folks," snarled a fat man with green sunshades and a chewed-up cigar.

"No more money, Nicky."

"Damn it, Carl, I'm on a roll. Going to win big."

The stickman said, "Let's roll them, sir."

"Yeah, roll them bones!" someone pleaded.

"Go on, Daddy, make it fine!"

"Please, please, please!" an elderly lady called.

Nicky rolled. Four.

There was an explosion of cheers and whistles, and then more people gathered around. I didn't want it to, but something went through me that said this was maybe Nicky's Big Turn. Then my hand was in my pocket pulling out money. I don't know how much. I squeezed in between a couple of guys, flipped it into the boat, where it fell out in the middle.

"No, no, no," the table boss said.

"Put your money on the edge there," the stickman said.

People stared like I was some bumpkin who didn't know the rules. I didn't care. I pointed at Nicky. "Just buy the man more chips."

Nicky peered at me like he'd just been saved and mouthed, Thank you.

"Whatever happens," I said, "it's fifty-fifty like you said."

He nodded. I was sure he knew what he'd nodded to.

Somebody said, "Roll number eight. He be cookin'! He be on fire!"

I couldn't watch.

The first time you take it sends a tingle up your spine. I couldn't tell you if it was a set of baseball cards or a catcher's mitt or what. But I took it and made it mine, whatever it was. Looked Ma right in the eye and said, sure, I'd found it along the road, just lying there, and picked it up. Looked her hard in the face and said that was the truth. Time after time, each time taking one more step away from her and her unhappy silences, backing away from the pit they called your conscience and I called a made-up thing to keep children in line out there in Albuquerque where there wasn't a thing to do but steal and keep things you stole in your room like trophies. Then I got older but nothing changed in the way I was turned and I couldn't tell you if it was a girl's virginity or a carton of cigarettes, a handgun or a new car. I just took it and made it mine. Got downright crazy and cussed Ma and moved away from home, all the way to Wisconsin, and began again. May didn't know this part of me, the down-and-dirty stealing part. But she was hot for me because of the mystery I carried inside. Like I was Jesse James or that Clyde. We'd eat out fancy and then make love in motels and I'd think how there was never going to be a day when she would be needing something I couldn't give her. Even if I had to up and rob Fort Knox. She'd never go wanting, never have that sad gaze that gets in a woman's eyes when she knows you can't give her what she needs. That is pure desolation and I made sure it never crossed her face. I can't tell you if it's your money or your girl or your house or your very soul I want the most. But I will take one, make it mine when the time comes. And if that works, then I'll take the rest, too. And I'll feel a vigorous thrill all through my body and think of May holding me between her strong legs. For there will be no end to it, no goddamn end of the road.

I went to the upstairs keno parlor and sat down and thought, Well, here I am and now what? Which is never a good position to be in.

"Love . . ." said the old man next to me. "Love and Merry Christmas."

It wasn't even summer yet. "Santy been good to you or something?" I asked.

"You bet he is. Santy always good to Mort."

"Santy is our man."

"Our man, right. I do loves Santy. And Miss Santy, too."

"Miss Santy?"

"You know, his daughter. She been in *Playboy*. Yes."

"That right?"

"I seen it. Miss Santy, it said. Written where they sign their name in curlicue. It said, 'Love and Merry Christmas, Miss Santy.'"

"Right."

"That's right. Miss Santy. Give me a number, pal."

"Eighty-eight."

"Love them ivories. Give me another one."

"Forty-one."

"Year of my first marriage. A good marriage. Now go on."

"Twenty."

"Hmm. Twenty. You sure?"

I said yes, marked the same. "Three-spot. We going for it?"

"You're the boss."

"I'll pay both. You get next time."

I went up, paid.

The cashier girl said, "He get you, too? He gets everybody for a dollar or two. You watch yourself now. He's a charmer."

We waited awhile. Then the microphone squealed.

"They be calling it now," my friend said.

We studied the numbers board.

"Number nine," the announcer guy said.

"No problem," said Mort. "Got plenty of numbers, plenty."

"No problem," I said.

The drink girl asked, "Another one here?"

"Sure. Get him one, too."

"He's been cut off."

"Cut off. What'd you do?"

The old man shrugged.

"Get him a drink," I said.

"Afraid I can't do that."

"Don't make a fuss," the old guy said. "I don't even need a drink. They're calling our game here. Come on."

I stood, handed her a twenty. "Get the man a drink."

"Why should I?"

She had on a deep-cut dress, so I poked a second twenty in there where it goes. She smirked. "You're fast. But he's still cut off."

"The hell he is."

"Have it your way. But he ain't getting another drink."

Then she walked off, with all forty dollars.

"Shit-fire," I said, sitting down again.

"Hey, hey!" the old man called. "We got eighty-eight! That's one!"

"All right!"

"Yes, sir. Miss Santy, she going to be good to us."

"You think so?"

"Say, son, it ain't the lady's fault. She's right to cut me off. I am an alcoholic."

"That's none of her business."

"It's none of yours, either. If you don't mind me —"

"I don't mind."

And I didn't. He was right. Time to catch myself.

"You know what?" he said. "You made me think of Venus then. She stuck up for me, too. Got them to give me a drink. She tipped a girl just like you did. Told her to get off her high horse. Bless y'all's hearts."

"Who'd you say?"

"Venus. My other guardian angel. So what's your name?"

"Venus who?"

"Just Venus."

"Black hair. Kind of tall?"

"Yeah."

"About forty-five?"

"Now I wouldn't talk about a girl's age. No sir."

"When'd you see her?"

"Long time ago. You looking for her?"

"Maybe."

"Good luck, and let me know if you do."

"I will."

Mort grinned and called, "Give us a forty-one! Forty-one, here!"

The guy reading the numbers frowned, drew the next number. "Six."

"That'll do, that'll do," Mort said. "You have to get your sixes out of the way. Making room here for forty-one. Making room."

"Name's Carl Stein. What's your secret, anyway?"

"Secret? I guess it's that if you've got good attitude, you've got the world, Stein. Forty-one!"

The call was ninety-three.

"Damn," I said.

"No problem, no problem. Forty-one! You've got to believe."

I joined him. "Forty-one!"

"Number twelve."

It went on: number fourteen, number eighteen, number seventy-one, number sixty-six, number forty, number eight, and so forth through all twenty numbers. Then it was over. We'd lost a grand total of two dollars.

"Hell's bells," he said. "Old forty-one wouldn't show. Next time."

"Play again?"

"Nah. I'll watch a game or two. You go ahead."

"How long you been in here?"

"Day before yesterday."

"Damn."

"My daughter drops me off. Comes back later and fishes me out. She knows I can't do any harm in here. I never have more than twenty bucks when I come in. Can't do no damage with that. Charlene's working all sorts of shifts over at the hospital and it's easier for her to have me here than at home alone where I can hurt myself. I eat in the cafeteria. They got TVs. They got table keno. I play a game or two, then come back here. It's all right. Except for number forty-one. Damn sombitch."

"Got to go, Mort."

"That right?"

"Take this." I handed him a hundred. "And you tell your daughter not to leave you down here so long."

His eyes were red. "That you, Santy?"

"You bet," I said.

It was time for me to go down to the first floor and see about Nicky.

"Hey, Carl, anybody ever tell you you look like Elvis? Well, all right, a very tall Elvis with different-colored hair. But Elvis nevertheless. The King."

"Full of shit."

"I swear." He waved his new sheet at me. "Now get me going."

I helped him up, got him moving toward the cashier.

"This'll be the one, Stein," he said. "All in the attitude."

Nobody could believe it, but Nicky still had those dice and the craps boat was loaded with chips. People were packed around that table carrying on as if it were some voodoo ritual. I stayed way back.

Here came Red. "I made that boy faint."

"Do I look like Elvis?"

"Yeah, he was kind of fat at the end, too. Who said?"

"I was just wondering."

"You better wonder into that mess there and save your friend."

"Nothing I can do. He's his own man."

"Want anything while we're waiting?"

A scream went up like someone being stabbed.

"Oops," said Lady Luck. "Seven."

The crowd fell back as if it'd been blasted away.

"What the hell," I said.

"Crapped out," Red said, and laughed. "I knew it. So long."

Off she went on the tide of folks getting away.

Nicky was draped over the edge of the table.

I got my hands under his arms and pulled him up. He was sticky with sweat. "Come on, pal. Come on."

"Damn," a guy said. "He was hotter than hell. Jesus!"

"Yeah!" bellowed another. "Damn fine roll, good buddy."

Nicky was breathing fast.

"Get you to a chair," I said.

Then he raised himself up and walked, more or less.

Everybody who hadn't run away stared.

We didn't get ten feet. "Hey, pick a number, Stein."

"Cut it out."

"What's your favorite number, Carl? Me, it's seven!"

More people scattered, like something evil had swooped in.

I steered him to the escalator and up we rode and then I thought, Why am I taking him upstairs when I should be taking him out of there? But straight ahead was the keno parlor I'd been in, lots of empty chairs. The one I dropped him onto, though, fell over and took him with it.

A floor-sweeper kid came and helped me get him up again, but didn't say a word or change his sleepy expression. Then he went back to flicking butts and cups and crap into his metal box.

I looked around for Mort, who was long gone, and wondered why I even gave a damn, but then I knew it was because I didn't want to look at Nicky gawking at the ceiling like someone with fresh brain damage.

Then I became aware of a young couple with matching gimme caps on backward, each clutching a half bucket of nickels like it was all the money they'd ever had, staring down with me at Nicky.

"What the fuck are you looking at?" I asked them.

The guy said, "We hear he lost six thousand dollars on craps."

"It was ten thousand," Nicky hollered. "Goddamn ten thousand United States dollars. Goddamn the whole fucking world!"

The kids shook their heads, waddled away.

"Want to do a five-spot?" Nicky asked.

I stared at him. Sweat was gliding through his hair and dripping onto the carpet. "Want me to help you get out of here?"

"Help me?"

"What do you want me to do? Get the car up to the door? What?"

"I want you to walk out of here. Just go."

Then he put his head facedown on the tablet.

Arctic air poured from the ceiling and bodies flowed back and forth. Bells rang in my head. Time to be out on a road to anywhere they didn't know you, didn't want to know you, couldn't care less. Out there with the wind and your own heart alone in the wind. Bells rang and rang until I turned to see where they were coming from. Believe it or not, someone had won the big one right there. A crowd was mobbing the winner, and then lights came on so bright I had to shade my eyes.

"Nicky, look. Somebody's won the jackpot!"

"Get lost," he growled. "Whoever the hell you are. Beat it."

Gianni, he wants me, I know. But I'm not going to let him have me. I won't. I will run my table and Gianni will have to be a man about it, pit boss or no pit boss. He smells bad, like these people at my table, all dirty, foul. I go through the motions of my job and think of steam baths and women in them together washing away all the grime of this life. I see strong-willed women with other strong-willed women knowing who they are and where they are going in this life. Not like these people. Tired carp in a slimy pool. Let them lose every dime they have. They don't know what they want anyway. I think of standing in the steam with strong women and holding hands with them and walking down the smooth steps into the warm water together to wash ourselves. Far away from the clinking of the white ball on the wheel. Far away from Gianni's bony hand reaching under my skirt. Far away where the steam billows and strong women move through the water in peace. Far away from Louisiana and back in the Far Eastern stretches of my heart.

I'd catch Elena standing in the damp shadows, arms crossed, waiting, eyes flashing like obsidian but the fire dying in them with each step Pullman made toward China's far desert, with each round I made of his house while rainwater trickled through the roof onto the floor and puddled. I'd see her leaning on the wet walls, staring, knowing she wanted me to go from there, to leave her alone until Pullman returned and took her into his bed again. I was a useless insect, drinking as much as my softening insides would hold, wandering through every room. Suspended out of time. Standing on the veranda imagining the ocean, the blue stretching out and away, but seeing only dark sweeping rain within rain. Hearing mud flowing through the jungle down the mountain.

One night I went to the old record player with the Sinatra record still laid upon it in the corner of the library. A battered speaker box sat in the window, pointing out and down over the slope. Had he danced with Elena there? Had they had candles going? Had they done that every night, all night, while ancient creatures crawled through the jungle and onto his lawn to commune with the moon? The books were black, claylike slabs. Who'd read them? Gloria? A dead woman's books arranged in a shrine where Pullman was high priest and Elena high priestess and Sinatra's voice the offering?

I played the record and sat in a wingback chair. Elena was near, watching, sometimes having a corn-paper cigarette and blowing long trails of blue smoke through the air. There were photo albums on the table and I opened them and looked back down the lines of Pullman's life.

Here he stood in a white suit with an ivory cane on the beach in front of the shell of a high-rise hotel. No date was written on the back, but it had to have been years ago because there were no other hotels in view down that stretch of beach, which I knew to be the big modern strip now.

Here he lay on a beach many years later next to a woman, the two of them on their bellies with their chins propped on their folded hands as they peered very seriously at whoever took the photo. Gloria. Every bit the looker he'd said she was, her face an open country of strong light into which I stared wishing that I could hear her speak or see her smile. Her blond hair, straight and long, thrown by the wind that day over onto his shoulders. I envied him the touch of that hair, the closeness of her body. Perhaps that had been the day they had been the most happy, with no needs or wants or desires that had not been fulfilled.

Numerous other pictures showed him conversing with men in expensive clothes, Americans, Mexicans, Asians, at cocktail parties on verandas of fancy houses, on lawns under exotic trees, in huge restaurants where waiters outnumbered diners. This was his business life and these were customers and associates and lawyers and officials, a galaxy of men revolving around him as he took the vast tracts of land that he had bought so cheaply and resold them bit by bit, making millions of dollars and countless friends, turning a sleepy port into a booming tourist draw.

I flipped the pages and watched his mansion get built atop the mountain. I saw the thickly grown slopes below it being opened up for the staircase down to the ocean. And the pool being blown out of the rock.

The mountaintop hotel came next, poking up out of the trees like a fancy cake. Then, on my side of the mountain, on the bay side, the jungle being peeled back, boulders being dynamited to bits or rolled down into the water, to make room for my place and the others around it.

I turned and turned pages, put down one album and took up another. Because it would be there. The photo of Frank Sinatra.

And it was. Centered on the black page by itself. A young Sinatra looking with Pullman into the water of the ocean pool. Pullman pointing at the water and Sinatra bending toward it. A school of pretty fish up from the deep?

How often had Frank come back to visit? Or had he? Did Pullman play "Strangers in the Night" to try to lure Frank back once more? I played the record, a little amused by it all, but also sad for him, and let my eyes roam over the photos. The yacht never appeared in any of them, but it didn't take much thought to know what he had done with those. Then I began to ask myself where all these people, these dozens of smiling friends from all over, had gone. Had they gradually drifted away in the sad years after Gloria's death? I suspected so. Leaving him just the occasional businessman to do another land deal with from time to time. Which helped explain why he would latch on to someone like me. Because he could see calamity in my eyes, disaster following me around. Because men like us couldn't help but be drawn to souls who lingered at the edge of life recalling days of abundant light.

As when May and Venus were overwhelmed with joy that Thanksgiving supper knowing without question that this had to be something like long-lost friends suddenly reunited. The candlelight dancing on their faces as they laughed and ate and drank as if it were a fete for them alone. The moment May's hand came to lie upon Venus's on the tablecloth, a simple movement that changed all moments after.

As when Gloria and Pullman lifted their champagne glasses toward each other and then touched them together and held them there while the yacht eased slowly through the Pacific evening. Keeping the rims of the glasses steady one against the other, their eyes unmoving, so that there was no possibility of any separation, no space there, only unity, as among all the parts of the ocean carrying them into the star-drowned night.

As when Carl Stein and myself slugged bourbon and shouted it up about women while we drove up and down back roads leaving a fog of chalk dust for as far as you could see. Like we were teenagers again doing what was forbidden. Like men had to do that kind of thing once in a while if they were going to stay men. Emptying a fifth of the stuff in the course of an afternoon and going so fast that the Suburban flew off the road coming over the crests of the hills but didn't flip because we yelled so loud in our insanity that Death got out of the way.

I saw Pullman walking proudly and much-noticed through the busy cities of China and then leaving the frenzy behind on slow trains and heading far out across orange-colored lands. Always in his white suit and donning his Panama, the dandy from the Tropics out for a stroll, dispensing coins here and there to beggars, stopping then and again to snap photographs with his expensive camera from America, reveling in the ancientness, everything of the past gradually falling away from him as he finally came to the desert wastes as to a place of trial. Would he, having entered, ever be able to leave? Did he ponder this as he paid off his guide and ventured forth like a man gone mad?

I played the record again and tried to imagine what it would have been like to go to China with him and walk into the desert at the heart of the continent, out among ancient bones in places where the wind hasn't ceased for thousands of years. An immense territory where I would feel incredibly small and where my failures would seem meaningless against the vastness of time? A place I would be too afraid to go into. Not wanting to be blasted and scoured and reduced to dust.

Venus was in a desert, too. Somewhere. In China, for all I knew, or down under the ocean, atop Red Rock in the wind, in the dimly lit hole with May, in the bathtub of a cheap motel somewhere with a man and the water sloshing over onto the linoleum as they glide together, ecstatic. In any of these places that were deserts one and all.

Places that might never be found, really, or might be empty if ever I left this rainy tomb and went out and returned to the other world again.

Was it the record that made Elena come and pull back the sheets in the dawn light, climb onto the bed, and get over me on all fours? Her breasts touching my chest. Her hair sliding over her head and around my face, full of sweet fire. Her mouth coming down and opening onto mine.

No one came and the telephone never rang. No letters arrived from China, no cables. As if he'd fallen off the earth. I went for days without dressing. Wandered like Elena, in a sheet, not eating, standing for hours in shadows, smelling leather, mangoes, mud.

Sometimes a light wind would push through the house. As if its source were sending a puff within, searching for life. I would go out on the veranda and look, but each time the rain fell only harder.

Pullman had told me one night before he left for China of wandering in old clothes through the slum that all his construction had created back in the hills behind the bay, up where the trees were all cut away and the tin roofs of hundreds of shacks made a rusted thatch. Feces and green slime ran in trenches and children saw through his easy disguise and followed him around. Men, drunk and red-eyed and ready to fight, barreled forth from the black corners of the steamy morning and shouted at him and spat with great force and then spat again. He said nothing to them, and then they went away, like dogs will do if you don't answer them. Then the women came forward, calmer, curious, and trailed him as he climbed through the slum, and they thought how holy he seemed, like a monk who'd come from afar, on a mission, no doubt, of some incredible importance that might change all things for the better at long last. They touched him and he spoke quietly to them and asked how many children lived there and no one knew how many and he asked if any of them went to school and everyone said no and he listened to them complain about water and food and the stinking air and the absence of hope. Knowing he had the power to change it, knowing it would be the simplest thing to do. Not because he wanted to be better than other men, but because he had created this himself. A murmuring crowd trailed him as he climbed past the foul hovels all the way up until he came to the top of the mountain where a boy whose name no one could remember sat in the shade of a tree. His eyes closed. Dreaming, or dead. Pullman bent down and touched the boy on the shoulder, but he did not awaken, did not break his glue-induced fantasy, or did not come back from the dead. And then he sat down next to the boy and leaned strongly against him like an older brother might do to get his attention, but the other made no move, and then the people watching concluded that surely he was dead and so whatever could all this be about? Then Pullman said he shut his eyes, too, and waited, feeling the weak heat of the boy's body coming through into his, remained there all through the rest of the morning and then through the afternoon and into the night until everyone had given up, no one daring to come and give him and the boy a poke to see what might have happened, whether they were acting or not, no one having the courage to do that, and gone away, leaving them alone. And when they had opened their eyes and looked out over the lights of the bay far below, Pullman heard the boy take an excited breath as if startled by the size of the galaxy of luxury, a flaring ring of blue and red and orange fire.

"Who are you?" the boy asked him.

"The man who brought the lights."

"There are a lot of them, more than the stars. How did you do this?"

"Money. Lots of North American money."

"Will I die here?"

"No. That's why I've come."

"To give me money? Give it."

"No. But I will raze this place and you will go and live in a house."

"Which house?"

"I will have them built, for all of you."

"A lot of houses? Where?"

"Here. When we've swept everything away and begun again."

"It is all right here. You can see a long way. Sometimes a very long way. Or that is what I pretend. That I can see past the edge of the sea. Look down there. Then go there. It is a place of green birds that fly and never land. The side of the world. An open place. Nothing like it is here."

"I will change this place."

"Your North American money . . ."

"Yes."

"I am dreaming of you, right?"

"No."

"How do I know?"

"You will have to believe me."

"All right. Then I will."

Giving the boy a friendly poke in the side with his elbow, Pullman said he'd gotten up to go back the way he'd come, only to find himself standing on his own veranda with a half-finished drink in his hand and staring out across the bay at the black hills above the hotels where he knew the darkened slum seethed in a vicious loathing of life and of all the expensive lights stretched out along the beach so that tanked-up gringos and their soft tanked-up gringas could promenade and murmur love words and make their cooing sounds to each other, there in Pullman's paradise, nothing like it on earth, no need to go another mile, this was the place, look at it pulsing like a luminescent monster spit forth by the sea.

Pullman said that he'd taken that message sent to him out of the squalor of the slum, out of the pained heart of the boy who dreamed in the shade of the tree of birds flying through another world, and had the place wiped away and a cinder-block home built for each family and a school built for the children and sewage pipes and streets put in and lights strung between poles so that there were no more dark places in which wives could be beaten by enraged men, in which children could inhale glue out of paper bags, in which policemen from the city could come and take the last hope straight out of the undergarments of young women who could not run fast enough through the spongy byways to escape them, in which old men lay down to die with a last cigarette butt smoldering on burned lips and their eyes upturned, bowls whose sides glowed faintly verdigris.

"Look there, Carl, and you can see it."

We were sitting on my deck in the lost hours. You could see it. Hanging back up in the hills behind the blazing hotels, a constellation of yellow lights strung across the blackness of the slopes.

"I never told anyone this. Even the people of the slum don't know. They say it was the government, I hear. It's fine that they think that."

"Do you feel like God, Pullman?"

"That's preposterous. But in touch with my heart, yes. I never set foot in that slum, Carl. I never saw a boy under tree. But the words came through me like a slow rain. I could only listen. And heed them."

I sat with him there watching the city without speaking and thinking how small all my thoughts were, how I'd never saved anyone in my life, how May's light-filled hair had plunged into the lake without the least resistance and the water had closed over it, how Venus had taken my chin into her hand the day she left me there and looked down into my eyes for something, I don't know what, and then turned to go with that tired sigh that spoke of her fatigue and misery and desire to test herself against the unknown, the better to shake off death and its haphazard ways of striking people down, the better to survive as May would have her do, as I would want, too. The yellow constellation glowed in the distance, delicate as a web, and I imagined the boy dreaming in bed of a country where the trees are filled with thousands of birds back from the beyond and resting at last.

Then the rain swept away with a sound like a door being opened, and I stood on Pullman's veranda listening. Elena brought soup in a wooden bowl. But who could eat? My ears were too full of the sound of no rain. Then we could hear the ocean breaking below in the man-made swimming pool. We hadn't heard that in many days, and I reached for Elena, as if she would celebrate this with me. But she was like a tired man and withdrew. The soup tasted like spiced oil.

I went down the stairs through the pale green light to Pullman's pool. Hung my legs over the stone deck and watched the sea push in, pull out. I studied the sandy bottom and followed the schools of red and blue fish. Imagined all the earrings and bracelets lost by beautiful swimmers in there, the laughter of women lounging in Pullman's court afternoon after afternoon with nothing more to do than bathe in the sea and soak up sunlight, than ask the waiter boy to bring another drink. While the master rested on a wicker throne in the shade, breathing deep and slow like the water surging in and flowing out of the bay of his own making.

A walkway led away from the pool along the edge of the ocean to another, deeper cove and Pullman's rusted yacht. There the wind was hotter and I grew sleepy as salt dusted my eyes. Cabin doors tapped in the wind. Along the deck were jagged holes. Liquor bottles lay all around with other trash and piles of half-burned cardboard and palm fronds left by people who'd sneak down the mountain for a night of boozing and whoring. Across the stern it read TRES ESTRELLAS.

I wanted to climb aboard, but held back. Returned quickly to the cooler air by the pool.

"Come back," he calls. "It's deep out there!"

I'm swimming out where Pullman's pool meets the ocean and plunges into the blue. I ride a slow wave back to the stone deck where he sits in the shade of a mango tree working on a purple soda pop.

"Who are you?" I ask, climbing out.

"Carlito. That's my name in Spanish. Do you fish?"

It's a boy with short white hair, maybe nine.

"My dad hates fishing. My mom, too," he goes on.

"Is that right?"

"They won't go near water. Scared to death of it. But not you, I see."

"I don't fish much, Carlito."

"I can show you how."

"Where're you staying, son?"

"At the hotel."

He points toward the abandoned hotel up there.

"But that one's closed."

"I know. My parents got mad and left."

"Pardon?"

"They said it was the worst place they'd ever stayed, and left."

"Left?"

"The other day."

"Do you know where they went?"

"No. But will you take me fishing?"

The pool is silver. The child breathes with a rasp.

"You know what?" he says, the voice deeper, as if a time has jumped forward. Now his face is gray and smeared, an old photograph. "You can fish for death. It's a funny red thing. And you know what it does?"

"What's that?"

"It can talk."

"What does it say?"

The voice goes high again, playful. "Oh, stuff like — hey, look!"

I look at the ocean pool.

"There's one right there!" he exclaims. "A death fish!"

I look hard at the metal surface, my heart pounding, but all I can see is my own sunburned face, wavering on the swells, mouth agape.

When I turn to him again, he is gone.

I did not understand what made Elena disappear the day I got over my uneasiness and climbed onto the abandoned yacht. Would she return when Pullman did? But once I had stepped aboard, it ceased to feel wrong, and I lingered there day after day. Again imagining

Pullman in China. Thinking that he might die there. Would word ever get back?

I knew people on the slopes watched me. Mexicans, crouching in the jungle, staring. What could that gringo be doing? Where was Señor Pullman? Had he maybe killed the old man? What had he been doing with the old man's maid? Or had he killed her, too? Someone call the *policía*. No, no *policía*, we will go in the night with our machetes.

Someone prepared food for me, but it was not Elena. No, it was an old thing, maybe her grandmother, who came into the house at odd hours, banged around in the kitchen and burned whatever it was, tossed it onto a plate, and left it for me. I'd seldom eat it, instead walking out of the house and down to the ocean pool. To watch the liners float by, decks lined with the faces of the rich. Sometimes I waved. Maybe somebody waved back.

It was the morning before Pullman left and I was watching a green snake move across the deck in the rain. It had come up out of the jungle and remained wound around the railing for a long time. Then it moved forth, stretching out, the longest one I'd ever seen, until it lay alongside the pool, immobile. As if at long last it had found its place. I'd never been afraid of snakes and this one did not alarm me. But I kept my eye on it and stayed still on my chair maybe six feet away. Pondering the one from the jungle and imagining its message. A stream of words about ancient places long since lost in the layers of green time reaching back to beginnings. It lay there for hours, through the middle of the day and into the afternoon, and I began to wonder if it had not come there to die. The rain rivered across the deck carrying bougainvillea petals and drowned insects and slid along the length of the snake and off the deck in waterfalls. Then it seemed that the visitor had moved slightly nearer. Only to stop again. And I began to think its thoughts. Slow thoughts that carried me away into the steamy jungle, down into the cemetery, past the knobs of blackened wax on the tombs where candles had burned. Slower and slower snake thoughts that turned me into a gray boulder overgrown with vines and clutched by tree roots and crawled across by families of silvery black rats, which of course knew all about snake time and feared it and kept an eye out always. Never sleeping. Never falling into a stupor and awakening in the night inside the snake. I thought these thoughts until the last light of the day and then watched the snake go quickly back where it came from. As if there were something urgent in which snake time turned into a flying chase in which there could be no pity.

The phone call finally comes one night. He speaks at a whisper.

"You took the woman, which I had planned, poor boy from nowhere. Do you realize how priceless she is? You took her with half a thought or two of pleasure, but none as to the value, and made her an old woman. I never expected more of you, though. For you are only walking around in my dream, among my things, my life, since you are without these things yourself. Aren't you afraid of dying before you accomplish anything?"

I sat up on the bed sweating.

Tried to see the night sky through the jalousies. A billion insects seemed to carry the air slowly this way, then abruptly throw it that way. There were no stars, only the black vault, and the memory of the rain awoke in me and I went out to see if a storm wasn't brewing.

All along the horizon, darts of lightning stabbed the sea. Tiny bells began to clang as wind heaved through the garden, through the doors and windows, like a big man trying to get through a crowd.

Pullman was right, this was not my true place and I had no right to believe his things were mine. To taste and take as I pleased, like a Carl Stein, like someone who didn't know better. I saw how I had been wasting what I had left of my life and asked myself how it was that I had not tried harder, not made every effort to revive the spirit of living that May had taught us, to latch on to my Venus as she prepared to go back north and keep her from leaving, how it was that

I thought I could let myself slip deeper and deeper into snake time and go its slow silent way into darkness and death, abandoning order and light.

The huge ocean rippled under the moon in the gusts of the storm plowing across it as though rushing to bring me knowledge.

I would go down and open up my house and live there again. I would go in the morning, ending this dead waiting, go backward into my life again because there was no way forward from Pullman's mansion, try to reorder my existence into a picture of someone who was Carl Blalock.

I sat on the veranda and let the wind push against my face and chest and it was warm and I slept only to dream again of the old man.

He is in a mud-brick building on the edge of the howling desert. Lying on his side smoking opium in the red glow of an oil lamp. While fellow travelers sleep the sleep of centuries and the cold sand piles up on the walls, burying them. He thinks of saying a few more things to me about living, about sailing and living without end, but knows that I can hear his words even if he does not say them aloud. Then he thinks of his green mountaintop and of the banded moonlight on the bay and of Elena's body like a long beach in the evening and tells himself to return. Only the body will not move. Cannot rise and dig its way out.

I began reliving in my mind the old life with Venus. There I was, out on the porch with her while the lawn went from green to blue, while the ice cubes melted in my glass, saying nothing at all until she sighed and went to make us both another one and I got up and lit the charcoal.

"You know that place we like to picnic at?" she asked.

"By Arrowhead Point."

"I read the other day some schoolkid found an Indian skeleton right at the edge of the water. She still had black rings on her finger bones."

I didn't say anything. Watched the flames dying in the charcoal. Waited for it to turn to ash. Then I'd put on the grill.

"She was only an inch under the mud. Kid stepped right on her. He'd found arrowhead flakes along the shore and was looking around. They figure she died maybe a hundred years ago."

"They can tell everything, can't they."

"I wonder what her name was."

I remembered it like it was a minute ago. How Venus scooted her lawn chair closer after the second drink. Hummed. Left the question in the air.

In that part of the night that is almost morning, I awoke to find a hot rain falling hard, battering everything with a sound like drum-roll. Only seconds later, however, it halted, as though on command. I stood and peered into the dripping yard. He was there. Strolling along the path under the wet trees in a white suit like a young man half his age. Carrying a huge red suitcase. Wagging his ivory cane.

"Carl, old boy!"

Straight out of China.

"Damn storm delayed my plane for hours. We sat in Mexico City since midafternoon. Never been so tired in my life. What time is it?"

I had no idea.

"Carl, are you not well?"

I felt cold mud rising around my feet.

"What is wrong?"

"Nothing. Welcome. Welcome back."

He came up the steps onto the veranda, took a long look at me as if to see how close to dying I might be, then turned and went clomping into the house. "Hello? It echoes in here! Elena? *Dondé estás?*"

He will be good now that I am inside of him a part of his body a memory like the taste of a mango so I go quickly under the yellow lights along the street behind the beach back to my home in the shadow of the hotels where Mother awaits me because I have her cigar the one she cannot finish the day without telling myself not to raise my head and look back up the mountain to see if there are many lights there in the mansion to see if the master is home from China if he and this Carl now are talking while the pretty record plays in the library among all the black books no one has read since Gloria drowned in the ocean and the perfume of my body floats on the night there with them and into the space between them and then into their minds at the same time so that they drop their eyes and peer into their drinks and see me looking up back at them in that way only a woman can if her heart is good and she wants to spread her love like a perfume that stays a long time in the air because it is expensive and maybe comes all the way from Paris if you are rich enough to afford it because it will make them wild in that way that a woman wishes so much for them to be so that she can lie back in the night very satisfied knowing she has found life in their hearts down in them where she need never fear where they will protect her and never let her go.

The next thing Venus knew Grover Hudspeth reached over and put his hand on her lap while his wife smiled and drove. "You like that?" he whispered.

Venus gazed over the Imperial's hood at the blacktop.

"Let's stop," said Emma. "We need gas."

"No, we don't," he said.

"Yes, we do, Grover. We have to stop."

Gently, Venus put his hand back on his lap.

The gas station was new, fancy. Grover got out, went and unscrewed the gas cap, set it on the fender, and stood there.

Waiting.

"What's he doing?" Emma asked.

"I'll help him," Venus said.

Venus climbed out, pulled her skirt down straight. "Grover?"

"Yes ma'am?"

The shiny pumps stood idle.

"It's one of those do-it-yourself joints."

"Oh." He reached for a nozzle, gave the hose a jerk, and pushed the end of it into the tank, which gave a hollow bang. Then he pressed the lever and considered the view from there of nothingness.

"Grover, I don't think it's pumping."

He peered at the pump. No lights, nothing. Then he mashed the lever again a few times, rattled the nozzle. "Think you're right."

"You have to have a credit card."

"Oh. Well, we can find a real gas station somewhere. Heck with this."

Venus waved at him. "I've got cards enough to get us to the moon."

She got the pump to light up. Then Grover went to work. It was amazing how much gas his car could hold. Every few minutes he smiled at Venus and she smiled back. As when there is a great understanding.

Grover said, "We must've been stone dry." He got out his billfold. "Can't have you getting this."

"Put that away. You keep your hands to yourself, all right?"

"I like you."

"But I can't be your gal, Grover."

"How do you know?"

"There's already a lady in your car."

"And I love her."

"You should."

"I wouldn't do anything to hurt her. She knows that."

"I know. So let's keep our deal, all right?"

She gave him a squeeze on the arm to say, Don't take it wrong. He didn't, and finished getting the clunky gas cap back on.

"Never in my life," he said, giving the station a final look. "Cemetery."

It was only a few miles to the casino and the old man kept his hands to himself. They listened to some church music and fevered preaching.

"Have you ever seen this many cars?" Grover asked.

"Not in my lifetime," Emma said.

Venus fiddled with her hair, pulled on it this way and that. "Why don't you folks get out at the front door and I'll go park the car for you?"

"That's very sweet," Emma said. "Grover, can you remember how long it's been since anybody's been this generous with us?"

"Can't," he said.

Venus left them in the waiting crowd, then tried to find a parking spot when there wasn't a chance. In no time she was a good ways from the casino. She couldn't help thinking about shooting on down the road into the orange-red evening. But then it'd be a stolen car. They'd chase her down and put her away. Which didn't seem what May would do. So she pulled over and lined the Imperial up with the other cars along a road with swamp on either side. Lay her head back on the seat and looked for long time at the water stains on the roof liner. Air was getting in behind the cloth, puffing it. The engine ticked as it cooled and she thought about dogwood, and abandoned cars full of dirty magazines rotting deep in the woods, flies all around. Like when she was a kid and things were either beautiful or evil.

She wished May were sitting next to her getting ready to go into the casino to play. To be two happy girls freewheeling through the world. Of course May would say, "You look like a million dollars, Venus," and Venus would say, "Is that for good luck?" And May would purse her lips, offended, and say, "No, I mean it, Venus. I always say what I mean straight out. Like, I love you, Venus Marie. Like, I never loved a woman as much as you. Like, it's all right that I love you and that you love me back, because it's our business and to hell with everyone if they don't comprehend it." Venus would lower her eyes and then raise them again and check her makeup a last time in the dim light in the rearview. "But where is all this love coming from, May?" "Coming from? Do you ask questions like that, truly? Don't do that, Venus. Whatever for?"

It was a long walk back along the road. Men in fancy cars and boys in beat-up cars offered rides, but Venus waved them away. Listened to the bullfrogs. Childhood tomboy memories rising up. Of empty dirt roads and maybe a catfish popping around in a bait bucket. The rank smell of crushed earthworms. Sticky fish slime on her hands. Thinking about the green turtles that rose from the deep and looked at her long and hard with their yellow eyes before dropping back slowly into the gloom.

Venus walked and walked toward the glowing lights and when she got there she went right up to the entrance and said, "My parents are in there. Do I have to stand in line?"

"Hey, Dan, what if her parents are inside already?"

Dan could have knocked you clean out of the state. "Anything that good looking can do whatever it wants. Let her in."

People booed. "What's the deal? Not fair!"

"Shut up!" Dan commanded.

"Free country!" somebody hollered.

"Who says?" Dan demanded. "Who?"

Nobody said anything.

Venus stepped inside, smiling at the flattery. Good looking, huh. She felt good in her clothes, it was true, felt good that men still peered at them and thought of getting them off her in a hurry. Wasn't it funny how the nicer the things you wore on your body, the more the men wanted to get rid of them? Like the prettier the veneer, the less they wanted it on you?

Because of what was inside. And what was inside of that, too.

She had all that, all right. Starting with some blue thong underwear. Why not? She could hear May chuckling about that. Not ridiculing her. Just the opposite. For it was an indisputably good thing, in May's book, for a grown woman to be wearing thong underwear under her short skirt if she wanted to. Hell, yes. That is, and here's what was funny, if she could put up with that damn strap coming up her ass.

Venus felt better than she had in weeks, and so it was very peculiar when a cloud of doubt blew through her mind because something spoke in her inner ear and said that Carl Stein would be there that night. Where did a thought like that get born, she wondered, as she sought a direction to take in the casino, suddenly unable to decide. How could trouble announce itself so clearly way before the trouble actually started?

Then she simply hoped it would not come to pass. And went over to a bank of slot machines, just for a quick test of her luck. Fed quarters into a hole, pulled the handle. Two cherries and a single bar. Two single bars and joker, something back. Three single bars, something back. Nothing, nothing, cherry. Cherry, double bar, nothing. Nothing, nothing, nothing. Cherry, triple bar, single bar. Nothing, nothing, joker. In no time she was down five bucks. But it didn't matter.

"Why, did you forget about us?"

It was Emma, panting, straw hat atilt and the red netting poking out as if it had exploded. She had rouged her cheeks, or was suffering from the heat. Her tiny white mouth trembled.

"Not at all, Emma. I was just getting warmed up here a little."

"Have you ever seen so many people? I can hardly breathe."

"Here are your car keys."

"Thank you. I hope you'll go back with us. How would we find the car without you? I know he's nasty. Always been that way. But he's as sweet as a puppy, you know. He didn't mean any harm."

The poor thing was shaking in her thin dress.

"I know," Venus assured her. "Are you all right?"

"I guess. Lot of noise in here."

"Have you lost him?"

"No. He's playing blackjack over there. His daddy taught him that game years ago. Only one he knows. You know what? He wins."

"That so?"

"Usually something. We don't come often, though. He says we don't want to make the authorities suspicious."

"I see. You want to play slots with me?"

"No, honey. I just watch. Until he's done. Then we go."

"You ought to play, Emma."

"Why's that?"

"You know you're going to lose. So you have fun. Put the money in, chitchat, have fun. That's what we're here for."

"Grover says you're never supposed to lose money. Fool if you do."

"You have to learn to lose some, I think. That's part of winning."

A change girl came by, so Venus got a couple of rolls of quarters, then a couple more, and a roll of dollar tokens for later.

"I'll show you."

Venus handed Emma a roll of quarters, then took one of her own and broke it open on the edge of the winnings tray. "Do like me."

Emma carefully unwrapped her quarters and held them in her hands and gawked at the machine in front of her.

"Now put them in up there," Venus said.

Emma obeyed, slipping one in.

"Now pull that handle. Or punch that button. Whichever."

Emma tapped the button with a long white finger. The machine clanged and clonged and stopped. Blank, cherry, cherry.

"Nothing happened," she said.

"You have to get them lined up to win."

"I see . . . What do I do now?"

"Put in another quarter!"

"Yes, another. And another!"

"That's right!"

"Until you're dead busted!" said a fat woman nearby.

"My," said Emma, seeing the woman's money tray. "She's rich."

"Nickels," Venus said.

"Still!"

"That's maybe ten bucks, Emma."

"That all?"

Emma clutched the rest of her quarters and watched the others play. She'd spent hundreds of hours wandering around that casino waiting on Grover to finish his blackjack, but it was like she'd never seen any of this before. Venus watched her watching awhile, then poked her and pointed at the place you put the quarters in. Emma obeyed, cheerfully, and soon, working hard at it, they were two gals lost in the madding crowd.

Once in a while loud bells went off. Venus looked up and tried to see who'd hit a jackpot. Her eyes searched but the light patterns spun, made her dizzy. Then, over in a corner, she spotted a flashing yellow light and heard a woman screech as her winnings clanked forth. She played her coins slower and watched the lady bawl and hold her hands to her cheeks, unable to believe her good luck.

People stared, but nobody tried to help. And the woman didn't ask them, either. Kept watching her money fly, once in a while slowly putting a handful into a bucket.

Then the coins stopped coming, people wandered off, and the gal slouched on her stool. Five thousand dollars, someone said.

"Be right back," Venus told Emma.

Emma wagged a finger at her that meant don't be bothering me, I'm a gambling fool now, that's right, I verifiably am.

This is how I am good to people, Venus thought to herself, this is the way it's done, and sidled up to the teary-eyed woman and said, "Never saw that many jealous faces. Could you use some help?"

"Looking for money, are you? Here."

The woman grabbed some quarters and tossed them, underhand. Venus put her hand out to catch them, but they all fell far short, scattered.

"Throwing it away now?"

The woman scowled. "Mind leaving me alone?"

She was a few years older than Venus and there was a wedding band on her finger but no man in sight. At her feet was a battered travel bag with its tow handle pulled up but slightly bent. Maybe she'd come all the way across the country to do this. Now she'd won five grand. What would she do? Go home to him and his foul mouth and their rude children? Go to a motel, make a warm bath, and slit her wrists with a Wilkinson Sword? Sit there and feed every quarter back in?

She had an eyeball that gazed over Venus's left shoulder.

"What're you staring at?"

"A winner," said Venus. "Wanted to let you know it's wonderful."

"Do I know you?"

"I'm sure you don't."

The lady's other eyeball wasn't right, either. It gazed over Venus's other shoulder. So that whoever this woman was with her crazy eyes, she wasn't looking at Venus at all. Which made her edgy. You could try to be nice to people, but when they scared you, you backed off. You didn't even say excuse me and good-bye, you just smiled and went your way.

To hell with the being-good stuff, Venus thought, hurrying.

"Now where're you going so fast?" the woman demanded.

"Have to see about a friend."

"I had a friend once."

What was this? Did the woman actually feel like talking after all? Venus came back, stood closer to her this time. "That so?"

"A good friend, too."

The victory tears had made brown channels in her makeup.

"They say you don't get too many of those," Venus said.

"Maybe not one in a lifetime. But I'm going to live again and again, so it doesn't matter right now because I've already had my one friend this time around. Then we had a fight and we don't talk anymore."

Venus wasn't sure she'd followed, but nodded anyway.

"I mean it, though," the woman said, fingering her coins. "I'm coming back. I'll be somebody else. But I'll be back. You know? Haven't you read that book about how we've all lived and died a jillion times and we come back and stuff and live again and again?"

"Don't guess I have."

She'd lied. She knew about that stupid book. It'd sold millions.

"Maybe in another life you did," the woman said.

"I doubt that."

"I've read it nine times."

"How many lives do you think you have?"

"This isn't like cats, sister. This is real. I was once Jackie Kennedy."

"Yeah?"

"Weird, huh."

"You're telling me."

"There's a glory to it all, see? We're all intersecting and crisscrossing each other and the longer we live and die again and again the more we'll all gradually come to understand that there's really no difference between me and you and the next person, that we're all one creature. You know?"

Venus watched Emma working her slot machine across the way.

"Jackie had these huge feet," the woman said. "Look at mine."

Venus looked down there. Size twelve, surely.

"You think it hurt her, too, to have big feet?" the woman asked.

"I've got size eleven," Venus said.

"Wow," she said, looking down. "And they hurt, right?"

"Not so much."

"Really truly?"

"You know, you ought to gather up your jackpot."

"Should I? Is that the way you are? Going around telling people what they ought to do? Maybe you were Jesus Christ once?"

Venus laughed. "Just trying to be helpful."

"Why?" the woman asked.

"Good luck, Jackie."

"What's luck got to do with it? And hey!"

"What?"

"I didn't say I am Jackie, I said I was Jackie. Now I'm Darlene Jung. Married a Korean, but he left me. I like his name, though, so I kept it. Always twenty-nine, right? Stay Jung. Get it? I'm from Bodie, Nevada. Out there in the desert where spaceships land."

Venus started to go, stopped. "You've been kidnapped by aliens, too, right? And they got you pregnant? And then you had an alien baby?"

Darlene gawked, one eye this way, the other that way. "Hey . . ."

"I'm sorry," Venus said. "You have a good time."

"Hey . . . how did you know?"

Venus walked away.

Emma had run through her quarters. "Busted."

"Let's have a cocktail, Emma."

"No ma'am. I will have a sodey, though."

Venus flagged down a waitress, a young thing shaped like a ball of dough with sticks stuck in it for legs and arms, and ordered a Coke for Emma, got a vodka-tonic for herself.

"Going to get likkered?" Emma asked.

"Why not?"

"You can if you want to. I'll drive us back. Don't worry."

"I'm not worried, Emma. Can I tell you something?"

"Of course."

"I may see someone here I know."

"May see?"

"I have a feeling."

"Yeah? A man?"

"Yes ma'am."

"How big a feeling?"

"Rather big feeling."

"That's good. I believe in big feelings."

The drinks came. It was time to hit the dollar slots.

May had had one feeling about reincarnation, Venus recalled. That it was a load of bull. The boys were out doing an all-nighter somewhere and May had brought over a bottle of Scotch. They'd never had a good drunk together. Venus got out glasses that hadn't been used in years.

The first drink went down fast. They slowed on the second, watching each other, starting to smile as the stuff heated the heart. The only light came from a lamp across the den from where they were sitting cross-legged on either side of the coffee table. It was past one in the morning.

Venus was thinking how she definitely was in love with May's looks. With her shapely cheeks, with the pools of green in her eyes, with all that radiant hair. She knew that she never got tired of staring at May and that sometimes in the night she awoke and knew that she'd been dreaming of staring at her. There was a kind of lovesick ache that she got, but she'd never told May about it. Never told her how she thought it would be sweet to sit naked with her, how it could only be heavenly to lie face-to-face on the floor staring at each other and not saying a word.

By the end of the third round they couldn't stop grinning.

"So, darling," May said. "I've got something I need to tell you."

Venus felt herself go weak in the middle. Was May going to say the very things she herself had been thinking? Was this the night they would stretch out together like alabaster goddesses? Venus felt giddy. Anything was possible. Nothing was over and done.

"What do you need to tell me?"

"That I love you, no matter what happens to us in this world."

Venus heard herself saying the same thing back, the way it was always said right back. But then she added, "I even dream of you."

"Dream of me!"

"It's okay, isn't it?"

"Like we might be lovers?"

Venus remembered dreaming of walking with her in the wind. Out where the sun came straight down upon them and made their hair glow golden, both the same. As they moved through grass hand in hand.

"I think so," Venus said. "Unless . . ."

"It's all right. I don't mind."

"You don't?"

"I can see it in your eyes, Venus."

"I love you like I've never loved anyone."

"How could we feel different?"

"I don't know."

"We couldn't. So we will feel like this because that's the way we feel. It's not like someone can tell us no. It's not like we need to be asking a thousand questions, either. This is just me and you."

"Yes."

They remained without speaking a long while.

Then they talked quietly of other things, about their husbands and how the sex had been good with them these last weeks, about the various strangers each had been with on slow days when no one was paying any attention to what went on behind motel doors, about the handsome new savings-and-loan manager they'd both had their eye on and the probable size of his well-moneyed member. There was laughter that rose to howls, and the Scotch went down hot and the cool night eased in through the screens and washed over their warm faces and necks.

Sometimes they would hear a car door and think it might be the boys. But then they wouldn't be in before dawn. Off night fishing, or maybe they were with some motel hookers. It didn't matter.

May kept fluffing her hair with her fingers and Venus let her eyes settle there as on a soft pillow. Yes, she began to see, she really was in love with May that way, physically. And, yes, she was also in love with the idea of having a love, be it a woman like May, a man like Carl Blalock, or men without names who came and went, so long as there was always that powerful overwhelming motion inside her. Of wanting to live so badly for the love that the will to live became a demand.

"Are you hungry?" May asked. "Don't you want some breakfast?"

"Now?"

"The all-night place is open. Let's go."

"No, May, let's stay here. I'm too drunk."

"Fiddle! How many times do you live?"

"A billion? But let's just drink tonight."

"I want pancakes. Bacon. The works. No, you only live once."

Venus looked at May's breasts in her thin white blouse where the light made them shadowy and maddening. And then she saw how May was looking at her breasts, too. Venus was sure they'd been sisters in another life. How else to explain? Thinking the same things at the same time?

Venus knew she was drunk but it felt like no other drinking she'd ever done. She pictured herself floating on a river through the country. Here she raced on the deep flow, there she spun to the bank. She lay back on the floor and watched lamplight catching on the ceiling cracks.

"I guess, then, you don't believe people who say they know who they were before?" she asked.

"You guessed right."

"Anyway, I was your sister once. I know I was."

"We're going to have to cut you off."

"No, listen."

"I always listen, Venus."

"I love you."

"And I you."

"But it's more than those words."

"I hope it is."

"A longer love. Across a huge expanse of time."

"Go on."

"Like a river that cuts through many places, many countries. Like it could never be stopped. Like it had always been there."

May frowned. "That's all right, Venus. For you. But it isn't right for me. I love you now is all. Not back then. Not tomorrow, maybe. Now."

Venus saw her idea shrink down. Whatever had she been talking about? What was this silly river of love across time?

"People lose sight of the big picture sometimes, get lost in nonsense," May said. "Worrying about the future and the past and time and death will only get you worked up so that you can't see the here and now."

Venus resisted the rush to be insulted, or hurt, and listened.

"Get unworked up about all that and start to live your life in the here and now. Every door opens. Every chance flows to you again. And you love what you love in the here and now with all the energy you can."

"But I will love you always."

"Do you know this?"

"Yes."

"I don't think you do."

"Why?"

"Put it this way, Venus. I wouldn't want to waste a minute thinking about the love I might give, but I'll spend as long as you want loving right now. In this moment."

"I think I see."

"In this moment."

"It's as if maybe you fear that everything could be taken away from you in an instant."

"That's exactly it, Venus."

"How very sad."

"Sad? Just the opposite. It frees you."

"But I know we were sisters, damn it."

May rapped the table and laughed. "All right, then, we were sisters."

"Always," said Venus, sitting up again.

"All right. But especially now. Right now."

"Yes."

"I am drunk! Will you kiss me, Venus?"

Venus didn't move at first, then she did, putting her hands on the coffee table and pushing up, and then they kissed on the mouth while the lamplight cut through the Scotch bottle and made a warped arc on the wall. The kiss was warm and tasted like cinnamon and peaches.

"I'm definitely drunk," May said. "Now can we go eat?"

May smiled so big Venus's heart pounded. "Of course."

"Good. By the way . . ."

"Yeah?"

"It is okay to get worked up about pancakes."

Venus knew better than to concentrate all that hard on the bars and cherries. Whatever came up, came up. If it was a lot, good. She paused, let the payback finish — ten this time, twenty that time — then scooped up coins and put them back in. Two by two. Pull. Three by three. For fresh luck she popped the spin button instead. Hummed a tune.

She imagined May bursting back out of the lake into the light with her eyes flashing like emeralds. Felt herself slipping at the sound of the dead woman's voice saying, "What's wrong with you, honey? All sad that I went ahead and left you? Well, don't worry your silly head. Come to sister. Come." Falling into May's arms and sinking with her into the cistern, the ice-cold water hitting her legs, locking them, and a downdraft yanking hard, like a child, insisting. May's mouth full of blue flames and her voice saying through the drowned world, "Sister, sister, oh my sister."

A siren sounded.

"Honey?"

The siren blew so loud Venus was sure it was the end of the world. After all those years of drills, the idiots had unleashed the package. She wanted to turn and see if everyone was running for their lives, but couldn't. Could only stare straight ahead, waiting for the blast of fire.

Then all the lights went out and a heart-shaking roar went up.

"Honey?" someone cried far away.

Venus clutched her red patent leather purse.

"Get away from me!" she shouted.

"Honey? Honey, it looks like —"

"Get away!"

"Like you've —"

The siren screamed higher and then there was a beam of light from above that tore through her. Coins poured over the lip of the tray.

Venus lifted her head. The sign atop the machine was flashing in red: $1,000,000 . . . $1,000,000 . . . $1,000,000 . . .

"I think you won, honey."

"Emma? Emma?"

"Yes, dear. I'm right here."

"Emma, hold my hand."

"Here, dear. Here."

Venus reached beyond the spotlight. Lots of hot hands grabbed on, pulled. She jerked back, as from jaws. What was it May had been saying just before she dropped into the cistern? Why couldn't she remember? Or had the end come in the middle of a silence? What was all this noise now? A million dollars? She stared at the black wall where the light ended. She heard deep rolling thunder. Perhaps it was someone else who'd won. She looked again at the flashing numbers. They seemed to be atop her machine. A tall man in a white suit emerged from the beyond. His lips were candy pink. TV cameras swung near.

"Louis Cleland, ma'am. Manager of the Iona Belle. Seems it's your big night! What's your name?"

"Pardon me?"

"What's your name?"

"Venus."

"Venus what?"

"Venus Millionaire!" Emma squawked from wherever she was.

People applauded, and a guy yelled, "You got that right!"

The manager flashed a smile, waved for quiet. Fiddled with his microphone. "Ladies and gentleman! May I have your attention, please?"

Thc roaring war for money eased slightly.

"Well," he began, "I think you've guessed it! We have our millionaire winner! Right here! Take a good look!"

The cheers came like a shock wave. Venus was sure she was being blown away into the unknown.

"And her name? Nothing less than the goddess of love. Venus! The very first Iona Belle Million Dollar Night jackpot winner! How about a big, fine hand for the lucky lady!"

The applause was full of whoops and hollers. And of things being poured in great quantities — dice, coins, chips, roulette marbles. Was this all it took to thrill people to the core, Venus wondered. Why cheer your heart out over somebody else's luck? Why was she asking herself this? And stop shaking! The shouts went on and on.

"So how do you feel, Venus?" the man asked.

"I don't know. I —"

"You don't know? She doesn't know!"

Everyone laughed. The microphone squealed.

"I mean, I don't know yet. I —"

"Tell us, Venus, did you feel lucky coming in here tonight?"

"That, no. Not lucky. No."

"Have you ever won big before?"

"No, never. No."

"How about that? And what're you going to do with all this dough?"

"I don't know."

"She doesn't know? Venus doesn't know!"

Someone cried, "Spend it!"

"A million dollars! Will you quit your job?"

"Well, I wasn't —"

"Of course you will! That's what all our Million Dollar Night winners will do! Kick back and relax for the rest of their lives! Thanks to the Iona Belle! And so to you I say . . . a million and one congratulations! And remember, folks, next time it could be you! Or you! Or you!"

Circus music boomed. Lights came back on and the ceiling opened and hundreds of dollar-bill-green balloons rained down. The siren on every machine was made to go off simultaneously.

"Yee-hai!" some kid screamed, waving his cowboy hat.

"We'll be glad to make the payout at your convenience," the manager said. "Again, congratulations." He kissed her on the cheek with those glistening lips. Then, with official ease, he opened a panel on her slot machine, made it stop cranking out coins, and reset it.

"Don't worry," he said. "Every last dollar will be in the check."

"Thank you."

"Your big day."

"I guess so."

"Enjoy yourself. It just doesn't get any better than this."

He said it in a defeated tone. Heading away, he yanked out a handkerchief and wiped away his lipstick and shook his head, miserable.

Then Venus recalled. She had been talking about how she hated shopping at the new mall out on the highway because it was always busy and people fought you for space in all the stores and bad music pounded you from the ceiling, and May had said, "Just try to be good, darling. Even when everybody else isn't. It takes courage to do that." Venus had stopped walking along the mud bottom of the lake and said, "What's that got to do with shopping?" But May had kept going. Toward the hole. And then it was over. Time jumped and May's body fell.

Venus picked up a token and put it in her machine. Bar, bar, nothing. A million murmuring friends surrounded her. She put in another dollar. Nothing, jackpot, cherry. She wanted nothing more than to sleep and dream of being Venus the Good. She tasted salt at the corners of her mouth.

"Here. It's free."

Emma. Handing her champagne.

"To you, honey."

"No," said Venus. "To you."

"Better, to this machine."

"To the machine!"

They downed them in one go.

A waitress refilled their glasses. "Congratulations, ma'am," she said. "On the house. Lucky you." There was no conviction in her voice.

Venus ignored her. "Play me a dollar here, Emma."

Emma reached into the pile. "Here goes."

Nothing, nothing, orange.

"Damn," said Venus. "Do it again."

"Then we better go, right?"

"Go?"

"Yeah. We have to tell Grover. He's hard of hearing, you know."

Emma was right. There was no reason to stay there. She'd won the game and now there was a new one to be played. Outside. Elsewhere.

Then Emma said, "You know what? I have a feeling that's him."

"Him who?"

"Him."

Venus turned.

It was.

The tall man with yellow hair.

"Am I right?" Emma asked.

"I don't know if I want to do this," said Venus.

"Do what?" he said.

Wind began slinging parking lot grit against the dark plateglass windows. A storm was coming in like a bulldozer.

Venus turned back to her slot machine, fed it. Cherry, orange, bar. Bar, bar, joker. Carl Stein was there now, right beside her, she told herself. Be nice to him this time? Or start yelling again?

Bar, bar, bar. Pay ten. Feed them back. Two by two now.

"So what do you want?" she asked him.

"I was sitting right over there," he said. "Right there with my friend Nicky. And you won a million bucks ten steps away!"

"Excuse me," Emma interrupted. "Venus, I have to find Grover now. Are you going to be going back with us?"

Venus told her yes. "Meet you at the door in fifteen?"

"Make it half an hour. Grover's slow to get away from his table."

Then Venus spun on her stool to look at him. His eyes were bloodshot and his matted hair needed a good wash.

"Look, about the money," he began. "That was the stupidest thing I ever did. I know that. Though it's not like you really need it now . . ."

Venus looked outside. You couldn't tell sky from ground.

"I've got it," he went on. "I mean, I can give it to you."

"What is it you want?"

"Nothing. I just want to give you the money I stole. Clean the slate. And say congratulations. You know."

"Forget that money."

"I can't do that."

"It's forgotten. You don't owe me a dime."

"Where's Blalock? You're not here alone, are you?"

"Why couldn't I be alone?"

Carl Stein's eyes flashed. "So you are . . ."

"No, I'm not alone."

"You're with that old lady?"

"Why don't you just go away for good?"

Strangers' hands began flying in to pat her. "You did it, lady! You did. What're you going to do with all that dough? Married? Need a broker? Honolulu here you come! Hell, go to Paree!"

"Back off," Carl told them, and they did, some. "So, Venus. What if I helped steer you through getting your money and getting out of here in one piece? Could I do that favor for you?"

"Why should you?"

"Something I did a long time ago. I owe you one."

"Long time ago? It was only a minute ago. A second ago."

He didn't say anything, scowled at the people pressing to talk to her.

"How many people have you done that to?" Venus asked. "How many people have you set up and then knocked down?"

Gently, he took hold of her arm.

"What're you doing?" she demanded.

"Trying to help you out here, Venus."

Then it was too late. He was easing her along.

"Why am I letting you do this?" she asked.

"Going to ask why you won a million, too? Helping you out is all."

With each step, the crowd parted. All she had to do was walk to the teller windows. All she had to do was let Carl Stein lead. And when she got there, all she had to do was say, "I'm Venus Blalock and I'm here to collect my one million dollars, please."

"Yes ma'am," said the young man in a silver suit. Then he raised his voice, as if speaking to everyone. "Paying out one million dollars!"

He reached for the big pink check, then held it up so all could see. Other men in silver suits gathered around and smiled. Then there was a cry as if somebody had been shot as flashes went off. She took the check from the man and swung her head around to look for the victim, for the body, and countless more flashes exploded.

But the next thing she knew Carl had gotten the check out of her hands and was holding it up high. “Smile at them, Venus. Smile big!”

Darlene Jung

Okay, so I am my own baby. So what? You can be anything you want in America. Though it's not really America anymore. And unless you're stupid everybody knows it's not really America anymore. That the aliens have taken it over and that we are their slaves, pawns in an intergalactic game. I like that word, *intergalactic*. Makes me think of all those space shows I watched when I was a pretty young lady and Mother left me in the trailer while she worked at the lightbulb factory in Bodie. Sometimes I get misty eyed about those days back then when I thought that America was American property and that nobody would ever take it away from us. What an incredible country! All ours, to do with as we pleased. Remember how you learned in school that we bought chunks of America for nothing, some beads? Now the aliens have it and I'm my own baby. It's bad some days. I get headaches thinking about how the spaceship lights cut through my head and made it throb while all the blue alien men made love to me against my will and got me pregnanter than a sow. And there I was fifty-two years old and living in Bodie with Mr. Jung. Only a few minutes went by in the spaceship up there before I had triplets. All of them looking like me. Then they put me to sleep back in my bed on earth, but when I woke up I was a pretty young lady again. And it was the middle of the night and Mother still hadn't come home from the lightbulb factory and it was very dark and nobody was packing lightbulbs at that time of night. Right away I took a shower to get the birth stuff off me. It was like car oil. It took a lot of soap and a long time. While I was in the shower I heard a thumping outside that scared the holy bejesus out of me and so I sat down in the shower and cried about everything. About my two lost space sisters who were me, too. Where were they? Why weren't they here helping me against whatever it was that was thumping outside in the desert? Where was Mother? Who was I now? What had happened to my middle-aged self lying sleeping next to Mr. Jung in Bodie, that woman the aliens kidnapped in the first place? My God, I was so confused, so sure that no one would believe me, that I decided right then, right there in that trailer, that my name was Jackie Kennedy and nobody could ever hurt me. I had the feet to fit the part. These big alien feet on my little body. And I was kind of cute, good ass, good tits, so there was that, too. So I said to myself, Jackie, get out of that shower and be brave, it's just an alien or something in the yard, go shoo him off. So I did. I went and opened the door that Mother said to always leave locked tight and looked out into our sandy yard. There was an alien. Tall, blue, luminous, you knew him well. He was the ringleader who had made me be born from the older woman I was before, see? It was him. He looked like he was pining about something, so I said, What're you out there thumping in my yard for? Get outa here! But he stood there, passing his hands through his body and twirling his eyes and whopping his big dino-looking feet against the sand and other stuff like a nervous teenager. Off out in the cacti you could see his pretty spaceship, blue and red lights glowing. I looked far down the road to town. No lights, no Mother. What was I going to do? I said, Get outa here, you! Then I heard him say, in the voice of our late president, I heard him say, Jackie, my darling? It was John. It was the King of Camelot. I felt dizzy and thought the world was coming to an end in some insane knot of stories. I said, This is death. This is the way you die. In total confusion. Having no idea what's up, what's down, what's anything. And there I was, saying back to him, Yes, John? Jackie, come to me, he said. Of course, I said, and did. And then we went to his spaceship and off we shot into the night. Sometimes I think I'm still gone with him. I don't know where, but

I imagine I'm still out there playing among the stars with that beautiful alien. I think, This isn't me. Me, I'm gone. Out there. With John. He smiles at me with all those glimmering alien teeth and steers from galaxy to galaxy and I dream of my lost sisters. That's what I get to thinking. It's not only a feeling. It's real. But, hell, it doesn't ever last very long and then there I am again having headaches and wondering if it was really my fault Mr. Jung left me and thinking why don't I do something really extravagant like go to a casino all the way over in Louisiana just to see what there is to see?

Imagine running into Venus the night she lands the jackpot. Brother, I was riding the tiger. As for Nicky, why say good-bye? He'd said his piece and let me go. I wasn't going to run back and ask any more questions or take any more chances. That was over and done.

On my advice Venus gave back the one-million-dollar check and instead took fifty grand in cash, paid all her state and federal taxes up front, and took the rest in another check for six hundred eleven thousand dollars. We wouldn't have any tax authorities on our ass and the fifty big ones would get us started.

There was no way I could talk her out of riding back to her motel with these two old people, though. Some friends of hers. No telling where she'd picked them up. No telling what they were up to, either.

They had an Imperial that had seen much better days and was parked at least two miles from the casino, meaning we had to walk forever out there in that wild wind in the dark to get to it. But it got us back to town in one piece, and then we went into Venus's motel room with some Scotch while the storm did its thing. Rain flew hard and the pool chairs and tables got flung into the green-glowing water, which was full of angry waves that popped up and splashed all over creation.

"Old motels go down first," I said.

"They sure do," said the old guy, Grover.

He'd spent most of his life fondling himself. But his wife, Emma, didn't say anything, like she'd given up trying to stop it.

Venus paced awhile from the bed to the window and back, then sat down and cried her eyes out. Making lots of noise, carrying on.

Emma went and hugged her.

Enough of that. I said, "More ice. Give me a hand, Grover?"

"Sure, bud."

Outside, the night air was full of flying drink cans, plastic bottles, dirt, newspapers. The ice machine was six or seven rooms down.

"Kind of like war out here," I said.

"Lost our Nathan in 'Nam. He was planning on the seminary."

"What?"

"Lost our only son in Vietnam," he yelled.

I looked at him. "My brother, Paul, too."

"Tell you what, though," he said.

"What?"

"Nathan and Paul, if they were here?"

"Yeah, what?"

"They would tell us to get back into the room now."

The ice bucket got sucked out of my hands.

"Lord!" Grover cried. He ran and flung open the door and jumped inside with the ladies and the fifty grand in cash and the check.

I stood by the ice machine a few minutes watching the late-night highway traffic, people heading here and there like nothing was wrong.

Then there was a long, hair-raising creaking sound, followed by a heavy rushing like a jillion birds going into flight, and then the ground shuddered as a giant oak crashed across the pool with a kick-ass *ka-boom*.

I sprinted for the room.

The others were sitting on the bed, waiting calmly.

"Grab the mattress and use it for protection!" I told them.

Nobody moved.

Grover wore a light smile. "What's the big deal?"

It was like he'd taken drugs in the one minute I'd stayed outside.

"Got to be a goddamn tornado!"

"Nah. Only some wind. Be over soon."

"That's right, we've been in lots of these," said Emma.

What was this? I smelled the air for marijuana. I looked around for pills. Or had these people escaped from an institution?

"Grover?" I said.

"Yes, Carl?"

"These walls are made of paper. They won't hold."

"Probably not."

"Don't expect they will," Emma threw in.

"Relax," said Venus. Her voice was metallic, like people who have a talking gizmo in their throat. "Nothing's going to get us."

I swear the walls moved. The air conditioner was ready to blow into the room. The lights dimmed to brown. Sharp whistling came and went.

"What's wrong with you people?" I hollered.

Venus said, "Park it, Stein. You're making everybody nervous."

"That's right," Emma said.

"A little wind," said Grover. "Be over in a minute. Get a grip."

Grip?

Then I felt very tired. Like all my energy had just been torn away. Thought, Maybe it is better to give up and just take what's coming. No dumber than anything else, right?

I started toward a chair by the window unit to sit and rest. Then I took another look at the throbbing air conditioner and changed course for the bathroom, put the toilet lid down and parked myself back there.

Puffs of wind came straight out of the walls. Any second and it'd all be over. I could see the cash and the check flying up to forty thousand feet. Then to a hundred thousand feet. And off into outer space.

Then it went black.

It was like some movie where the lights go out and there's a commotion, people jumping around and knocking things over, and then the lights come back on and everything is in a different place and everybody is somewhere else. That's what happened. And the Big Winner was gone, red purse and all.

"Where's Venus?" I shouted. "Where's the money?"

The old folks stared at me. "We don't know," he said.

The door opened as I reached for it, slammed into the wall, broke from one hinge. Venus was out by the fallen oak with her purse flying from her neck. Her long black hair swirled in the green motel spotlights.

"For Jesus' sake, save her!" the old woman cried.

"What the hell did you let her go out for!"

Grover got up. "You can't talk to my Emma like that!"

I reached back and popped his brown cheek. He dropped slowly, not quite knocked out, a green and red mess dangling from his nose.

"Baby, my baby," she said.

"It's all right, Mama," he said.

He sagged into a chair.

I got out there to Venus. "Get back inside!"

"Is all that money really mine?"

I pulled on her arm. "We have to go in."

"You're going to try to get my money."

"I'm trying to get you inside before we both get killed."

"You're going to try. I'll let you try, though. So I can show you wrong from right. No one's ever shown you wrong from right, Carl."

"I'm not going to try!"

"Yes, you will. Because you're Carl Stein and Carl Stein does that to people for a living. But I'll show you."

"Show me what?"

"That you don't have to be Carl Stein. You can be someone else."

Enough bullshit. I grabbed her and hurried her stumbling to the room. Put her on the bed, where she started saying no one had the right to bring her in from the storm when she damn well hadn't been ready and who was I to be helping her when she didn't want any help! Emma threw in with her and then Grover started in again, but in another voice, like the storm had kicked him in the head again, changed him into someone else.

"Who are you to try to stop the clocks of destiny?" he shouted.

"Who are you against this? Against the tide of history and men's ancient travails? Remain calm. Have dignity! Have courage in the face of your demise, I tell you! Do not fear death."

His eyes rolled back and he thrust his hands up high and turned a circle. Emma pranced on the carpet as if she, too, had been possessed, raising and dropping her dress. "Tell him, Grover! Tell him!"

Grover hollered, "For, behold, the day cometh that shall burn as an oven, and all the proud, yea, and all that do wickedly, shall be stubble. And the day that cometh shall burn them up, saith the Lord of hosts, that it shall leave them neither root nor branch."

He grabbed his crotch and pulled up hard.

I raised my fist to hit him again. He backed away.

Venus lay on the bed, watching like a sleepy child.

What was that about wanting to save me? I didn't like the sound of it. Ah, but this was a lot of dough right here within reach, the other side of me said, so what difference did it make what she tried to do to me?

Grover bellowed more things in weird tongues as around and around he spun with Emma in his arms. Venus smiled at them.

I guarded the broken door, listened to the howling.

It seemed a lifetime passed, or maybe several, before the old folks finally wore themselves out with their insanity and collapsed onto the bed. His cheek was puffed, blue. Her dress was torn up one side.

Venus, trapped in a daze, stared at the rattling window.

"You want a drink?" I called.

She didn't answer.

I got the bottle and drank for the both of us, my back against the shuddering door, and worried through the rest of the storm.

After a lot of cajoling I got Venus to leave the old folks sleeping at the motel once the wind and rain had died down and the sun had come up in the nasty, tired-out sky. We took her hail-dimpled Impala back to my place. We'd go back for her friends later, I lied, after we'd rested.

I went into the kitchen, got a butcher knife, and started hacking at the ice that'd built up in the freezer. It was hard as granite.

Venus sat on a stool. "What's in there?"

"Give me a minute."

"What are we going to do with ourselves now, Carl?"

I stopped. "What?"

"There are big decisions to be made. I have money now."

She patted that red purse sitting on her lap like a throw pillow.

"For the moment you can watch me until I'm done here," I said. "Then you can walk if you want to walk. But let me finish here first."

She let a half smile come, like she liked tough stuff.

"So what's in there?"

I chopped. Two or three minutes went by.

"I can't believe you punched Grover!"

"He was out of his mind."

"What if they wake up dead?"

I looked at her again. Pointing the knife at her without thinking, then lowering it. "Who are they, anyway?"

"I have no idea."

"No idea?"

"They were just there. By the pool. Wanting to go to the casino, so I went with them. Seemed friendly."

"Cult people or something. Circling before the hit."

"Come on!"

"I'm telling you. Circling like vultures. They'd have your money in a flash. Can't you see that?"

"I don't think so."

"Suit yourself."

I turned back to hacking the ice.

She shuffled in to the living room, turned the TV on loud.

A few more stabs and then I had it. The big black-eyed-peas box with the bank bag and their money. I took it in to her. She had stretched out on the recliner and held the remote in her hand like a gun to be fired.

"Something I owe you," I said. "Maybe we can call it settled now."

She put down the zapper and looked into the bag. "What's this?"

"Money from the safe."

She said nothing.

"What I did was wrong," I said.

"You're saying you were wrong?"

"It was foolishness. Taking advantage of people. Running roughshod over everything we had. Even after May died. Now I can set it right."

"Like it didn't happen?"

"No. It did happen. But now maybe we can forget it."

"You want me to forgive you?"

"Up to you."

She looked at the storm report on the TV but didn't say one way or the other.

Then I asked, "So where's Blalock?"

"Puerto Azul, I suspect."

"What happened?"

"Everything." She took out the cash and counted it, sort of. "It's almost all here." Then she sniffed it. "Smells like vanilla."

I looked back into the kitchen. The freezer was still open. At the edge stood an ice-cream carton I'd destroyed to get at the black-eyed-peas box.

I slouched on the couch. It was like a damp sponge. And thought, Here I am. In this room with a jackpot queen and trying to get her bundle. Who else in the world was doing what I was right then? Not a soul, and I liked the feeling.

"I had to get out of there," she said. "I was thinking of May all the time and how the road might be an answer to my pain. Puerto Azul pinned me down and I was sure I was drowning myself in that deep blue bay from staring at it drunk every day. Because that's all we did. Drink. It took me forever to get up the willpower to go, though. I'd slipped down deep. But then one day I was able to do it, go. I don't know how. Like walking up out of the bottom of the ocean."

I stared at the ceiling light. The cover was full of dead bugs. I remember thinking, All right, we've heard the sad tale, so what now?

"It's over with Blalock, then?"

"I don't know."

"All right."

"All right what?"

"I mean, I understand. You're going to see about him later."

"Or not." She turned off the TV. "It is very strange to be here with you, Carl. But then it's like I can finally talk."

"That's good."

"I guess it is."

"Sure it is."

"You're right," she said, then popped the recliner back up so hard it threw her on to her big feet. "You know what May would say to us?"

"What?"

"To live our lives now. Grab them and live them. They're our lives, remember. And we've got hundreds of thousands of dollars to play with. What're we sitting here feeling sad and gloomy for? Jesus Christ!"

I smiled and felt like hundreds of thousands of dollars myself.

"You don't live your life like you have a gun to your head then you're not alive, Carl. You're stone-cold dead."

She fired the TV remote at me. She was grinning like she'd just figured out everything there was to know in this world.

There was a clunk in the kitchen. The ice cream had hit the floor.

I had her saying we. I had her saying we and hundreds of thousands of dollars all in the same sentence, too. My heart raced, and I stood up and grabbed on to her hard, like maybe she was going to blow away if I didn't leap. It made her laugh, a nice womanly laugh, and she was soft and easy in my arms.

I'd never say it outright to anyone, but I knew I'd miss Nicky when a quiet time came along. It's one of the great sad things, ain't it? The one Ma told me about that time long ago when she sat me down on the porch in the orange Albuquerque evening and said, "You have a left hand and a right hand. Look at them." I looked at them. Both dry and red but huge. Like hers. Then I looked at her and she said, "You'll have only so many real friends in a lifetime and how many do you think it'll be?" I flashed her ten, twenty, thirty, and she laughed. Said, "Take your right hand and hold it up," and I did. Said, "Hold up one finger, then one more." There were two fingers now and I looked at her and she looked at me and then we looked out at the brown yard. Then she said, "Maybe." Maybe one. If you were real lucky, two. I'd miss Nicky some. Then get past it fast, like always, like I did Blalock, fast as the road carried me away.

We hugged and both enjoyed the hugging, and then it was over. She sat back down on the recliner as if we could take as long as we wanted to decide what next.

I said, "I wonder what Blalock would say to all this. Getting most of his money back, finding out his wife has just won the big jackpot, everything. Going to call him?"

She kicked back flat again. "Can I tell you a story, Carl?"

There was a sticky sweetness in her voice, but then you have to let them talk the way they want to talk when they want to talk. "Sure."

"The first summer Carl and I were married it was so hot and dry you couldn't get the hard white light out of your eyes. One night I sat up in the bed with my eyes burning and stinging and called for Blalock, but he'd already gotten up and gone to work like he'd do in the middle of the night sometimes to avoid the heat. We were living in town then and everybody's windows were always open. There was a young girl who lived next door and she heard me and came outside in her gown and over to the window and asked what she could do to help. She was maybe twelve. Then I realized I'd been dreaming my pain, that there wasn't anything wrong with my eyes except being afraid of all that light. I told her that I'd only had a nightmare and thanks for coming to see me but that she ought to get home, and she said she had dreams, too, that woke her up and got her upset and wanted to know what mine'd been about. So I told her. About being in a world where the lights never ever go out. And she said, 'I have that one all the time. It's okay. Everybody here has that one. Maybe you ought to wear sunglasses to bed.' We laughed and held hands. There was a universe of lightning bugs out flying and we watched them thinking they were the prettiest things that'd ever been created."

I studied the bugs in the ceiling light again.

"Well, of course, the next day that hard white light was right back and cutting through the top of my head while I was out doing errands. But when I got back about lunchtime I saw that girl sitting on her porch by herself. I knew something wasn't right and went over there."

"I'm going to take a shower now."

"But I'm talking."

"Talk to me in the shower. Got to clean up."

I undressed, started my shower.

When she didn't come in I called, "Where are you?"

"In the middle of my story, damn it."

She was right there. I yanked the curtain back. She had her blouse off. Just the skirt on. Her tits pointing right at me.

"Run a lady a bath."

I jammed that drain shut, cut the shower off and let the faucet run. Everything was speeding up.

She finished undressing and opened the curtain. "Make room."

I got down by the faucet, knees to chest, left her the rest. She got right in, put those long legs right around me, slid down low.

"You have to listen to the end," she said.

I cut off the flow, leaned back the best I could. It was a small cheap-ass tub and water splashed onto the floor. I saw her blue string underwear lying there on her skirt.

"So I went over and said, 'What're you doing, Georgette?' That was her name. The saddest child who ever lived. I pulled on her chin, made her look at me. I wish I hadn't, though. She'd aged ten years."

"What happened?"

"Every stick of furniture in the house was gone. There weren't any papers or anything. Dead empty. Just the buckled hardwood floors, shadows of pictures on the walls. Everything gone."

"Bastards."

"I can't fathom why they did that. How parents could do that to their own child."

"White trash bastards."

"You know, it was her idea to walk me through the house and show me the emptiness. She took my hand and led me through. Like walking through a tomb. God, it still makes me sick."

"What happened to her?"

Venus got water into her hands and brought them up and pitched the water onto her face, leaned back and eyeballed the sagging ceiling tiles.

"I took her home and she stayed with us a couple of days and then out of the blue our phone rang and it was some relative of hers from up in Oklahoma, and then a couple of days later this white-haired older man in an expensive car came and picked her up and took her away.

"I got letters all through her high school years and pictures of her getting more gorgeous by the minute. Then more letters and more pictures of her getting even prettier when she went off to California to be in the movies. Then she began calling me on the phone when things started going kind of nutty out there. She went from one man to the next and none of them was kind to her. It was a nasty cycle of drinking and drugs and sometimes getting hurt very bad, and then one year I didn't hear anything more. Not a word. It's been fourteen years. Nothing."

I didn't know what to say.

"She was as beautiful as May."

I reached over and ran a hand up and down one of those soft legs. "My God, Venus."

"What?" she asked.

"It's a terrible thing."

She reached down and took my hand off her leg and gave it back to me. I didn't say anything, let it drop into the water.

She said, "You remember our first run-in at the casino? I went home to Red Rock after that. Not quite sure why, though, until I got there and realized I'd wanted to see if Carl had maybe come back from Mexico. And he had. Only it was the strangest thing. The house had been emptied. Not only had he come back, he'd packed up everything and taken off. And I thought, Well, it's my turn now to be the one abandoned, isn't it?"

"Like with the girl," I said.

"He'd closed the books. Which was always his way, everything neat and tidied, like he kept that damn store of his. All right, I was the one who pulled out of our lives down there in Mexico. But it was way too soon for him to be suddenly rising out of his own fog and coming back to Texas to shut everything down. Feels like he did it all in a big rush."

"He must think you're not coming back."

"I don't know what he thinks."

"If I know Carl he was shutting a door that maybe you'd left open a little. It'd be easier for him that way, I mean."

"You don't know Carl. If you had, you'd never have stolen from him. Am I right?"

I went ahead and got out. She stretched out, slid down.

I dried and got my trousers on, sat on the bed.

"But I've been thinking," she said, "that it doesn't have to be this way. I mean, things don't have to turn out nasty every time. I won the jackpot. Isn't that proof enough? That chance is alive and well?"

There was a suck and splash and in she came.

"Don't you think so?" she asked.

I went to get a shirt out of the closet.

She followed me. "Well?"

I looked at her naked and dripping on the carpet in my closet.

"Sure, Venus. Chance is alive and well."

"Things can be good. Turn out good."

"Yes they can."

"In that case, I want to go to Mexico again."

"You said it was all you could do to get out of there."

"I don't mean down where he is. But out in the desert. Out in the light. Out where it's dry. Where it's dry land for as far as you can see. And sit out there enjoying sitting on my money and preserving the goodness it's created. Until I figure out what I'm going to do."

"Let's think about that."

"What's there to think about? That's where I'm going."

There was a knock on the door.

"Who is it?" I called.

"Lisa."

"Who?" Venus asked me.

"Neighbor. Get something on."

I went and opened up. Lisa'd been crying.

"Can I come in?"

"Well, I have company and —"

She pushed past me. "Someone broke into my apartment in the night during the storm." She hit the couch, huffed. "Got a beer?"

"Out of beer. Somebody threaten you?"

"Threaten? I slept through the whole thing? Me, fat stupid Lisa!" She slapped her forehead.

I thought of Nicky. "Did you call the cops?"

"Nah, what can they do?"

"What did they take?"

"All my mirrors. Why would someone want to take Lisa's mirrors, Carl?" She started sobbing. "Why'd they do that to me? Jesus Christ!"

I got on the couch, put my arm around her. Who would take a girl's mirrors? "We'll find those mirrors," I announced.

She brightened like the sun popping out. "Yeah? How?"

"Well . . ."

Venus came out in just a towel.

Lisa lifted my arm off, sat up. "Oh. Oh, hello there."

"Hi. I'm Venus."

"Nice to meet you. I'm Lisa."

"Sorry about your mirrors."

Then Lisa stopped blubbering and looked Venus up and down trying to figure out who she was. "Oh, I can make more. What a storm, huh?"

"So, Carl, how're you going to find the mirrors?" Venus asked.

"Don't worry," Lisa said. "They'll show up."

"Show up? They've been stolen," said Venus.

"Well, some of them. One or two. Maybe one."

"One? I don't get it."

I did. There hadn't been any break-in or anything. She'd thought that I was alone and had decided to make a play for me, something.

"Well, Lisa," I said. "I'm going to be leaving Iona today."

"Like for good?"

"Yeah, back on the road. Got another job."

"Where?"

"Del Rio, Texas," I said, making it up.

"Del Rio? God."

"It's a job."

"Doing what?"

"Running a boys' club," said Venus.

I looked at Venus. Where'd that come from?

Lisa said, "Boys' club? That doesn't sound like you, Carl."

"He'll be great at it," said Venus. "Helping others in need."

"Whatever," I said. "Lisa, want me to come see if I can't fix your door lock before we leave?"

"Go have a good time in Del Rio. You can keep the mirror."

It was right there on the wall, no bigger than a paperback.

"You made that?" Venus asked, going to it.

"I can make you one, too, if you want."

"Yeah?" Venus took it off the wall and looked into it. Turned it right and left, brought it close to her face, held it far away. "You can see yourself again and again. How many times is that?"

"Yeah, it's special," I said.

Lisa said, "The number is twelve."

"Twelve of me? That's wild. All so tiny . . ."

"That's right," Lisa said. "Every one you. Through time, too."

"So, did you get robbed or not?" I asked.

"Guess not."

"Yeah, she guesses not," Venus echoed. "So let's drop it, Carl."

"You two are crazy," I said.

"How far is it to Del Rio?" Lisa asked.

"Why don't you come with us?" asked Venus.

Time to take charge again. "Lisa, go back to your apartment and your life. Venus and I are going to Del Rio. I'm sorry."

"Hey, I wouldn't go to Del Rio if you paid me ten thousand dollars! Good of you to invite me, though, ma'am, but I'm not a destitute idiot. I have a life, yes, Lisa Joyner has a life. Of my own. I make mirrors and sell them. That's what I do when I'm not wiring houses or offices. And I'm going to get a white dog and name her Rabbit. So, you see, you didn't have to invite me to Del Rio. In fact, I bet you did that because you'd rather not be alone with him during the next phase of his game."

"A dog named Rabbit. I like that," Venus said.

"I've got to pack, Lisa," I said.

"Lisa's leaving," Lisa said.

"It's been nice knowing you."

"Who says we know each other? But you can keep the mirror."

"I will."

"No you won't, but that's all right. Pleased to have met you, ma'am."

Venus could've been her mother. "Lisa, I'm sorry."

"I could believe you, ma'am. I really could."

Then she went out into the daylight, leaving the door open.

I went and shut it and said, "I'll get packed."

Venus didn't say anything, climbed onto the recliner and found a home-repair show to watch. They were explaining how to change a door lock.

First, though, I drank my one last beer in the kitchen. Tried to convince myself that I hadn't hurt Lisa bad. I hadn't wanted to, but I had. So there I was.

When I went back into the living room Venus was gone. I looked in the bathroom, the closet, then back through the apartment. No Venus.

Then she grabbed me from behind. "Hey!"

I pulled free. "What the hell?"

She had put on clean clothes, makeup, nice shoes. "Let's go."

"Where?"

"Down into the Mexican badland desert. See what there is to see."

The deal was starting to spin away from me. She was thinking fast and I was going to have to speed up or lose her.

"We don't have to decide everything right now."

"But my mind is set. And I'm the Million Dollar Lady, remember?"

I finished gathering up my junk. Stuck that mirror in with a few clothes and left the rest behind. Including the Falcon. Plunged head-first into a rich new world.

It was five after ten in the morning when Venus paid cash for the new Suburban. Like we were a family and had kids. The dealer must've thought we were a mirage. Until she put down those new bills.

"I've decided you're right," she said as she drove off the lot, leaving her old Impala parked by the entrance. "Those old people, the Hudspeths? They were definitely up to something."

"I'm telling you."

"So we're going to leave them put."

"Fine with me."

"I liked Emma, though. She made me think of Mama. Of what I always thought my mama would be like had she lived to be older."

"When did your ma die?"

"I was twelve. Up there where you once cut trees in the Ozarks. Backwoods. We spun off the road and flipped. Dad died next to her. And there I sat in the backseat unable to move not because I was hurt but because my life had crashed. It was hours before anybody saw the car off in the trees and stopped. In the night. An old man and his wife. Kind of like the Hudspeths. Weird. They took me to go get the police while my dead parents lay out there in the dark. I sat up front between the old people and bawled and the woman hugged me and the old man said Bible verses."

I didn't know what to say, kept my trap shut. A woman was sure to have these spells, and my only job was to not make fun and thereby keep her trust. If that's what you could call the weak hold I had on her then.

She drove us out of town. Where the land went up some, I looked back at Iona below and how the river cut it in two. A freight train with a yellow engine snaked along the far bank. In my mind I put a penny on the track like back in Albuquerque and ran back into the head-high weeds to wait for it to be flattened. Sometimes you didn't find it after, though.

"Open the glove," she commanded.

I don't know how, but in there was an unused map of Mexico.

"How about that?" I said.

"How about that. Now, find the road to La Purísima. South of Saltillo. We hit Laredo, then Monterrey, then Saltillo, then La Purísima. Best motel in the desert there, Las Palmas."

"You know it?"

"Stayed there every trip down to the ocean." She ran down all the windows and the steamy day poured in. "Be navigator. Read the map."

I stabbed the button to make my window go back up, turned a vent so the cold air blew on my face. "How long's it going to take?"

"Who knows? Let's do like when we were kids!"

"Crossed the Mojave with Ma and my brother, Paul, once when I was a kid. But it scared the shit out of me. Being out there in the night."

"You, scared?"

I slept and woke a few minutes and slept again and let her drive. I dreamed of having all those dollars to myself and the most astonishingly lovely woman who'd ever lived. Not Venus. Not May. But Georgette. The abandoned babe. And all we did was make love on the floors of that emptied-out house in Red Rock while the white light outside burned up the earth and the wind blew and blew. When I woke up the last time we were squealing down a mountain road in the middle of another day.

Venus was flooring it to pass a truck. "My thirty-ninth one. Thirty-nine gasoline trucks. How many gas trucks can there be in Mexico?"

Her eyes had black crescents under them. We were about halfway around the truck. Bastard was speeding up.

"Honk at him," I told her.

"They honk back."

"Honk!"

She honked and it got stuck, but the idiot let us pass. The horn blew on and on.

"A jillion-dollar jackpot and I get a bad horn!"

She pounded her fist on the horn. It stopped.

"More like it. Don't touch it now. Not for anything."

We were coming off a steep ridge into a valley full of cacti, a brown-green ocean of nothing but heat and dust and emptiness.

"La Purísima's out there!" she shouted.

"Yeah?"

She chucked the map into the back. "Only a couple of hours to go. We'll get bungalow seven, be in the pool before dark."

I stared out at the road running straight as a rail to the end of the world, wondering how we'd gotten there so fast. Like she'd taken us through some time tunnel. But I didn't say it.

Grover Hudspeth

Now what of sex and the intellect? Does one not shape the other? Does one not have a whip hand over the other? Nothing new here, my fellow inmates, indeed. But, I ask you, is there a way to break the bond? To liberate the man, the woman? Mahatma Gandhi foreswore meat in order to calm those fires and to feed the heart and mind with other things. And yet it is a vow not easily kept. One's suffering may or may not lead to an enlightened state. I therefore wish to argue — gentlemen, ladies, doctors, nurses, guards, wardens, people at large — that there is nothing whatsoever wrong with touching yourself, so long as you continue, simultaneously, to reflect profoundly upon the great matters, upon the vitality of life, of the ring of pretty women's shoes through deeply shadowed alleys in summer, of winning just a little sweet something at the blackjack table each time, nothing too big but not too small either, just a little quiet hundred bucks or so, of Everyman and Everywoman going his or her way toward unseen destinies while the sun hangs timeless overhead and clouds boat this way and that, of gentle rain atop the roofs of all mental institutions in which great men and great women lie quietly as smells of cafeteria-style food waft through the corridors and through white-painted cell bars and into hairy nostrils, smells of corn and peas and chicken-fried steak and mashed potatoes and gravy and Jell-O, of the sleek beauty of an instant erection, of the corralled beast that flings itself against the railing and bursts forth into the windy freedom of the endless prairie, of the gracious blow one delivers with anything at hand to the head of the nearest guard in order to take him or her out of his or her misery here in such low-paid employment, that is to say, baby-sitting such infantile madmen and madwomen as us, we the utterly confused, the totally confounded, the miserable victims of the eternal stretching machine of the mind, pulling first this way and then that way and then both ways at the same time until we are mere parts, morsels, detached limbs with nothing to lose but our insanity, our will to fight, our will to rise to and deliver the coup de grâce to the nearest authority and flee back into the world given to us as our birthright, whether clear of mind or not clear of mind, whether pure of heart or sinful, whether right or wrong, our world for the taking, if only you will rise with your forks, with your knives, and deliver the blow! Lo, even now they hunker, afraid! Rise, rise, rise! Rise and charge them! Tomorrow we will sail the boundless sea! Rise, children, rise!

Carl Blalock

A speedboat swings into Pullman's ocean pool and cuts its motor. There are three women aboard in black evening dresses. They don't see us in the shadows of the mango tree and carry on as if they have every right to be there. One of them looks like May, another like Venus, the third like Elena. I want to hail them. But Pullman shrinks down on his chair, in no mood. So I wait, listening to the goddesses chatter.

"I'm telling you, this place has been abandoned for years! Back in the old days there were jet-set parties here. Frank Sinatra would sing beside a white piano, right over there! I even danced with him once!"

It is the one who looks like Elena, somehow speaking loud American, shading her eyes and pointing at us. I am sure she can see us.

"Frank Sinatra?" It is Venus. "Who needs Sinatra when you've got Carl Blalock! Now there's a man for you! He didn't have to sing!"

May stands up, undoes something at her shoulders, and her gown falls. She stretches, naked in the light, and flings herself into the water.

Elena and Venus stare at her swimming down. Pullman closes his eyes. I wait for May to come back up. But she doesn't. The women in the boat wait. I try hard to see her in the pool, but the light shimmers.

"If only we could swim that way," says Venus. "She is a fish."

"Do you want to try it with me?" Elena says. "She will be there if we swim down to her and she will show us what to do."

"Do you think so?"

Then Elena drops her dress, lifts her brown arms, and plunges in. Venus bends over the back of the boat, following her with her eyes. I call my wife's name and she looks up. She hears something, but she does not see me. Pullman snores lightly. I want Venus to take off the dress and stand there in the sun. I do not want her to go into the water yet. I call her name again. But now the others have come back up.

"Did you see what I saw?" May cries. "Did you see it, Elena?"

"Oh, yes!" she answers.

They are close together in the water.

"What is it?" Venus asks. "What did you see?"

"Come look!" May cries.

Venus disrobes in an instant. I stand up. She dives in and the light scatters and I cannot see her. The others kick the turquoise water and giggle and swim around as the boat bobs on deep swells.

"It's a long way down there," Elena says.

"She'll make it. She's strong. She'll see it all right!"

I go to the edge of the pool. They don't see me, and then I disrobe and dive in. All is liquid light and I swim toward the white flash of Venus's body, far below, down where the pool ends and plunges off a sea cliff. Soon, though, I lose her and my ears fill with pain. Where is she going? What is there to see? I turn to go back up, but there she is swimming next to me. She is pointing and I can see something far below where the cliff reaches the bottom. My ears stop hurting. I don't need to breathe. She holds my hand and we swim toward this deep place. I'm not afraid. She speaks to me without words and then I see that the deeper we go, the more light there is, bands of color, and clouds of fish again. Then, far below, we can see the bottom of the speedboat, and it is as if we are rising slowly to it. We kick hard and she speaks to me without words, saying, Swim hard with me. We swim with all our strength and burst out into the air.

"Did you see that, Carl Blalock?" she shouts.

I pull her to me and hold her in the water.

"We have to do it again, and again!" May yells.

She seizes Elena's hand and they dive down. Venus and I watch them. They go down through the shifting colors. Venus and I look into each other's eyes and see the magic of the pool in them reflecting back in a million shiny pieces that waver and blend and make a universe of hope.

"You know, Carl, I didn't go to China."

We had finished our supper and gone into his library.

"Where, then?" I said.

"To the moon."

"Pardon?"

"To a place where you come face-to-face with the unimaginable. Some of the astronauts found God on the moon. In that infinite timelessness. The deserts of China and the moon are one and the same."

"You found God?"

"God? Not at all. But something maybe more powerful."

Then I remembered. "I dreamed you phoned me from China."

"From the moon? Marvelous!"

He tilted back his head and the lamplight made his eyes sparkle.

"You were lying in an opium den," I said. "That's what it seemed like. Phoning me from there and telling me to get on with my life."

He leaned forward. "What, opium? Hardly! But I was sick with a stomach ailment for a long time in a place that had a share of addicts and whatnot, an old customs post at a frontier so ancient no one knew the name of it anymore, what purpose it served. Far out in the desert where there was a constant wind and the air was choked with gray dust."

"That was the place . . ."

"Was it? Everyone's eyes were red from the dust and we kept bumping into each other in the hallways of the post and shouting at each other in different languages. I had come to see the desert and you couldn't take a step out the door without risking your life. You could have been blown away and no one would have given it a thought.

"The wind howled like someone's eternal suffering. The sun neither rose nor set and there was no way to tell time. I slept curled up under a greasy blanket and dreamed of the coolness of my ocean pool. When I awoke I would make my way to a tiny room where a woman with a huge round face made tea and gave me bread. The tea was red as blood, and I chewed the tasteless bread for hours, grinding the grit of the desert with it. The sour drink made my stomach knot more than before, and I would hurry back to my sleeping spot and lie beneath my cover.

"Men with stringy beards would look at me, come and hold candles over me, shout words in their languages, give me a kick now and then. I quit replying after a while. Quit going to have the tea and bread. Quit moving and imagined that I had found the right place to die, a wasteland where the wind never stopped and burly men were always trying to provoke you into a fight with knives or rocks. Time after time they gave me a boot in the gut. I rolled over and ignored them.

"Until one of them grabbed me like an empty sack and held me up off the floor and shook me. 'Land's sakes, man!' he hollered into my face. 'Are you going to lie there and die? Is that what you're doing?' He had a British accent, huge buttery cheeks, and the breath of something dead. I couldn't answer, only stared into his bloodshot blue eyes. He shook me until I could be shaken no more, and then I bellowed into his sweat-drenched face, 'Let go of me, you damn idiot! Let go of me!'

"I fell like a stone. Only when the falling should have stopped, it didn't. It kept going and I with it. Down and down into some infernal hole with the gray sand of the East filling in atop me. I cried out in this nightmare for the British officer to save me. 'Indeed, that won't do!' I heard him say. 'Courage, man, courage!' I cursed him and bellowed and swiped at the sand as angry as I've ever been in my life. "Right-o!' I heard him shout. 'That's the spirit! Fight it, old boy! Bloody fight it!'

"And I did. I started to swim up through the sand, which then became as smooth and easy as water. I swam and swam, higher and higher, and then I broke free, into my blanket. I sat up. Nearby some men were squatting in a circle arguing with each other over a card game. Wood-fire smoke hung in the air. The wind had stopped and you could hear everything, voices, footsteps, coughing, laughter. Quickly, I made my way through the halls and outside into the light, which was dim and seemed to come from all directions. Then, to one side, colors appeared, pink and orange and yellow. Nearby, the old woman who'd fed me poison was laughing, her broken teeth showing, and I laughed with her as we shaded our eyes and watched the sun roar up. Then she pointed into the desert and said, in shy English, 'Moon, mister. Welcome moon!'

"There was no one else outside but us, and do you know I found her attractive? That dumpling? I found her intensely desirable and I took her hand and we walked straight for the sun. At first she laughed, but then she saw I was serious and began to be the one who tugged us along, on out into the open, through all the sculpted swirls of sand, on and on. I don't know how long we walked, always in silence, stopping at the same time to see the same shape or color, starting again at the same moment. But it seemed a great time passed before we arrived back and found a few of the men standing outside the customs post, as if waiting for us. I thought there would be trouble. But they were all smiling, and some clapped me on the back and shouted what had to be vulgarities. I knew what they were saying and looked at the woman. She was embarrassed and hid her face with her scarf and went inside to work. The men laughed and tramped inside, too.

"It was getting fiercely hot. I stood there and realized that to wander out into the middle of nowhere as I had done in order to die in that abstract place, out where life hardly had any meaning at all amid the furious elements, would be to go the way of sand, unseen. You would not have known, and who else would have cared? So it would be the ultimate example of futility and selfishness. This was clear to me finally.

"But most important, Carl, more important than that, I knew I needed to tell you this story. To hold one more session in our own *Thousand and One Nights*. Do you see?"

"Of course I do."

"Do you? Do you see that I learned of the mortal danger of allowing sorrow to steal my life away from me, seize it for fifty years, keep me from believing in anything but the memory of the nights out on the yacht with Gloria? For fifty-one and a half years, holding me prisoner. In a cell, this mansion, where even the embraces of the maids who came into my bed only brought back more details of waiting for Gloria's body to rise.

"That night in the desert I saw more stars than I'd ever seen in one night, an ocean of them, of every color. I lay on the cold ground and swam in the stars and felt warmed to my bones. Knowing that I had seen something out there, even in this eighty-third year of my life. And it returned me here. To tell you. Completing the circle. Do you see?"

Pullman didn't ask what had become of Elena. I'm sure he guessed what had happened in his absence, but he left it alone. Then he hired a new girl, Maria, and again beauty flowed through the mansion. There were damp footprints on the tiles. There was the smell of lime and watermelon. She filled the rooms with blue hibiscus flowers.

I lingered there a number of days and nights, talking with him, walking with him in his garden, swimming with him in his pool. Thinking how it was like being with a father on whom I leaned for guidance and knowledge. I drank with him, and laughed with him, and rode about town in the beat-up jeep he'd always driven down there. He seemed to want to live at a hundred miles an hour now, and more than once he dragged me into nightclubs where we stayed until morning. Because there was no reason not to, I supposed. Because after, at dawn, weaving through the streets, he liked to take me down to the beach to see the fishermen rushing their boats out of the waves. Where a frenzied market began as we gazed into the holds of the boats at piles of creatures from the deep, some dead, but many still quite alive and looking out at the world. He always bought a few kilos of this and that and had me hold the bag all the way back up the mountain to the house. Where Maria would fix it up for our lunch while we drank more to chase away our hangovers and sat on his veranda trying to detect a breeze while the smell of fish cooking came to us from the back of the house and birds called in the jungle and anchor chains rattled as another ocean liner pulled into the bay to dispatch hordes of tourists into the city.

"Tell me again how there was nothing here when you came," I said.

"Only a couple of wooden shacks back over there where you could pull up and maybe sometimes get gasoline for your boat. Nothing else, no hotels, no stores, no palm-lined avenues, no airport."

"Now all this . . ."

"One thing has led to another. Don't think I didn't see it all the way it is now, though. I knew very well what I was doing."

"It's a great place. Pullman's city."

"Great . . . and out of control most of the time. I often feel like I'm in a fort up here in my house. That I've unleashed some strange forces that might turn on me at any time."

"Forces?"

"Jealous rabble. They've often risen up throughout history . . ."

"The government would protect you."

"You mean the oligarchs of the ruling party? You've got to be kidding. If trouble ever broke out here, they'd disappear in a second. They'd abandon me to the people. Who would steal every last thing I have. That's the way it is. And the people would be right to do it."

"How?"

"No man really deserves to amass all I have amassed, Carl. It's as if once the ball got rolling, there was no stopping it. Sure, a fortune is something you make. But there's a threshold to it. And once you get over that threshold, it snowballs. Money pours in. And then you don't know what to do with all of it."

"I could think of a few things," I said, laughing.

"Indeed you could. A boat, a house, a plane, another house, whatever. Easy. Then what? What if you still had millions? All right, some land, more land, some hotels. Then what? What if you still —"

"You're kidding, right?"

"Kidding?"

"Money is a burden?"

He frowned. "Don't laugh at this."

"I'm not."

"The money puts you in a prison and then you strive to get out of it the rest of your life."

"I don't think I'd feel that way."

"You would if you were to think about it."

"I don't know."

"I'm not asking you if you know, Carl. I'm telling you the way it is. Christ, sometimes you're pathetic."

"How am I pathetic?"

He waved me away, and that was the only time he ever did that.

I rose and went to bed. Fell to sleep easily, in spite of the harsh words. Perhaps because I'd already made up my mind to go.

I am lying in bed, exhausted from swimming in the ocean, when a crowd of children in white smocks runs in off the veranda and surrounds me. They are speaking many languages, arguing among themselves, and this goes on for a long time. Then one, a darling of a blonde, like a little May, steps forward and says in adult English, "The punishment for running away from your life will now be carried out. Do you have any last words?" I look at her green eyes and teased-up hair and shake my head no. She smiles sweetly, and I believe she and all the others are going to help me, lend me their tiny hands and guide me, point the way to go, rush along with me for a while, and then bid me farewell as I disappear into a warmly lit future. But then she screws up her mouth and spits on my face. One by one the others join in. Then they are all spitting on me. It goes on and on and I call out to Pullman as if my life were at stake. He does not hear me.

The next morning I told Pullman of my decision. Because something had spoken to me and said I, too, had come to a far place and had stood there too long not knowing how to advance, only to see that I, too, needed to set aside all the moments that led to May plunging into that hole, and all the moments that followed and brought destruction to all that I had with Venus, turn around and retrace my steps until I was back to someplace where I belonged.

But he surprised me again. Saying in a kind tone, softly, "Of course you can't go now, Carl. We're going to be busy, you and I. I'm not done with you at all."

"Busy?"

We were having breakfast by the ocean pool.

"Will you help me fix up my yacht? I want to take it out for cruises. We'll troll and enjoy ourselves. How's that sound?"

I stared at the slices of fruit on my plate. I knew without hesitation that I didn't want anything to do with reviving his yacht.

"Don't you like to fish?" he asked. "What's the matter?"

"Nothing."

Nothing more than the images of Gloria and May both alive and standing on the yacht in the sun running their fingers through their hair.

"Good," he said. "Then we'll get started right away."

Part of me fled the scene, went back to my house down the mountain. Not to stay there, but to pass through, grab clothes, see the bay a last time and hope the deep blue picture would stay sharp, and then to go back to dry Texas soil, mounds of shiny nails, piles of yellow lumber, and huge red-flocked Christmas trees. Where I would live again in the still-unsold house where Venus and I had spent all those years. Reading in the mail the names of the motels in other states where she had charged another room on our credit cards as she sped from place to place with no plan in mind, no return route. Waiting for weeks and then months and then halting the wait finally because what was the use. Going forth then like a man who suffers from not hunting to get myself a woman to take behind a candy-orange door on the back wing of the motel west of town where the sun would be setting, going straight down into the ground right there where I could see it happening as I watched from the window after I'd had sex with her. Maybe the nameless woman would call out to me from the bed and then maybe I'd go back to her and do it again with her and think about Mexico, Pullman, and the Pacific. And while I did if I was very lucky then maybe Venus would not take over that body beneath me and hold me.

"First, I'll see about getting the motor fixed," Pullman said. "You and I can do a lot of the rest. What do you think?"

I reached for my orange juice, which abruptly slid out of reach.

"Another one," said Pullman.

The glass bumped along, then dropped onto the rock deck.

"The ones that wake you up in the night are the worst," he said. "A strong man shaking your bed like a shoe box."

Maria came and slowly picked up the pieces of glass.

"I don't know much about boats, but it's in pretty bad shape," I said.

"Let's take a look. We'll have a list to start."

Pullman walked quickly, as if he were going to break into a run. Was this something else that'd come over him in China?

That night he told me, "In the first dream I had in China I am walking along a path in a forest of blue trees. Suddenly there is a tremendous light in my eyes. A great Buddha head blocks the path, giving out a light so strong I can neither go forward nor turn and run, only wait. And after a long time a skinny white boy takes my hand and says, 'Say hello to Buddha, mister. Then he'll let us by.' I say hello and Buddha's face changes to a cool blue and a door opens in the mouth. The path leads into a garden and we go along a trail of white pebbles."

I held this image like a precious stone and saw in its facets a world where the blue light would carry me like the ocean away from the shore, far enough and long enough that I would cease fearing the depths below.

He made her rise the first morning we worked on the boat.

"Do you still think about Venus?"

I stared at him. "Sometimes a lot."

"Gloria is waiting for me someplace."

I didn't know what to say. My mind filled with an image of snow falling in a forest and two men tramping along, small and bent, far below the towering trees. It was a light snow and there was no wind and the two men didn't talk because there was no longer any need for words.

Pullman went below deck. Came back with paint scrapers.

"Here. Let's do the railings first." He was shining with sweat.

Men he'd hired helped with the worst things. Fixing a big hole in the deck where someone had made a fire. Throwing out garbage, cleaning away the filth of years of disuse, scrubbing everything down.

"Where did you get it?" I asked.

"A Greek. Paid far too much. Nineteen forty-one. He'd brought it all the way from Piraeus, fleeing not just the war but the tax authorities. I spent a fortune for it, and then another to restore it. And for my efforts? It brought me only pain and death."

"Then why bring it back to life?"

"I intend to see that this boat finishes in a deep trench out there."

"We're going to sink it?"

He laughed. "Not on this trip, anyway. But we will."

"Don't think I'll join you on that one . . ."

He smiled but didn't look steady, and then I saw that his skin had turned a shade of purple, as if his blood pressure were skyrocketing.

"It also occurred to me upon my return from China that I had not taken you out on the ocean. Have you ever?"

"Never had the occasion."

"Every man has to go out there once."

"That right?"

"How could he not do so? How could he not know the sensation of losing all footholds? We mere regular men cannot go into outer space, and yet the ocean can take us to something quite similar."

"Way out there?"

"Carl, let's paint it flaming pink! They'll see us miles away!"

"Who?"

"Anybody! Everybody! Let's be flamboyant."

"Flaming pink . . ."

"Outrageous, no?"

Then I laughed. "Flaming all-get-out blazing pink, then."

He frowned. "Pink yacht paint. Can it be found? I have to make some calls. Then, yes, we'll change the name, too. Call it the *Pink Rose*."

He hurried up to the mansion to use the telephone.

Then he went to bed for a few days with a bad cold. Dozens of pots of pink paint came, and I painted. Guzzling beer and getting sunburned. While the pump sucked bilgewater from the bowel of the boat and spit it overboard. While the workers replaced windows, sanded and polished the deck, fixed doors so they would open and shut again, put in a new two-way radio, hoisted a Mexican flag at the back. Gradually the *Pink Rose* began to resemble a yacht again. It had a motor from a World War II tank, he'd told me, and those things being indestructible, a boat mechanic he'd found soon had the thing going. It got fired up for the first time the day Pullman climbed out of bed and came down to the dock in his blue silk robe. When he saw the pink paint job, he hugged me.

"The most outlandish ship on earth. Good job, Blalock! Bravo!"

He was still wobbly from his ailment, so I helped him to a deck chair where he could look into the hold at the man finishing with the motor.

"Sounds like before," he said. "You could go anywhere in this boat. That motor's got more guts than a five-star general." The vessel vibrated. "We leave in the morning. We'll fish a week."

But he was still feverish and his face looked like damp gray paper. To wait until he was better, I managed to put off our departure a couple of days by pretending that there were still things to done, stocking food, getting fuel and water, running motor tests.

Pullman pouted over the delay, waiting on a chair by his pool. Like an old woman, I thought, angry because her taxi has not come on time. I made sure Maria kept a cold drink in his hands.

Meanwhile the mechanic and I took the yacht out maybe half a mile, where he showed me the basics of handling it. But you never really have control. You can only steer and hope. That much I saw on the first spin in outer space. After that it was even more of a miracle to me.

Then one morning it rained again and he said, "It's the day."

"In a downpour?"

"Twenty or so miles, you come out of the rain. Enter open ocean."

"That far?"

He went out on the veranda and took a long look at his garden. Then he flung the contents of his breakfast cocktail onto the lawn.

"Aren't you ready yet?" he demanded.

"Well, there are some very last things to —"

"That's not what I meant!" He eyed me like a preacher. "This is not simply fishing. And we're not going to drink, either."

"All right."

"We're going to show you the ocean, Carl. Out where you can't see anything but water."

"Fine."

"Is that all you have to say?"

I sent to the market for bait, loaded on more food, got rid of the alcohol. Pullman was right. Time to dry out, see the endless water.

Maria came to see us off that afternoon and waved so long she had to hold her arm up with her other hand. Pullman watched her from the back of the boat, but he didn't wave. He'd said his good-byes to her before dawn when the rain had started and they had lain listening to it.

The dock shrank away, and then Pullman came and stood with me at the wheel. The tank motor roared like an airplane. The sea was dull, flat, and the rain came down straight like oil. The yacht gashed the water, and we looked back at the two pale waves smoothly spreading out.

"Did you bring the record player?" he asked.

I shrugged no. His face turned red and he went below into the cabin.

Then I understood. What else had a man done on a yacht alone after his wife had fallen into the sea but listen to the record? He'd drifted out there listening to Sinatra sing that song day after day, night after night.

I secured the wheel and went down where he sat at the table under the swaying lamp. The new varnish threw a coppery light across his face. Sweat dripped onto his hands. He smoked a cigar.

"I don't remember —"

"Of course you do, Blalock. We talked about it several times. You blanked it out. Now here we are without the record player."

Smoke and motor fumes stung my eyes.

"You know what I wanted to do?" he said. "I wanted to listen to it a last time out here and then toss it and the record player into the sea."

"Scare the fish."

"Likely." He eased back against the wall, relaxing. "You know, I am grateful you stayed in my house while I was in China. Not just anyone could be trusted to watch over it. And so I'll be sad to see you leave it."

"I was glad to oblige."

"And now what?"

"I'll go back to a place called North Texas."

"And Venus?"

"I don't know. That page is being turned."

"But, you know, it's not like it is with me and Gloria. Gloria's gone. But Venus isn't. What I mean is, I think you could find her."

"That wouldn't be easy."

"Easier than you think, I suspect. Find her and finish burying the Steins. Like I am going to finish burying Gloria. It's time to finish these things. Don't you see that this is the problem? Inertia after disaster?"

"How do you see these things?"

"A moment of clarity?"

"Clarity . . ."

"I don't get many."

I looked out a porthole. "All I see is rain."

"It will stop."

"Does that, too, mean something else?"

"I don't know about that, Carl. What I do know is there was a great and pitiful loneliness in me that you've helped chase away."

"I only house-sat awhile."

"Before, after, during. You were there. And I thank you."

"Carl Blalock, Texas drunk, Texas nobody. Tune in for more episodes of *More of the Same*. Minus some other actors, that is."

"Is all this self-ridicule real, Carl?"

"It's raining like a mother."

"Let it rain. Let the other Carl be here now. The one who doesn't worry about the old Carl or want to be him. Let the new one be here out on the ocean for the first time. Doing this thing he's never done."

The cabin rolled slowly side to side.

"I need a beer," I said.

"There's other things you learn on the moon."

Meaning out at the end of the world in China.

"Like what?"

"Like how fragile everything is, how tenuous."

"Boat on an ocean," I said.

"And that it takes some people, like me, a very long time to see things. Perhaps a whole lifetime. But so long as you do see something when you finally arrive then you have not failed."

I listened to the rumbling motor and thought about the bottom of the ocean plunging down into the violet and then into the black as we idled along far above. Said nothing, studied my dirty hands, wondered if I might not get sick to my stomach. Thought of having never been this far off the rock that had lain under my feet nearly half a century.

"Maybe you were thinking all along that I was going to give you a lot of my money," he said. "I could have made you a rich man for the rest of your days. Out of friendship. But I won't. That's not what you need."

"I didn't ask —"

"Of course you didn't. But perhaps you wanted to. Somewhere inside yourself you wanted to. And that's all right. But I'm not going to."

"Look —"

"When the time comes my associates will dispose of everything," he said. "There won't be anything you need to do."

"What're you talking about?"

"Go your way knowing that you've tasted the ocean air and felt the power of swells rising up from far below. They will carry you, you know. Far inland. But you won't be the old Carl Blalock. You'll be a new man, full of strength to break free. Full of the strength that Elena and Venus and May put into your soul. The strength to live your life as if it were an incredible exception in the universe, to exist for the time allowed you as if it were the most fantastic gift to be found in all infinity. And the strength to let go of your life when the time comes."

"Let go of it?"

"That's another thing you learn on the moon. Not to cling to your life as if it were a cliff, a thing you'd never think of letting go."

I felt a lightness working through me, as if the weight of my body were being stripped away for good out there on the open sea.

He leaned forward against the table and cradled his face on his fists, neither sad nor defeated, but more like someone waiting for the next part of a play to begin. His eyes flicking this way and that.

"Is it because I'm eighty-three? Is it because the only true light I ever knew lies somewhere below us in the darkness? Is it because I want you to jettison all that is death and go and live? Go and be generous with Venus? Give to her unboundedly and bring your lives to a higher place? It may be all these things. And other things. Things I cannot know, that cannot be drawn out and made into words. Though they have this terrible and final power over me, driving me. Quite like the moon. Quite like this ocean. Always there, pulling and pushing. Leading me to places I never thought I'd be. From which I must go forward yet again into the unknown because not to do so is to die a much worse death."

I waited there with him awhile, afraid like that day at the lake when there was nothing to be done because it was too late. But he said nothing more, and I went back up to the wheel. Hoping, stupidly, that he'd forget about all that and come up and fish and talk about regular everyday things. So that we could be like normal men. So that the big picture wouldn't hang there in the air like some black curtain in which he claimed to see all things and in which I could see only vague outlines.

I steered the boat out to sea. We had no map. But then I knew that we didn't need one. No more than he'd needed one in the desert. If only for once in my life, I stopped worrying about maps. What was the use? I knew where we were going, and it was like heading into a wilderness from which I would return as changed as he.

I played out a sad scene in my mind where Sinatra comes into the library and says, "You're making me sick of that song, William!"

Pullman apologizing, scurrying to the record player, knocking the needle off with a screech. "Right, Frank. Drink? Something to eat?"

Frank laughing. "You're my pal, William."

"Does that mean you'll stay awhile?"

"Well, now, William . . . I have so many gigs, you know. I have so many people to see and parties to attend and, well —"

"Please, Frank!"

"William!"

"I've been playing this tune for years and hoping you'd come here and now you're here, see, and you won't stay for a drink with me?"

"A drink? Sure. Then I have to go."

"That's all right. No problem."

Frank sitting down by the record player and having a look at the record while Pullman makes the drinks and blue and red and green parrots waddle on the bookshelves and squawk.

"You've about worn this record through, William."

"I'll get a new one."

"One of my finest sellers. Nobody played a note that wasn't there, you know? Very professional. I wouldn't have it any other way."

"Immemorial, Frank. Now here you are having a drink with me. Want to go out on my boat later? We could go swimming out there."

"I'm really afraid of deep water, William."

"That's all right. Lots of guys are afraid of deep water. I'll tell you what they're afraid of, too. Of Gloria."

"Who?"

"Gloria. Or Venus. Whoever she is. Your love. Your one love in this life. Because she's down in there, Frank, and it's impossible for you not to think about that. Impossible not to think while you're dangling there in the black that something is going to grab hold of your foot and pull you down in an instant. Your long-lost love, back with a vengeance. Wanting you to be with her down in there. Dead. You know?"

"That's rather curious, William. Perhaps you've been living here alone too long."

"But don't you see my point? It's only fear at work here. Nothing's going to get you in the deep water, Frank. You can get in. Let yourself go in it. Float. Sink. Swim. Whatever. There's nothing to fear."

"I wish I could believe that but —"

"Sure you can."

"How?"

"Because if you don't, then you can't live your life."

"That right? Look, I really have to go soon, you know."

Pullman gawking at Sinatra, seeing that young-boy face in all its radiance, that handsome brow, and those blue eyes . . .

"One for the road, then?" Pullman asking, spilling some of his drink.

"Haven't finished this one yet, William," Sinatra saying, checking his platinum watch. "About out of time here anyway."

"That's all right. Glad we could talk."

"Always good to see you."

"Will you be back this year?"

"Maybe next year."

"Right, then."

"Thanks for the drink."

"Anything for my pal Frank. You're sensational."

"Hey, like that song!"

Hours later Pullman came up on deck. We'd emerged from the rain and I'd turned on the floodlights. We looked like a hotel.

"Ready to fish?" I asked.

"I'll watch you."

He dropped onto a deck chair and curled forward like he was seasick.

I baited with a long blue sardine, cast her long and far. Then parked the rod in its slot, kept an eye on the tip.

"Being out here," I began, "reminds me of this old boy who had this shack down the Brazos River from our house when I was a kid. Right on the water. Daddy'd let me go down there if I'd been good and it was always like a reward because it was pretty far from the house and that meant I was to be trusted. I'd always get there early and fish until sunup and then old man Thornton would come out of his shack and fish with me. Catfish, bass, shad, carp, turtles, you name it."

"Turtles?"

"Ugly things. Catch one and you had to cut the line. That meant a treble hook and a couple of sinkers. That used to piss me off, but old man Thornton would be quiet whenever it happened to him and that way showed me how to rein in myself because I was often tempermental. I figure the old man was kind of a teacher. He told me about Old Blue."

"Old Blue," Pullman said, liking it.

"There's an Old Blue in every river in creation, I guess. You hardly ever catch one, though. Old man Thornton said one time he'd put a chicken heart, still beating, on his line and chucked it in back over there in the shade under the bank. Sure enough, in no time, something very very big swallowed that sucker and —"

Pullman fell asleep. I watched the ocean and my rod. Then he got to snoring. I really wished I had a cold beer. I'd have had that sucker down in no time, tossed the bottle as far as I could. Had another. Stayed up all night and hung on to the pink railing watching for those fish they say come up glowing like neon lights. I wanted to see some of those. Something gorgeous that came all those miles up to the surface to you.

When I awoke, the motor was off, the lights were off, and Pullman's chair was empty. I looked out at the ocean. How long had I slept? There was no way to know. I called out for him, but the sound of my own voice turned against me and I lunged forward and looked into the water. It was done. I'd been asleep. He'd lowered himself into the black and let himself go. In silence, the water hardly moving, the water smoothing over again. Had he been dreaming and then awakened to see me sleeping? Had he said something softly to me before going? Had I been dreaming, too? Of waking and seeing him lower himself into the black and smile up at me, like a quiet invitation? Did I follow him? I wasn't sure of anything, and sat there far outside the realm of time and reason with my white hands holding firmly to the railing.

Then, slowly, I took up the story I'd been telling. Louder than before, as if he were floating on his back out there listening to me.

"Of course . . . the line broke . . . and Old Blue got away. He always got away. And old man Thornton just shook his head and sighed and said, 'You know, boy . . . I'm going to buy a Cadillac with my Raleigh coupons pretty soon and drive out of here and quit fretting about Old Blue.' He'd say that and smoke his Raleighs one after another. And when we'd finished fishing, when the day was done, we'd take our mess of fish up by his shack and gut them and rinse them in a tin bucket. 'Now you give those to your mama and you tell her to fry them up and get some okra going and corn bread and pour you a tall glass of cow's milk, you hear?' Then he'd take me inside his shack and get out a big cardboard box full of tan cigarette coupons. There had to be thousands of them in there and he'd pull them out to show them off and start counting them and humming to himself while he smoked some more. After a while we'd be sitting there in the shadows saying nothing. The old man would fall asleep and I'd peer out the rusted front-door screen at the last light on the river. It would get so quiet the only thing I'd hear were bullfrogs and snakes moving through the weeds and turtles sliding through the deep, down with the branches and stumps and trotlines. When it got darker I'd push the door open real careful so it wouldn't wake him and go out into the grass that came up high as my ears and stand there waiting for a breeze. And imagine I was out on the ocean . . . on a big boat . . ."

I looked at the water and thought I could jump in and go down until I found him and take him in my arms and swim even farther down.

Down to where we break through into the air again and he takes a breath and I swim toward the boat with him. He weighs practically nothing and stares at me like a baby with his mouth half open and I feel sick for trying to save him. Then I stop swimming and hold him, and he looks at me and I look at him, and then I let him go again. Really do the right thing this time. Like Daddy'd said I'd have to do in this life if ever I was going to know God, the sum of things. Softly, he sinks into the black. Then I feel my body go slack and I let myself go under, too. Taking a mouthful of the sea of colorful stars. Thinking of May. Of Venus. Feeling a cold tug, like a child insisting, or maybe it is God, taking me down. But I am not afraid at all. Because I know I will come back out into the light.

Maria was waiting on the dock late the next day as if she hadn't moved. I said nothing to her as I stepped off, and she went aboard to look for him. I went along the walkway past the pool and then up to his house, thinking how the land had changed from rock into cloth that would tear through. I went to the library and played "Strangers in the Night" because there was no choice but to do that. I drank bourbon and wandered the halls wishing Elena were there to take me into her fires. She'd known my pain, hadn't she? Then I was Frank, many sheets to the wind. Strolling through the rooms of the house atop the cloth world and singing for love, white bird in the heart of the jungle. Yes, I was Francis Albert Sinatra that final night. The witty crooner, the carefree cartoon man. All bad things wiped away from the world. My eyes shining like blue suns, mouth opened in song. Until the needle halted again at the place it often did. "Ever since that night . . . that night . . . that night . . ."

I slept in Pullman's mansion a last time and dreamed of Venus wearing nothing but red panties, a red bra, and a floppy red straw hat.

"Well, did your buddy jump in the ocean and die? Crap out on you? Poor thing. Well, here I am. Fix us a drink, will you?"

Like that, there we are on the deck of our house. I sing the Sinatra tune and make big tall piña coladas, come back and snap my fingers so there's a sailboat race to watch.

"Nice boats, but do me a favor," she says.

"All right."

"Don't sing. You could never sing."

"Then I won't."

"But you've learned to make a hell of a drink! How's that?"

She sucks on it until the straw finds no more. Then a breeze comes.

"Maybe I ought to get dressed. Going to catch cold. You kept the clothes I left here, didn't you?"

I hadn't. She knows it, too, but pretends it's all right, gets up and walks toward the bedroom.

"Who needs clothes, anyway? Did Pullman go in with his clothes on? Or did he dive in naked?"

I shut my eyes and open them, and then there is no Venus. Trash and dead leaves kick along the deck. Maria stands dark and still at the gate.

"Go away," I say.

But she pushes on the gate and it squeaks fiercely as she steps inside.

"Dondé está el señor? Dondé está?"

I bolted upright. Maria was at the bedroom door. I fell back on the sheets. She shouted at me and waved her arms, then went quickly away. I sat up, awake as a cat. Was she going to call the police? I'd done nothing wrong, had I? I'd gone fishing with a rich old man and fallen asleep and he'd gone swimming alone while I slept and never come back. Of course you pushed him into the sea, they would say. How could I have? But no one would hear of it and they would cast me into a hole.

I left the mansion, went to my place. Began gathering a few things to take with me, then stopped. Turned to see the fishing boats coming in as the pink light grew over the mountains to the east. Had strange thoughts. Of Mama saying once when she was very old that if you dug far enough below the Panhandle you'd come out in China. Of Pullman sailing arms-out down into a luminous ocean trench like a man flying. Of May's skeleton standing at the bottom of the cistern as if she were waiting. Of Venus wanting me to climb upon her and make that universe of us be born again. In the end I left everything there as it was, and it would be as if I had disappeared into the air.

The sun was only just up when I got to the bus station, where I bought a ticket for some obscure place, it didn't matter where. So long as I went away in the least visible manner. Not on an airplane. But among people going where tourists never go. I climbed into a bus full of workers. Found no place to sit and stood in the stairwell and waited for the driver to show up. As if I were one of them, another night worker going home. Only I wasn't, and every shut eye watched me, every nostril breathed me. Everyone was a police officer waiting to make the arrest.

As I looked out the door of the bus, I saw Seidensticker ambling along the sidewalk with a boy. They were talking heatedly and the boy was giving him a hard time about something. Seidensticker kept saying, "All right, all right." Then they went into a bar. There was a burst of laughter once they were inside, and a lot of high-pitched yelling, and then music blasted forth like a burlesque show had begun at that instant.

Again snow falls on a forest where Pullman and I are walking with guns and dogs. But there is nothing to shoot and we go along looking at the naked black trees without talking. The dogs whine. Our boots squeak in the snow. There is something out there, maybe a bear, maybe a twenty-point buck, but we won't know it until we see it. And so there is no hurry, no rush, we are strong men going our way, and the thin snow falls ever more slowly.

When the driver of the bus arrived we left right away, as if there were some urgency. And like a beast heading back into the bush with its prey, the red bus groaned up into the green mountains.

Capitán Ernesto Díaz

This American. Do you recognize him? No? Think carefully, for it is a matter of murder. Yes, the William Pullman case. No, we have not found his body. Do you recognize this man? Yes? He bought many shirts here. When? Only a few days ago. I see. Did he say anything at all? Are you sure? I know you are busy, but it is a very important case, for you see Señor Pullman was a most prominent citizen. What's that? That's not very kind, señora, the man is dead. That's not my concern. You'll have to speak with the land rights office. No, I don't know. I'm sorry for your brother and his property, all right? Now, you're sure you haven't seen the American since the last time he was in here? I'm doing my job. Please don't shout at me, señora. It is not necessary to shout. Are you trying to anger me? I must ask you to stop screaming at me, señora. I don't know about the land! Be quiet! That's better. Remain civilized. You remember nothing else, then? Well, thank you for your time. Good day, señora.

I'm telling you, Esteban, we will not solve this one. Isn't it clear to you? The boss is having us run around in circles to show we've done something. They know what happened. The gringo pushed the old man out of his boat out there on the sea and then ran away and they'll never find him. Why? Because it's a big world, Esteban! You mean why did he kill him? Don't you know, Esteban? Money! It could only be money. And now the gringo has to be a thousand miles from here with the money! So why're we having to run all over town asking these questions! No one knows a thing! Some have seen him, others maybe, and no one has anything special to report. He was just a gringo. Now he's committed murder and gone to hide. This is not the first time such a thing has happened, is it? Of course not. Why are you shaking your head, Esteban? What's that? It had to have been murder. What are you talking about? The gringo helped the old man kill himself? That's insane, Esteban. Have you been drinking again? You're shaking your head again, Esteban! No, this was not about being charitable to the very old! This is not the Netherlands, you fool! You have some mixed-up ideas! Now how about lunch? I can't stand this heat! Quit shaking your head!

Venus

The Las Palmas motel in La Purísima still had everything Venus needed, even if she was the Million Dollar Lady now. Like always, she got bungalow seven, a little back from but facing the pool, though Stein wasn't the same señor she'd been stopping there with for years.

"I'm getting old," she told Estella, the manager. "Need some rest. Too much running, too many miles on the road, you know?"

"No old, no old!" Estella screeched. "You beauty, you young!"

"We could argue about this."

"No, no argue. Venus still heaven."

As Estella's boys took care of their bags, Venus told Carl that the jackpot was not to be mentioned to anyone. But he only trudged into the room and fell onto the bed. "You're paranoid, Venus."

"And you're Carl. But not for long. There'll be a new Carl soon."

Estella's boys waited at the door. Venus dug in her purse and gave each five dollars. Waving the bills, they darted away in the sunshine.

Venus looked out at the rectangular pool and the wind-beaten palms planted around it. The neglected lawn had turned as gray as a field of ashes. A red cement donkey stood to one side, one ear broken off. A white boy, alone, fiddled with a paper kite. No wind.

Carl went to piss. "What do you mean 'new'?"

"We're going to have to talk," Venus called. "First about money."

He pissed a long time, then came back. "And?"

"If we'll agree that it's okay that you want some of my money, then we can quit thinking about that and go on to thinking about other things. When we get to a bank, I'll set you up."

"Set me up?"

"That way we're past it. And on to bigger things."

Carl's eyes widened.

Yes, Venus was sure, a packet of her money would change everything. Carl would become another man.

Then his eyes narrowed. "So you're buying me?"

"Would a hundred thousand dollars do you? Would that get you going with the flow? Couldn't you be a gentleman with a lady for that?"

"You're tired, Venus."

"Tired? Fix me a drink."

The fridge was crammed with samples.

Trucks wailed down the highway like ghosts.

When evening came, Venus said, "Time for the surprise."

She led Carl out onto the tiny porch with its tin roof. The air was still deathly hot.

A fat guy on the diving board yelled, "Hey, Marvin! Marvin! You watching, Marvin?"

Marvin didn't answer.

"This is your surprise?" Carl asked, stepping down onto the fried lawn. "We don't have to listen to this."

"Come back and sit. I want to show you my surprise."

"Marvin, if you don't look up here I'm not going to dive! Marvin!"

"Hey, you!" Carl shouted.

The guy stopped bouncing. "You talking to me?"

"Damn it, Carl," Venus said.

"That's right, I'm talking to you. Hold it down, will you?"

The guy began bouncing again. "Yeah, sure. No problem." Slowly, the board speeded up. "Marvin! Marvin! Marvin, you watching?"

"Hey, didn't you hear me?" Carl cried.

"What did you say?" the man shouted, waving his arms in a circle as the board lifted him higher. "Marvin, who is this guy? Huh, Marvin?"

Carl dropped it, got back on the porch. "Stupid assholes."

"Now, that's not our new Carl, is it?"

"Cut it out with the 'new Carl' stuff."

Venus pointed at the sunset, which had just ended, a towering orange show over the mountains. "Isn't that something? Like a giant furnace."

"Long as it cools off."

"Come on, Carl. Try to relax with me here."

"I am relaxed. And I am with you here."

"Those mountains . . . they're full of ghost towns, silver-mining towns. They pulled millions of dollars out. Then everything dried up."

"Been reading your tourist guides?"

Venus took a slow breath. "I think it's spooky. All of Mexico is spooky like that. In America you look at something and you can hardly imagine it having a past. But down here everything is much more."

"Yeah?"

"And then there's the high-pitched laughter you hear in the night."

"What?"

"It's spooky the first time you hear it, but then you know it's the sound of happy people. And then you think how happy the people down here are even though they don't have anything. They're up all night. How did they get so happy?"

"How do you know they're happy?"

Carl went back inside. Venus thought, What good did it do anybody to think the worse thing when you could think the better thing?

"Where have you always wanted to live, Carl?" she called.

He didn't answer.

The two guys at the pool waddled off wrapped in their expensive towels, the fat one talking loudly about some restaurant in Chicago where they were going to go as soon as they got home, the skinny one not saying anything and watching the ground as if maybe there were snakes.

Then an American family plodded past, checking in. Their clothes were cheap and they had one suitcase, which the father was carrying.

"How're you doing?" Venus asked them.

"Bushed!" the lady said. "Nineteen hours from Laredo. Never again!"

"We had three flats," the daughter said. "Daddy fixed every one."

They went to bungalow four. The kids stood in the door and looked toward the pool. Then the mother pulled them inside and shut the door.

Venus decided to give them money, too. Set them up, get them out of their misery. Give them a chance to enjoy their lives again.

Then Carl was back with another drink. "Carmel, California."

"What?"

"Where I always wanted to live."

"What's in Carmel, California?"

"A life of leisure looking out at the ocean every morning."

"Don't you like Mexico?"

"Tired old place where nothing's ever going to happen."

"Nothing? Everything happens here, Carl. Life happens here. There's laughter in the night . . . And up in the mountains, haciendas full of huge green plants in tall orange pots. Clay tiles and raindrops soaking into them in the night. The moon racing along just out of reach and a family walking down the road, arm in arm, laughing while the cook stands in his restaurant door under a yellow light and watches them go . . . There are black-haired girls in white dresses flowing into churches and kneeling before the Virgin and whispering about boys while the old ladies move about like witches and hiss at them to be quiet. There are sad tilted spires and facades leaning back into the soft earth, and the onyx shine of Spanish royalty in the wet eyes of the Indians . . . It makes me dream. And when I'm dreaming, I'm alive."

"You're alive all right, Venus."

They watched the light dying and the first stars coming out. He'd come around, Venus was sure. It was already happening.

Then she thought a swim might help her relax, but as the idea came into her mind the fat man was heading back to the pool and talking to Marvin about Sheila and how he wasn't going to put up with Sheila's mouth much longer and screw the kids who'd never loved him anyway. Then he was back on the board. "Marvin! You watching, Marvin?"

Carl said, "This place is a joke," and went into the room again.

Venus rubbed her eyes, wished she wasn't getting sleepy.

"Marvin! Marvin! Marvin!"

Enough was enough. "You! On the board!" she cried.

The guy stopped bouncing. "You talking to me?"

"Dive, will you?"

The guy pointed at her. "Marvin? Did you hear what she said?"

"Yeah, I heard her. So do it, will you? You're embarrassing me."

The fat guy laughed, gave the board a big push and, arms straight out, rose high into the air. Venus put her hand over her eyes. There was a shout, then a *boom*. Venus looked. The splash made a tall beautiful striped fountain of red water and blue pool light, and then dispersed. Doors opened at every bungalow and people stared out.

"Holy Jesus!" the guy yelled. "Did you see me, Marvin? Marvin!"

Carl stuck his head out. "What the hell was that?"

Venus liked to get the check out from under the lining of her white pump when Carl wasn't around, unfold it and look at it, think some more about dividing it all up. So far there was Carl, the family in bungalow four, Estella, Estella's boys, the maid who cleaned their room, and the fat guy at the pool, to shut him up. How much for each, though? Would she hand it all out the same day? Make it a party?

Mama and Dad had never once let on, but Venus had had a sister, a gorgeous creature who hadn't died in secret at birth, who'd lived beside her all these years, been right beside her through everything, all the good and all the bad, whose sweet voice spoke to her now, saying, "Yes, give all the money away, Venus, and then go your own way. Carl isn't the answer to anything, either." She sounded right.

Venus was standing up to her neck in the pool. The water shone like a mirror and she squinted. Carl still didn't know how to swim and stayed seated on the edge with his legs in.

"What do you want out of life, Stein?"

"To hold your check. Where're you hiding it? Are you really going to give me some like you said? Or were you kidding?"

He really did want to know. He was planning every minute.

"Be patient, Carl."

"Time I've got."

It sounded like a murderer waiting for the blood to run out of his victim to be sure she was dead before he went for the stash.

The midday heat pressed upon them. Out on the highway old women and old men waved down tourist buses to sell iguanas.

Venus said, "One time Blalock and I came through here heading back to Texas and we stopped where this guy was selling pretty clay pots. I picked out a couple and Blalock paid him and then the guy stepped into a stick-and-newspaper shack he'd made to keep out of the sun and led out a boy, maybe six years old. Nothing was said and the boy looked at our shoes. We examined the boy a moment and then Blalock picked up our pots and started toward the car. But the father said, 'Two hundred pesos. He starves with me.' Blalock put the pots in the Suburban as if the man hadn't said a word, told me to get in. I touched the boy's face and then got in the car, just like that."

Carl looked into the pool through his green shades. "Yeah?"

"I can still see that boy's eyes."

"Pretty sad."

"Carl and I couldn't have children."

"I didn't know that."

"I would've taken that kid."

"I can see that."

"But I didn't. I didn't do the right thing."

"Then neither did Blalock."

"No, neither of us did."

"Well, it might have been illegal or something. I mean, I'm no expert but how would you get back across the border with a Mexican kid?"

"We could've found some solution."

"I doubt that."

"We just didn't try."

Venus looked at Carl, then at the wide-open sky, then dropped down under the water, opened her eyes, and peered through the water at his wavering white legs. Stayed there watching for a long while, then burst free.

"Jesus!" he said. "What're you doing?"

"Getting wet. What?"

He shook his head. "I don't know. You scare me sometimes."

"There you go again about being afraid. What is it?"

"Come on. We're going to fry out here."

Venus swam to the other end of the pool, hung on to the edge, and slowly kicked her legs. The silver water rippled thickly. "So what would you have done?" she called.

"What?"

"About the boy."

"Taken him, I guess. Tried to figure it out."

Definitely a liar. Venus got her hair wet. Then she put her head under the surface and opened her eyes again. Listened to her sister's voice. "Why aren't you doing what you've already decided? The money's seized you by the neck, girl! Get rid of it, quickly! Go your way without regret. Can't you hear me, sister?" When she came back up Carl's tracks on the sidewalk led back to the bungalow. He was right. Time to get inside. Into a cool place where she could think again. Give it all away? Really?

They'd rest indoors afternoons, let time float by. Venus would play solitaire on the coffee table with the air conditioner blowing on her. If he was good and asleep, she'd get out the casino check yet again. Read the numbers, her name. Shiver at the thought that it wasn't worth the paper it was printed on, that when she went to cash it, it would all turn out to have been a TV stunt. Peer around to see if there wasn't a hidden camera filming her. Never finding one, of course, but getting a good look at the zigzag cracks between cinder blocks, the black-felt painting of a bloody bull and matadors, the battered lamp shades, and the tall man from Wisconsin lying on his side of the sunken bed, snoring. It was easy for her to put Carl Blalock in the place of Carl Stein, remember sitting there at the same hour in the same season years ago wondering if she would be parked just like this someday with the cards in front of her. Which made a strange circle of time, from which she immediately broke free. Getting up and putting the check back in her white pump.

He said, "Don't you ever rest? Damn."

He hadn't opened his eyes. Drool lay on his cheek.

Venus put on a white blouse to cover her brown suit with faded yellow flowers and went out. There was a gift shop next to the restaurant. Maybe it would have something she liked. Her sandals slapped her heels as she followed the path among the painted rocks and yuccas. Where it came close to the road she watched the buses and trailer rigs. Dust clouds drifted away into the scrub and rocky waste on the other side.

"Excuse me, but aren't you the Million Dollar Lady?"

Venus set the black onyx queen back on the chess table.

"I'd like to apologize for my brother's perpetual bad behavior in the pool," the man said. "I'm afraid he'll never change. That is no excuse, however."

"Don't mention it. We may even get used to it."

"That's very kind of you. I'll tell him that you have accepted his apology."

Venus turned around. His red hair sat on his head like a helmet. He had a thin white face. The eyes were streaked different colors.

"They seem obsessed with chess, wouldn't you say? I've never seen so many chess sets, have you?"

"I was looking for a new swimming suit."

"And you found they don't sell any. I did as well. Andy and I, my brother and I, we're here on rather short notice. And you?"

"Short notice?"

"Well, it happens that Andy is a stockbroker and you can't always go on vacation when you want to. We live in Chicago. Do you know it?"

"Excuse me, but I have to go. Nice talking to you."

A pastel blue appeared in his face. Venus had the feeling he was going to block the way and looked at the bead curtain for the shopkeeper.

"Well, you see, I'm a reporter for a large metropolitan daily and —"

"I have to go."

"Then you're not the Million Dollar Lady? Have I erred?"

"Don't know what you're talking about."

"Is he keeping you from talking?"

"Who?"

"The man you're with?"

"No, he's not. I mean . . . I have to go now."

"In this heat? Don't you feel like melting? Andy insisted, you know. He said, 'Marvin, let's get out of the country for a couple of weeks and rest.' I said, 'Where do you want to go?' He said, 'Way down in the middle of Mexico, you know, like last time.' So here we are. Running away again."

"From what?"

"I mean, on vacation. Ten days already . . . He told us your deal, you know."

"Excuse me?"

"So what're you going to do with the money?"

"I don't know what you're talking about, mister."

"Marvin. Marvin Thomas."

The bead curtain rattled, but no one emerged.

"Are you so afraid of something you can't tell me?"

"Not at all."

"Then will you go for a walk with me tonight?"

"Walk with you?"

"Yeah, I walk out there."

He pointed out the window at the closest mountain.

Venus picked up a white marble pawn. "I don't think so."

"It's not the same at night as it is during the day. It's astoundingly beautiful. You've never seen anything so perfectly wild."

Venus laughed. "No, I don't think so."

"You know you're beautiful, don't you?"

"Excuse me?"

"I'm sorry. I go too fast. Let my words out before I know it."

"You do seem to be going pretty fast."

"But will you go for a walk with me later on? Perfectly innocent."

"Why should I go for a walk with you out there?"

"Why not do it because you've never done that before and have always wondered like those who are deeply curious about this world just what it would be like? Is that not a good enough reason, Mrs. Blalock?"

"Venus Miller is the name. My maiden name is Miller."

He pulled out his billfold. "My card."

MARVIN THOMAS, it said. REPORTER, CHICAGO DAILY MAIL.

"Meet me by the restaurant at eleven? Can you do that?"

"I can do anything I want," Venus said.

Marvin laughed. "Hey, if you've got a million bucks, you can do whatever the heck you please when you please. Am I right?"

"Marvin?"

"Yes?"

"Why do you say heck when you mean hell?"

"Oh. We couldn't even say darn in our house."

Carl had the check out when she came back in, but handed it straight to her like a boy caught playing with something that wasn't his.

"I was only looking at —" he said.

"They have tequila in the shop. Run get some. I forgot my money."

"I wasn't going to do anything with it. All right?"

She said fine and out he went. Whistling like everything had been solved. Then Venus decided, No, she definitely wasn't going to give her money to anybody. What had she been thinking? What had her sister been thinking? It made no sense at all, no more than anything that you couldn't turn around and take back. No, she wouldn't help set up Carl, or save some starving people, or anything like that. She'd hold on to her money as tight as a baby does candy. What else was going to save her? That good, churchy feeling of doing right? Who was she kidding? It took money to be safe in this world. Piles of it.

There was no use trying to find a better hiding place for the check, either. If Carl was around, it was vulnerable. So she put it back in the same shoe. Then she rechecked the cash in her purse for the bundle from the casino and the bank bag from Carl's old heist. All there.

She put on a cotton dress, combed her hair and fixed it in a ponytail, and thought looking in the mirror how pulled-back hair made her younger. "Not a dime for anybody," she told her sister.

"What?" asked Carl, coming back with the tequila.

"Nothing."

He set things up on the table by the air conditioner.

"Could use some music," said Venus.

"Sitting on this money and we don't even have a transistor."

He poured the stuff.

"Here's to it," he said. "Let's get down!"

Venus thought that it certainly didn't take much to make him believe he was in heaven. Then she threw back her tequila.

"Do me again."

"Met the weirdest guy. Reporter. Asked me about you."

"Yeah?"

"He said I'd already told him about your jackpot and so why didn't I go ahead and tell him about you. I told him I'd never seen him before in my life. And I hadn't. But I said you were a famous dancer."

"Dancer?"

"I was just trying to say anything to keep —"

"Well, I can dance. Sister taught me. She's very good."

"Didn't know you had a sister."

"Lives way up north now."

Carl grinned. "Speaking of dancing, I used to have this buddy who lived next door and had this gorgeous wife. I'll never forget one night we were sitting in their living room carrying on and he said to her, 'Honey, why don't you strip for us now.' 'You mean like a strip show?' 'Yeah, like a real strip show. That way we don't have to drive to the club tonight. What do you say? We're friends here. I'll get a record going you like and you strip like it's real. Nothing'll happen.'"

"Did she?"

"Best I've seen. What was her name? Melody? Melody dancing to a tune!"

They had another round.

"You want me to strip?" Venus asked.

"I was just talking."

"No, you weren't. Besides, I feel like it. Then we can make love and see where that takes us."

"Takes us?"

"It may not take us anywhere."

"I don't know . . ."

"What's the problem? All you have to say is, 'Strip for me, Venus,' and then by God I will. Why not? It's what you want, isn't it?"

Carl looked her up and down. "Yeah?"

"Yeah."

"All right. Then, strip for me, Venus."

"You got it."

Venus stood up and slowly unbuttoned her dress, down to her

belly, then eased the straps off her shoulders and let it fall. Then there was nothing else to strip away. Carl didn't speak. She stepped out of the pool of the dress, watching him carefully. Flames rose through her body and wavered in the blue light. She could hear sweet music.

It was awful. The booze gave every motion a sickening heaviness as if gravity had been juiced up. He cut the light off, she put it back on, he cut it off again, and then there was no turning back. He was loud and rough, and it lasted only minutes. Then he fell away. It wasn't supposed to be that way for Million Dollar Ladies, Venus thought. She stared at Carl's white buttocks and saw herself out there in the scrub and rocks, far away, walking with Marvin. Her brother, the one who hadn't died in secret at birth, confident, level headed, well mannered. And they would find her sister, too, out there. Under the moon. And the three of them would sit and talk and be a family again, warm and whole.

Carl rolled toward her. "Do you want to do that again?" But before she could say no, he flopped back where he'd been. "You wore me out."

The travel clock said eleven. Time to go.

He was waiting on the steps of the restaurant, finishing a cigarette. Vacant eyed, like he didn't have a thought in his head. Wearing the same red plaid shorts, aqua-blue golf shirt, orange sandals.

"You've done this plenty of times before, right?" Venus asked.

"Nothing to it."

"Let's go, then."

They went across the parking lot to the road and stopped. Truck lights sliced the night. Hunched-over people moved along like refugees from a war. It was a long time before they could cross safely. But when they could he took her hand and they ran hard, like children into a park.

From the other side the lights of the motel seemed like decorations on a lost ship. He tugged on her arm, led her with strength she hadn't expected. She could feel the check under her heel in her Million Dollar Shoes and worried that it might give her a blister.

"You sure you know the way?"

"Sure I do."

He kicked a rock a couple of times, sending it thudding along a short ways until it stopped in the dust. He whistled something complicated.

"You always take a pretty girl with you?"

"Pardon?"

"You have them stashed all over out here, right?"

"That's not funny."

"Funny?"

"I assure you, Venus, there is no reason to be afraid of anything. We're simply following a path here that leads up the mountain to a place where you can look out and see a bona fide ghost town."

"A silver-mining town?"

"Ah, you read about them, too. That's right. They're numerous around here. Abandoned museums of time. Nothing quite like it. I hope the moon will be up. When the moon is up things get interesting."

She brushed the unsettling contours of his words, sure that they meant much more than she understood. But he was right, the taking of the odd direction, the bold movement toward unknown things, the test, it was these that pushed the heart faster and widened one's tired eyes.

The path had lots of forks, but he never hesitated.

It seemed only a few minutes passed before they came to a place where they could look down and see the road and the lights of La Purísima back on the desert floor, already distant. There was the derrick out in front of the motel, the tall blinking red letters LAS PALMAS struggling to send their neon message into the emptiness. The pale light of the swimming pool glowed like a landing pad for no one.

Then he said, Let's go, and they went up higher and slipped around a ridge onto the far side where they faced the open night.

"The way I see it," he said, "if you don't go and see the things you're curious about, then you're not alive. You're loitering at the edge of life. Like when you're in the car driving through the mountains and looking out at them and thinking how you'd like to stop and climb right up to the top of one?"

"Yes," said Venus.

"That longing to get out and walk all the way."

"Would you rather be alone out here?"

He stopped with a skid, reached out to the rock face to steady himself. "Much better to share. Don't you think so?"

"I guess."

"I talk too much about personal matters, don't I?"

"That's okay."

"No, it's not, Venus. It's a sign I'm not totally sure of myself yet."

"Pardon me?"

"Don't listen to me. I'm babbling."

"Why?"

"Being out here does it to me."

"Does what?"

"Freaks me out!"

"Well, don't get too freaked out."

The trail kept going up. Venus noticed a lightness in her step, a giving back from the earth, as if it were hollow and they were walking on the roof of something deep, an abandoned silver shaft, something. Agave reached up out of the rough ground with fistfuls of spears. Unseen creatures skittered among the boulders and birds called to each other.

"We'll come to the place where you can see the ghost town if the moonlight's right," he said. "Hey . . . if the light's really right, we could go climb right on up to it. What do you say to that?"

"You're not putting me in any danger, are you?"

"Something wrong?"

The voice was harder. She said no, kept following. Maybe he wasn't any more dangerous than a boy out exploring. But it was the middle of the night, she reminded herself, and he was kind of odd. How would he ever protect her from anything? Would he know how to suck snake venom out of her leg if he had to?

She studied the stars. There was only one patch of them, though, overhead, colorless. She would swear their footsteps echoed.

"We're going to fall into a hole out here, Marvin. Or die from a bite."

"I know the way. Don't worry."

He was farther ahead now and talked louder. "So, Andy and I came all the way up here one time after we ate some peyote buttons."

"Drugs?"

"Andy got the stuff. Tasted horrible. But, heavens, there were some strange things to be seen that night!"

"I don't do drugs, Marvin."

"It was exhilarating."

"It was, huh."

"Yes, to see the rocks move around. Become things. Animals, people. I swear there was one rock that we both hallucinated on, thinking it was a god of the Aztec empire speaking right to us. Might have been."

"That's insane."

"There's a lot of things in these rocks we can't know directly. People sitting back in the motel can't know this. You can't know these things without trying to go and be near them, let them touch you."

He had stopped where the path abruptly came to an end and the void took over and motioned for her to stay well back from the precipice.

"Here we are. And do you know what that old god told us both?"

"The drug god?"

"Are you ridiculing me, Venus?"

"No. But where are we? What're we supposed to be seeing here?"

"That old god said to Andy and myself to first and foremost beware the silver sickness, the evil greed of wealth, and to cast away all riches before they enslave us. It spoke in plain American. We laughed our heads off, then went back to the motel and lay in bed sick for four or five days."

Venus didn't like the undertones, didn't like this place, and stood straining to see into the gloom that lay all around them.

Far above a passenger jet rode silently over the roof of the night.

"I think it's time you took me back now," she said.

"What? Why don't we sit down here for a while. The moon's going to come up over the cliff behind us and it's going to shine right on the ruins of the town over there. I don't know this place's name. Maybe it was all so long ago it doesn't have a name anymore."

"How far away is it?"

"A mile or two only. Up that way. You can get there from here but it's hard and the moon must be with us."

"Quit talking like you're in a ghost movie."

"What?"

"I don't like the way you keep saying things as if you meant something more that you don't really want to tell me, something that's going to happen."

"See what a million dollars has done to you?"

"Stop that."

"It's an old story, Venus. The corruption of the soul by money."

"My money."

"I don't want your money, Venus. I'm simply walking you around in the night to see if we can't enjoy ourselves. I'm not going to touch you. Nothing. You're not afraid of me or something, are you? Heavens."

She felt uncertain again, disarmed. Perhaps he wasn't up to anything, perhaps she was letting her fears run away with her. Why couldn't she give him the benefit of the doubt, go with the flow here, stop resisting?

He took something out of the pocket of his shorts — a wad of newspaper, it seemed — unfolded it, took up something and put it in his mouth. "Yuck! As bad as last time. Horrible."

"You're eating those drugs!"

"Why not, Venus? I'm experimenting again. I'm living again, being directly in touch with the things of this world. What's wrong with that?"

"I didn't come out here to do drugs, Marvin."

"You don't have to. I just want you to be with me is all."

He chewed and laughed and said again how filthy and bitter it tasted. Then he spat it out and stuck the rest of whatever it was into his pocket.

They waited.

Venus could feel a rumbling in the depths of the earth, like ocean waves rising into pockets along a coast and breaking against walls.

"Hear that?" she said.

He had lit a cigarette and lay on his back. "Wind or something."

"Coming from in the ground."

"Nah, that's the wind. You get weird currents up here. It goes flying in strange directions. Want me to do you the echo of a lifetime?"

"No."

"You okay?"

"You keep asking me that."

"Do I?"

"Stop it anyway."

He didn't answer.

She sat down a short distance from him and watched his cigarette turn to a sharp orange tip, listened to the paper burning. He didn't seem like her strong brother now. And her sister wasn't around like she'd thought she'd be. Then she noticed the cold on her arms and legs.

"I know we ought to get back now."

"We have to wait for the moon."

Venus stood up. "I'm going back."

"The moon's coming, Venus."

You couldn't see much of anything. Even the patch of stars had gone out. She began to walk away from him and the frightening edge. But as soon as she'd taken a few steps she called back. "Marvin, come on."

"Huh?"

"Come on now. Take me back down before those drugs kick in."

"Waiting on the moon, I told you. Don't be wandering around. You'll go over the edge or slip down a mine shaft. How could I find you?"

Venus squatted, put her hand to the gritty earth. It felt warm and she spread her fingers upon it.

"What're you doing, Venus?" He flicked his lighter a couple of times. "Huh, Venus? Please be careful."

"Feeling the ground. We're on top of something empty."

"It's a maze of shafts and pockets like Swiss cheese. Come back, will you?"

"I'm going back down."

"I need you here. To stay up here with me."

"I'm going now, Marvin."

"Wait."

She turned again to go and her eyes fell upon the face of the moon reaching up over the ragged ridge as if to catch them at some sinful task.

"Here it comes!" he shouted.

It shone weakly but put enough light on the twisting path that Venus could see the edges, the drops, the soaring rock, and make her way among the jaggedness, around bends, the slope downward steeper than before.

"Do you see it? Huh, Venus?"

She wished he wouldn't call her and walked more quickly, the mountain's drop propelling her with lead force. Any second now, she was sure, and the lights of La Purísima would arise and she'd know the way.

"Where are you?" he shouted. "You can't just leave me!"

This time she looked back, but the moon had already found a thin cloud and the pile of black rock above looked down menacingly, as if he had become one with it and would come crashing down upon her.

"Don't take another step, Venus! You'll step into a shaft and fall deep into the earth! Do you hear me?"

"I hear you, Marvin," she said softly, as if he were at her side.

"Good. Thank God. Don't move now. Keep talking to me. I'll come down following your voice. Keep talking and then I'll walk you back. It wasn't really peyote. Just some candy. I was only kidding!"

The moon came and went like a spotlight improperly used and then she spied him on another path on another slope of the mountain, his back to her, rushing along. There was something in his hand and it glinted once, then again, and she understood that he carried a pistol.

"Venus! I've caught my leg in a hole! Venus, come and help me. I can't move. You can't leave me here, Venus!"

She could still see him hurrying along the ridge, looking for her. Damn liar. He really had taken her out there to attack her. He'd have distracted her with the drug story, then pulled the gun and forced her stay out there for hours, made her tell him where she had the casino money hidden, and when she'd finally broken down and told him it was right there in her shoe, right there under her foot, he'd have pounced on her like a coyote. Then shot her when he was done and taken her check and finagled some way to cash it and been rich the rest of his foul days.

"Venus!"

The voice echoed and she thought she would cry for fear that he would begin firing the gun in all directions in the hopes of hitting her.

"Venus, where are you? Do you see the motel lights? Do you?"

Yes, she thought, now I can see them. Right there, blinking in silence, marking the way. A mile or two, but there, reaching out like the living.

"Venus? Where are you? My leg is caught under the rock! Aren't you going to help me, Venus?"

She wouldn't. The liar couldn't touch her now. The liar was going around the mountain the wrong way drugged up and spinning toward his own bad end. The liar could go die like an animal out there. Where they would never find him no matter how long they looked. I'm walking away, you son of a bitch. Toward the lights. Toward the town, and life.

"Venus? Where are you? Venus! I've taken the wrong fork! You've got to help me! I did take peyote, I swear now I did. And now I'll never find my way back. I lied about my leg, though. I'm not caught. But I'm hallucinating now and . . . Venus, are you there?"

She left him for lost.

La Purísima beckoned as she went toward it but grew no closer. It seemed to want to remain far away, much farther than they had come. But that was all right. She was not frightened anymore of the night, and took her time. Walking through the empty foothills, one easy step after another, past gaping openings of bottomless shafts but fearing none of them.

Thinking of May down in her grave and how all the graves that lay under the earth must connect with each other so that there is a single world under the ground where the bones lie. It was a terrible and lonely place that sometimes seemed to resemble the world of the here and now, and Venus knew that she'd failed these months to know the difference. To see this world above of openness and far horizons as the one May would have her hold on to. To see that death had drawn her life down into the other world for a while and that it was time to break free, snap the bond and walk again in the light and air and hope.

Venus walked slowly through the desert. Leaving May behind. And then telling her sweet lost sister once more that, no, she hadn't come all this way just to hand over her fortune to someone or anything like that. Imagining her sister's disapproving frown, but then hearing her sigh and then seeing her nod in the moonlight that painted her skin yellow and made blue stripes in her long black hair like in one of those old sepia photos. And then the two of them continuing on, their shoes kicking up silvery dust, which lingered around them like it did when men walked on the moon. Venus leading the way and her sister ceasing to resist and all the bones lying well behind them in the far places under the ground where they belonged.

Dawn brought her into La Purísima. Square-headed dogs sat in the glow of red and green lights slung over the street. House after house was dark, door open. Empty bottles, fruit rinds, exploded firecracker husks, cigarette butts, dry horse droppings lay all around. As if there'd been a grand fiesta the night before. Before everyone, abandoning all, had melted away. Leaving only the growling dogs.

She walked to the square, stopped. A bus sat idling, smoke drifting from its tailpipe. The motel lay at the end of the street where the highway passed, and all she had to do was return there, go inside, and lie down next to Carl as the sun rose. And yet here was this beckoning bus.

As she drew near she saw that it was quite full, that it had likely only been stopped there a few minutes. All manner of goods had been piled atop it, and at every window a face stared hard at her as she came along the filthy street in a white dress streaked with dirt.

The driver would be back soon, working his zipper back up and sucking a cigarette, a bottle of something poking out of his back pocket. Any second he would show up again, and off they'd go.

The faces shone faintly pink as the early light appeared over the low roofs.

Without another thought, Venus climbed aboard.

There were ripples of laughter as she stood looking at them all.

But then it grew quiet as she came down the aisle and silently took a seat next to the traveling gringo, the one they'd all been laughing at for days, the one who kept riding from here to there with no purpose. A man she evidently knew well.

Was she an angel? they wondered. How else had she known he was here with us on this bus if she wasn't an angel? Of course she was. The women reached out to touch her. An angel, no doubt about it.

And then the angel lay her head on his lap. He looked down at her, nervously at first, then calmly, and put his hand on her long hair and stared straight ahead as if the world had been set right in an instant.

"What's the matter with all of you?" the driver growled as he climbed back into his seat. "You look like you've seen a ghost."

There was a strange glowing all through the bus.

"Someone burning candles? No candle burning, hear?"

Some nodded. Others pretended to sleep.

Sister

I always knew you would figure out things, Venus. There was never any doubt in my mind. After all the twists and turns since May went down in the hole, I knew you would find your way. Will you come with me, then, and play again in the old house? Will you go with me again into the grass and lie with me and watch the sun? Can I touch your hair again? Will you eat pears with me? I know you will. And death will sink into the earth far below us, never to rise again and knock us around. You and I are dolls that never grow old. Forever beautiful and good. And we will lie there and laugh together while our men search around for us calling playfully. We won't answer for the longest time, and then, taking a deep breath, we will spring into the light to grab them.

It was late morning when someone pounded the door.

"Hey, Marvin! You in there? Marvin?"

I jerked it open. "What?"

His face was sunburned bad. "Andy Thomas. Have you seen my brother, Marvin? Is he in there?"

"Why would he be in here?"

"Can I look around? Where is the woman who —"

He pointed past me. The bed I'd left was empty. No Venus.

"Damn!" he let out. "Something's happened to them. Something bad has happened. I'm getting the Federales. We'll have to start a search."

"What?"

"They're lost, you idiot!"

"Lost?"

"Are you drunk? Can't you understand English when it's spoken to you? Lost on the mountain! Are you coming or not?"

"No, no," I shouted, waving him away. "Get out of here."

He raised an open hand up high and gasped like he was going to hit me. "I could . . . I could . . ."

"What?"

"I . . . I . . ."

I shook my head at him. His hand dropped back to his side.

I slammed the door. Was this a joke? Where was Venus anyway? I looked out the window. Everything was drowned in white. No Venus in the pool, no Venus on a chair sunning, no Venus anywhere.

The fat guy headed toward the office, elbows out flapping, unbuttoned beach shirt flying from his shoulders like a goofy Superman's cape. I thought maybe I should've been following him, but then there are insane people who get started on these things only to find out nothing has really happened. The loved one was only in the john, officer, sorry, yeah, should've thought to look there, stupid me.

Then I checked. But Venus wasn't in the bathroom.

So where? Out in the desert traipsing up a mountain? With the snakes? What for? Made no sense. There was just no way . . . no, no, she'd be right back. She was over in the gift shop or something, yakking with Estella, buying us a bottle, whatever.

I wanted to know right away, though, where that casino check was, and went to see which shoes she'd worn. It was those white pumps. I sat down on the floor and stared at the rest of her goddamn shoes. Listened for a while to the air conditioner rattling. Then I made a leap into the closet to see if she'd left her purse and the cash. This time somebody up there was watching over Carl Stein, for there it was right where she'd tossed it. And there in the bottom of it was the cash envelope, twenty-one thousand left, and the bank bag with bunches of crisp twenties still tucked in there just for me. A sea breeze blew through me and there I was far away from the desert floor on a white beach being oiled up by some —

"Hey!" It was the same fist on the door. "You still in there?"

I rammed both stashes back into the purse, then thought better and stuffed them into my suitcase.

"Open up! They really are lost! Hey, open up!"

I threw it open hard, startling him. "Who says?"

"Estella. She saw them cross the highway last night."

"What's out there?"

"Taken her up to that ghost town. There are mine shafts all over."

"What ghost town?"

"Up on the mountain. I've been there, too."

"They'll be back."

"Are you listening? Been eleven hours since they were last seen."

"Not going to worry."

"Not going to worry? It's your wife!"

"Not my wife."

"No?"

"A living breathing person who can do what she pleases. And with whoever she pleases, right? Who're we to say, No, she can't?"

"Huh? You can't just sit here and not do anything."

"Want me to walk around there with you to find them? They could be anywhere, pal, and they're probably off in some other motel. Or maybe you can't stand the idea of your brother getting laid? Is that it?"

"What'd you say?"

I flung shut the door. He kicked it a couple of times, then went away yelling and everybody came out to see what the commotion might be. Everyone got out of the pool, too, and stood around like sheep.

Five sizzling minutes later, though, it was like nothing had happened.

The kiddie-screaming at the pool got going again, and the family of four emerged from their bungalow for a picnic in the sun. I stayed at the window trying not to think about the crap that was starting to happen and watched as the woman put a bloodred blanket down and the children set the food on it. The daddy stood to the side smoking a cigarette. All four of them were sickly. Then they sat and clasped their hands and prayed. In no time their faces were cooking like meat under a broiler.

The cops showed up and talked with Andy Thomas outside the motel office. A couple of times he pointed at my bungalow, but then they all started gawking at the mountain. The dust closed in behind them as they crossed the highway, and I shook my head in disgust over the whole show and thought, Go tramp on up there, you idiots, what're you going to find?

I lay on the bed looking far into Lisa's mirror and thinking about Venus maybe being truly lost and how you can't begin to predict what's going to happen in this life, then broke off from that line of ignorance and chucked the thing against the wall. It shattered and the pieces lay on the floor like weird petals.

I went out on the porch into the deep afternoon and sat on the warm concrete steps. The cop cars were baking in the parking lot. Unbelievably, the family was still out there, picnic stuff stored away, the four of them holding their faces up high as if to a sun god. I dared to look up at the blazing disk of it, too, and for a few moments a black stain floated across things as I peered out at the desolate sand and scrub.

Dead or alive? Hell, she and what's-his-name, Marvin, they'd come walking down the road together around sundown like it was nothing to have been out there messing around and when they got to the motel they'd answer the cops' questions for a while and apologize and everything. Venus would come into the bungalow and go in to take a long cold shower without saying a word because it was none of my business, not now, not ever, and I wouldn't ask. I'd go to the door and listen to Marvin arguing with his brother at the pool. I would turn and see Venus come naked out of the shower and grin like she'd won another game.

Or they'd not ever appear. It would get dark and still there'd be no sign of them.

Waiting, I thought about being out in the open that time the ex-preacher man Ma was seeing took me along with the deer hunting party but said, No, you're not old enough to be shooting so you go goof around while we kill deer but be sure you don't go too far or something because I might not be able to find you or you might get yourself shot. I remembered walking and walking and then turning on my heels in the vastness of the hills and feeling the power of being lost. I remembered standing there hearing the wind and thinking how glorious it was to be totally alone. I saw how that moment had come again there in Mexico, the points of the compass meaning nothing at all.

I waited for a long time watching that family cook itself out there. Then I decided that, No, they weren't worshiping a sun god, they were gazing directly my way, maybe praying for me and my goddamn soul.

"What the hell're you looking at?" I called out.

The daddy shook his head as if to say, We weren't looking in your direction, mister, and the wife said something to him and he nodded.

"What're you assholes sitting out there for?" I insisted.

Clearly but without shouting, the man said, "May Jesus save you."

"Better save yourselves, mister, and get out of that sun."

He shook his head no again, as if I were beyond communicating to, and then they stood and brushed off crumbs. His wife folded the blanket while he gathered up the picnic things. Then they pulled hard on the arms of their kids, who both said ouch on account of their sunburns but looked back and grinned at me because I'd used curse words. It was not my way, but I waved to them, creating a little inside thing between me and them because it wasn't their fault having parents with no more sense than that, which kept them gawking backward with innocent affection in their eyes until they got to their bungalow and the daddy quickly herded them inside.

It was midnight when the search party came back, a dozen flashlights twitching. No Venus, no Marvin. Only the fat brother trailing the cops, head hanging low. They asked me a few questions and I tried to answer. And then they told us that it was all very clear, the American woman Venus Miller and the American man Marvin Thomas had gone for a walk where they shouldn't have and had fallen into some deep place in the earth where they would never be found again. An old silver mine. They hadn't found a trace, nothing. Shoes? No, they hadn't found any shoes. The mountain had swallowed them, they said, and no one had any business thinking the mine could be searched for Americans with no more sense than to wander where they had no business being.

Andy followed the cops to their cars, yelling and whining, but they pushed him and cursed at him and spat on the dust and drove away.

I waited on my porch while the fat boy stared across the road. A great deal of time went by before he shook his head at the desolate scene as if the curtain had fallen on a very tragic play and came over and plopped down on my steps like an uncooked biscuit. "What kind of a country is this?"

I shrugged.

"There's not even a body," he said. "That's not right."

"Nobody checked the other motels?"

"Don't start saying that shit again, do you hear? My brother had no intentions toward the woman. He was being stupid trying to take her up there and show her that ghost town. He knew better. Stupidity."

After a while I said, "Until there's evidence to say different, they could be anywhere. I'd advise you to be ready for them to show up right out of the blue anytime."

He groaned loudly and went his way.

When he got to the pool he stopped and gazed into it.

"Jump in," I said. "Do you some good."

"The hell with you, pal," he replied.

Then he went around the pool and into his bungalow.

I drank and waited and looked over there at his closed door, thinking how it was really beginning to look like the Million Dollar Lady would end up robbing me of the jackpot that'd been coming my way. Then I asked myself if I really had done something to deserve this. Even when I knew damn well I had — all my life.

For the next few days I drank, waiting and lamenting the missing fortune, wishing Venus would emerge from wherever she'd gone just tired and maybe a little hungry. Then I went to the closet one morning to pack because to wait any longer was to let gravity take over my life. I looked at Venus's shoes. Somebody had lined them up nice and neat like she was something special. Then I remembered it was me. And then I saw it was kind of like arranging flowers on a tombstone. Which was silly, so I shifted the jewels in the proverbial kaleidoscope, got a new pattern going. One where I'd put the keys in the ignition and drive Venus's Suburban somewhere. Roar out of this scene. Take my dollars and go the way I've always gone. Pick a dot on the map. Go there without thinking. Then trace the straight line from that dot to the next. Go all the way to the sea and start back. Or all the way up into the highest mountains and then back down. It didn't matter. Any way would do.

I could taste freedom as strongly as that hard orange piece of candy May gave me after we made love the first time. I lay on the soaked sheets and clung to that sweat-slicked creature and tried to put my exploded thoughts back together when there came her hand and she said, Open up, and set that sweetness onto my tongue. Suck it slowly, she whispered, I have a whole bag of them.

I went around and around the bungalow checking for forgotten things.

I looked into the bathroom mirror and thought how I had become as bitter as rind. Then, like anybody, I had the next thought, but then I am not a man who can pull the trigger on a gun to my own head. Which left me as I was. To go from here to there, between the named or between the nameless, bigger than life or verifiably invisible.

I lay back on the bed and watched dust in a blade of morning light passing between the curtains and thought of all the unknown universes.

I held a pair of Venus's high heels over my face, turned them, studied the cracked leather. These meant nothing to me, though I had picked them up from the closet floor. They'd have gone on the feet of any woman. Then I suddenly remembered they were the ones she'd had on the first time I found her in the casino.

I didn't move for the longest time, holding those red shoes over my face, feeling warm sand flow up from my bowels and into my mouth until my tongue lay buried. Then I lowered them and set them on the bedspread and thought of her long legs going up high.

"It is Jesus who helps us."

The voice was not hers, and there had been no knock at the door. It was the preacher daddy, his big head cutting the sunlight at the window, dark eyes looking through the crack in the curtains. Every day I'd watched him come closer, as if trying to get a bird's trust.

"Get away from there," I said.

He rapped the glass hard, as if he did not mean to be turned away, then popped the door a few times. "Your loss can heal you, my friend."

"Get the fuck away from my door!"

"Maybe we could talk a few minutes. I'm not going to preach to you. Trying to lend a hand."

I sat up. "Get out of here."

"Listen. Janice doesn't think I ought to be over here and I didn't either for a while, but then we got to talking about what happened to your wife and to that man she was with and I said to Janice, I think enough time has passed that I should go over there now and see if I can't help him. This coming even after you said what you said to us that day in front of our children. I don't hold your talking like that against you, though. I want you to know that. I would've cursed out the first people I'd seen, too, after finding out my wife was missing."

"Go away."

"This isn't about Jesus or God or the church. Just about men needing to talk. I live with Janice and she's all right but she's not a lot of fun, and so whenever I get a chance to do some straight shooting with a man, I go for it. Nothing quite like it, in the end. We used to do that dove hunting, me and my buddies. Talk it all out long and hard so that by the time you got back home to the wife and the children, well, you'd said it all and that was that and there was no sense giving her or the children any part of your personal troubles in this life, all the more so since you'd seen with your own eyes the glories of the outdoors and thanked God for all that bounty put there to liberate you from all the ugliness there is, which will never end until he slams the book shut."

It was as if it had begun to rain and it would not stop. I went and stood behind the door and listened to the deluge.

"You follow me?" he asked.

I didn't answer. It had way too much church spin for me.

"I know you can hear me in there, friend, and if you'd rather we left the door between us closed like this, that's all right. I can talk to you straight through the wood. I've been known to talk holes in wood."

I opened up, still a little angry, mostly curious. But the first thing I saw was something I really hadn't wanted to. Out past the deep red face of this Good Samaritan I could see Andy Thomas back bouncing on the diving board and hear him hollering at the preacher's children in the water to hurry up for Christ's sake and get out of his way. For an instant it seemed that time had rolled backward . . .

"I'm going to dive, so move aside! I'm going to dive!"

"He's a big one," my savior said.

"Well, it looks like he's done mourning his brother," I said.

"Everything has to end. And that's good."

Maybe this guy was just an old dog. Sweet and stupid, with maybe a flicker of smarts. I took a gamble and offered him a drink. He didn't hesitate and had the screen door pulled open as soon as I unlatched it.

We hadn't gotten the first shot of tequila down and some cigarettes going before he said, "None of my business, but I can't figure how you can sit here in this motel and not move on. Don't think I'm ministering, though. I'm asking is all. Not that I'm an expert on knowing where one's supposed to be . . ."

I thought for sure I was offended, then dropped it. "I had a life, and I still do, mister. The truth is this. My wife, I mean, the lady I was with, she had struck it rich in a casino, had a check for several hundred thousand dollars on her out there walking around with the fat boy's brother."

The man nodded gravely. "And so the money is gone, too?"

"That's right."

"Kind of leaves you stuck?"

"Yes and no."

He gave that some thought. "You still waiting on her to show up?"

"I think I'm about done with that."

"A person could wait a long time here."

"A person could."

He thought some more. "We're going to Ecuador to work for a missionary school. Janice will teach school and I'll teach the Bible."

"Ecuador."

"Equator runs through it. That's how far down there it is from here."

I hadn't ever given the equator any thought, but by the time we got the second shot of the stuff down and glowing inside our guts, I asked, "How long does it take to drive to Ecuador?"

"Maybe two weeks from here. Depends."

"I still have her Suburban."

"We have a clunker that needs an alternator before it's going anywhere. That's how come we've been sitting here. A person can wait a very long time for American car parts in La Purísima."

"I could drive you to Ecuador."

"I couldn't allow that, mister."

"Why not?"

"We don't have any money to speak of."

"I've got a little," I admitted. "Won't be hurting."

"We couldn't give you a job when we get there, either. Sorry."

"I don't care. I'll take a look at the equator and then head out someplace else. That's the way I am."

"Tommy Vinson," he said. "Mart, Texas."

"Vincent Lewis, Salt Lake City," I said.

"That's a long haul just to go look at the equator."

"I like to move around."

"What kind of work, Vince?"

"Same as yours. Lord's work. I also can build a cotton gin or fly a crop duster or put on a roof or play the piano and sing 'Amazing Grace.'"

Half true, half fib, like always it didn't matter. Vinson looked around the room as if seeking evidence for my claims. And the longer he did that, the more I thought he was counting the empty bottles and the pieces of Lisa's busted mirror that I hadn't bothered to pick up.

I swept in with some more fake bona fides. "Long line of preachers on my daddy's side going back up the line, way back into colonial times in the Carolinas. That's what they've told me anyway."

"I think Janice has got some South Carolina folks."

We had a third one and I went and pissed and came back and opened the curtains so we could see out. The fat boy was scolding the children and there was fierce squabbling going on around the diving-board ladder.

The preacher said, "Well, Vince, here we are."

"A strange place on this earth," I said.

"Never know where you're going to be, what you're going to do," he said. "I've done a little bit of everything. Don't regret very much, though. Except those years when I was in my twenties and I was a con. This drinking with you brings a lot of that back to me now. And you know what? It's kind of like looking back upon the vision of a lithe woman you've known and cared for. She was something else again, but that was then and it's over and done with."

"How do you give up being a con?"

He smacked his lips as if tasting something right out of the air and smiled at me like maybe I might've had a personal reason to be asking that. Then he said, "I don't know. You go to Ecuador, I guess."

"That's pretty far off the map."

"But then that could be a good thing. Maybe it'd be the place a man could start over from. The equator is the middle of the world."

I considered that. And thought, Well, maybe something really could be gained from driving all the way down to where they marked the middle of the earth and standing on the line in the straight up-and-down light, one foot in the North, the other in the South, and looking up at the sun out of the hole I'd made of my life.

Then I'd figure out how to con him and his church for a few bucks and go my way.

I poured us another one. He grinned like it was a very pleasant surprise, after all, to see how another man would want to pull up and go to Ecuador just like that, then signaled for us to belt them down in a hurry. For there came his Janice across the lawn like a locomotive.

"I'm in big trouble," he said.

"I'd still like to drive you to Ecuador."

"That won't be necessary. I'm going to be dead directly."

"Like in three seconds?"

"Too late to pray."

It was maybe five o'clock in the morning when I woke up with a definite thought like a guy who knows he might not have come home from the bar with his own billfold. I went to the suitcase where I'd put the last of the money. And sure enough, as if I'd seen it coming in my sleep, the money was gone. My Ecuador pal had cleaned me out. I went to the curtain, flung it back, and tried to decipher the night. The pool lights were off. But in the last of the moonlight I could see what I didn't want to see. The Christian family's beat-up black bomb with its perfectly good alternator gone from its spot. It was like in a movie when the bad guy gets it. And with that, the thin floor opened up, dropping me down a shaft into a world of dust where there were no endings, no resting places, no signs. Leaving only a disk of weak light far above, the place that I'd never get back to no matter how long I tried.

May

You know, Venus, it is not the way you think it is when you go down in there. There is no fright, no pounding of the heart, no desire to call out and be helped. There is nothing but silence and you in the middle of it, floating. You stare like someone in a movie theater who is so caught up in the story on the screen that you become the woman in the film, you become the image, the one with the golden hair and the silver mouth that shines blue inside when she parts her lips and looks at you knowing that you and she are one now forever. It lasts only a moment, then it is over.

Carl Blalock

I knew I had a little story going again when she walked down the aisle of the bus and sat down beside me as if she'd only gotten off for a while to stretch her legs. And it was going to be a fine story, born in the dawn light slanting through greasy, cracked windows. I could hear a choir singing gloriously. Everyone on that bus heard it. I could tell from the way they were smiling as Venus lay her head on my lap and closed her eyes.

Then suddenly I knew this town, the squat buildings, the low wall around the motel with the rusted oil derrick sign blinking in the dawn. Of course this was where we would find each other again. Of course this was where she'd run to, an oasis in the middle of nowhere, a resting place on the long road to and from the ocean where we'd sometimes lingered dreaming a day or two in the transfixing sunshine and then working out some of the knots in our bodies with each other's help late in the night.

The bus pulled out on the road, gears winding high and higher, horns and guitars blaring from the tape deck, the passengers crossing themselves furiously as we swung from the right lane to the left and into the path of a gasoline truck and then back into our own lane.

Venus slept. I tried to imagine her dreams as we rolled through the desert that morning. Like me, she'd brought no belongings, no baggage. As if, like me, she'd wanted to start over in the purest way possible.

So I knew she was dreaming of a big new wedding. The one where everyone comes and sees how it all worked out for her, and for me, after all the mess. We were both roughed up and older in too many ways to recount, but we had come through, somehow, and so we were there before the congregation to say so, to let them know they could stop holding their breaths for us. We'd found our way.

She slept deeply, beads of sweat on her forehead. Then she frowned. As if remembering something? Or seeing something just ahead? I drew a line across her wet skin and the frown went its way.

I gazed out at the desert. Soon we'd cross more mountains and descend onto another plain, make the run to the border.

I slipped my fingers into Venus's damp hair.

"America," he said.

Across the aisle, a teenager, heading north for a job. His head wobbled from fatigue or drunkenness.

"America and wife. Good. Give me dollar?"

A woman bundled up in shawls hissed at him to leave me alone. He slumped against the window, muttered curses. I rummaged for paper pesos and gave him most of them. He nodded thanks, tucked them away, and closed his eyes. The woman frowned at me, but I shrugged. For what else was I going to do? When I had everything now?

Everyone slept as we climbed into the mountains, rising up for our final dive back to the earth. As Venus dreamed our new beginning and the bus swerved, dodged death at every curve. Pigs squealed in crates on the roof and a rooster broke free and flapped down the aisle. But no one awoke. Because everyone was off to the dream wedding.

High on a plateau in the mountains, in the cool damp clouds, where all are seated at a long table covered with food and drink, every soul in the countryside lined up in their Sunday best, with me at one end in a fine white Mexican wedding shirt and crisp white trousers, and Venus the Angel in a fine white wedding dress at the other. A cloud of green birds comes through the air and settles on the table, on shoulders, on hands. And everyone looks at these birds carefully because no one has ever seen birds like them before and they surely have come a long way.

Late afternoon had come when Venus and I went to the back of the bus to watch the purple-brown slopes of the mountains slide back down into the earth the same slow way they had risen for us each time we'd driven out there to that place where men and women measured themselves against rock and got a glimpse of who they were.

At midnight we crossed the river at Laredo without our passports, with nothing to prove who we were, and spent more than twenty-four nervous hours getting new documents and becoming Americans again. With our old names and old faces, old birth dates. But we were not the same people who'd started out on that trip.

It was the dead of night when they finally let us go without one question about Pullman, a fact for which I had no explanation other than the luck of slow-moving news. Or because the gringo being sought by the Mexicans wasn't me at all but the other Carl I'd left behind down there somewhere.

We got a room in the first hotel we found. Fell onto the bed and lay staring at each other in the light of the yellow neon sign until dawn, when I reached for her and we held each other. Making life. A life much bigger than either of ours. With strong arms and yet at ease, able to lie there body to body, unmoving, until morning's sleep carried us in a boat down a green river. Pullman is with us, sitting up in the front with Gloria, holding hands with her and watching the water road through the jungle. Now and then turning to smile at us as if to say, We are almost there.

I told her about them as we rose from the bed, got back into our filthy clothes, and walked out of the hotel. First the story of Gloria and the pink yacht. Then of the final night on the sea, how I had let him go. Then how I had fled the place because so much would not be understood, so much would be twisted into something it wasn't. How I had gone quickly, abandoning all, and wandered not wanting to find a place to be, only wanting to keep going. Not thinking I would ever find her, either.

Then Venus told me that there had to be a reason for us ending up in the same place again and that we must never again lose hold of it. She could not name this reason, but said it had to be something much more than mere chance. Something that had been flowing between us since the beginning but that we'd lost sight of in the mayhem after May's death.

We were standing on a bluff at the milky green river. A brown lid of smoke hung over the border town across the way. Beyond, we could see the beginnings of the vast desert, but not the mountains anymore. We had come a terribly long way, back to the flatness of the earth. Where if we were to be anything at all upon its dull surface, then we would have to build it, lift it above the sun-swept nothingness. Or risk sinking back into the dust, strangers one to the other. We had tempted that fate . . .

"It took a final long walk in the desert," she said, "for May to lose her grip on me. Now it's done. I've left her out there, down below it, in the hidden place where she should be and where I need no longer wander."

"I picture Stein in a dark prison cell."

"No, put his bones out there with her, too. So they'll be together . . . and gone from us. Bones under the Mexican ground."

I took her hand and held it. Thought again of May telling the story of listening to the voice of the wind with Carl out on a mound of orange rocks in the desert. But there was no wind there on the border that afternoon. Nothing to move the air. Yet I could hear so much even without sound and began, like her, to see how we were leaving all our guilt down in Mexico, over May's demise and over all that occurred after the moment that her head went under. Abandoning it in the desert, far below the moon-colored rocks strewn upon the wide stretches of emptiness.

Venus peered at me, hiking her eyebrows. "You all right?"

"I am."

"You're going to be even more all right."

"How's that?"

"I have a little surprise." She took off a battered white pump and handed it to me. "Take a look in there."

We went to the biggest bank in town and startled all the people there, then to a car dealership and startled the people there, too, and then we drove out of there in a new navy blue Suburban.

We went only a few miles from the border, though, before we stopped again, this time at a nicer place. Leaped onto the bed and lay there with the bundles of casino money parked between us. The air-conditioner roar cutting us off from the world.

"I guess this is the second miracle," I said.

"Definitely. And it's going to produce the third one. Help us find just the place we need to be."

"Think so?"

"Without a doubt."

She went for glasses in the bathroom and poured us a Scotch. We sat on the bed and clinked a toast. Then slowly reclinked it for good measure.

"You know," she said, "with all this money we could hire someone to always be there to make our drinks and hand them to us on little napkins."

"That'd work for me."

"And fix us good things to eat. By our pool."

"A pool that takes you half an hour to get to the other end of."

"Oh, I like that," she said. "Blue tiles. And no matter where you stop to rest along the way there are big blue towels on the edge waiting for you. And when you get out, you'll be able to see real far. Way off."

"Are we on a mountain again? By a bay?"

"Out on the plains. Tall grass all around. With the wind blowing through it. And our big white house sitting right in the middle under a soft blue sky. I once saw a place like this."

I thought of those trips we'd made to go see my dying mama and then again about the day we'd buried her and how the wind blew straight through me as if I weren't there, as if I were the one who'd passed on. I also remembered getting back into the car after the funeral and sitting behind the wheel thinking of the steep cut in the ground for the coffin when Venus had come walking up to my window, the wind tossing her hair all around, and leaned in and given me a long kiss that made me want her more than ever. There, twenty yards from my dead mama, out on the pancake earth.

"Then we'll find that house," I said.

"We don't have to find it. We can have it built. Way out somewhere."

"With that long pool."

"We don't really have to have a pool."

"No?"

"Maybe we'll just be happy with all that grass."

"Sure, Venus."

"An ocean of grass."

"I like that."

"Never cut it, either."

"Never. No work."

"No work. Not ever."

Late in the night it rained and I cut off the air conditioner, opened the window, and let the air in. In a while I would go get us coffee across the road and then drive us north in the early light on the wide gray highways for as long as it took to get to the place we were going. A big white house at the end of an empty dirt road, ancient pear trees all around, grass left to grow for the wind to do with as it would.

Venus will love it and disappear for hours in that grass. I'll stay up on the porch where I can see a broad river way back over there. Later she'll come and slowly put slivers of pear into my mouth and then the falling light will push us off the steps for a walk on the road. After a while one of us will say something about the perfection of this place, and we'll stop and look back at our house on the grass ocean. Then we'll start back toward it under the stars. We'll turn on every lamp once we get there, and then step out again into the grass that comes up to our shoulders and look at the golden windows as she sails through the night.